James Thomas, Andrew Galatian

Indian and Pioneer History of the Saginaw Valley: with Histories of East Saginaw, Saginaw City and Bay City, from their earliest Settlements

Also Pioneer Directory and Business Advertiser, for 1866 and 1867

SALZWASSER
VERLAG

James Thomas, Andrew Galatian

Indian and Pioneer History of the Saginaw Valley: with Histories of East Saginaw, Saginaw City and Bay City, from their earliest Settlements

Also Pioneer Directory and Business Advertiser, for 1866 and 1867

1st Edition | ISBN: 978-3-75257-905-5

Place of Publication: Frankfurt am Main, Germany

Year of Publication: 2022

Salzwasser Verlag GmbH, Germany.

Reprint of the original, first published in 1866.

INDIAN AND PIONEER HISTORY

OF THE

SAGINAW VALLEY,

WITH HISTORIES OF

EAST SAGINAW, SAGINAW CITY AND BAY CITY,

FROM THEIR EARLIEST SETTLEMENTS.

—ALSO—

PIONEER DIRECTORY

—AND—

BUSINESS ADVERTISER,

FOR 1866 AND 1867.

COMPILED AND PUBLISHED BY

THOMAS & GALATIAN.

JAMES M. THOMAS, A. B. GALATIAN.

EAST SAGINAW, MICH:
LEWIS & LYON, BOOK AND JOB PRINTERS.
1866.

PREFACE.

We present this our first publication of a Directory of the beautiful Cities of East Saginaw, Saginaw City and Bay City, and of adjoining villages in the Saginaw Valley, trusting that its merits will be sufficient to give it a cordial reception by the people. Our aim has been to make a perfect and reliable work, and in striving to do this we have spared neither labor nor expense. If we have succeeded, well; if not, we have failed after earnest effort. The difficulty of procuring accurate information on all the subjects presented in this work, has been great; and while there are possibly, some errors, we are yet able to say, that this Directory is as nearly accurate as any work of the kind ever published.

We found the flourishing towns in the Saginaw Valley new, comparatively; the project of forming a combined directory of them was new; and the labor and care attending the compilation of such a work for the *first time* in any locality, is not easily understood by those who have had no experience in the matter. We say this, that the effort may not be viewed too critically.—The great amount of labor necessarily laid out in procuring the historical portion of this work has delayed its publication several weeks beyond the time originally designated. For this delay we ask the indulgence of our patrons.

To Hon. C. P. Avery, of Flint, we are under great obligations for the services rendered in furnishing the Early Indian and Pioneer History of the Saginaw Valley—a history that cannot fail to be read with deep interest. To the Rev. J. A. Wight,

T. W. Watkins and William McCormick, of Bay City; William H. Sweet, Esq., and Lester Cross, Esq., of Saginaw City; we are indebted for aid extended in procuring the local history of their respective places of residence; and to William L. Webber, Esq., for reliable Salt statistics. We are also under obligations to Mr. L. R. Elliott, for assistance in compiling the history of East Saginaw, to J. S. Estabrook, Esq., for statistics of Lumber, Shingles, &c., and to others who have rendered us aid and information. We return our cordial thanks to the business men of the Valley, who have extended to us a liberal patronage.

For the superior typography of the work we are indebted to Messrs. Lewis & Lyon, of the *Courier* Office.

The binding is the work of Mr. Albert H. Frey, and well attests his superior mechanical skill.

THE PUBLISHERS.

INDEX.

FOLLOWING INDIAN AND PIONEER HISTORY.

EAST SAGINAW.

SAGINAW CITY.

BAY CITY.

[For Advertisements not indexed, see fly-leaves and outside cover.]

THE TREATY OF SAGINAW OF 1819.

Indian and Pioneer Incidents of the Saginaw Valley.

BY CHARLES P. AVERY.

The various Indian nations within the United States having been always treated as independent powers, although living within our borders, and after the Revolutionary War, as well as after the War of 1812, as helpless, and their tenure as frail as tenants at sufferance, no negotiation or agreement with them, as nations, would have been deemed valid unless entered into by the President and approved by the Senate of the United States—the treaty-making and the treaty-ratifying powers.

The action of the President and Senate was an indispensable pre-requisite to any valid disposition of their possessory rights, and as a power delegated by the States, under the national Constitution, it took precedence of all action on their part.

Although living within our borders, and answerable to our criminal law for all violations of the peace and for crimes, we have always granted them the right of internal or domestic polity, and at no time when they have lived in bands, according to the custom of their fathers, have we sought to throw over them our civil code. Where individuals of those races have separated themselves from their tribal associations and have lived isolated, they have been generally treated as citizens and made amenable to our civil code regulating the rights of property, real and personal, its descent and distribution.

As a fact in the history of nations, it is certainly anomalous and singular that there should have been and now are distinct and independent governments within the limits of our national sovereignty—instances of an *Imperium in imperio.*

But such has been at all times the fact from the early history of the Republic down to the present time; a course of action and a treatment of that unfortunate and now fast disappearing race of people, inaugurated and insisted upon by the great and good Washington with his refined and high sense of national equity.

By this view which he and successive administrators of our national affairs took of their condition, we recognized the possessory rights of the Indians. They were substantial rights which could only be parted with at treaties fairly made, at public and open councils of the natives, where the General Government should be represented by its agent, and everything done fairly, freely and without the least taint of authority or duress.

This was the theory of those councils, and the wise and humane intention of Washington and of the Government. If violated in any instance to the injury of the weaker party, and there were doubtless exceptional instances of such violation, it should be attributed to corrupt individual action and not to the expressed and well known instructions of the proper department of our Government.

The first treaty of importance which was made for the extinguishment of the Indian title to the soil of what now comprises the State of Michigan, was the one entered into by William Hull, then Governor of Michigan, as a territory, and *ex-officio* Superintendent of Indian Affairs, with the natives at Detroit, in 1807, when a tract of land in the south-eastern part of the State was ceded by them to our Government.

Detroit and a belt of land adjacent to it, lying along the river and lake, six miles in width, were not affected by this grant, we having before that succeeded to the possessory rights of Great Britian to the District of Detroit, so called, which she had held for a series of years, co-extensive with the claims of her predecessor, France; and which by the Treaty of Greenville, made by General Wayne, on behalf of our Government, in 1795, had been re-assured to and made perfect in us.

With that exception, the title to the south-easterly part of our State was obtained from the natives by the treaty of 1807.

The northerly line of this grant included only small portions of what are now the counties of Lapeer and Genesee, and was a little north of their southern boundaries, thus leaving the Saginaw River and its principal affluents, the Flint, the Cass, &c., entirely unaffected by the provisions of that treaty.

This portion of the State remained in Indian possession, with the rights of the natives intact and unaffected, until the Treaty of Saginaw of 1819.

In that treaty we are particularly interested, for the cession of lands then made by the natives, with the reservations therein provided for, include the rich and flourishing valleys of the Saginaw and its tributaries.

General Cass was commissioned to act as the agent of the General Government in securing to it this important addition to our territory.

He was then in the vigor of his manhood, with a laudable ambition to achieve a national reputation and to identify himself by his exertions with the acquisition of such a valuable body of land, and feeling that the influx of immigration, then beginning to be felt at Detroit and its vicinity, required a wider domain for it to spread over, and with the greater security it would give to life and property of settlers upon the domain which had been acquired by the previous treaty, he felt the importance of the enterprise into which he was about to embark, and that if successful it would be an achievement upon which any statesman might well ground a claim for the gratitude of those then living at and near Detroit, and might be excused if he looked to such achievement as the ground-work of future national honors.

He appeared upon the Saginaw, upon the site of what is now Saginaw City, on the 10th of September, A. D. 1819, with his staff of interpreters and assistants.

They made the journey, the whole distance upon horseback, from Detroit by way of Flint, and thence down the river by the way of what was until lately the Indian Reservation of Pe-won-ny-go-wingh, which was at that time the tribal home of the Chief Ne-ome and his successor in the Chieftanship, Tone-dok-a-ne.

Before starting from Detroit the General had directed Mr. Louis Campau, who had been since 1816 an established Indian Trader at that point upon the Saginaw, to build the Council House and make the necessary arrangements for the reception of the Commissioner and his company. No other man could have been so appropriately selected to meet the Commissioner's expectations and aid him in the details of the enterprise.

Mr. Campau yet survives, an aged gentleman but with an accurate memory, a fine representative of the better class of early French pioneers, a liberal, public spirited and worthy citizen.

Two government vessels, laden with stores for the subsistence of those upon the treaty ground, were sent around by lakes St. Clair and Huron. On one of these was a company of United States soldiers, commanded by Captain Cass, a brother of the General, who had been ordered to the treaty ground for the protection of those in attendance.

By the time the Commissioner, with his staff of interpreters, secretaries and assistants had arrived, Mr. Campau and his employees had constructed the Council House. It was spacious and commodious, extending several hundred feet along the bank of the river, a few rods back from the shore, and of the requisite width to accommodate the large number of natives who were expected to be present. Situated nearly between the present site of the Webster House and the river, but severel rods farther down on the slight ridge or second rise from the shore, its position was commanding and pleasant.

Trees conveniently situated, furnished the columns of the Council Hall, and boughs interlaced above made the roof. The sides and ends were open. It was of an order of architecture not recognized by Ruskin, Downing, Upjohn or any professional writer upon that branch of science. It was doubtless more nearly assimilated to that Temple described by the Great Poet of nature, Bryant, in the opening of his Forest Hymn, one of the finest of all his fine poems:

> "The Groves were God's first temples; ere man learned
> To hew the shaft and lay the architrave
> And spread the roof above them, ere he framed
> The lofty vault to gather and roll back
> The sound of anthems"

A platform made of logs, faced or evened by the axe, elevated about a foot above the ground, and broad enough to accommodate upon rustic benches, Commissioner Cass and the other officials, occupied the central portion of the Council Room.

Huge logs in their native roughness had been rolled in upon the other space to be used as seats by the native lords of the soil when in solemn council. The bordering woods were dotted with temporary wigwams, hastily and rudely constructed by the natives for the accommodation of themselves and families during the pendency of the negotiation.

Among other preparations, temporary but convenient additions to his trading house had been made by Mr. Campau, sufficiently spacious to make a good sized dining room for the large number of officials present, and comfortable quarters for the Commissioner. The number of Indians present at the time of his arrival was not as large as was expected. Messengers or runners had been sent among the different bands, some living quite remote from the place of holding the Council, to notify them of the proposed treaty, and others were sent out for like purpose after the fact became apparent that some localities were not properly represented.

The number present upon the treaty ground on the day when the third, which was the fullest Council that was held, has been variously estimated from one thousand five hundred to four thousand. They were mainly Chippewas, but not all. There were present some Ottawas of pure and mixed blood, and although in our State papers the parties to the treaty are spoken of as the United States on the one side and the Chippewa nation on the other, there are the names of Chiefs and head-men affixed to the treaty who were of Ottawa descent.

There were but three regular Councils or audiences held during the ten or twelve days that the negotiations were pending. At such formal Councils the chiefs, warriors, head-men and braves, only were called and admitted into the Council Hall, although the sides being open and the opportunity for hearing and seeing unimpeded, the Indian women and their children gathered in timid groups close by. They were silent but by no means disinterested spectators of the solemn negotiations proceeding within, which involved no less than a full and final surrender of the burial places of their fathers, the ancient hunting grounds of their people, the fair and beautiful heritage of forest and corn ground, lake and river.

At the first Council General Cass made known to the natives through Henry Conner and Whitmore Knaggs, experienced and highly respected Indian Traders, and as interpreters most competent, the object of his journey from Detroit and the general purposes of our Government. He endeavored to impress upon them the paternal regard which their Great Father at Washington had for their welfare, and the hope that the peaceful relations which had existed between them since the close of the war should be rendered perpetual. He reminded them of their condition as a people, the swelling of the wave of civilization toward their hunting grounds, the growing scarcity of game, the importance and necessity of turning their attention more to agriculture, and relinquishing the more uncertain mode of living by the chase, and the better condition they would ultimately be in by confining themselves to reservations ample for the purposes of agriculture, to be provided for them by the proposed treaty, and the cession of the residue of the territority then occupied by those who were there represented, upon such terms and guarantees as their condition required, including therein stipulated annuities.

He was answered by their chief speakers with a gravity and eloquence peculiar to Indian Councils.

Three Chiefs of high repute acted as speakers for the Indians, who survived for some years after the treaty, and were known to some of the earlier settlers in the valley. Their names were oftentimes pronounced by our early traders and pioneers differently, and are found in documents with different orthography, but as they appear at the foot of the treaty they are Mish-e-ne-na-non-e-quet, O-ge-maw-ke-ke-to, and also at the first Council Kish-kaw-ko.

At the subsequent Councils the latter was not present, except at the last, and then merely to affix his totem to the treaty after it had been engrossed for execution. He had put himself out of condition at the close of the first day by drinking, and remained in a state quite unpresentable as a speaker for the residue of the time.

He was an Indian of violent temper, and in the excitement of liquor was reckless in the commission of outrage. Subsequent to the treaty, after many acts of violence, he was arrested and died in prison at Detroit.

He was less dangerous in his wigwam quietly drunk than in the Council Room tolerably sober.

The chief speaker, O-ge-maw-ke-ke-to, opposed the proposition made by Commissioner Cass with indignation. His speech as remembered by persons still surviving, who were interested listeners, was a model of Indian eloquence. He was then quite young, not over twenty-five years of age, above the average height, and in his bearing, graceful and handsome; although in the later years of his life he was often seen intoxicated, he never fully lost a look of conscious dignity which belonged to his nature as one of the original lords of the soil.

In true eloquence he was probably hardly surpassed by the Seneca Chief, Sa-go-ye-wat-ha (Red Jacket). His band lived at the Forks of the Tittabawassee, and like the famous Seneca Chief he wore upon his breast a superb Government medal.

He addressed the Commmissioner: "You do not know our wishes. Our people wonder what has brought you so far from your homes."

"Your young men have invited us to come and light the Council fire. We are here to smoke the pipe of peace, but not to sell our lands. Our American Father wants them. Our English Father treats us better. *He* has never asked for them. Your people trespass upon our hunting grounds. You flock to our shores. Our waters grow warm. Our land melts like a cake of ice. Our possessions grow smaller and smaller. The warm wave of the white man rolls in upon us and melts us away. Our women reproach us. Our children want homes. Shall we sell from under them the spot where they spread their blankets? We have not called you here. We smoke with you the pipe of peace."

To this the Commissioner replied with earnestness, reproving the speaker for arrogant assumption; that their Great Father at Washington had just closed a war in which he had whipped their Father, the English King and the Indians too; that their lands were forfeited in fact by the rules of war, but that he did not propose to take them without rendering back an equivalent, notwithstanding their late acts of hostility; that their women and children should have secured to them ample tribal reserves on which they could live, unmolested by their white neighbors, where they could spread their blankets and be aided and instructed in agriculture.

The Council for the day closed. The Commissioner with his staff of earnest and devoted assistants, composed of gentlemen distinguished at Indian Councils, Whitmore Knaggs, known to the natives as O-ke-day-ben-don, and beloved by them; Henry Conner, known to them as Wah-be-sken-dip, meaning literally white-head, significant of the color of his hair; Col. Beaufait, G. Godfroy, sub agent, John Harson and other gentlemen of deserved influence with the Chippewas, all retired to their lodgings disappointed and anxious, while the Chiefs and head-men of the natives retired to their wigwams in sullen dignity, unapproachable and unappeased. Certainly a very unpropitious opening of the great and important undertaking and trust which General Cass had in hand.

The juncture was a critical one, and for a full appreciation of it a brief allusion to the relative status of the two who were about to become contracting parties to the treaty, but whose minds had not yet met, becomes pardonable if not necessary.

The proposition for a cession of the Indian title came from us not them. Their possessory control by our uniform recognition and action was as yet perfect. For any lawless or vindictive act upon the treaty ground there would have been immunity from immediate punishment, and probably ultimate escape. The whites, comparatively, were few in number. The military company on board of the schooner, anchored in the stream, was quite inadequate to successful resistance against an organized and general outbreak.

Sufficient time had not elapsed to wash out the bitter memories of border feuds, of fancied or real wrong. Foot-prints were yet fresh upon the war-path. Indeed only the fifth summer had passed since that war had closed, which had laid low many Chippewa warriors. Our Commissioner and his staff of assistants had placed themselves voluntarily within their strong hold upon the Saginaw, to which no pale face had penetrated throughout that formidable struggle, unless as pinioned and care-depressed captives, with the exception of the single memorable instance of the daring trader, Smith, to rescue from captivity the children of the Boyer family, who had been taken captives with their father from their homes upon Clinton river, near Mount Clemens.

Here, within a half dozen summers previous, they had drilled in martial exercise, trained themselves to warlike feats, and prepared for those deadly incursions into our frontier settlements, and for those more formidable engagements where disciplined valor was called upon to breast their wild charge. After the bloody raid, to this valley they looked as to a fastness, and to it returned with their captives and streaming trophies.

And here too had been for generations their simple altar in the unpruned forests, their festivals, called by us without reference to their true significance their dances, when thanks went up to the Great Spirit for the yearly return of the successive blessings of a fruitful season, following to its source, with direct purpose and thankful hearts, the warm ray which gave to them the trickling sap, which reddened the berry, which embrowned the tassel of the corn and perfected their slender harvest.

Ne-ome, the chief of one of the largest bands of the Chippewas, occupied and assumed to control the most southerly portion of their then national domain.

The Flint river, with its northerly affluents was by the line of the treaty of 1807, left a little north of the border in full Indian possession. It was called by the natives Pe-won-nuk-ening, meaning literally the river of the Flint, and by the early French traders, La Pierre, as was the principal fording or crossing place of that river, called by them Grand Traverse, a few rods below the Flint City bridge. By the Chippewas the site of that city was called Mus-cu-ta-wa-ingh, meaning the open plain burnt over.

That river, after leaving the northerly part of Lapeer County, bears southerly to the Grand Traverse (City of Flint), and then curves northerly to meet the Saginaw; the crescent, which it thus describes, lying upon the southern border or nearly so, of what were the home possessions, intact and unaffected by previous treaties, of those bands of Chippewas whose chiefs and head-men met General Cass in Council at Saginaw.

Well beaten trails upon the Flint and its tributaries, reaching to their head waters and upon all the affluents of the Saginaw, all converging to the main river as the centre, forming a net-work of communication which might not inaptly be compared to an open fan, with the handle resting upon the treaty ground, gave the Chippewas, upon the banks of those streams, unobstructed access by land, as well as by canoes upon the rivers, to the Commissioner in Council. The advancing wave of white settlements had already approached and in some instances had without authority, encroached upon the southerly border of their network of trails upon the Flint.

In point of location, geographically, Ne-ome and his powerful band stood at the door, the very threshold of the large body of land which our Government, through its faithful and earnest Commissioner, wanted. To any one standing at Detroit and looking northerly to the beautiful belt of land lying westerly of the river St. Clair and Lake Huron, it was plain that the old Chief, Ne-ome, stood, unless well disposed toward the treaty, indeed a lion in the path.

Ne-ome was honest and simple-minded, evincing but little of the craft and cunning of his race, sincere in his nature, by no means astute, firm in his friendships, easy to be persuaded by any benefactor who should appeal to his Indian sense of gratitude ; harmless and kind.

In stature he was short and heavily moulded. With his own people he was a chief of partriarchal goodness, and his name is never mentioned by any of the members of his band, even at this remote day, except with a certain traditionary sorrow, more impressive, in its mournful simplicity, than a labored epitaph.

After General Cass had made known the purpose of the Government in calling the Council, he found the Chippewas as before detailed, with minds by no means disposed to treat or cede.

There was a power behind the throne greater than the throne itself. That power rested in the hands of an Indian trader who was known to the Chippewas as Wah-be-sins, (the young swan), and to the border settlers as Jacob Smith. He had been for a long time a trader among the Indians at different points on the Flint and Saginaw, both before and after the war of 1812. His principal trading post which he made his permanent one, the same year of the treaty, was at the Grand Traverse of the Flint, in the First Ward of that City, near where the Baptist Church now stands.

By long residence among them he had assimilated his habits and ways of living to those of the natives, even to the adoption of their mode of dress, and spoke their language fluently and correctly. He was generous to them, warm-hearted and intrepid. Though small in stature and light in weight, he was powerful as well as agile. Like most men living upon our Indian frontier, he had become the father of a half-breed family, one of whom, a daughter, by the name of Mo-kitch-e-no-qua, was then living.

Skilled in woodcraft, sagacious and adroit, he may be said to have equalled, if not excelled, the natives in many of those qualities which, as forest heroes, they most admire.

Brought into almost daily intercourse with the large band of Chippewas upon the Saginaw and its tributaries, the opportunity was at hand of ingratiating himself into the confidence of the chief and head men of that influential branch of the natives known as Ne-ome's band, and it is safe to say, that of the one hundred and fourteen chiefs and head men of the Chippewa nation, whose totems were affixed to the treaty, there was not one with whom he had not dealt and to whom he had not extended some act of friendship; either in dispensing the rites of hospitality at his trading post, or in substantial advances to them of bread or of blankets, as their necessities may have required.

He had entrenched himself in their friendship, and, at the time of the treaty, so nearly had he identified himself with the good old chief, Ne-ome, that each ever hailed the other as brother. Even to this day, Sa-gos-e-wa-qua, a daughter of Ne-ome, and others of his descendants now living, when speaking of Smith and the old chief, invariably bring their hands together, pressing the two index fingers closely to each other, as the Indian's symbol of brotherhood and warm attachment.

Upon the treaty ground the two friends acted unitedly and in perfect unison.

Smith had no position at the treaty, either as interpreter for or agent of Gen. Cass. He was personally known to the General, for when not at his trading post he was at Detroit, where he had a white family, but it is evident that he was looked upon with some distrust by the Commissioner.

For days the most active efforts of the authorized interpreters and agents of the government were ineffectual in conciliating Ne-ome, O-ge-maw-ke-ke-to and the other chiefs. Not a step of progress was made until Mr. Knaggs and other agents, who assumed, but with what authority is somewhat doubtful, to speak for the government outside of the council room, had promised the faithful Ne-ome that in addition to various and ample reservations for the different bands, of several thousand acres each, there should be reserved as requested by Wah-be-sins, (Smith,) eleven sections of land of six hundred and forty acres each, to be located at or near the Grand Traverse of the Flint. Eleven names as such reservees, all Indian names, were passed over to Mr. Knaggs on a slip of paper in his tent.

A council was again called several days after the first one and fully attended by all the chiefs and warriors. This with some other points of difficulty had become quieted. The storm which at first threatened to overwhelm the best efforts of the Commissioner and the active agents had passed over, and in its place a calm and open discussion ensued of the terms and basis upon which a just and honorable treaty should be, and at length was concluded. There was but one more general council held, which was mainly formal, for the purpose of having affixed to the engrossed copy of the treaty, the signatures of General Cass and the witnesses, and the totems of the chiefs and head men of the Chippewas and Ottawas.

A removal of the Chippewas west of the Mississippi, at least west of Lake Michigan, was one of the purposes sought to be gained by our Government at the treaty, in addition to the cession of the valuable body of land lying upon the Saginaw and its affluents. In the instructions from the War Department to the Commissioner, this purpose is set out among others; but it was discovered by the General, soon after his arrival at the council, that it was impossible to carry out that part of his instructions which related to the removal of the Indians, without hazarding the consummation of a treaty upon any terms.

This country had been so long occupied by their people, and was so well adapted to their hunter state, in the remarkable abundance of fish in its rivers, lakes and bays, and in the game yet left to them and not very materially diminished in the forest, that they were not inclined to listen to any proposition of removal.

The exterior lines of the territory ceded at this treaty, were as follows: "Beginning at a point on the present Indian boundary line which runs due north from the mouth of the Great Au Glaize, six miles south of the place where the Base Line, (so called,) intersects the same," (in the north-easterly part of what is now Jackson County;) "thence west sixty miles," (to a point in Kalamazoo County;) "thence in a direct line to the head of Thunder Bay River; thence down the same, following the course thereof, to the mouth; thence north-east to the boundary line between the United States and the British Province of Upper Canada; thence with the same to the line established by the Treaty of Detroit, of 1807; thence with the said line to the place of beginning."

An amusing incident occurred at the close of the treaty. Although hardly rising to the dignity of history, it is so illustrative of the state of things upon the treaty ground, that it may be worth preservation even if a little below the gravity of historical record.

The execution of the treaty was consummated about the middle of the afternoon of the last day. The silver, which was to be paid to the Indians upon its completion, was counted out upon the table in front of the Commissioner, for distribution.—The Saginaw chiefs and head men being largely indebted to Mr. Louis Campau, for goods before furnished, had put themselves under a promise to him that he should receive at least fifteen hundred dollars of the amount, in satisfaction of his just claims.

The Commissioner informed the Indians that all of the money was theirs, and if it was their will that Mr. Campau's debt should be first paid to him, to so signify and it should be done. Three other traders were present with goods for sale, and were by no means pleased to see so large a proportion of the money thus appropriated. Smith was one of the three traders. He urged the turbulent and besotted Kish-kaw-ko and his brother to object. They addressed the Commissioner: "We are your children; we want our money in our hands."

In accordance with this wish, the Commissioner directed the money to be paid to them, and Mr. Campau received none of his pay from that fund To use Mr. Campau's language: "I jumped from the platform and struck Smith two heavy blows in the face; he was smart as steel, and I was not slow; but Louis Beaufait, Conner, and Barney Campau got between us and stopped the fight. So I lost my money and they cheated me out of a good fight besides." "But," continued Mr. Campau, "I had my satisfaction that night. Five barrels of whiskey were opened by the United States Quarter Master for the Indians.— I ordered ten of mine to be opened, and two men to stand with dippers at the opened barrels. The Indians drank to fearful excess. At ten o'clock the General sent Robert Forsyth to me, to say: "The Indians are getting dangerous; General Cass says, stop the liquor." I sent word back to him, "General, you commenced it."

"A guard was detailed to surround my door. Soon after some Indians from the Bay were coming to my store, and the guard tried to keep them out with the bayonet. In the scuffle, one of the Indians was stabbed in the thigh. The war-whoop was given, and in fifteen minutes the building containing my store and the General's headquarters, were surrounded by excited Indians with tomahawks in their hands. They came from all points. Cass came to the door of his lodgings, looking very grotesque, with a red bandanna handkerchief tied about his head, exclaiming "Louis! Louis! stop the liquor; we shall all be killed. I say stop the liquor, Louis." I said to him, "General, you commenced it; you let Smith plunder me and rob me, but I will stand between you and all harm."

He called out to me again, "Louis! Louis! send those Indians to their wigwams." I said, "Yes, General, but you commenced it."

Mr. Campau said in closing, "I lost my money, I lost my fight; I lost my liquor; but I got good satisfaction."

Mr. Campau left his trading post at Saginaw City, for a permanent removal, in June, 1826; his brother, Antoine, succeeding him. The building has but recently been removed and will be readily called to mind, upon the west side of Water street opposite Wright & Co's Mill, as the residence until within a few years, of that genial old Frenchman, J. Baptiste Desnoyers, who made the dilapidated tenement, with its rickety stairs and loose flooring, seem cheerful with his cordial welcome.

It may be mentioned here that for one year, (1819,) Mr. Campau also occupied a trading post on the site of what is now East Saginaw, near where the Methodist Mission House was afterwerds erected; but finding the Indians discontented, he soon abandoned it. Their announcement of dissatisfaction was sudden and unmistakably pointed: "We gave you the other side for trading; go there."

In the fall of 1826, he became the proprietor of two fractional quarters, by government entry, covering what is now a large part of the site of the flourishing city of Grand Rapids.

He has been emphatically the father of that flourishing inland town. Selling his fine landed estate with the greatest liberality; endorsing freely for enterprising new-comers to that place; associating himself with every worthy enterprise—the sequence we readily anticipate—embarassment and straitened means; the classical but very inconvenient *res angustae* at home; an humble but cheerful cottage, with a limited garden-plat, upon the secluded outskirts of his once lordly possessions. In connection with these facts how pleasant to read a paragraph, which appeared recently in the Detroit *Free Press.*

"*A Nice Thing Nicely Done.*—Under this head a Grand Rapids paper gives an account of a Christmas present to Louis Campau, Esq. The presentation was made by a number of leading citizens, and consisted of a purse containing $1,040."

The same autumn of the treaty, (1819,) Smith, whose influence with the Indians was so marked on that occasion, built a trading-house, rough and of limited dimensions, near where the Baptist Church now stands, in the city of Flint. He lived there during the trading season, making occasional visits to his family in Detroit. In 1825, he died, from neglect as much as from disease, at his trading post, after a lingering and pitiable sickness. A good hearted Frenchman, by the name of Baptiste Cochios, who was with him upon the treaty ground in 1819, and himself an Indian trader, having his posts upon the Flint and on the Saginaw, performed for the brave but unfortunate man the last sad rites of humanity. An Indian lad, who had lived with Mr. Smith for several years and attended him in his sickness, was the only household mourner.

He was the same Indian whose name was associated in later years as co-plaintiff with the Messrs. Dewey, of Flint, in several actions of ejectment brought to recover from the occupants Section Two, on which the First Ward of that city is situated. The proof however showed that his real name was An-ne-me-kins, and that he was not the genuine Me-ta-wa-ne-ne, for whom a section of land was intended and reserved in article third of the treaty.

A few Indians gathered in mournful groups about the grave, as the remains of the unfortunate man were committed to the earth. Ne-ome was there, his trusty and reliable friend, mute with grief.

With that feeling of gratitude which belongs to the Indian character, and which takes rank as a cardinal virtue in their untutored minds, the Indians proved true and faithful throughout his sickness to the last.

The brave, warm-hearted, generous Indian trader, Jacob Smith, the earliest white pioneer upon the Saginaw and the Flint, lingered and died in sad condition, and but for the good Cochios and his Indian assistants, would have gone to his grave uncoffined.

Within a few days after his decease, his son-in-law, C. S. Payne, came out from Detroit, to the trading-house which had so recently been the scene of such long and unrelieved suffering, and gathered up most carefully and carried away the few poor remnants of the earthly stores left by the noble-hearted Indian trader.

Sa-gos-e-wa-qua, the daughter of No-ome, in recounting this history, expressed herself with a sententious brevity peculiar to the Indian and worth recording. "It points a moral," if it does not "adorn a tale." "When Wah-be-sins (Smith) sick nobody come. Him sicker and sicker; nobody come. Wah-be-sins die, little tinker come and take all him blankets, all him cattle, all him things."

No-ome soon followed his friend Wah-be-sins to the Spirit Land. He died in 1827, at his tribal home, a few miles above Saginaw City, enthroned, in patriarchal simplicity, in the hearts of his people, beloved, mourned and faithfully attended, through a long and severe sickness, by his children and relatives.

Judge Gardiner D. Williams became an Indian trader at Saginaw City, in the spring of 1828. His brother, Ephraim S. Williams, joined him in the autumn of that year. They occupied the little red building at the foot of Mackinaw Street as their store, where they continued to trade until 1840.

They were the sons of Oliver Williams, who emigrated from Old Concord, Middlesex County, Massachusetts, before the War of 1812. He became a merchant at Detroit, and at the opening of hostilities was engaged in the commerce of the lakes. His vessel was captured at Mackinaw and himself taken prisoner.—His vessel was in the enemy's fleet at the memorable battle of Lake Erie, which has immortalized the name of Perry, her name having been changed by them from the "Friend's Good Will," to the "Little Belt."

In March, 1819, he established himself, with his family, on what was afterwards known as the "old homestead," near Silver Lake, three miles north of Pontiac, where the two sons remained until their removal to Saginaw City, in 1828.

Reaume, a Frenchman and an old Indian trader, was at that time and at that point, the agent of the American Fur Company. He and the Messrs. Campau had had personal difficulties of long standing, which had become an inveterate feud, creating unprofitable divisions with the Indians, amounting with them to fierce partizan hatred. The current was turned against Reaume, and his personal safety becoming endangered, his store was kept closed too much of the time for him to continue a profitable agent for the company at that post. Judge Abbott, the Company's Superintendent at Detroit, selected the Messrs. Williams as the successors of Reaume, who came on as before detailed, and became the owners of his interests at Saginaw City, and also at the Little Fork of the Tittabawassee, (Midland City,) where he had another post. Dequindre, an active young Frenchman, had been his local sub-agent, until a vicious Indian by the name of Wah-be-man-ito or White Devil, forcibly took possession of the post, driving out the sub-agent, who fled for his life, for several days roaming about, lost in the woods, and ultimately coming into Saginaw City with his feet frozen. The Campaus had a rival post at the same place, and by the abandonment of the other, the valuable trade of the Tittabawassee was left wholly in their hands.

The winter after Mr. E. S. Williams had establisned himself at Saginaw City, he was deputed to take stores to that point and re-open the trading-house. He chose for his asistants, Jacob Graveradt, and the two younger Roys. Prudent friends endeavored to persuade him not to embark in an enterprise so evidently fraught with danger,but the Company's interests required the venture, and he soon with his assistants presented himself at the post. A short time only elapsed before Wah-be-man-ito resumed his attitude of hostility. He was on his way with his outfit to the trapping ground, somewhat in liquor.

He stopped at the door of the trading post, and with an insoent and defiant bearing, which a half-drunken Indian only can assume, demanded liquor. "Mish-sha-way," (Mr. Williams name, meaning Big Elk,) "give me whiskey." It was refused. He placed his hand upon the handle of his tomahawk, and repeated the demand more fiercely than at first, and was met by another refusal as defiant as his last demand.

He sprang for Mr. Williams with his tomahawk upraised, and aimed a blow at him which, if it had not been dexteriously avoided, would doubtless have proved fatal. With a well seasoned hickory club Mr. Williams defended himself, knocking his assailant down and being about to repeat the blow the discomfitted hero begged for mercy.

After getting upon his feet and recovering from the stunning effects of the blow he walked out of the trading house and sate down in front of it in apparently deep thought. He soon after called to Mr. Williams and expressed great mortification at the outrage he had attempted; and to confirm his sincerity promised that his next furs he would bring to his *new friend* Williams.—He kept his promise faithfully and became the fast friend of the man at whom, within an hour previous, he had aimed a deadly blow.

The Messrs. Williams sooon after bought out the trading post of Antoine Campau who had, as before stated, succeeded to his brother Louis, which quieted the dangerous spirit of rivalry that had already culminated in some serious affrays between the Indians and others who had become parties to the feud. Among other agents who had residences, at different times, at Saginaw, were Sherman Stevens, the father of the distinguished actress Miss Sara Stevens, who has achieved in the drama no ordinary position. To considerable solid acquirement he united a vein of romance and sentiment which made him at that time a genial companion and a rare social acquisition to the limited society of Saginaw. He was master of the Chippewa dialect and spoke the language fluently and well.

Archie Lyons was another trustworthy agent of the Messrs. Williams, whose history is identified with the Saginaw Valley prior to the Treaty. He was a fine penman well educated and a musician of no little skill. He was located at the little Forks of the Tittabawassee (Midland City) and in coming down from that point, on the ice, upon skates, for the purpose of playing the violin for a dancing party at Saginaw City he was drowned.

His track was found upon the ice the next day, to the edge of the hole into which he had skated, leaving no doubt as to his fate.

His, widow, a bright and agreeable woman, of French and Indian extraction, who rejoiced in the almost unpronouncable name of Ka-ze-zhe-ah-be-no-qua, became afterwards the wife of Antoine Peltier of Pine-ne-con-ning; a second marriage that was undoubtedly justifiable if her object was to free herself from her most remarkable Indian name.

The Messrs. Williams had another agent, Mejeau, an Indian of quarter blood; an accurate clerk although he could neither read nor write. Thousands of dollars passed through his hands yearly. His mode of keeping accounts was the same as that usually adopted among the agents. A straight mark symbolized one dollar. One O a muskrat or a quarter of a dollar. Two O's a half dollar. Instead of the name of the Indian his totem was drawn upon the book and prefixed to his accounts. O-ge-mau-ke-ke-to's totem was a long fish, a spotted pickerel, which he made with some skill, another's was a beaver, another's a bear &c.

Judge G. D. Williams, died at his homestead at Saginaw City on the 11th day of Dec. A. D. 1858, beloved and mourned.— His brother, Mr. E. S. Williams, is still living at Windsor, opposite Detroit, with his constitution unimpaired by his early border life, and a strength of muscle still intact, that would make any modern Wah-be-man-ito tremble in an encounter.

John or Jack Smythe had a trading house, from 1830 to 1832, at Saginaw City a little below the Campau trading house. It stood there until within a few years and will be remembered as a building with a thatched roof. He was a trader of but little prominence.

The writer of this article is indebted to Mr. E. S. Williams for the facts of the following incident, which occurred while Mr. Williams was a resident of Saginaw City and of which he was personally cognizant, one of the most romantic and remarkable affairs to be found in our border annals.

Some few years after the treaty and soon after Judge Jewitt, Col. Stannard, and the Messrs. Williams became residents of Saginaw City this incident occurred, strongly illustrative of frontier life and of Indian character.

Nah-way-go was a young Saginaw Brave, living in his earlier life at Green Point and his later years upon the Lake Shore.— He is described as a model of native strength and grace.

While living at the former place he killed a son of Red Bird who lived on the Tittabawassee Reservation. The relatives demanded satisfaction and by Indian law his life was the forfeit. He presented himself at the chief mourner's wigwam where the warriors of the family of the deceased had assembled and informed them that he had come for them to strike at his heart. He bared his bosom and took his position for the selected number to pass by him and inflict the knife wound. They passed and inflicted, as they hoped, the mortal thrusts. That done and Indian usage being satisfied he was making the best speed he could, with his streaming wounds, to his own wigwam when he was struck in the back by a cowardly Indian, inflicting a severe stab but as it appears, like the other blows, not fatal. He was yet enabled to reach his wigwam where his young wife was awaiting in anxiety, his return. She received him and bound up his wounds. He was restored after fearful suffering.

Finding the coward afterwards upon his hunting ground, who had inflicted upon him the wound in the back he visited him summarily with Indian vengeance; death.

Soon after the Indians were assembled in large numbers at Saginaw City at a "payment." An altercation ensued between Black Beaver, an Indian of considerable note and the young Brave, Nah-way-go; the former reproaching him with the outrage he had committed upon the Indian who had struck him in the back. Nah-way-go defended the act as just and brave.— The reproof was repeated and upon the instant he slew Black Beaver.

This was near the site of the Emerson mill on the east side of the river; Black Beaver and his band were there encamped; on the west side and below the city, on the open plain, Nah-way-go and his band were encamped. After the bloody deed he crossed over to the west side among his own people.

A warrant was at once issued by Col. Stannard for his arrest, acting as Justice. Nah-way-go fled back to the east side of the river and accompanied by a friend secreted himself in the woods upon what is now the site of East Saginaw.

He preferred to trust himself on the same side of the river with the tribe whose leading warrior he had stricken down than to endure the mortification of arrest and punishment by the white man's law.

He sent word to two of his white friends, Antoine Campau and Mr. E. S. Williams desiring, them to cross the river and come to the woods, in which he was secreted, when by giving a signal he would come to them.

They did so and he soon made his appearance. He informed them that he had sent for them for advice; that the white man's punishment, imprisonment, was only fit for cowards; death by the hands of his own race was glorious, in comparison, if any relative of Black Beaver should choose to make it a cause of vengeance.

They advised him to cross back to his own camp, present himself to his people and let the affair take the course warranted by Indian usage.

The arrest by the officer was waived and he presented himself at his own camp openly.

The hour for the burial of Black Beaver arrived. An immense number of Indians were gathered as mourners and spectators at the place for burial which was between the old Campau trading house and the river. The body had been placed in the coffin.— The relatives with their faces streaked with black paint had gathered about it. The few white settlers then in the Valley were all there as spectators. The fearful outrage, so near to their own doors, had absorbed and engrossed the attention of all.

While the solemn Indian rite was in progress over the remains of their favorite warior, Nah-way-go was seen approaching from his camping ground.

He was dressed in full and careful costume; tomahawk and knife in girdle and a small canteen of whiskey at his side; his whole appearance imposing and gallant.

He made his way with a lofty and majestic step to the centre of the mourning group.

Walking, with measured step, to the side of the coffin he placed upon it his tomahawk and knife.

He filled his calumet with kinikinnick, composedly and with diginity. After smoking from it himself first, he passed it to the chief mourner, who declined it. He passed it to the next and the next with the same result.

He passed his canteen of whiskey with the same formality and with the same result. They declined to partake.

He then undid the collar of his hunting shirt and bared his bosom, seating himself with calm dignity upon the foot of the coffin.

He turned his face full upon the chief mourners and addressed them :

"You refuse my pipe of peace. You refuse to drink with me. You wish my life. Here it is. Strike deep. Strike not in the back. Strike not and miss. The man that does, dies when I meet him on our hunting ground."

Not a hand was raised. Upon the dark and stoical faces of that cloud of enemies, by whom he was surrounded, no feeling found expression except of awe; no muscle moved.

He rose, and towering to his full fine height, exclaimed:—"Cowards, cowards, cowards."

As composedly as he had taken them out he restored, unmolested, the tomahawk and knife to his girdle and, with his canteen at his side, walked away from the strange scene as lordly as he came.

He had awed his enemies and was evidently master of the situation.

Removing soon after to the lake shore, away from the scene of his early feuds and fearful exploits he fell ultimately upon the hunting ground in a personal recontre with a relative of one of his early victims

A forest hero! as fearless as Rob Roy, as chivalrous as Rhod-erick Dhu. The theme is worthy of the pen of a Sir Walter or the epic verse of Whittier, Hosmer or Street. It is certainly somewhat above the flight of a plain prose pen.

Mr. NORMAN LITTLE may well be called the projector and father of the enterprising city of East Saginaw.

Mr. Little was the son of Docter Charles Little of East Avon, Livingston County, New York, who had become a pioneer there as early as 1797, emigrating from Columbia County, Connecticut. He practised his profession for forty-two years in Livingston County.

In 1822, certainly a very early day in the history of Northern Michigan, the Doctor formed a very favorable opinion of the Saginaw Valley from an inspection of the then imperfect maps of this part of the State, and deposited with Chancellor Farnsworth at Detroit sufficient money to secure the lands to himself, by government entry, which he deemed the most valuable upon the Saginaw. In 1823 and 1824 he again visited the valley and traced all the tributaries of the Saginaw and had the entries made, which he deemed desirable, immediately, upon the opening of the Land office.

He entered lands upon the Saginaw for several miles extending, from the lowest point of East Saginaw, all the way, with occassional exceptions, to Green Point, including in his purchases the site of what is now the flourishing village of Salina, and on the other side of the river, for several miles from Saginaw City to the Tittabawassee and also above upon that stream. Doctor Little was familiar with and had passed over the site of Rochester N. Y., in an early day, many times, when it was a silvan waste and had seen that and other localities which could have been purchased at nominal prices, converted, as if by magic, into busy marts. The same money which he had been loaning to the farmers of Livingston at seven per cent., if invested in such localities, would have returned him a princely income. Acting upon a theory which had been thus practically impressed upon him, and with a foresight eminently wise, he made the entries spoken of. Like causes in Michigan have produced effects similar to those in Western New York and his descendents feel and appreciate his far seeing sagacity.

After a life of eminent usefulness he died at the homestead in 1842. His son Norman Little, partaking of the enterprising spirit of his father came through to Saginaw City by the Indian trail at an early day. In his company were some eight or nine others from Western New York. They made their intended explorations and returned.

Mr. Norman Liltle removed from Littleville and became a permanent resident of Saginaw City in 1836. He bought the sight of that place, the Military Reserve, for himself, Mackie, Oakley and Jennison of New York City. Price $55,000.

The purchase was made of Dr. Millington of Ypsilanti who had bought of the Government at public sale for $12,000.

Mr. Little came from Detroit in June 1836 with Governor Mason by steamboat up the Saginaw, the first steam vessel, it is said, that ever ploughed the waters of that river.

The expenditures of the firm of Mackie & Co., of which Mr. Little was a member, in their efforts to build up Saginaw City by the erection of various expensive structures, which still stand as monuments of their enterprise, amounted to a large sum, and followed so soon by the financial crisis of 1837 and 1838, it is not to be wondered at that trouble and embarrassment ensued, causing further active efforts on their part, at that time, to build up Saginaw City, almost entirely to cease.

Disappointed but not discouraged, Mr. Norman Little turned his attention to the east side of the river and, in 1850, induced Mr. James M. Hoyt of the old firm of Eli Hoyt & Co. of New York City, and his son, Mr. Jesse Hoyt, to become interested, with himself, each one third, in the site and business of East Saginaw.

They had been business acquaintenances and old friends for many years, when Mr. Little resided at Littleville where the father and son had both shared his hospitality and knew the intrinsic worth and goodness of his character.

To consummate the enterprise two hundred and twenty acres, upon the site of East Saginaw, and other property amounting to 2,400 acres, on the same side of the river, were bought by the partners; a portion from those who had purchased of Dr. Little's estate and some from Messrs. Carroll, and others of Livingston County, New York.

From an enterprise, thus inaugurated by Mr. Norman Little, East Saginaw entered upon its career of remarkable prosperity, and his memory may well be cherished, with a tender care, by those now enjoying the fruits of his far-seeing wisdom; especially when they call to mind the struggles through which he passed and the courage with which he carried his plans through to a glorious fruition.

Mr. Little removed from Saginaw City to East Saginaw, for a permanent residence, in the year 1852, where he continued to reside until his decease in 1860.

To great energy of character and a physical endurance, not a little remarkable, Mr. Little united a mild and benevolent disposition and a truly social nature, which rendered him, to the latest moment of his life, an object of affectionate regard to those who were his juniors and of uninterrupted attachment to the friends and associates of past years. To the latter he ever remained constant and true, for friendship, with him, was a sacred sentiment, admitting no cold and heartless change. They could not and did not forget him. He could not and did not forget them. True friendship and a spirit of universal hospitality belonged to his nature and became substantial characteristics. In his view they were cardinal virtues.

But few of this class of pioneers now remain.

The ancient landmarks are fast disappearing.

"Time rolls his ceaseless course."

Mr. Harvey Williams, whose history is identified with the Saginaw Valley since 1834, was for many years, prior thereto, a resident of Detroit, where he was engaged in the foundery business, was a skillfulll machinist and was sometimes employed as a mill-wright.

Mr. Williams deserves something more than a passing notice as one the very few yet living of the earlier stock of emigrants from the Eastern States to this then remote territory.

1815 was the year of his emigration from Charlton, Worcester County, Massachusetts, to Detroit, where he continued to reside until the time of his removal to Saginaw City, where he entered into the lumbering business, building there the first steam sawmill north-west of Detroit and giving his attention to that until 1838, in which year his well known integrity of character caused him to be employed by the State in the opening of roads. He constructed the road from Flint to Saginaw City, *via* Bridgeport, and, in the various enterprises of that era, which had for their object the improvement of the communications with the Saginaw Valley by water as well as by land, he was among the foremost. And through his influence the Light House at the mouth of the river was established and for a year was taken charge of by him.

In the winter of 1822 —3 Mr. Williams made a trip from Detroit to Saginaw in performance of a contract made by himself, and Col. John Hamilton yet living at Flint, with the Government to take supplies through to that point for the use of the garrison established there in 1822. On this trip they were accompanied by Mr. E. S. Williams and Schuyler Hodges, late of Pontiac, as guides and assistants.

At Saginaw City he found Mr. Louis Campau and Reaume, interpreter Archie Lyons, Provensal, Indian blacksmith. and two or three others engaged in the fur trade, the only white persons there except the two Companies of United States Infantry at the Garrison.

These troops were of the 3d Regiment and had been ordered from Green Bay to occupy the Post, for the protection of the Saginaw valley and adjacent frontier.

They were under the command of Major Daniel Baker and remained at this point a little more than a year. After losing some valuable officers, Lieutenants Baker and Allen, and many from the ranks, by disease. they received from the War Department an order for their removal to Detroit. The locality was considered at that time and doubtless was exceedingly unhealthy. The flooding of the valleys of the Saginaw and its tributaries, the spring previous to their removal, by the rapid melting of the unusually heavy body of snow then upon the ground, had, with the excessive heat of the following summer, generated endemic diseases which baffled the best medical skill.

The venerable and beloved Docter Pitcher, of Detroit, who was then Assistant Surgeon in the regular army, and had reported to Major Baker at this time, was in attendance upon the Garrison.

His skill and efforts did much to prevent and alleviate but could only partially stay the progress of disease.

The Fort was abandoned in the autumn of 1823, an event, which from the reasons assigned for its discontinuance, tended to draw away attention from the Saginaw valley and retard immigration.

On the route from Detroit to Saginaw City Mr. Williams and his company found but five or six settlers; at Pontiac, Orison Allen, Mr. Oliver Williams at Silver Lake, Alpheus Williams the father of Harvey, at Waterford, Jacob Stevens at Grand Blanc, Edward Campau a half breed, who had lost an arm, (the Now-o-ke-ghick named in article 3d of the Treaty,) and the unfortunate Smith at Grand Traverse (Flint). Of Mr. Jacob Stevens, there should be, if the annals of that locality were within the scope of this article, a more extended notice. He was a true type of the gentlemen of the old school, to whose moral and physical courage, as a pioneer, was united a rare intelligence, marked by a literary taste showing itself conspicuously even in the few scattered remnants of his correspondence which have come down to this day.

In 1837 Mr. Williams built, for Messrs. Mackie & Co., of which firm Mr. Norman Little and himself were members, having each one-fifth interest, the Saw mill, since known as the Emerson mill. The year previous he had erected the first frame dwelling house, near the mill, on what is now the site of the city of East Saginaw. Of the latter place he has become a permanent resident quite recently.

For several years he lived at his homestead at the mouth of the Kaw-kaw-ling, (the name of which Mr. W. says is O-gah-kahning) a few miles westerly from the mouth of the Saginaw, where he traded largely with the Indians and was engaged very extensively in the Lake and Bay fisheries.

So fair and upright have been his dealings with not only, his white neighbors but also with the natives, that he has secured to himself the sincere and unchanging respect and regard of all.

Those friends, who have shared the hospitality of his house, upon that bleak promentory which projects into the bay, particularly in midwinter, when the winds from the north have been abroad in their wrath, know how to appreciate the warmth of his welcome at the threshold; the hospitable, savory board, the profusion of which was only equaled by its neatness; the luxurious beds for tired, chilled limbs; and last, but certainly not least, that glorious barrel of "Bay water," which had taken on a remarkably fine flavor, as we were assured by 'uncle Harvey,' by its having been so long 'rocked in the cradle of the deep;' the stories of the olden time, Indian and pioneer incidents so pleasantly interspersed with the "night-caps;" all—all never to be forgotten memories—

"Such things have been and were most pleasant."

Under the name of Buena Vista the little hamlet of settlers, in the vicinage of the Emerson mill, was formally organized into a Township and in its first annual township election, of 1848, its destinies were swayed by a constituency of solid yeomanry, numbering five, composed of Curtis Emerson and Charles W. Grant Esquires, the two Messrs. Willey and Stephen Warner.

This small settlement, whose destinies were soon to be united, by social and commercial ties and a common bond of interest and brotherhood, with those who, under the influence of that excellent gentleman, Norman Little, and his brother Col. W. L. P. Little, established themselves, somewhat later, upon what is now the busy mart and central part of East Saginaw, received, in February 1855, their common franchises as a village and, in February, 1859, their charter as a city.

The philosophical and just thinker and writer, De Tocqueville, whose "Democracy in America" has taken its place among the standard works of the age upon governmental polity; a work which as well honors his heart as his head, was desirous, upon his arrival in our country in 1831, to visit some of our outposts upon civilization's extreme frontier. He desired to look in upon some of our remote, primeval vallies, the then almost unoccupied cradles of future populations.

He selected the valley of the Saginaw and we find him at that time, in the consummation of his purpose, crossing from the east side of that river to Saginaw City in a canoe, swimming his horse behind his frail bark and remaining for a few days at the latter place to indulge himself in his philosophical observations at that advanced outpost of civilization, then numbering within its limits less than forty people old and young.

He says in a way which seemes, if the expression can be pardoned, like a prophetic *on-look* into the future:

"In a few years these impenetrable forests will have fallen; "the sons of civilization and industry will break the silence of "the Saginaw; the banks will be imprisoned by quays; its cur-"rent which now flows on, unnoticed and tranquil, through a "nameless waste, will be stemmed by the prows of vessels.— "More than one hundred miles sever this solitude from the great "European settlements and we were perhaps the last travelers "allowed to see its primitive grandeur."

The glorious anticipations of the French traveler and *savant*, bearing now upon them almost the look of inspiration, have become, under the shield and arm of those Republican Institutions, which he so much admired, and the spirit of which he so justly interpreted, the well established realities of our day.

Those Pioneers of stout hearts and strong hands of Saginaw City:—The Messrs. G. D. and E. S. Williams, Eleazer Jewett, Abram Butts, Col. Stannard, Judge Elijah N. Davenport, Thos. Simpson, (familiarly and humorously known to the early inhabitants as Lick-se-bo-gee) Benjamin Cochios, Harvey Miller, Albert Miller, the Messrs. Gotee, the Messrs. Little, Hiram L. Miller, George W. Bullock, Charles L. Richman, James Frazer, Eliel Barber, Nelson Smith, T. L. Howe, Samuel Gordon, Joshua Blackmer, Charles S. Palmer, Joseph Malden, Perry G. Gardiner, Doctor George Davis, Anthony R: Swarthout, James Busbey, William F. Moseley, John Smith, William McDonald, and other gentlemen of enterprise and distinction: And of East Saginaw—Curtis Emerson. Charles W. Grant, Messrs. Norman and William L. P. Little, W. F. Glasby, the Messrs. Willey, Moses B. Hess, George Oliver, Adoniram Dan, Alexander English, the Messrs Curtis and others who have identified themselves with the developements of this favored locality: and of Bay City—J. Baptiste Truedell, Sydney S. Campbell, James McCormick, Albert Miller, Cromwell Barny, Daniel Chapel the Messrs. Tromble, Captain Israel Marsac, James Watson, Benjamin F. Pierce, Frederick W. Backus, Israel Catlin, James G. Birney, Curtis Munger, not omitting here the name of Mr. James Frazer, the later years of whose life were identified with this place; the announcement of whose death yet lingers so painfully in our ears; all of whose names, together with many others not here enumerated, are worthy of an enduring place in the early annals of this storied Valley—*Nobiles Fratres*—have worked out the prophecies of the French philosopher, De Tocqueville, to a perfect solution, a full fruition, and have stamped upon the friendly predictions of 1831 the undying impress of Truth.

BATTLE OF SKULL ISLAND.

The following communication was prepared by William McCormick, now an honored citizen of Portsmouth, which we publish by request:—

Messrs. Galatian & Thomas, Gents:—I modestly offer the following narrative for publication in your history of Saginaw. Being one of the early pioneers of this valley brought up on the frontier with no advantages and no society except the hardy adventurer and the Indians,it must not therefore be expected to find the theme as interesting as if penned by a more skilfull hand. My father emigrated to the Valley when I was but ten years old; my associates were mostly among the Indians, which language I became almost as familiar with as my own; and for a great many years was engaged in the fur trade. During this time I used to go up the different tributaries of the Saginaw to buy furs, and on nearly all such occasions I found indications that the Saginaw Valley was inhabited by a different race of people prior to the present Indians. On nearly all the tributaries can be found mounds filled with human bones which I have opened for my own satisfaction and found them lying in all directions showing they were thrown together without any regularity, upon which I became satisfied they were killed in battle. This awakened in me a curiosity to find out what people they were, and where and what had become of them. I often questioned the Indians in regard to it, but they would invariably say that there were two or three very old Indians living on the Bay that could tell me all about it, telling me their names. Accordingly in one of my journeys to the bay I sought out the Indians in question, I think this was in 1834. I found him a very old man, I asked him his age. He said he thought he was a great deal over 100 years. His faculties were as bright as a man of 50. I told him I understood he could give me the tradition of his race. He said he could as it was handed down to him by his grandfather, who he said was older than he was now when he told him. For fear I should not get it correct I called to my aid an educated man who was part Indian, Peter Grewett, a man well known by the early settlers as an Indian trader and is still living I believe in Gratiot County, and has spent his life with the Indians, in in the fur trade, and was for many years in the employment of the American Fur Company.

The old Indian (Puttaguasamine, which was his name) commenced as follows: He said the Socks occupied the whole of the Saginaw river and its tributaries, extending from Thunder Bay on the north to the head of the Shiawassee on the south and from Lake Michigan on the west to Detroit on the east. The balance of Michigan was occupied by the Pottawatomies, and the Lake Superior country was occupied by the Chippewa and Ottawas, while the Monomonies was at the head of Green Bay in Wisconsin, and another tribe west of the Mississippi, which he called the Sous. The main village of the Socks stood on the west side of the Saginaw river just below where the residence of Mr. Frank Fitzhugh now is, and opposite the mill of the Hon. N. B. Bradley.

The Socks were always at war with their Chippewa neighbors on the north and the Pottawatomies on the south and also with other nations in Canada, until at last a Council was called consisting of the Chippewas, Pottawatomies, Monomonies, Ottawas and Six Nations of New York. At an appointed time they all met at the Island of Mackinaw, where they fitted out a large army and started in bark canoes, and came down the west shore of Lake Huron. They then stole along the west shore of Saginaw bay by night, and lay concealed during the day, until they arrived at a place about ten miles from the mouth of Saginaw, a place called Petobegong. Here they landed part of their army, while the rest crossed the Bay and landed to the east of the mouth of the Saginaw river in the night. In the morning both armies started up the river, one on each side, so as to attack both villages at once. The army on the west side attacked the main village first by surprise, and massacred nearly all; the balance retreated across the river to another village, which stood near where the Court House now stands, near the ferry, in Portsmouth. At this time that part of the army that had landed on the east side of the river came up and a desparate battle took place in the vicinity of the residence of Wm. R. McCormick, that being the highest land and where they had attempted to fortify themselves; and at the present time by digging in this hill you will find it full of human bones which were killed in that battle. Here they were again defeated; they then crossed the river and retreated to Skull Island, which is the next island above what is now called Stone's island. Here they considered themselves safe as their enemies had no canoes and they could fortify themselves. But the next night after their retreat to the island the ice froze thick enough for the allies to cross, which they did, when another massacre ensued; here they were all exterminated with the exception of twelve females. Since which time this island has been called Skull island, from the number of skulls found on it in after years.—The allies then divided, some going up the Cass, some up the Flint, others up the Shiawassee, Tittabawassee and so on, where there were different bands located. But the largest battles were fought on the Flint; one about half a mile below the present city of Flint on the bluff. Another Indian traditionist says another reinforcement met them here coming through from Detroit, here there is a large number of mounds filled with bones which can be seen at the present day. They then came down the river and fought another battle on the bluff about a mile above the present village of Flushing on the farm formerly owned by a Mr. Bailey. Here there is also a large number of mounds yet to be seen, and, if you shonld dig them open as I have, you will find them filled with human bones.—

The next battle was fought about 16 miles below Flushing on the farm formerly occupied by the late James McCormick.

There were several battles fought on the Cass, at what is now called the Bend or Bridgeport Center, where there was a fortification of earth work which was plainly to be seen 35 years ago. The next important battle was fought on the Tittabawassee just above the farm on which the late James Fraser first settled when he came to the Saginaw valley. This differs from the rest as the remains of the slain were all buried in one mound, and it is a very large one.

After the extermination of the whole nation, with the exception of the twelve females before spoken of, a council of the allies was then held, to know what should be done with them. Some were for torturing and killing, others for sparing their lives, finally it was agreed they should be sent west of the Mississippi, and an arrangement was made with the Sioux that no tribe should molest them, and the Sioux should be responsible for their protection, which agreement was faithfully kept. The conquered country, of which the present Saginaw valley is a part, was then divided among them all as a common hunting ground. But a great many who came here to hunt never returned nor were ever heard of. It became the opinion of the Indians that the spirits of the dead Socks still haunted their hunting grounds and were killing off their hunters; when, in fact, it was a few Socks who had escaped the massacre and still lingered around their hunting grounds watching for straggling hunters and killing them where ever an opportunity occurred. Ton-do-gong, an Indian chief who died in 1840, told me he killed a Sock while hunting when a boy, this must have been over 80 years ago, and up to a few years ago the Indians still believed there was a Sock in the vicinity. They had seen the place where he had made his fires and slept. I have known them to get together and not hunt for several days for the reason, they said, there was a Sock in the woods, they had seen where he had slept; I used to laugh at them but it was of no avail, you could not make them believe otherwise.

But to go back to the Indian tradition, the country was considered as haunted, and no more Indians came here to hunt, although game was abundant. Finally, it was converted into what would be termed among civilized nations a Penal colony; every Indian who committed a crime would flee or be banished to the haunted hunting grounds (Saginaw valley), to escape punishment, for the Indian laws were more severe and strict then, than now. This was long before we became degraded by coming in contact with the whites, said the Indian.

The Chippewas becoming the most numerous finally their language predominated, and at the present time the Indians in the Saginaw valley do not speak, in all respects, the same as the Chippewas on Lake Superior, from which they originally sprung; showing that the mixing of different nations in the Saginaw valley has been the cause of the same. Put-ta-gua-sa-mine said his grand father told it to him when he was a boy, which was 90 years before, and that it had been handed down to his grand father from his ancestors and was a custom with him to repeat it often to his people, so that the tradition or history should not be lost, and a successor was always appointed in case the traditionist should die, that the history of the nation should not be lost, and be handed down from generation to generation.

I have talked with two other old Indians on the same subject, and their tradition is precisely the same, word for word with one exception; they say the battles on the Flint were fought by the army coming from Detroit. I have no doubt the above is a correct narrative, as much so as if it had been written at the time and handed down to us as a matter of history.

I cannot close this rough narrative without a kind rememberance to those early pioneers who shared our privations and our happiness. I say privations, they certainly were; for weeks and months there was not a barrel of flour in the valley; our nearest mill was Pontiac, and nothing but an Indian trail; we had to get to Flint the best we could, and then bring it down the river in canoes. But we always had one resource that never failed us, which was to pound corn in a mortar. If one had a few pounds of flour he shared it with his neighbor, in fact they were more like relatives than neighbors. Perhaps it would be interesting to your readers to know who those pioneers were, or some of them: Gardner and Ephraim Williams, Judge Jewett, James McCormick, who lived on the Flint, James Fraser, Judge Davenport, Judge Miller of Portsmouth, Thomas Simpson *alias* Lix-a-bo-ga, and Judge Stowe of Flint.

But they are all passing away. PIONEER.

SALT.

Although the question as to the existence of a salt basin here was demonstrated as late as 1860, yet it was agitated when the country was quite new. It was known that many surface indications or deer-licks were found, and most of these were called salt springs. When Congress in June 1836 passed an act providing for the admission of Michigan into the Union and for settling the Northern boundary of Ohio, it was among other things provided that "all the salt springs within the State not exceeding twelve in number" with six sections of land adjoining each might be selected by the State, and in pursuance of this act, the Legislature of Michigan by act of July 25th, 1836, authorized the Governor of the State to make the selection. Most of the lands were selected in the Grand River Valley, but one tract was selected on the Tittabawassee river at the mouth of Salt river, and by Act approved March 24th, 1838, the State Geologist, (Douglas Houghton) was "authorized and directed as soon as "practicable at one or more of the State salt springs to commence boring for salt." An appropriation of $3,000 was made to defray the expenses of the work. Pursuant to this direction Dr. Houghton selected one point in the south-west corner of Section 24, in township 15 North, of Range 1 West, on the west side of the Tittabawassee river and about half a mile below the mouth of the Salt river, and commenced operations.

His report will be found in Senate Documents for 1839, page 1; we make the following extracts:—

"The brine springs of our State, like those of Ohio, Pennsyl- "vania, and Virginia, emanate from a rock which lies deep "being covered with a mass of rock and earthy matter which "(in order to procure salt water which can be economically "used) it is necessary to penetrate. In this respect they differ, "most essentially from those of the State of New York, for in "that State a simple earth excavation has proved amply suffi- "cient to ensure an abundant supply of water of a superior "quality.

"The appearance of a salt spring at the surface is, of itself "very far from being evidence of the existence of water of value "below. It is only a single link in the chain of facts."

"The State salt lands on the Tittabawassee river, in Midland "County are peculiarly eligbly situated being a few miles below "the head of navigation of that stream. and embracing the "mouth of Salt river. A re-examination of this saline district, "showed it to be more extensive than had been supposed, and it "was in consequence of this, in connection with the strength and "purity of its numerous springs, deemed a strong point for "commencing operations."

He states that he commenced active operations at this point about the middle of June, 1838, and that during the remainder of the year there had been expended $2,118 67 on this work.—That the shaft was begun on the bank of the river, and he adds:

"It is proposed to sink this shaft already commenced to the "rock which may be estimated to lie at the depth of something "over 100 feet and to secure it carefully from the influx of fresh "water—having accomplished this, the salt rock, which will "probably be found at this point to lie at a depth of between five "and seven hundred feet, will be reached in the usual manner "and until this be fully accomplished, we cannot hope to arrive "at any satisfactory conclusion on the subject."

In his report dated January 6th, 1840; (Senate Doc. 1840, page 153), he says the indications at the shaft are such as to "add "confidence to the hope before expressed of eventual success, in "the object sought, if the plan proposed be carried out."

On the 5th of January, 1842, he reports (House Doc., 1842, page 15) that the shaft has only reached a depth of 139 feet, as the result of nine months continuous labor of the contractor.—

Great difficulties were experienced in sinking the iron tubes in consequence of the character of the materials passed through, consisting of clay, sand, gravel and boulders. He repeats his confidence in the final result; but looks for no beneficial results until a depth of at least 600 feet shall be reached.

But notwithstanding his confidence, which was shared by the Legislature, as appears from the report of the committees to whom his several reports were referred, when the appropriation was exausted the great expense of the work at such a distance from machine shops, and from a base of supplies, together with the financial difficulties of the State, was such that it was thought best by the Legislature to abandon this shaft, at least, until some future period.

During the several years that the work was in progess Dr. Houghton passed much of his time in Saginaw, and in his intercourse with the people, fully impressed them with the same confidence which he had in the existence of a salt basin in this valley. He informed them that the act under which the appropriation was made, required him to commence on the State salt spring land, but that it was his opinion that the centre of the basin would be found at or near the mouth of Tittabawassee river, about two miles above the present site of East Saginaw.—And after the work was abandoned by the State, Hon. Norman Little and others continued firm in the belief founded upon their confidence in the opinion of Dr. Houghton, that a shaft had only to be sunk to the depth of from 600 to 1,000 feet to find strong brine at any point in this vicinity. But the experience of the State led them to believe that it was no idle task to make the experiment, and that whoever should take the risk would be obliged to invest a large sum, which, in case of success, would benefit his neighbors as much as himself. Thus matters stood until the session of the Legislature in 1859, when a bill was introduced to appropriate $10,000 to aid in developing of salt springs in the Grand river valley. As soon as the pendency of this Bill was known at East Saginaw, a public meeting was called and the unjust discrimination in favor of Grand Rapids was bitterly complained of. It was believed that the chances of success at Saginaw were at least equal to those of Grand Rapids. As the country had become better known about Saginaw, it was found that the surface indications of the existence of brine were abundant, and were found existing in the greatest profusion at about an equal distance from the point selected by Dr. Houghton as the centre of the basin, and almost in every direction from that centre.

This meeting was held at the office of Chas. B. Mott, Esq., on the 26th of January, 1859. And on motion of Hon. N. Little' Dr. Geo. A. Lathrop was called to the chair and W. L. Webber was appointed Secretary.

Dr. Lathrop on taking the chair stated that from an examination made by himself and from information from others he had no doubt of the correctness of the opinion entertained by Dr. Houghton, but as a large outlay would be required, and as it was a matter of general and public interest, it was thought best to apply to the Legislature for some encouragement. Other gentlemen present expressed great confidence in the existence of strong brine, and a committee consisting of Hon. Norman Little, Morgan L. Gage, Dr. Lathrop, and W. L. Webber. were appointed to draft a petition to the Legislature and also a bill for such aid and protection as in the opinion of the committee the Legislature would be likely to grant. The committee believing the Legislature would be more readily disposed to encourage the enterprise by a bounty contingent on the success of the experiment than by direct appropriation, proposed a bill on that principle, and the result was that the Bill to appropriate $10,000 for Grand Rapids was laid aside and this bill, with a few amendments, was passed and was approved Feb. 15th, 1859. The Act exempts all property used in the business from taxation and provides for the payment of a bounty of ten cents per bushel on all salt made.

Beloiving that the State would in good faith carry out the provisions of the Bounty law, in case the company should succeed, and induced to embark in the enterprise by their faith in the result, on the 30th of March, 1859, a subscription book was opened for the formation of a corporation under the general manufacturing law of Michigan, for the manufacture of salt, said company to be called the "East Saginaw Salt Manufacturing Company," to have a capital of $50,000 to consist of two thousand shares. In two days the whole amount was subscribed, and on the 16th of April 1859 the articles of association were signed. The names of those to whom this valley and the State at large are indebted for the final settlement of the question as to the existence of brine, with the proportion of each in the venture, will appear in the list following; showing the names of the parties associating in the first instance:

William L. P. Little	120	Shares.
W. L. Webber for Webber & Wheeler,	120	"
James L. Ketcham	120	"
George A. Lathrop	120	"
D. G. Holland	120	"
M. B. Hess	120	"
A. English	120	"
John F. Driggs	120	"
Wm. J. Bartow	120	"
Wm. F. Glasby	120	"
Jesse Hoyt	180	"
Chas. B. Mott	120	"
H. C. Potter	120	"
C. B. Jones	120	"
John Derby	120	"
Wm. C. Yawkey	40	"
Geo. W. Merrill	40	"
D. W. C. Gage	20	"
O. P. Burt	20	"
C. H. Gage	10	"
Perry Joslin	10	"
Total	2,000	"

The first Board of Directors consisted of Dr. Lathrop, President, W. L. P. Little, Treasurer; W. L. Webber, Secretary; and Messrs. Chas. B. Mott, James L. Ketcham, Moses B. Hess, H. C. Potter, George W. Merrill, and W. F. Glasby.

As soon as the Company was fully organized a conditional purchased was made of ten acres of land just at the lower part of East Saginaw, from Mr. Hoyt to sink the well upon, it being agreed that if brine was not found, Mr. Hoyt would relieve the company from payment for the land. A committee consisting of Geo. W. Merrill and S. R. Kirby was employed to visit Syracuse, in the State of New York, to learn what kind of a building and what kind of machinery were wanted to bore the well. On their return proceedings were at once instituted to erect a suitable building, to procure machinery, and to commence active operations. Being entirely new to all the employees, the work progressed slowly in comparison with work of that character at the present day, and although greatly encouraged by every change as the boring proceeded, yet, the board determined not to deceive themselves, nor others, by their discoveries. It was not until the 7th of February, 1860, that a report was made by the Board to the stockholders. From this report we make the following extract:

"We have been aware of your natural anxiety for informa- " tion during the progress of the work, but the Board of Direc- " tors at an early day adopted the policy of studiously witholding "the facts developed from time to time, however encouraging, "lest they might excite hopes which the final result would fail "to satisfy. We are happy now to assure you that Saginaw "possesses salt water, second in strength and purity, and we " believe in quantity to none in the United States."

The report then gives the details of their boring and the analysis of brine and closes with the assurance that at as early a day as practicable, the manufacture of salt would be commenced in at least two blocks. The effect of this report on the community is stated by the *Courier* of February 9th, 1860, to have been "like an electric shock."

We give a condensed view of the borings of the first well which was 3⅝ inches in diameter, as kept by Dr. Lathrop who gave it his daily personal supervision:

At depth of	Intervening Thickness	Thickness of formation	Description of Rocks, &c.
0	92	92	Alluvial and Diluvial materials. Sal. 1°.
92	79	79	Brown sandstone with angular grains.—Temp. 47°; Sal. 2°
171	40		Shales, first dark, then light.
211	23		Sandstone and 3 or 4 feet of COAL. (Highly arenaceous Fire Clay !)
234	12		Shales, below, dark bituminous.
246	10		Sandstone with thin seams COAL.
256	38	123	Shales. Temp. 50°. Sal. 14°. Discharge 80 gal. per minute.
294	105	105	White Sandstone.
399	65	65	Limestone embracing 6 beds of 'sandstone.' from 6 inch to 2 feet thickness, (the uppermost bed five and half feet,) and terminating in an arenaceous limestone with shaly matter.
464	3		Shales.
467	20		Sandstone, Sal. 26°.
487	29		Shales.
516	43		Shales with intercalated sandstones 6 in. to 2 feet thick. Sal. 44°.—60°.
559	10		Fine sandstone, blue. Sal. 64°. at 568 ft. ["Waterlime !"]
569	15		Dark shales.
584	11		Fine blue sand stone, ["Waterlime !" 3 1-2 feet shale at 590 1-2 feet.
595	3		Greyish, coarser sandstone with angular grains.
598	7		Dark shales.
605	15		Sandstone, hard, becoming micaceous—at 610 ft. calcareous.
620	7		Dark shales.
627	6	169	Limestone, hard, brown.
633	14		Fine sandstone, continuing at 647. Brine nearly saturated.

This shaft was afterwards sunk to a depth of 742 feet to red shales. The Company at once ordered the sinking of a second well, and pursuant to the act under which they were incorporated, increased their capital stock to $250,000, the new stock being all taken in proportion to the previous stock by the shareholders. The two blocks were completed and the boiling of salt commenced the later part of June 1860, but no salt was packed until July 1860. From that date until July 1861 the total production of this Company was 10,722 Barrels, of 280 pounds each. For the year ending July 1, 1862, the production of this Company alone was 32,250 barrels.

Immediately on the fact being demonstrated that strong brine of excellent quality existed here, other companies were formed, who could now safely prepare works for manufacturing salt while their wells were being sunk, and although six years from the making of the first salt in the valley has not elapsed, the manufacture has assumed gigantic proportions.

COMPARATIVE PROGRESS.

The manufacture of Salt was commenced at the Onondaga Salt Springs, in New York, June 20, 1797.

Salt made 1st year;	5,095	barrels.
" " 20th " 1816	69,733	"
" " 40th " 1836	382,572	"
" " 41st " 1837	433,455	"
" " 66th " 1862	1,810,775	"

At Kanawha, Virginia, Salt was manufactured as early as 1804.

Made in 1829	130,000	barrels.
" " 1860	700.000	"

SALT MADE IN SAGINAW, MICH.

1st year, 1860	4,000	barrels.
2d " 1861	125,000	"
3d " 1862	243,000	"
4th " 1863	466,356	"
5th " 1864	529,073	"

The first investment in the salt business on Saginaw river, was by the East Saginaw Salt Manufacturing Company, at East Saginaw, in 1859. Present value of the salt investment in the Saginaw river district; nearly two and a half million dollars—about the same value it was estimated all the salt works in the Onondaga district would hold at the end of the year 1860.—[Report Supt. Onondaga Salt Springs, for 1859, p. 15.]

"Fifty years of progress in the manufacture of salt in the Kanawha Valley did not eqaul the progesss made in four years in Saginaw Valley, and forty-two years progress at the Onondaga Salt Springs, the leading salt producing locality in the United States since 1797, did not equal the progress made there in five years. In 1860, a gentleman who was for some time Superintendent of the Onondaga Salt Company, and for years one of the most careful, practical and successful salt manufacturers in New York, who possessed the fullest knowledge of all matters pertaining to the question of markets as well as manufacture, gave it as his opinion that it would be at least five years from that time before the annual product of Saginaw Valley would reach one million bushels—200,000 bbls—and that before then the demands of the Western market would be increased to an extent which would require this amount in addition to the customary supply from the Onondaga Company. How that prediction was verified in regard to the Saginaw manufacture, may be seen by reference to the foregoing table. The product for the 3d year, 1862, being 1,215,000 bushels. The shipments of Saginaw Salt to Chicago, for 1864, the "5th year of manufacture," were 343,887 bbls, an excess of 120,887 bbls. over the entire receipts of domestic salt in that market for 1860, and 12,115 bbls. more than were received there during the past year from the Onondaga Company.

We append a statistical table of the salt business of 1865.

SUMMARY.

Number of Companies in operation,	67
" Blocks,	118
" Kettles,	4,210
" Solar Covers,	4,949
" Acres Land,	9,475½
Investment,	$2,269,500
Salt made in 1865, (barrels)	529,078
Men employed,	892
Cords of wood consumed,	109,368
Aggregate value of wood.	$286,545
Value of barrels used,	$238,074
Aggregate value of salt at shipping point.	$1,190,410

"The disproportion between the aggregate value of wood and the number of cords given, is explained by the fact that many works where mill fuel is used have given the value without any estimate as to number of cords. As at present carried on, the demand for wood for salt manufacture in the Saginaw Valley will require each year the timber off from about 3,000 acres of land.

LUMBER.

The lumber tract comprised in the Saginaw Valley is probably the most extensive as well as the most valuable tract in the world. Its extent is measured by thousands of acres, and the quantity of timber is so great that it must afford an abundant supply for several generations to come. The quality of lumber is unsurpassed.

In 1861 a quantity of deals were shipped to Quebec and those were of such a quality as to call out the following from the Montreal *Gazette*:

" The deals that have reached Quebec this season from the " district of country known as the Saginaw Valley, in Michi- " gan, are allowed to be the best quality that has been placed on the " market."

A portion of these deals were shipped from Quebec to Liverpool, England, by Messrs. Farmer, DeBlaquiere & Deeds, whereupon their correspondent advised these gentlemen that the shipment was of the best quality ever offered in that market.

The great advantages of the Saginaw Valley over other lumber districts, lies not alone in the superior quality of the article produced, but also in the peculiar facilities for manufacture and shipment. The numerous tributaries of the Saginaw river, reaching in their ramifications into the very heart of the heavily timbered districts, afford abundant avenues for the easy transportation of logs in rafts and floats to the mills. These being mainly located on the navigable portion of the river, vessels can take their cargoes of lumber direct from the mill docks, and thus a great saving in the cost of preparing for shipment as compared with other localities where lumber is necessarily transported many miles on wagons or by Railroad. Another advantage over many timber sections is that shipments of lumber may be made direct from the mills in the Saginaw Valley to all parts of the world. Direct shipments have been made from Saginaw to nearly every Eastern, Central and Southern State, to California, Liverpool, London, France, the Sandwich Islands, Australia, Valparaiso, and many other foreign ports, and everywhere it stands unrivalled as to quality.

The kinds of lumber produced are White Pine, or cork pine, as it is sometimes termed, straight grained and free from pitch, the most valuable, and from which the upper qualities are made; Sapling Pine which cuts mainly into fencing, flooring, common and lower qualities, and Norway Pine, firmer, but free from pitch, and peculiarly adopted to bridge and car building purposes, deck plank etc. Hemlock is also found in abundance and is worked into fencing and joists. Small quantities of White Wood, Black Walnut, Cherry, Ash and Oak are also sawed for local use.

The evident advantages of the Saginaw lumber district in quality and variety of the article produced, and its peculiar facilities for reaching the best markets, has attracted the attention of heavy capitalists from the east, and we may look for a rapid and unparalleled developement of the resources of the locality.

The Saginaw River is the great outlet through which the vast quantity of lumber that enriches the acres of the lower peninsula must find its way to market; and along the shores of the navigable portion of this stream are located the numerous mills which prepare the lumber for transportation to distant ports; much of the business energy and capital engaged in the production of lumber is also located on the Saginaw River, and these facts make it a matter of importance that fuller statistics should be given in this work.

The Saginaw River, reaching from the village of Salina to the Saginaw Bay—about twenty-five miles—is navigable for the largest class of lake vessels. A few miles up from where the stream ceases to be navigable for large boats, the River divides into four channels, known as the Cass, the Flint, the Shiawassee and the Tittabawassee rivers—the two former coming in from the eastern part of the lower peninsula, the Shiawassee from the southern, and the Tittabawassee from the northwestern portion.

These streams divide and sub-divide into numerous water courses, too shallow to be navigable, yet sufficiently deep and wide to allow the free transit of logs through them to the larger streams and to the mills. The four principal rivers mentioned, which, at their confluence, form the Saginaw river, extend, in their numerous ramifications, throughout the greater portion of the Saginaw lumber region, and afford the most feasible outlets for the vast supply of logs along their shores. Indeed there is no other natural outlet for the extensive lumber tract of the lower peninsula than that through the Saginaw valley, and whatever of lumber is taken by any other route to market from this district, must be taken at such an additional expense as to make it far less profitable to the producer than if taken by this natural course.

Such, then, is the relation of the Saginaw Valley to the great lumber producing section of the lower peninsula of Michigan. Now, let us glance at the lumber section itself, and we may then form an estimate of its importance to the State at large, and of its intrinsic value to the district most intimately connected with its production and sale.

The lumber region comprises, in whole or in part, the following counties; viz:

Midland, Isabella, Gladwin, Roscommon, Huron, Salinac, Lapeer, Genesee, Tuscola, Saginaw, Gratiot, Clare, Iosco, Ogemaw, Montcalm, Mecosta, Ingham and Livingston. The four first named are wholy within the lumber section, while the remainder are in part covered with heavy timber lands. The whole region comprises several hundred square miles of territory.—This large section of land is drained almost exclusively by the tributaries of the Saginaw river. It is calculated that pine territory will average five thousand feet per acre and the estimate therefore is that it will take over twenty years to exhaust the pine at the present rate of consumption; and, besides the pine timber, there is an immense amount of hemlock and oak.

It was not until the year 1848 that this began to be looked upon as a lumber region; and from that time until 1850 the business was not very extensively carried on. In the latter year, with but seventeen mills in operation, the business began to start up, and its increase has since been rapid. From 1851 to 1857 large tracts of land, then in the hands of the Government, were taken up, and the business assumed mammoth proportions, A number of additional mills were put into operation, increasing the whole number to thirty-three. The seventeen mills, operating in 1850 had a capacity of 25,000,000 feet per annum. The thirty-three mills, in 1857, had a capacity of 75,000,000 feet. In 1860 the number of mills was forty-one, with a capacity of 125,000,000 feet. There are now in operation on the Saginaw River, proper, fifty seven mills, with a capacity for sawing 300,000,000 feet per annum. The introduction of improved machinery has increased the annual production of lumber far beyond the increase in the number of mills in the valley.—The estimated value of the pine lumber cut during the past year, is $4.200,000. It finds a market in all the eastern States, *via* Buffalo, Oswego and Ogdensburg; in Cincinnatti and all parts of Ohio, *via* Cleveland and Sandusky: in Kentucky, Indiana, Illinois, Missouri, Kansas, Nebraska and southern Wisconsin. A large portion of the lumber consumed in the western States mentioned finds its way thither *via* Toledo and Chicago. Even Philadelphia and Baltimore, among the eastern cities, receive a large share of their lumber from this region. Nearly all the old producing sections such as the Susquehanna, the Chemung, and the Alleghany districts have ceased to be producers and have become consumers of lumber. Ohio has but recently become a market for the best qualities of Saginaw lumber.

As a matter of statistical information we may state that in the year 1865 the Tittabawassee river rafted out one hundred and fifty millions; the Cass, fifty millions; the Flint, thirty millions, and the Bad river—a tributary of the Shiawassee—twenty millions of feet of pine saw logs, board measure, besides which, many logs came from other sources.

There are fourteen shingle mills on the Saginaw, Cass and Tittabawassee rivers, which made last year (1865) sixty-five million shingles. There are also a large number of stave factories, and the quantity of staves produced is no small item in the aggregate of commercial wealth centering in the Saginaw valley.

LIST OF MILLS ON THE SAGINAW RIVER.

SALINA.	No. of feet sawed in 1865.
Bundy & Lowman,	5,250,000
Sutherland,	500,000
J. F. Rust & Co.,	3,500,000
SAGINAW CITY.	
Green & Harding,	3,500,000
Forest City, (Lee & Leavitt),	5,300,000
Heather & Allison,	3,500,000
V. A. Payne,	5,300,000
Williams Bros, (two mills),	5,000,000
Wright & Pierson,	3,000,000
Barnard & Binder,	new ——
EAST SAGINAW, FLORENCE AND CARROLLTON.	
Curtis & Corning	4,000,000
N. H. Chapman & Co.,	4,000,000
Chapin Mill,	5,000,000
Briggs,	4,000,000
F. P. Sears & Co.,	7,000,000
Geo. C. Warner & Co.,	6,550,000
Warner & Eastman,	3,800,000

Lee, (2 mills)	4,300,000
Little, Col. W. L. P. & Co,	4,100,000
Holland Mill,	3,300,000
Garrison,	4,200,000
Seth McLane,	3,500,000
Bliss, Grant & Sailor,	3,200,000
Chicago Salt & Lumber Co,	3,000,000
Merrills,	5,650,000
Shaw & Williams,	6,500,000
W. R. Burt,	5,300,000
Gould,	3,000,000
E. C. Litchfield,	6,000,000
Hall & Co.,	new——
Buttman & Co.,	new——
Oneida Salt and Lumber Co.,	8,000,000
Rust, Eaton & Co.,	9,453,500

BAY CITY AND PORTSMOUTH.

Watrous & Southworth,	3,000,000
Youngs,	1,250,000
Miller & Post,	4,000,000
Peters & Lewis,	4,000,000
J. J. McCormick,	4,400,000
J. F. Rust & Co.,	4,000,000
Watson,	3,000,000
N. B. Bradley,	6,800,000
Wm. Peters,	7,200,000
Miller & Co.,	6,000,000
H. M. Bradley & Co.,	4,000,000
Catlin & Jennison,	3,500,000
Fay & Gates,	4,500,000
James Shearer,	6,815,000
Samuel Pitts,	6,800,000
Dolson & Walker,	1,500,000
McEwen & Fraser,	6,000,000
Braddock's Mills,	3,000,000

WENONA, BANGOR AND KAW-KAW-LIN.

Huron Salt & Lumber Co.,	3,180.000
Sage & McGraw,	9,000,000
Drake Mill,	3,000,000
Bolton,	5.500,000
Taylor & Moulthrop,	6,000,000
Moore & Smith,	7,000,000
Kaw-kaw-lin,	5,000,000

EXPORTS FROM BAY CITY FOR 1864.

Lumber, ft.,	141,806,391
Salt, bbls.,	397,295
Shingles,	7,321,500
Lath,	8,831,850
Staves,	1,794,876
No. of vessels cleared during the season,	852
Average per month,	107

EXPORTS FOR 1865.

Lumber, ft.,	154,727,945
Salt, bbls.,	259,061
Shingles,	6,420,250
Lath,	8,011,080
Staves,	3,957,366
No. of vessels cleared during season,	1004
Average per month,	125½

THE SAGINAW RIVER FISH TRADE IN WINTER.

We extract the following from the *Saginaw Daily Enterprise*, in regard to the fish trade of the Saginaw River:

" A new and important branch of trade has grown up in the Saginaw Valley within the past two years, opening a market for an article of which our streams, bayous, and the bay shores, afford, as yet, an ample supply. We refer to the trade in Fresh River Fish, which are shipped *as* fresh fish, undressed and unsalted, during the cool season. This trade opened during the winter of 1864–5, through the enterprise and negotiations of "uncle" Harvey Williams, the pioneer, and still leading, fisherman of this region. During the early part of that season, Mr. Williams was consulted by a member of a New York firm, who was investigating the practicability of arranging a fishing ground where white fish could be caught alive and kept in ponds, to be taken out as wanted. That scheme Mr. Williams considered impracticable, as there was no suitable place on the bay shore for carrying it out. But while discussing this question, the idea of sending our common river fish to the New York market was suggested, which Mr. Willlams thought *was* practicable, and volunteered his services, free of charge, during that winter, to inaugurate it. Consequently the fishermen in his employ were offered four cents per pound, and the traffic commenced. The fish found a ready sale in the eastern markets, and preparations were made to go into it on a more extensive scale during the past winter.

"The fish are caught under the ice, by cutting a series of holes and passing the nets under from one hole to another.—Various kinds of nets and seines are used, the manner of operating being somewhat different with each. The fishing grounds are in the Saginaw River and bayous connected therewith, and in the bay; and perhaps one hundred men are engaged in it.—The kinds caught for this trade are the pickerel, pike, black bass, calico bass and perch. Bull heads and suckers are also caught, but only for the home market. The prices paid have been for pickerel, pike and black bass, 6 to 7½ cents per pound; for calico bass and perch 3 cents.

"The fish are put up in barrels, frozen or nearly so, and then shipped by express to New York, Cincinnati, and other points; for the trade has greatly expanded, a wider market is found, and other operators are engaged in it. The express freight is 5 cents per pound, deducting the weight of barrels. A Detroit firm, however, ships to that point, as railroad freight.

"The amount shipped by the general dealers engaged in the business, from the 1st of January to the 1st of March last, is as follows: Harrison & Co., 35 tons to Wm. Davis & Sons, Detroit; H. Williams, 20 tons, to New York; McKay, Braddock and others, about 8 tons. In all, 68 tons from *under the ice.*

"The development of this trade thus opens a market for an article that scarcely brought a remunerating price, and for which there was before only a limited local market.

HINTS TO TRAVELLERS.—The FLINT & PERE MARQUETTE, the FLINT & HOLLY and the DETROIT & MILWAUKIE Railways form a straight connection from DETROIT to SAGINAW. These roads by a *compact* entered into, between their several managers, run their cars, the same as if they were owned by one Company, over one and the same road; thus avoiding any change between Detroit and Saginaw. Passengers coming here from the East will find it to their interest, to purchase through tickets to East Saginaw, at the office of the Great Western Railway Company, as these Roads run in connection, and a great deal of time and trouble will thus be avoided.

TO BUSINESS MEN AND PLEASURE SEEKERS.—To those about traveling Eastward either for pleasure or business, we will hazard a suggestion, as to which route is the safest, cheapest and most pleasant. In leaving Saginw Valley, of course there is but one route; the Flint & Pere Marquette, Flint & Holly, and Detroit & Milwaukie Roads over which to get to Detroit. From Detroit take the Great Western Railway, of course; as this is the only route that goes directly to SUSPENSION BRIDGE and NIAGARA FALLS and passes through the famous OIL REGIONS of CANADA. To speak in tones of praise of this well known and well conducted route, would seem almost useless; for every person must be aware that their track is the smoothest to ride over, and their cleanly Palace Cars, the pleasantest, and the polite and assiduous attentions passengers receive from its employees, the most agreeable, of any route, to or from the West. This road in all its appointments is most perfect; and its *management* faultless.—Take the Great Western route by *all means!* and we will guarantee you will be delighted with your trip. To those going to New York and points in New England, we would especially recommend the Erie Railway from Buffalo. This Road is the *Broad guage* line, with wide and roomy cars, magnificently finished and furnished, like the "Great Western" of Canada, you will meet with polite and attentive conductors, a smooth and easy track to ride over, luxurious sleeping cars on all night trains, and a safe, comfortable and speedy transit. A *double track*, having been laid almost the entire distance from Buffalo to New York, renders it less liable to accidents than other roads not so provided. Without any interest, further than the advancement of the comfort and pleasure of the traveller, we would in all candor, recommend the above routes.

EAST SAGINAW AND BAY CITY LINE.

THE NEW AND SPLENDID LOW PRESSURE STEAMER

EVENING STAR,

T. M. HUBBELL, Master,

Will make regular trips between EAST SAGINAW and BAY CITY during the season, for passengers and freight, in connection with trains on Flint and Pere Marquette Railway.

THE NEW AND SPLENDID UPPER CABIN STEAMER,

L. G. MASON,

STEPHEN MEANEY, Master,

Will make regular trips during the season—running alternate with the "EVENING STAR,"—between EAST SAGINAW and BAY CITY, touching at intermediate landings.

☞ FOR FREIGHT OR PASSAGE APPLY ON BOARD.

Saginaw, Alabaster, Tawas, Sauble River, Harrisville and Alpena.

1866. **1867.**

THE STAUNCH PASSENGER PROPELLER

SKY LARK,

ALFRED G. RIPLEY, Master.

Will make regular trips during the season between SAGINAW and ALPENA, connecting with the F. & P. M. RAILWAY, touching at Alabaster, Tawas, Sauble River and Harrisville. Through Tickets may be procured at the D. & M. Railway Depot, Detroit.

☞ Fare as cheap as by any other route. For Freight or Passage apply to

GOODING & HAWKINS, AGENTS, East Saginaw, Mich.

HART & MONROE, AGENTS, Bay City.

ERIE RAILWAY.

BROAD GAUGE--DOUBLE TRACK.

FROM

Buffalo, Dunkirk or Salamanca,

TO

NEW YORK, BOSTON,

And all New England Cities.

☞ Four Express Trains Daily. 460 Miles without change of Coaches, saving 22 miles in distance. Close connections made at Buffalo with GRAND TRUNK RAILWAY TRAINS, at Dunkirk with Lake Shore Railway, and at Salamanca with Trains of A. & G. W. Railway.

☞ EASTERN PASSENGERS should bear in mind that by purchasing Tickets via the ERIE RAILWAY, all the modern improvements in Railway Traveling are secured.

☞ There is no change of Coaches between Dunkirk, Buffalo, or Salamanca and New York, by which a good night's rest is secured, and the unreasonable changes incident to other lines entirely avoided.

New York and New England Passengers securing Tickets by the Erie Railway ☞ can depend upon making the connections at Dunkirk, Buffalo and Salamanca, as when necessary, Trains on this Railway will wait from ☞ One to Two Hours for Western Trains and make regular running time through to New York.

☞ Tickets reading FROM DUNKIRK are good via BUFFALO.

The best Ventilated and most LUXURIOUS SLEEPING COACHES in the World accompany all Night Trains on this Railway.

☞ PASSENGERS holding THROUGH TICKETS to any point in New England, will be transferred with their Baggage, through New York FREE OF CHARGE.

Be sure and secure your Tickets via ERIE RAILWAY. For sale at all principal Ticket Offices.

HUGH RIDDLE, Gen'l Sup't N. Y.   F. E. MORE, Western Pass'r Ag't, Chicago.   WM. R. BURR, Gen'l Pass'r Ag't, N. Y.

GREAT WESTERN

RAILWAY

TICKET AGENCY

No. 103, BLISS BLOCK.

EAST SAGINAW, - - MICHIGAN.

TICKETS TO

New York, Boston, St. Paul, St. Louis,
Albany, Syracuse, Cincinnati, Chicago,
Rutland, Vt. Kansas, Springfield, Milwaukee,
Philadelphia, La Crosse, Washington, Green Bay,

AND ALL POINTS

EAST, WEST and SOUTH.

☞ Information concerning all Routes furnished on application TIME AND MONEY SAVED BY PURCHASING THROUGH TICKETS.

A. FERGUSON, Agent.

ENTERPRISE COMPANY

Steam Printing House,

Office, Corner of Water and Tuscola Streets,

EAST SAGINAW, MICH.

The Daily Enterprise, Issued every morning, (Sunday excepted, contains the Latest Dispatches, General and Local News, and circulating among the lumbermen and other business men of the Saginaw Valley, is by far

The Best Medium for Advertising in Northern Michigan.

The Weekly Enterprise, Issued every Thursday, is a very large sheet, filled with the choicest of reading, and is decidedly *the best Family Newspaper* published in this part of the State.

A limited number of Advertisements only admitted.

The Office, furnished with a large assortment of JOB TYPE *of the Latest Styles* and superior MACHINE PRESSES including a

FIRST CLASS HOE'S DRUM CYLINDER,

Is prepared to do all kinds of

PLAIN & ORNAMENTAL JOB PRINTING,

On short notice and reasonable terms.

HAND BILLS, CIRCULARS, LETTER HEADS, TICKETS,
POSTERS, BILL HEADS, CARDS, &c., &c.

— ALSO, —

Book and Pamphlet Work.—Law Cases and Briefs.—Lumber Inspection Bills.—Shipper's Bills.—Commercial Blanks of all descriptions.

Steamboat & Railroad Printing, Colored & Fancy Work.

Bank Printing, Drafts, Checks, Certificates, &c., &c.

☞ **GERMAN PRINTING Correctly and Neatly done.**

☞ All communications should be addressed to

ENTERPRISE COMPANY,

EAST SAGINAW, MICH.

ST. NICHOLAS

RESTAURANT.

F. G. CASEY, PROPRIETOR.

Bliss Block, opposite Bancroft House, **EAST SAGINAW, MICH.**

TARSNEY, RICH & CO.,

DEALERS IN

GROCERIES & PROVISIONS,

SOLE AGENTS FOR

FINLEY & WILDER'S

Celebrated Ale and Porter,

AND

Wholesale and Retail Dealers in

FOREIGN AND DOMESTIC LIQUORS.

No. 126, North Water Street,

EAST SAGINAW, MICH.

CHAS. SCHUERMANN,

(SUCCESSOR TO BINDER & CO.)

Wholesale and Retail Dealer in

Groceries,

Provisions, Flour, Feed, Paints, Oils,
Crockery, Glass and Stone Ware.

Forwarding and Commission Merchants.

ALSO, AGENTS FOR

WARD'S DETROIT, TOLEDO, AND LAKE SHORE

LINE OF STEAMERS.

Store and Dock, No. 211, North Water Street.

BAY CITY, MICH.

 THE STEAMERS 

SUSAN WARD & SAGINAW

WILL PLY REGULARLY BETWEEN

East Saginaw and Detroit,

TOUCHING at all INTERMEDIATE PORTS.

LEAVING DETROIT FOR SAGINAW EVERY

Tuesday, Thursday and Saturday.

LEAVING BAY CITY FOR DETROIT

Mondays, Tuesdays and Saturdays.

For Freight or Passage apply to

CHAS. SCHUERMANN,

BAY CITY MICH.

HISTORY OF SAGINAW CITY.

Saginaw City the County seat of the County of Saginaw, is situated on the west bank of the Saginaw river, eighteen miles from Saginaw Bay, and one and one half miles below the confluence of the Tittabawassee and Saginaw rivers, and is navigable to this point for vessels drawing not to exceed eight feet of water at its lowest stage; a depth sufficient to admit the larger proportion of vessels used in the navigation of the great chain of Lakes with which it connects. A ridge of land extending upwards of two miles, running parallel with the river and a short distance from it, rises to a height of twenty-eight feet above low water mark, and affords the most delightful locations for the construction of private residences. That part of the city between this ridge and the river is used for commercial, manufacturing and mercantile purposes. A public square occupies the centre of the City upon which stands the Court House of Saginaw County; an imposing edifice, and one of the finest of the kind in the State of Michigan; and also a brick building containing the County Offices, on each side of this square four handsome Churches are erected besides the Union School House, and the County Jail.

The locality of the site of this city far surpasses that of any of its sister cities in the valley, and perhaps is unrivalled in that respect by any city in the west.

In the year 1820 the United States Government established on the site now occupied by the central portion of Saginaw City a military post, which was maintained but a few years; about the same time the American Fur Company established a trading post at or near the stockade erected by the Government, which was maintained until the year 1846. The affairs of the Company for several years were managed by Wm. McDonald who continued to reside at this place until his death, which occurred in 1851; and also by Gardner D. Williams until the Company ceased to carry on operations here. At the time the Government took possession of the place for military purposes, the entire country was an unbroken forest. The stockade was constructed on the brow of the hill, near the present residence of the Hon. P. C. Andre, overlooking the river, and during the time the troops were quartered at this place, they cleared the bottom land between the stockade and the river. The troops were finally withdrawn, and the military post abandoned by the Government; the necessity of maintaining a military post at this point no longer existing. As early as the year 1852, John Farly and Samuel McClusky caused a portion of the territory now occupied as the city, to be plotted by the name of the Town of Saginaw. But few lots were sold by the proprietors of said plot, and with the exception of a rude hut constructed by a half-breed known as Jack Smith, and a block house by Louis Campau in the same year, no improvements were made on the plot thus laid out. The block house erected by Campau was a novelty in regard to the manner of its construction, every portion of it including the roof and floor (excepting the chimneys) having been constructed of timber hewn by the hand of the early pioneers. It was massive in its construction and withstood the ravages of time—a monument to the indefatigable industry of the early French pioneer—until 1862 when it was destroyed by fire.

In 1835 Samuel Dexter caused another portion of the present site of Saginaw city to be plotted; known as the plot of Saginaw City; including the N. E. quarter of Sec. 26, Town N. R. 12, 4 E. But few sales of lots were made by Dexter; and in 1836, he disposed of his interest to Mackie, Oakley & Jennison of the City of New York, who associated with them the late Norman Little, under whose auspices the present plot of the City of Saginaw was created; embracing the Dexter territory, together with the whole of said section on both sides of Saginaw river, and portions of adjacent territory. This was the era of gigantic land and other speculations. Mr. Little moved to his new home from the State of New York and entered energetically on his mission – that of building up a city. He was the main spring —the propelling power in the movement – attracted by the wealth of the forests of the valley, its salubrious climate, the unrivalled water communication connecting the far interior with the great chain of Lakes; and its fertility of soil—enthusiastic and far-sighted, he then predicted the future growth and greatness of the valley, its eventual developement and position; and although the financial revulsion of 1837 compelled a suspension of the improvements begun and in contemplation by him, resulting in his pecuniary prostration and removal from the place for a time, yet his conviction of the ultimate destiny of the valley was so strong, that he returned again in 1850 with abundant capital with which to mature his earlier plans. Fortuitous, circumstances compelled him to re-commence his labors on the opposite bank of the river at East Saginaw. Mr. Little lived to realize his earlier hopes and predictions in the fullest fruition and now sleeps beneath the sod of the valley he so long and ardently loved. During the year 1836 the Webster House, two large warehouses, one on the river and one on Washington street, the residence of the late Gardener D. Williams, Hiram L. Miller, and several other buildings were erected. The crisis of 1837 paralysed to a great extent all progress for years, the city exhibiting comparatively little advance until 1850 and 1851. This may be said to have been the dark age of the Saginaw valley. Gloomy as it was, it did not stand still. The energy displayed by its early settlers, and those who followed them thither by no means slumbered, steadily though not rapidly, they pushed forward improvements throughout the city. School houses – the Court house - and warehouses were put up, and the business of the place increased although to a considerable extent embarrassed for want of direct and frequent communication with the outer business world.

During this period Nelson Smith, Esq., then a resident of this city, constructed the first schooner permanently used in the carrying trade of this city—the Julia Smith, which for a number of years was the principal medium for the transit of merchandise. An occasional vessel arrived from Detroit, but no regular line of communication was established until the year 1850.

Among the first settlers of Saginaw City were Eleazer Jewett, Gardner D. Williams, Abram Butts, James Busby, Harvey Williams, Elijah N. Davenport, Hiram L. Miller, Charles D. Little and James Fraser. The first white child born in Saginaw County was Mary Jewett, the daughter of Eleazer Jewett, now Mrs. Dr. N. D. Lee, a resident of this city. The first male white child was Wm. Williams, son of the late Gardner D. Williams, who also is a resident. The first event took place in March, 1834, the second in March 1835. Both were born within the present corporate limits of the city of Saginaw. At the date last mentioned the families of the persons referred to formed the principal portion of the white population of the valley. A few adventurous French *voyagers* from Detroit and Canada *attaches* of the American and English fur Companies, squatted in various localities upon the river, engaged principally in hunting and Indian trading. The Chippewa Indians at this early period were almost the sole possessors of the valley, and in the year 1832 numbered some 3.500 souls. The abundance of game in the forests of the valley, of the fish in its rivers, and the romantic scenery, made the present site of this City and Greenpoint adjacent thereto, a favorite resort and camping ground, and was called by them Ka-pay-shaw-wink, signifying the Great Camping Ground. In the year 1837 the small-pox committed fearful ravages among this band of Saginaw Indians, carrying off nearly two-thirds of their number. The principal remnant of this band have been removed from the valley and now occupy lands in Isabella county where they are gradually passing from a semi-civilized state into a higher grade of intellectual and moral being. The river bank in the central part of the city was set apart and reserved by them as a place of sepulture for their dead. The rude hand of progress in the developement of the present higher order of things temporal, has not spared the quiet repose of the illustrious Indian dead, who for so many years has slept "the sleep that knows no waking" beside the much loved stream; and the spade and pick of the modern vandal, as he makes excavations for the foundation of some stately warehouse, manufactory or other improvement, throws up to the eyes of the curious spectator the bones of these once swarthy braves and their burial paraphanalia with as little remorse as the grave digger in Hamlet.

"Alas poor Yorick."

Our fellow townsman, Dr. I. N. Smith, has formed from these exhumations a considerable anatomical collection, and has arranged the same in such a manner that reflects credit upon him.

The inhabitants of the valley at the present day can form but an inadequate idea of the toil, suffering and privations of its pioneers at the time of its early settlement. No steamer then disturbed the surface of the Western Lake or River, no steam whistle broke the "expressive silence" of the broad expanse of prairie and forest. The Indian roamed the monarch of the valley; its stillness broken only by the crack of his rifle. The surface of its silver streams disturbed by nothing save the noiseless dip of his paddle, and stealthy progress of his canoe as he followed his precarious calling, in search of food or furs.— No road save the Indian trail winding its devious way from settlement to settlement, then far apart, through swamps at times almost impenetrable, and streams unbridged and frequently impassable. The North star and the pocket compass at all times were more reliable as indicating the route the traveller desired to pursue than the "blase" or the "trail."

Obstacles such as these were sufficient to deter all save the most hardy and resolute of purpose from seeking a home in this now populous valley. But to the men whose names we have herein given, as the early pioneers, these obstacles presented no terror; men in whose vocabulary there was no such word as "fail." These with their equally indomitable wives, penetrated the almost impassable swamps, forded turbid and swollen streams upon Indian ponies or sleds drawn by oxen; or trusting themselves to canoes upon streams obstructed at every turn by masses of impenetrable drift-wood, making long and tedious portages a necessity; camping out in the forest night after night. made cheery by the light of the camp fire, illuminating its green arches, which afforded them their only shelter from the fervor of the mid-day sun, or the fury of the storm. The settlement thus begun was gradually increased. The ring of the hardy woodman's axe usurped the sound of the crack of the Indian rifle, and the settlers log cabin the site of the Indian wigwam. Slowly but steadily the forest shrank back from the river before the steady assaults of the pioneer; and the place of worship, the school house, the store and the workshop soon became realities—*fixed facts*—The "latch string hung out" on the door of every house or cabin; hospitality was the rule—the want of it the exception.

A small remnaent of this grand pioneer stock, the original thereof, still remain in and about Saginaw City, enjoying the well earned fruits of their early labors, and now as then, dispensing with the dignity of maturer age, that genuine charity and hospitality which from early habit has become as it were a rule of actions with them. Innumerable are the blessings enjoyed by the citizens, not only of this city but of the adjoining country; the result of the admirable foresight, and indomitable courage and energy of the pioneers of this valley, a greater portion of whom have passed away.

To the greater portion of the population of this county they are but little known. Those who survive and *knew* them in days "lang syne," will not cease to cherish the memory of the warm and open-hearted hospitality—the open-handed liberality—the genuine man and womanhood of the pioneers of Saginaw valley.

In 1850 the City of Saginaw contained six wholesale and retail stores, five carpenter and joiner shops, three boot and shoe shops, three blacksmith shops, one bakery, one steam saw mill, one paint shop, three hotels and three grocery and provision stores and two other places of retail trade.

Hon. Gardner D. Williams was the first Mayor elect. He was re-elected the succeeding year to that office. His death occurring before the expiration of his second term, Hon. Hiram L. Miller then Recorder of the city acted as Mayor until the election of Geo. W. Bullock, Esq., who held the office for two consecutive terms. Hon. John Moore succeeded Geo. W. Bullock, Esq., and was re-elected, P. C. Andre, Esq., was elected for the next term, followed by Stewart B. Williams who was succeeded by the present mayor, Wm. M. Miller, Esq.

The population of the city was 536. Up to the year 1857 the City of Saginaw formed a portion of the township of Saginaw, a City charter was granted by the Legislature of the State which went into operation in the spring of that year.

The projection of the plank road from East Saginaw to Flint, and its construction in 1851—thus completing an available communication to Detroit—infused new life into every department of trade throughout the valley. A semi-weekly line of steamers plied regularly during the season of navigation between this place and Detroit, and two steamers between Saginaw City and Bay City.

The population of the city and business in all its various branches rapidly increased. In 1851-2, the Union School House was constructed, five churches commenced, and three of them completed.

The principal business up to this period, and up to 1860 and 1861, was the manufacture of lumber, which during the two years prior to that time had attained great importance and formed the principal business not only of this city, but of the entire valley.

The discovery of salt in 1860, and its almost immediate development, gave additional impetus to trade. The second salt well in the valley was sunk and went into successful operation in this city. The sinking of this well and one at East Saginaw, rendered success in the manufacture of salt no longer doubtful.—Capital, and busines men from all parts of the country were attracted hither by the prospect of success then presented and assured.

All branches of trade were beneficially affected thereby, stores, shipyards, steam and other manufacturing establishments, spruug up as if by magic. The capital of the city increased during the three years succeeding 1860 one hundred fold, the population of the city doubled, brick stores, large manufacturing establishments, tasteful dwellings and Churches were erected The Saginaw River was alive with commerce; regular steam lines of communication established between this City and Detroit, Buffalo, Cleveland, Toledo, Chicago and Gooderich; and lines of stages to all the towns in the interior. So large an accession to the wealth and population of the City, enabled the government of the city and its inhabitants, to expend large sums in the improvement of streets; laying side walks and drainage of the surrounding country. At present the streets throughout the entire city are in most excellent condition; miles of side-walk leading to every mans' door, renders pedestrianism at all times and in all weather no unpleasant task. Two additional brick school houses have been erected, and a third at an estimated cost of $10,000 is to be commenced the ensuing season. Besides the facilities created for education under the general laws of the State, there are several private schools of a high order of merit; The Riverside Seminary now in successful operation taking the lead. A Street Railway from this City to East Saginaw has been completed and is now in successful operation. Steam ferry Boats during the season of navigation ply regularly between the two places.

The city contains five Hotels; but these are inadequate to accommodate the travelling community, and the construction of a sixth has already been commenced by William H. Taylor, Esq., on the corner of Court and Hamilton streets, which, judging from the design of the architect, promises to be one of the largest and finest structures in the State.

The city contains seven Churches, viz: Presbyterian, Methodist, Episcopalian, Roman Catholic, Baptist, Lutheran and Dutch Reformed. Two Banking Houses, two Real Estate Brokers offices, two Photographic Galleries, two Masonic Lodges, one Odd Fellows Lodge, one Lodge of the order of Good Templars, one Lyceum, a well organized Fire Department, fifteen Physicians and Surgeons, five Dentists, fourteen Lawyers, one Weekly Newspaper, (Saginaw Valley Herald), one Newsroom, seven Clergymen, three Book Stores, six Dry Good Stores, eighteen Grocery and Provision Stores, one Feed Store, three Drug Stores, two Wholesale and Retail Hardware Stores, six. ready made Clothing Stores, one Hair and Ornamental Jewelry Store, one Hat and Cap Store, one Crockery and Glassware Store, four Boot & Shoe Stores, two Bakeries, two Confectionary Stores, six Meat Markets, four Barber Shops, two Tobacco and Segar Stores, two Livery Stables, one Ship-yard, six Blacksmith Shops, six Cooper Shops, four Paint Shops, three Cabinet Ware Rooms, ten Architects and Builders and one Telegraph office.

Manufacturing Establishments—eight Steam Saw Mills, eight Salt Blocks, three Shingle Mills, one Flouring Mill, one Salt Mill, two Door, Sash and Blind Manufactories, two Planing Machines, four Stave and Heading Manufactories, five Carriage and Sleigh Manufactories, one Gun and Rifle Manufactory, five Cabinet Ware Manufactories, three Steam Boiler Machine and Engine Manufactories, three Tin and Sheet-iron Manufactories, one Segar Manufactory, Four Restaurants and twenty-five other places of retail trade.

The population of the City in 1860, was 1,712. The present population is 5,426. It is confidently anticipated that the construction of a Rail Road connecting this City with the Detroit and Milwaukee Rail Road at Owosso will be completed during the ensuing year, thus affording the citizens of the Valley direct communication with Chicago, Cincinnati and the far west. The completion of this Road will give an additional impetus to the trade by opening new avenues for the transit and sale of the salt and lumber of the Valley. In short we predict that the next ten years will produce improvements in trade and an accession to the wealth and population of Saginaw City as great as we have shown that of the past ten years to have been. Its position as a commercial town with the unrivalled water communication, surrounded by a country abounding in mineral and agricultural wealth, all unite to make it what we confidently predict it will become, the Queen City of Michigan.

George W. Bullock was born in Savoy, Berkshire County, Mass., August 27th, 1809. At the age of seven he removed with his father to Warren Co., Pennsylvania, where after having arrived at sufficient age, he learned the carpenter and joiner's trade. In 1831, he left the old familiar home scenes to pursue his fortunes as a pioneer in the then "far West," and arrived at Monroe, Mich., where he carried on business as a builder for five years.

In 1836 he came to Saginaw, and here continued the building business until 1844, which he then relinquished and commenced merchandizing. He carried on the dry goods business in a building situated on Hamilton Street, until within one year previous to his untimely decease, which occurred June 6th, 1861.—He was engaged quite extensively in the salt and lumber business in connection with his mercantile trade, and was the first President of the first salt company organized in Saginaw. He owned the largest share of the stock in this company, and devoted a large share of his attention to its interests. It was here he lost his life by the explosion of one of the salt vats. In company with the late James Fraser, deceased, he built the road leading from this city to Bay City. He was a public spirited man, and done much for the improvement and advancement of the place. He was elected one of the first Aldermen at the organization of the city government, and afterwards held the office of Mayor for two consecutive terms.

He caused streets to be laid out, and adorned them with shade trees, and also erected several substantial buildings. He built the first brick dwelling house in Saginaw County, which he occupied as his residence. It is situated on Court Street, and is a beautiful structure; having ample grounds, which are laid out in the most tasty and elegant style. It really bears a home like appearance of ease and comfort. The Episcopal Church, (St. John's) is largely indebted to his zeal and liberality in the erection of their beautiful edifice on Washington Street. As a man he was frank and open hearted, genial in his manners, with but few equals in genuine hospitality. Let his virtues be emulated.

Charles L. Richman, was one of the early pioneers of the valley, having come here in 1836, in company with Norman Little. At Detroit they chartered the steamer *Gov. Marcy*, and were the first who ever navigated the Saginaw River by steamer. He was born in the city of Philadelphia, in the year 1800. He was for several years a clerk in a dry goods store at Canandaigua, N. Y., and first entered into business on his own account at Naples, Ontario Co., N. Y., in 1828. From Naples he went to Moscow, Livingston Co., N. Y., and opened a dry goods store, where be remained till 1836, when he came to Saginaw. He cantinued the mercantile business in Saginaw until his death, which occurred September 6th. He always manifested great interest in the growth and prosperity of the town, and done a great deal in an unostentatious manner for its material advancement. He was unassuming in his manners, but genial and affable in disposition. He represented Saginaw County in the State Legislature, in 1846. He ran against the late Hon. James G. Birney, then living at Lower Saginaw, now called Bay City.—He was a firm supporter of the Episcopal Church, and shortly previous to his death was largely instrumental in the erection of St. John's church, on Washington Street. Few men had more friends than the subject of this memoir, and his loss was felt to be a severe affliction to the whole community. "Death loves a shining mark."

The House Furnishing Emporium of Elliott & Harrison, at East Saginaw, contains all the various articles in the way of China and Crockery ware that are known to the trade. In addition to these the stock of Carpets, Oil Cloths, Mirrors, Plated Goods and Cutlery, kept at their establishment, is desirable in style and low in price; and the demands of the trade, both wholesale and retail, are met by the proprietors in a way that gives universal satisfaction. The Saginaw City Railroad, terminates on Water Street, very near the Emporium, which affords a convenient mode of access for residents of Saginaw who desire to purchase supplies of House Furnishing Goods.

Benjamin Geer commenced business in this city November, 1864. He occupies a fine, large store, and keeps the largest and best selected stock of goods in the city, consisting of Dry Goods, Groceries, Boots and Shoes, and numerous et ceteras. Mr. Geer's reputation as a Merchant, and a fair and upright dealer, stand above reproach, by means of which he has secured a large and lucrative patronage. Mr. Geer sells his goods at a very low figure, having adopted the principle of "quick sales and small profits," and is always pleased to show his stock whether a purchase is made or not. Give him a call.

ST. JOHN'S CHURCH.

In the year 1836, there could have been found in all the Saginaw Valley, but three communicants of the Protestant Episcopal Church—Mr. and Mrs. Busby and Mrs. Amanda Richman. Not till the year 1841, was there a service of the church held in what then constituted Saginaw County. During that year the Rev. Daniel E. Brown, of Flint, visited the new settlement, and for several years he held occasional services here. At length in 1851 a parish was organized, and the Rev. Joseph Adderly was called to take charge of the same. He was succeeded in 1852, by the Rev. Daniel B. Lyon, who remained but one year. In 1853, the Rev. V. Spaulding was called to the Rectorship. The number of communicants reported to the Diocesan Convention that year was eleven. On the 20th February, Bishop McCoskry made his first visit to this parish, and on the 11th April, following, he returned to lay the corner stone of the present church edifice.

In June, 1858, the Rev. V. Spaulding resigned; the number of communicants having now increased to twenty-four. In the following year the Rev. Edward Magee accepted a call to the Rectorship. A debt of $400 had hitherto prevented the consecration of the church, but this indebtedness being liquidated, on the 9th May, 1860, Bishop McCoskry consecrated the church by the name and title of "St. John's." In the year following, the Rev. Mr. Magee tendered his resignation; three communicants having been added during his pastorate. He was succeeded in 1862, by the Rev. Osgood E. Fuller, who remained three years; the number of communicants having meanwhile almost doubled, there being no less than fifty-one reported to the Convention in 1865.

The present Rector is the Rev. John Leech, and the number of communicants is eighty-eight.

The church has attained its present growth with but very little assistance from abroad. During his incumbency the Rev. V. Spaulding went East, and procured $500 to assist in the erection of the church edifice, and by the advice and with the consent of the Bishop, the late Charles L. Richman solicited aid for the same object in several of the larger cities in the State of New York.

He there obtained the sum of $600, together with the baptismal bowl and communion sett presented through him, by the late Mrs. Ebenezer Hale, of Canandaigua, N.Y. The bible and prayer book, still in use, are the gift of our late lamented townsman, George W. Bullock. Through the commendable exertions of the ladies of the congregation, a new bell will in a few weeks send its sweet music from the tower of St. John's, along the rich and busy valley of the Saginaw.

FIRST PRESBYTERIAN CHURCH.

The First Presbyterian Church of Saginaw City, the oldest church of the Saginaw Valley, was gathered by the ministerial labors of Rev. H. L. Miller, during the years 1836 and 1837, and organized March 1st. 1838, with the following members:

Norman Little, Jane A. Little, Elizabeth Rice, Thomas Smith, Wm. Heartwell, Mrs. Harvey Williams, T. L. Howe, Mrs. T. L. Howe, Hinds Smith, Mrs. Julia Smith, Mabel Terrill, Mrs. H. L. Miller.

An occasional circuit rider of the Methodist Church had visited this region prior to 1836, holding an isolated religious service, but the labors of Mr. Miller constituted the first regular permanent ministry of the Saginaw Valley. Failing health compelled him to terminate his ministerial service in 1839, but continuing to reside here, his name and influence has been identified with the entire history of the church of which he was the founder. His successors in the ministry and the periods of their service, have been as follows:

Rev. C. F. Foot, stated supply, January, 1840, to May, 1840.

Rev. Harvey Hyde, stated supply, March, 1842, to May, 1844.

Rev. C. H. Baldwin, stated supply, January, 1846, to July, 1847.

Rev. Louis Mills, stated supply, November, 1848, to July, 1849.

Rev. D. M. Cooper, Pastor, June, 1851, to April, 1859.

Rev. D. H. Taylor, stated supply, March, 1861, to March, 1865.

Rev. J. W. Hough, Pastor, July, 1865.

The church was organized as a Presbyterian church, but during the first years of its existence was not under the care of any ecclesiastical body. In 1842, its form of government was changed to Congregational, and it was connected successively with the Eastern and the Genesee Conferences. In 1853, it returned to the Presbyterian polity, and became a member of the Detroit Presbytery, being transferred to the Saginaw Presbytery upon the constitution of that body in 1856.

While it was a Congregational Church, its deacons were Geo. Davis and Albert Miller. Upon its return to the Presbyterian polity, H. L. Miller, Robert Ure and Geo. Davis, were ordained ruling elders, and Alanson Griffis, deacon. Subsequently Geo. Davis having deceased, and Robert Ure and Deacon Griffis having removed, Timothy Barnard and Wm. A. Carpenter were ordained ruling elders, and D. F. Mitchell, deacon.

Mr. Miller first preached in a carpenter shop, upon the site of the house now occupied by Capt. Richman, corner of Washington and Ames Streets. Subsequently in the Post Office, nearly opposite the hardware store of D. H. Jerome & Co.; at times in the office of Norman Little, then on corner of Washington and Madison Streets, and for a period in a building known as "Mechanics' Hall, standing on the site occupied by the house of E. Briggs; on Washington Street, since removed and now occupied as a dwelling by F. P Woodruff, corner of Fayette and Ames Streets. In 1837, was built the first public building in the Saginaw Valley, serving the manifold purpose of church, school house and court room. It stood in the rear of the present court house, and on the erection of that building was removed to the site now occupied by the Jail. This building now occupied by the Methodist clergyman as a parsonage, served as the place of worship of the Presbyterian Church until the erection of the present house of worship. This edifice, on the corner of Court and Harrison Streets, was the first building in the Saginaw Valley set apart to the purposes of religious worship. Its erection began in the spring of 1851, and was completed in the autumn of 1852. The cost of the building was a little more than $3,000. Its architect was H. C. Weston. Its completion at that early day when the church was still feeble, was chiefly due to the liberality and untiring effort of its first minister and his lady, who still live to behold the fruits of their early labors and sacrifices in its behalf. It was dedicated December 12th, 1852, the service being preached by Rev. R. R. Kellogg, of Detroit. Measures are now in progress for its enlargement to a capacity suited to its present needs, with the addition of a conference room, with rooms for Sunday School and Pastor's use.

The whole number of members connected with the church since its organization is 175. Its present membership 100.

METHODIST EPISCOPAL CHURCH.

Rev. Andrew Bell, Stephen Lytle, Levi D. Chamberlain and Lovina Hart, were in 1850, appointed a Board of Trnstees for this society.

The first class consisting of only three members was organzied in 1851. Of these Mrs. John Moore, alone remains. Rev. C. C. Olds, their first Pastor, was appointed to the charge the autumn of the same year. The Pastors since then have been George Bradley, Addison C. Shaw, Samuel Clements, Jr., John Levington, Theron C. Higgins, Wm. Fox, Arthur Edwards, Jr., Reynor S. Pardington, Isaac C. Cochran and A. R. Bartlett.—The church now numbers 83 members. Its Sunday School, under the care of D. B. Ketchum, Esq., has 18 officers and teachers, and more than 160 scholars.

The official list at the present time stands as follows:

A. R. Bartlett, Pastor; Anson Abbott, Local Preacher; Stewards—Smith Palmer, R. A. Bounting, Edwin Saunders, Lorenzo B. Curtis, Jas. Penoyer, D. B. Ketchum, Major W. Hollister, A. C. Abel; Class Leader, S. F. Green.

The building now used as a parsonage, was dedicated as a chapel in the summer of 1854. The present chapel was dedicated February, 1864.

GERMAN EVANGELICAL LUTHERAN CHURCH OF THE HOLY CROSS.

The first church built in Saginaw City was the church of the German Evangelical Lutheran Congregation, unaltered Augsburg Confession—"the Church of the Holy Cross." It was built in the year 1851, and enlarged in 1859.

The congregation was organized in the year 1848, by the Rev. F. Sievers, of Frankenlust, Saginaw County. The services were held in private houses and in one of the Court House rooms till 1851.

The congregation belongs to the "German Evangelical Lutheran Synod of Missouri, Ohio and other States," and strictly adheres to the unaltered Augsburg Confession and all the other symbolical books, as contained in the "Book of Concord," published in 1580.

The first regular Pastor was the Rev. Ottmar Cloter. His instalment took place at one of the Court House rooms. In 1857, he received and accepted a call of Synod to work as a missionary among the Indians, (Chippewas) in the State of Minnesota. His successor was the Rev. T. A. Hugli, who two years afterwards accepted a call of the Lutheran congregation in Detroit. Then the Rev. Martin Gunther, formerly of the State of Wisconsin, was elected Pastor; he was installed on the fourth day of March, 1860, and is the present Pastor.

The congregation has a parsonage, two burying places and two parish schools. Owing to the increase of scholars, a third teacher will be called as soon as possible.

The number of voting members at present are eighty-seven.

MASONIC.

Saginaw Valley Lodge of A. F. and A. Masons, was organized and received their Dispensation February 19th, 1864, with the following officers:

Dr. D M. Bennett, W. Master; Wm. McBratnie, S. Warden; T. L. Jackson, Jr. Warden.

They received their Charter at the next session of the Grand Lodge in the year 1865, with the same Master and Wardens for the year 1865.

Their officers at the present time are, Dr. D. M. Bennett, W. Master; Wm. McBratnie, S. Warden; W. M. Smith, J. Warden. Number of members at the preset time, 43.

GERMANIA LODGE, No 79, F. & A. M. was organized in March, 1854, under dispensation, with eight Charter Members. The present number of members is 34.

The first officers installed were M. C. T. Plessner, W. M.; Count Solms, S. W.; G. Liskow, J. W. The present officers are W. M., M. C. T. Plessner, S. W., Wm. Seffardt, J. W., A. Achard, Secretary, G. Schultz, Treas. E. Bark, S. D., Henry Barnhardt, J. D., John Bauer, Tyler, Romeyke.

Stated meetings on Friday, on or before the full moon of each month.

I. O. O. F.

Saginaw Lodge No. 42, I. O. of O. F., was instituted February 9th, 1849, by P. G. Charles D. Little, special D. D. G. M.

Its first officers elected were as follows:

W. L. P. Little, N. G.; J. S. Woodruff, V. G.; J. B. Chamberlain, Secretary, J. Bookstaver, Treasurer.

This Lodge, as well as a few others in the State, for a time suffered from adverse circumstances but has steadily kept its course and outrode the failure which threatened it. It is now in a flourishing and healthy condition, numbering eighty-six members with almost nightly acquisitions to its membership.

Its present officers are, W. E. Smith, N. G.; J. Sutherland. V. G,; A. D. Lacy, Treasurer; J. Cook, Secretary.

The Lodge room is neatly furnished and tastefully decorated with appropriate emblems of the fraternity, and being well ventilated will compare favorably with any lodge room in this part of the State.

WASHINGTON ENCAMPMENT, No. 19 I. O. O. F.

This Encampment was instituted by Most Worthy Grand Patriarch, Dennis, on the 9th of May, 1866; originating with thirty members. Its officers are, A. G. VanWay, C. P.; W. McRath, F. P.; D. H. Buel, S. W.; A. O. T. Eaton, J. W.; B. Rice, Treasurer; A. F. Rockwith, Scribe.

GOOD TEMPLARS.

Saginaw Lodge No. 172, I. O. G. T., was organized at Saginaw City Feb. 13th, 1864, with nineteen charter members, and increased rapidly for six months, when a reaction took place and was reduced considerably in the number of its members, although its efficiency was not materially lessoned. It has become firmly established and for the past few months has rapidly increased in numbers and influence. It meets every Tuesday night in its Hall on Water street. Its present officers are:

Wm. H. Tutle, W. C. T.	Rev. A. R. Bartlett, W. C.
Jennie Alexander, W. V. T.	F. W. Holister, W. M.
Anna Alexander, W. S.	Adda Palmer, W. D. M.
E. C. Newell W. T.	Mrs. Linaman, W. R. H. S.
Miss Miller, W. I. S. G.	Kate Eaton, W. L. H. S.
———Sutton, W. O. S. G.	Henry Ketchum, W. A. S.
Thomas Lawrence, W. F. S.	

OTTO H. G. MOORES commenced business in 1861. He came here in 1849, and worked for Daniel Johnson in his steam mill. In 1850 he wént to East Saginaw and helped clear away the trees preparatory to building the city. The next year he engaged as clerk with Thomas Whitney in his lumber business and remained with him till 1858. Then he came to Saginaw City and engaged as bookkeeper for D. H. Jerome, continuing with him till 1861, when he commenced the grocery and provision business, in which he has been engaged ever since, at his present location, No. 317 South Water Street. Mr. Moores enjoys the reputation of an honest and upright man, and is much esteemed for his good traits of character.

Saginaw County Officers.

Sheriff—Jesse H. Quackenbush.
County Treasurer—Thomas L. Jackson.
County Clerk—George Schmidt.
Register of Deeds—James N. Gotee.
Judge of Probate—Otto Roeser.
Prosecuting Attorney—Chauncey H. Gage.
Circuit Court Commissioner—John J. Wheeler.
County Surveyor.—Lewis Loeffler.
Coroner—John Erd.

Saginaw City Officers.

Mayor.—William M. Miller.
Recorder—A. F. R. Braley.
Aldermen 1st Ward—Jas. G. Terry, Ami W. Wright.
" *2d* " Ezra Rust, Richard Khuen.
" *3d* " Geo. F. Williams, Geo. R. Stark.
City Attorney—A. S. Gaylord.
Treasurer—Edwin Sanders.
Marshal—C. E. Brenner.
Street Commissioner—Charles T. Brenner.
Board of Health—W. D. Lee, D. F. Mitchell, Theodore Krauss.
Constables—Chas. E. Brenner and August Miller.

SAGINAW CITY DIRECTORY.

ABBREVIATIONS.—For ab., read *above*; bds., *boards*; bet., *between*; carp., *carpenter;* cor., *corner;* col'd *colored;* E., *East* h., *house;* lab., *laborer;* manuf., *manufacturer;* manufy., *manufactory;* N. *north*; propr., *proprietor;* res., *residence;* S., *south.*

The word *Street* is implied.

A

Abbott Anthony, farmer, h 903 N Fayette.
Abley John, cooper, bds 812 Monroe.
Abel A C, foreman for Miller & Norton, h Ames.
Abel John H, carp, bds Ames.
Achard William, (Seyffardt & A), h 411 Cass.
Ackley Chas H, book keeper, h 906 N Hamilton,
Ackley Frank C, jeweler, 102 S Water, h 906 N Hamilton.
Actor Antoine, mason, h 1011 Mackinaw.
Adams G, grocer, 113 S Water, bds 408 N Hamilton.
Adams J F, grocer, 203 N Water, h 306 N Webster.
Adams Joseph E, (Andre & Adams), h 406 S Webster.
Adams Thomas, clerk, bds Washington House.
Adams Thomas, grocer, bds 111 Adams.
Aldor Frank, lab, h 1003 N Fayette.
Alexander Daniel, (col'd), lab, h 811 Cass.
Alexander Mrs Janette,(col'd) h 811 Cass.
Alexander Richard, saw manuf, bds Webster House.
Allen Charles, carp, h 910 N Bond.
Allen Frank, carp,h 911 N Fayette.
Allen James, millwright, bds 611 Adams.
Allen William, sailor, bds 623 N Water.
Allenberg John, lab, h 905 S Harrison.
Allison D W, (Heather & A,) bds N Water.
Allor Frank, lab, h 1007 N Fayette.

Almy Miss J, 208 Cross Road.
Alvord Wm, lumberman, h 605 N Granger.
American House, John Friedlein propr, 105 N Franklin.
Amoit Louis, saloon, 207 N Water, h same.
Amoit J O, clerk, h 326 N Water.
Anchart Geo, lab, h 606 N Fayette.
Anchutz Henry, 609 Van Buren.
Andre & Adams, (Alex A & Joseph E A), furniture 117 S Water, manuf, 602 S Water.
Andre Alex A, (A & Adams), h 201 S Washington.
Andre Elias, h 502 N Washington.
Andre P C & Co, (P C Andre, A F Douglas & Wm H Childs), boots & shoes, 108 N Water.
Andre P C, (P C A & Co), h 206 Court.
Andre & Stark, (P C A, G R & H J Stark,) dry goods, 202 N Water.
Andrew Richard, gardner, h 912 Monroe.
Angetts John, lab, h 702 Mackinaw.
Anschutz George, lab, h 401 N Webster.
Anschutz William, lab, h 401 N Webster.
Arhat Sebastian, shoemaker, h 508 S Fayette.
Armstrong ——, millwright, bds 611 Adams.
Armstrong W A, photographer, 101 S Water, bds 606 N Washington,
Arnold Silas, lab, bds 709 N Water.

B

Bachman Conrad, lab, h 504 S Mason.
Baker E L, dentist, 314 S Water, h same.
Ballintine Samuel, wagon maker, h Hamilton.
Baptist Church, —————, Pastor, 202 N Fayette.
Barber Joseph, wholesale liquor dealer, 318 S Water, h 904 S Fayette.
Barck Edward, grocer, 214 S Water, h same.
Barkham E J, miller, city mills, h 511 Van Buren.
Barlow John, machinist, h Hamilton.
Barnard John L, lumberman, h 801 Mackinaw.
Barnard Joseph, (Newell, Barnard & Co), bds 803 N Hamilton.
Barnard Lacy, lab, bds 709 N Water.
Barnard, Newell & Co, (Newell & Joseph Barnard), lumber & salt manufs, 118 N Water.
Barnard Newell, (Newell Barnard & Co), h 807 N Hamilton.
Barnard Parish, lumberman, bds 803 N Hamilton.
Barnard T, h 803 N Hamilton.
Barney M C, carp, res Salina.
Barry Sidney, mason, bds 623 N Water.

Bartlett Joseph, carp, h 911 N Bond.
Bartlett A R, pastor M E Church, h 106 S Washington.
Bartram & Gardiner, (Wm H H B & Edwin B G), proprs Saginaw Valley Herald, 108 N Water.
Bartram W H H, (B & Gardiner), bds 601 N Washington,
Bates W H, carp, bds Webster House.
Bates Zury, salt boiler, bds 520 N Water.
Battell Timothy, bds 205 S Harrison.
Bauer ——, lab, h 307 S Mason.
Bauer Jacob, mason, h 302 S Granger.
Bauer John M, carp, h 308 S Webster.
Bauer John, engineer, h 602 S Webster.
Bauer Peter, grocer, 104 N Water, h same.
Baurick Lewis, (Byagelmeyer & B), 306 S Water, bds same.
Beach Joseph, clerk, bds Fayette.
Bean John, sawyer, h 510 S Bond.
Beals Zina P, clerk, h 403 S Water.
Beck J G, cabinet maker, h 112 Cross Rroad.
Beehler Reinhard, dentist. 121 N Water, h 108 N Hamilton.
Beldoff Henry, mason, h 1102 Mackinaw.
Befill Frank, lab, bds 709 N Water.
Belisle Charles, blacksmith, 504 N Water.
Bell Charles, blacksmith, h Hamilton.
Bellgard Joseph, shoemaker, h N Water.
Benedict Miss Kate, music teacher, Riverside Seminary, bds Court.
Benito Leander, blacksmith, 503 N Water, h 102 Madison.
Benjamin Charles, lab, bds 709 N Water.
Benjamin David, lumber insp, h 311 Wayne.
Benjamin D M, cooper, h 1308 S Fayette.
Benjamin Frank, lumberman, h 302 S Harrison.
Benjamin R L, h 1308 S Fayette.
Bennett Denis, lumbermam, h 1308 S Hamilton.
BENNETT D M, physician, 102 S Water, h 907 N Hamilton.
Bennett Dimick, lumberman, h 202 Perry.
Bennett Joseph, grocer, 401 N Water, h same.
Bennett Washington, lumberman, h 111 Adams.
Benson M, lab, bds American House.
Benson Wm H, steamboat captain, h 918 N Hamilton.
Benton Louis, engineer, bds 111 Adams.
Bernhard Henry, clothing, 301 S Water, h 308 S Fayette.
Berridge Jonathan, h 1002 Adams.
Berry Jas L, foreman mill, h 409 Van Buren.
Berry Thomas, cabinet maker, bds 111 Adams.
Biesterfield Henry, carp, h 509 N Fayette.
Bigelow Wm, carp, h 302 N Hamilton.
Binder Wm, salt & lumber manuf & express agt, 204 N Hamilton.

Birdseye Lucius, Principal Union School, bds 907 N Hamilton.
Bither Asa, lumber manuf, h 1008 S Fayette.
Bitkie Charles, carp.
Black James, sawyer, bds 1315 S Water.
Blackmore Joshua, deputy sheriff, 104 S Washington, bds 611 Adams.
Blacks Faltin, jr, cabinet maker, bds 305 S Granger.
Blacks Faltin, sen, bds 305 S Granger.
Blaker John, harness maker, h 805 N Fayette.
Blanchard Augustus, book keeper, h 608 Adams.
Bliss L W, physician. h 702 S Fayette.
Bliss Wm, lab, bds 1315 S Water.
Bloomer Mrs B, h 307 S Hamilton.
Bluhm Henry, lab, h 511 Lyon.
Bolun Frederick, sawyer, h 701 S Bond.
Bolt Charles, bds 413 N Water.
Bolton Edward, engineer, h Water.
Bounting R, carp, bds Madison.
Borethel Nathaniel, cooper, h 1305 S Hamilton.
Bostick A, blacksmith, h 408 S Fay.
Bostick, Alonso, h 304 S Harrison.
Bostick Austin, carriage manufy, 110 & 112 Van Buren, h 304 S Hamilton.
Bostwick Austin, lab, bds 304 S Hamilton.
Bounting Richard, carp, bds 411 Madison.
Bradley A, builder, h 411 Madison.
Brady James E, shoemaker, bds Van Buren.
BRALEY A F R, (Miller B & Co), bds 406 Court.
Braley Phineas D, lumberman, h 203 Stevens.
Braley Phineas, jr, lumberman, bds 203 Stevens.
Braley Russell, shingle bolter, res Tittabawassee.
Brenner Chas, h 210 S Granger.
Brenner Edward, bds 210 S Granger.
Brenner William F, lab, h 803 Adams.
Bretzelbauer Wolfgang, lab, h 403 Jefferson.
Briggs E A, bds Dunbar House.
Briggs Ebenezer, salt & lumber manuf, h 407 N Washington
Briggs E M, book keeper, bds 407 Washington.
Briggs J W T, carp & joiner, bds 412 S Water.
Briggs L W, carp, h 508 S Webster.
BRINK G J, propr Dunbar House, 404 & 406 S Water.
Britzman Henry, lab, h 911 Throop.
Broader John, carp, h 411 Adams.
Brockway Abel A, treas Tittabawassee Company, h Mackinaw road.
Brogan Andrew, lab, h 565 N Granger.

Brophy John, teamster, bds 412 Throop.
Brooks ——, dry goods & groceries, bds 201 N Hamilton.
Brousseau Julius, lawyer, 108 S Water, h 1102 S Washington.
Brown A, lab, bds 709 N Water.
Brown Charles, lab, bds 623 N Water.
Brown H, lab, bds 709 N Water.
Brown John, carp, h 408 S Granger.
Brown John, jr, ostler, bds 408 S Granger.
Brown P L, physician, 112 Court.
Brown W J, salt boiler, bds 409 S Water.
Bruno John, engineer, h 111 Jackson.
Bruyea Joseph, lab, bds 709 N Water.
Bryant Andrew, lab, bds 709 N Water.
Bryant George, lab, bds 709 N Water.
Buck Ferdinand, lab, h 712 Mackinaw.
Buel David H, builder, 203 N Harrison, h 410 Franklin.
Buel O L, carp, bds 410 Franklin.
Bullock Henry, driver express wagon, h 611 Clinton.
Bullock Mrs L, h 407 Court.
Bunting Samuel, engineer, city mills, h 701 S Water.
Burdick Charles P, carp, bds 1108 Van Buren.
Burdick Chillus D, carp, bds 1108 Van Buren.
Burdick William P, carp, h 1108 Van Buren.
Burke Chester W, carp, h 501 Jackson.
Burlison Charles, book keeper, h 611 Jefferson.
Burnham C, carriage maker, h 402 N Washington.
Burnham Charles, boat builder, bds 402 N Washington.
Burnham Joseph T, lumber manuf. 205 N Water, h 508 N Washington.
BURROWS GEO L, banker, (& Rust Eaton & Co), 205 Court, h 206 S Washington.
Bush Wm, carp, h 806 Jefferson
Busha Joseph jr, carp, h 905 N Bond.
Busha Joseph, sen, h 907 N Bond.
Butman Myron, lumber manuf, h 407 N Hamilton.
Butman & Rust, (B & A R), lumbermen, 205 N Water.
Butts Abraham L, h 203 N Washington.
Butts Charles H, carp, bds 203 N Washington.
Butts J I, sawyer, bds 203 N Washington.

C

Cain John, blacksmith, h 702 S Granger.
Camp Abram, lab, h 602 Miller.
Campau Joseph, lab, h 606 S Hamilton.
Campbell Archibald, lab, bds 610 Adams.
Campbell, lab, h 504 N Water.

Carpenter S P, lab, h 406 S Mason.
Carpenter William A, merchant tailor, 105 S Water, h 205 S Harrison.
Carr James, bds Dunbar House.
Cary Harrison, engineer, h 1103 Court.
Catholic Church, R Vanderheyden, pastor, 602 N Washington.
Chambers Edward, painter, bds Cross Road.
Chapin Arthur B, lumber manuf, bds Webster House.
Chapin O D, lumber manuf, bds Webster House.
Chapman Albert, h 611 Court.
Chapman N H, & Co, (N H C & J Donley) lumber manuf, office 205 N Water.
Chapman N H, (Chapman & Co) h 611 Court.
Chapman B, raftman, h 810 N Fayette.
Chatterton D D, cooper, h 406 S Bond.
Cheadea John, lab.
Cheadea, Oliver lab.
Cheeseman F, carp, h 1102 S Fayette.
Childs Miss Mary, teacher penmanship, Riverside Seminary, bds 106 N Hamilton.
Childs Mrs Emma. h 106 N Hamilton.
Childs William H, (P C Andre & Co) h 106 N Hamilton.
Churchill John C, (Linderman & C) h Hamilton.
Clark A D, Farmer, h 609 Van Buren.
Clark E L, h 601 N Washington.
Clark James W, lawyer, 205 N Water.
Clark Warren, h 803 S Fayette.
Clark William A, lawyer, h 412 Monroe.
Clayton Isaac, gardner, 1012 Throop.
Clermont William, lab, bds American House.
Clifton F G, machinist.
Clinton Andrew, lab, bds American House.
Close William, shoemaker, bds 512 Ames.
Cobb Henry B, lab, bds 709 N Water.
Cole Jacob, cooper, h 1305 S Hamilton.
Cole Mrs D, h 701 Mackinaw.
Common Council Room, 108 S Water.
Conley Bernard, mason, h 211 Cross Road.
Conley Hugh E, lab, bds 709 S Water.
Conrow John, lab, h 507 N Fayette.
Consha W, lab, h 702 N Bond.
Cook Joseph, (C & Loxley) h 122 S Water.
Cook & Loxley, (J C & J E L) tinsmiths, 122 S Water.
Corbit Robert, lab, h 805 S Porter.
Corning, lumber manuf, h 306 S Fayette.
County Clerk's Office, 104 S Washington.
County Treasurer's office, 104 S Washington.

Court House, 102 S Washington.
Crabner Conrad, lab, h 302 N Granger.
Crabner C B, lab, h 207 Granger.
Cranson William N, carp, h 407 N Granger.
Cross Ira W, lumberman, h 503 N Washington.
CROSS LESTER E, lawyer, 108 S Water, h 205 N Washington.
Cross Lester E, bookkeeper, bds 503 N Washington.
Cross Samuel N, bookkeeper, bds 503 N Washington.
Culver Edwin, painter, h 412 Jefferson.
Curran Samuel,blacksmith, bds 623 N Water.
Current William, carp, h 1210 N Hamilton.
Curtis Chester, physician, 121 N Water bds American House.
Curtis L B, lumber manuf, h 703 S Washington.
Curtis Thomas, h 403 Cass.
Cushen Terry, lab, h 701 N Porter.
Cushway Benjamin, blacksmith, h 111 Court.

D

Dadge E W, carp, h 512 Monroe.
Dashner Louis, lab, h 507 Throop.
Davis George W, saddle & harness, h 402 S Porter.
Davis Robert, carp, bds 622 N Water.
Davis Robert, saw filer, h 503 Stevens.
Day, ——, lake capt, bds Exchange Hotel.
Dean A C, lab, bds 709 N Water.
Dean John, lab, bds American House.
DeBrest Arnold, shoemaker, h Hamilton,
Deder Wolfgang, carp, h 902 Throop.
DeGroff John, h 505 N Hamilton.
Delavergne Joseph, cabinet maker, bds Webster House.
Delavin J cabinet maker, bds East Saginaw.
Dennis, bds 202 Jackson.
Dennis Joseph, h 111 Lyon.
Denny Samuel, lab, bds 520 N Water.
Dibble John B, architect, 216 N Water.
Dickinson Charles, lab, bds 511 Jefferson.
Diedke Charles, carp, h 604 Mackinaw.
Dieter J S, lab.
Dieter Samuel, engineer, h 707 N Water.
Dingman, ——, bds 809 S Hamilton.
Dingman Calvin, fireman, bds 1308 S Hamilton.
Ditmare Christie, lab, h 811 Throop.
Ditmare Ernst, lab, h 811 Throop.
Ditmare Gustav, lab, h 811 Throop.
Ditmare Lewis, lab, h 811 Throop.
Doebel John, lab, h 807 Lyon.
Donley James, (Chapman & Co), res East Saginaw.

Doran W, farmer, h 1107 Throop.
Dougherty M, ship carp, h 409 N Fayette.
Douglass A F, (P C Andre & Co), bds Cass.
Dowe Thomas, sawyer, h 704 S Water.
Duffany C, lab, h 1213 S Water.
Duglos Charley, shoemaker, h 1012 Adams.
Dunbar Alexander, carp, h 210 South Granger.
Dunbar House, G J Brink propr, 404 & 406 S Water.
Dunbar W, telegraph operator, bds 606 N Washington.
Durand George H, cartman, 701 N Water.
Durand L T, student, bds 701 N Water.
Durand Miss Maggie, ass't teacher, Riverside Seminary, bds 701 Water.
Dushane Anthony, lab, bds 111 Adams.

E

Eastman Alvin, grocer, 204 S Water, h same.
Eaton A O T, druggist, h 701 N Webster.
Eaton Daniel L C, insurance agt, 205 Court, h 205 S Washington.
Eaton F L, Justice of the Peace & lawyer, 205 N Water, h 208 Franklin.
Eberhardt Charles, barber, h 419 Lyon.
Edgers Joseph, lumberman, bds Dunbar House.
Edgers Christian, shoemaker, h 1002 Court.
Eggleston Charles, lab, bds 709 N Water.
Eib Philip G, shoemaker, h Mackinaw.
Eiler Matthias, lab, h 808 Mackinaw.
Eiler Nicholas, lab, bds 808 Mackinaw.
Eiler Theodore, lab, bds 808 Mackinaw.
Elliott Ira, lumberman, 605 S Granger.
Elliott James, lab, bds American House.
Elliott John, lumberman, bds 605 S Granger.
Elliott S, lab, bds American House.
Emendorfer F B, boots & shoes. 123 N Water.
Ementerver Frank, shoemaker, h 203 N Harrison.
Emerson Edward, lab, bds 709 N Water.
Emerson James, lab, bds 709 N Water.
Episcopal Church, Rev John Leach, pastor, 105 N Washington.
Epting Emil, druggist, 110 & 112 N Water, h same.
Erhard Sebastian, shoemaker, h Mackinaw.
Evens Alonzo, cooper, h 1407 S Washington.
Exchange Hotel, Henry Heinka propr, 301 N Water.

F

Fanning Michael, mason, h 504 S Porter.
Farrall John, carp, bds Hamilton.
Farrington Henry, h 512 Ames.
Fay B M, banker, h 706 S Washington.
Fay Michael, lab.
Feeney John, lab, bds 709 N Water.
Feibish Philip, agt for N Nathan & Co, bds Washington House.
Felcher George, h 505 S Webster.
Felcher & Green, boots & shoes, 311 S Water.
Fellows Albert, sawyer, h 805 N Bond.
Fellows Edward, lab, h 803 N Bond.
Fellows Hiram, lab, h 807 N Bond.
Fellows Linus teamster, h 902 Clinton.
Férguson Charles, lab, h 805 S Bond.
Ferguson Stephen, lab, h 710 N Oakley.
Ferris Heman B, deputy Co Clerk, 104 S Washington, h 802 S Washington.
Fetter N, lab, h 601 N Bond.
Finningan Mrs Mary, h 704 N Harrison.
First Ward School House, 605 N Harrison.
Fish & Co, (B P F & W S), groceries 309 S Water.
Fish B P, (B P F & W S), bds 412 Franklin.
Fish Benjamin F, h 301 N Hamilton.
Fish Benjamin, drayman, bds 601 N Hamilton.
Fish & Burnham, boat builders, 610 S Water.
Fish Charles, bds 202 Jackson.
Fish F L P, (F & Burnham), h 202 Jackson.
Fish W S (B P F & W S), bds N Washington.
Fisher Andrew, cabinet maker, 601 N Water, h same.
Fisher Benjamin F, h 701 N Hamilton.
Fish Frank, blacksmith, h 605 S Washington.
Fisher Martin, saloon, 310 S Water, h same.
Fiske Leonard, teamster, h 511 Williams.
Fitts Miss Elizabeth, Principal Riverside Seminary, bds Dr. Lees'.
Flake John, ship carpenter.
Fletcher Alex, arcade saloon 314 N Water, h same.
Flour D, lab, h 1315 S Water.
Foley Peter, lab, h 708 Jefferson.
Forbes Benjamin, millwright, h 710 S Webster.
Forbes William, lab.
Forrest Valley Salt and Lumber manufy, Swift, Lockwood & Leavitt proprs, 1401 S Water.
Foulds Joseph, lab, h 1105 Adams.
Fournia, —— lab, h 608 S Webster.

Fradd William, carriage maker, bds 420 S Water.
Franke Mrs Lena, milliner, 119 N Water, h same.
Franke Louis, physician, 119 N Water, h same.
Fraser Sylvester, carp, bds 712 Clinton.
Frazee H, carp, h 208 N Hamilton.
Frazee & Long, (Waldo F & John L), carps & joiners, 424 N Water.
Frazee Waldo, carp, bds 408 N Hamilton.
Frazee Waldo, (Frazee & Long) h 408 Hamilton.
Frazer Allen, lab, bds 623 N Water.
Frederick Frederick, (Kunidnger & F) h Hamilton.
Freelang Garrett, painter, h 902 S Washington.
Freidlein John, propr American House, 105 N Hamilton.
Freiderich Wolfgang, butcher, h 112 Cass.
Frost James, carp, h 412 Mackinaw.
FROST N M, tobacconist, 205 S Water, h 806 S Washington.
Fruchtel Henry, carp, bds 502 Throop.
Fuehr August, tanner, h 712 William.

G

Gale J M, flour & feed, 213 S Water, h 305 S Fayette.
Ganschow Frederick, pattern maker, h 206 Williams.
Ganschow Rudolph, wagon maker.
Ganspauer John, boots & shoes, 215 N Water, h same.
GARDINER EDWIN B, (Bertram & G), h 205 N Washington.
Gaylord Augustine S, (G & Hanchett), h 901 N Washington.
GAYLORD & HANCHETT, (A S G & B H), lawers & insurance agents, 205 Court.
Gaylord H R, bds 901 N Washington.
Geer Benjamin, dry goods & groceries, 106 S Water, h 406 N Washington.
Geiler August, drug clerk, bds 110 N Water.
George John, lab, h 1107 Van Buren.
George Nathan, machinist, bds 408 N Hamilton.
German English School, Caspar Hess teacher, 412 Adams.
German Lutheran school, C H R Schafer, teacher, 105 S Washington.
German Lutheran school, Christopher Eberharat teacher, 506 Ames.
German Lutheran Church, Rev Martin Gunther pastor, 101 S Washington.
Gibson John A, foreman mill, h 305 S Porter.
Gilmore George, (G, Phinney & Co), res Portland, Me.
Girard Joseph, lab, h 801 N Harrison.
Godfrey Frederick, mason, bds 411 Madison.
Gooding J K, lumber manuf, h 609 N Fayette.
Goodman Rev J S, Pastor Baptist Church, h 808 N Hamilton.

Good Templars Lodge Room, 109 N Water.
Goodson Mrs R C, 406 S Washington.
Gotee James N, register of deeds, h 502 Adams.
Goty Isaac, lab, 502 N Water.
Gould C H, millwright, h 405 N Harrison.
Grabner Adam, h 108 Court.
Grabner Christopher, bds 108 Court.
Grabner John, cigar maker, bds 108 Court.
Gradt Francis J, cabinet maker, bds American Hotel.
Graham C lab, h 911 Adams.
Green J H, book keeper, h 807 N Washington.
Green C H, lab, h 808 S Harrison.
Green & Harden, salt & lumber manufy, 1515 S Water.
Green John, lab.
Green Miss Mary, clerk Post Office, bds S Water.
Green Mrs Mary, h 906 N Porter.
Green Samuel F, shoemaker, h 210 Williams.
Green Washington, salt & lumber manufy, h 404 N Washington.
Green William, (Marrow & Co), bds Exchange Hotel.
Greer E, sawyer, bds 514 S Water.
Greer Jacob, sawyer, h 616 S Water.
Greer John W, cooper, h 312 Williams.
Grenney William, carp, h 401 N Harrison.
Grier Louis, sailor, bds Exchange Hotel.
Grout Gardiner K, deputy U S assessor, 205 Jefferson, bds 507 Adams.
Grover James C, boarding house, 809 S Hamilton.
Grover J C, groceries & provisions, 501 S Water, h 809 Hamilton.
Grover J H, clerk, bds 809 S Hamilton.
Gruber Louis, bartender, bds 414 S Water.
Gruhnler Christian, saloon, 206 Franklin, h same.
Guilliot Eugene, lab, h 1711 Jackson.
Guillott Joseph, painter, h 408 S Mason.
Guillott Mrs Esther, h 711 Jackson.
Gymnasium, 202 S Fayette.

H

Hale Charles D, lumber manuf, h 401 Jackson.
Haley Mathew, lab, bds 709 N Water.
Hamell John, lab, h 912 N Harrison.
Hamilton George, conductor street cars, bds 201 N Hamilton.
Hammond Z, lab, bds 709 N Water.
Hanchett B, (Gaylord & H), h 605 S Washington.
Hang Roman, carp, h 502 Throop.
Hanline Andrew, lab.

Hardenberg Howard, h 305 S Hamilton.
Hardin H G, Sag City Flouring Mills, 501 & 503 S Water, bds 121 N Water.
Hardin W H, salt & lumber manuf, rooms, 121 N Water.
Harding W, (Green & H), res N Y.
Hardy William, lab.
Harkin Barney, lab, bds 409 N Water.
Harper Edward, (col'd), barber, bds 107 Cass.
Harrington Dwight, (Miller & H), h 412 Clinton.
Harrington M T, bds Dunbar House.
Harrington Truman, ostler, bds Dunbar House.
Harris Mrs Ann, h 809 N Water.
Harrold M, fireman for Miller & Norton.
Hart Isaac, (H & Zivi), 104 S Water.
Hart & Zivi, (J H & J Z), clothing, 104 S Water.
Haskell Truman H, lab, bds 112 Lyon.
Haskell William, caulker, h 112 Lyon.
Haug Philip, carp, res E Sag.
Haug Roman, carp, 407 Ames.
Hawes, bookkeeper, bds 301 N Washington.
Hawker William, gunsmith, 208 N Water, h same.
Hawkins J A, cabinet shop, 103 Jefferson
Hawkins J S, furniture ware rooms, 218 and 220 N Water, bds Webster House.
Hay James, (Rust & H) h 601 S Washington.
Hay Thomas, h 412 Van Buren.
Hayes Carlos, lab, h 511 N Granger.
Hazel L P, carp, bds Webster House.
Hearns James, carp, h 807 N Water.
Heather Alexander, lumber manuf, bds 606 N Washington.
Heather & Allison, (E H & D W A) lumber, salt and pine land dealers, 105 S Water.
Heather E, (H & Allison) bds 606 N Washington.
Heather James, lumber manuf, bds 606 N Washington.
Heilprun Christian lab, h 806 Jefferson.
Heisrodt William, engineer, bds 1312 S Water.
Helmer William, lab, bds N Water, near bridge.
Hembling Noah, blacksmith, h 510 S Bond.
Henika Henry, propr Exchange Hotel, 301 N Water.
Henry Mrs P, h 401 Van Buren.
Herald Matthias, fireman, h 812 Throop.
Herbage John, painter, 413 S Water, bds 502 Cross Road.
Herbert Edwin, painter, h 308 Lyon.
Herman John G, lab. h 104 N Hamilton.
Heipschman John, lab, 1001 Adams.
Herrig Bernhard, grocer, 205 N Water, bds S Washington.
Herrig Frank, clerk, h Franklin.

GAYLORD & HANCHETT,

Attorneys at Law.

Office in Burrows' Block, No. 2 5, Court Street,

A. S. GAYLORD,
B. HANCHETT.

SAGINAW CITY, MICH.

JAMES W. CLARK,

Attorney and Counselor at Law,

And Solicitor in Chancery,

No. 205, North Water Street.

SAGINAW CITY.

GEORGE B. WHITMAN,

Commission Lumber Dealer.

PARTICULAR ATTENTION PAID TO THE PURCHASE OF LUMBER AND LOGS.

Will attend promptly to Inspection and Shipping of Lumber, Lath, and Shingles, from any point on Saginaw River.

No. Genesee Street, EAST SAGINAW,
And No. 205, North Water Street,

SAGINAW CITY, MICH.

J. W. RICHARDSON,

Saddle & Harness Maker,

AND DEALER IN

Saddles, Bridles, Harness, Whips, Fly-Nets, Cards, Combs, Brusher, &c.

No. 328, North Water, cor. Jefferson,

SAGINAW CITY.

Special attention given to fitting out lumbering establishments.

Herrig Nicholas, saloon, h 411 Jackson.
Herrig Peter, clerk.
Hess Caspar, teacher German English School, 412 Adams.
Hickey Edward, carp, h 702 Lyon.
HILDRETH, H L, (H & Kinsey) bds 301 N Washington.
HILDRETH & KINSEY, (H L H & N B K) proprs Saginaw Iron Works, 402 N Water.
Hilliard E G, furniture manuf, 402 N Water, h 412 Madison.
Hillsley John, lab, h 906 N Bond.
Hoffman John, painter, h 307 S Hamiton.
Hollandmoertz George, carp, h Granger.
Hollington John, lab, h 108 S Bond.
Hollister Major W, blacksmith, 506 S Water, h 604 S Fayette.
Holmes Charles, cabinet maker, bds 306 S Water.
Holmes Jabez, lab, h 306 S Water.
Honeywell Samuel, engineer, bds 623 N Water.
Horton H W, conductor S R R, bds 606 N Washington.
Horton Thomas, lab, h 1101 S Water.
Hortwick Mrs M A, h N Water. near bridge.
Hose Mrs Caroline, h 910 Court.
Hough Rev J W, Pastor Presbyterian Church, h 906 S Washington.
Hough Robert, lab, bds 614 S Washington.
Houton Baldwin, lab, bds N Water, near bridge.
Hubbell L, dentist, 121 N Water, h 912 Cass.
Hudges Richard, carp, h 704 N Fayette.
Hudson J A, dry goods, 201 N Water, h 409 Franklin.
Hughes Abram, lumberman, h 312 Mackinaw.
Hughes Peter, restaurant, 409 S Water, h same.
Hulburt John, cabinet maker, res Salina.
Hunt E R, bds 606 N Washington.
Husick John, lab, h 707 Court.

I

Inker John, lab, h 407 S Harrison.
Ipe Phillip G, shoemaker, h 611 Mackinaw.
Ippel George, (Trakat & I) h 405 N Fayette.
Ittner Frederick, shoemaker, h 406 N Harrison.

J

Jackson Thomas L, County Treasurer, h 305 S Granger.
Jacobson Louis, actor, h 310 S Hamilton.
Jerome D H & Co, (D H J & J G Terry) hardware, 401 and 403 S Water.
Jerome D H (D H Jerome & Co) h 311 Van Buren.
Jerome Frederick, clerk, bds 803 S Washington.

Jerome H R, lumberman, h 302 S Webster.
Jerome J H, physician, 205 N Washington, h 405 N Washington
Jerome Mrs M, h 307 Jackson.
Jerome Timothy, livery stable,222 S Water,h 803 S Washington.
Jorsey Nathan, carp, bds 410 Franklin.
Johnson Charles, lab, bds 912 Monroe.
Johnson Mrs H S, teacher Union School, h 309 Clinton.
Johnson William P, clerk, bds 309 Clinton.
Jones Edward, blacksmith, bds 305 S Hamilton.
Jose William, (Wallace & Jose) h 612 Adams.
Judge of Probate's office, 104 S Washington.
Jungerheld Henry, saloon, 110 Court, h same.

K

Kagel Christian, teamster, h 903 Adams.
Kampfert Frederick (Wurtzel & K) h Cross Road.
Kelley Jacob, lumberman, bds 307 S Hamilton.
Kelly Patrick, lab, bds 807 N Water.
Kelly William, engineer, h 412 Throop.
Kendall E H, carp, h 707 N Water.
Kennedy A, lab, bds 623 N Water.
Kennedy S W, printer, h 312 Court.
Kennedy Thomas S, jailor, h 312 Court.
Kenyon Franklin, machinist, bds 408 N Hamilton.
Kessell Frederick, cooper, h 1004 Mackinaw.
Kessell Ernst, cigar maker, bds Mackinaw.
Ketchum Daniel, bookkeeper, h 409 N Harrison.
Ketchum Henry bookkeeper, bds 409 N Harrison.
Khuen & Epting, (R K & E E) 110 N Water.
Khuen Richard, (K & Epting) h 207 N Hamilton.
Kimball Mrs C. dressmaker, h 312 Ames.
King Mrs L W, h 702 S Washington.
King Nicholas, carp, h 207 N Harrison.
King Stephen, lab, h 207 N Hamilton.
KINSEY N B, (Hildreth & K) bds 201 N Hamilton.
Kirby Ernest, lab, bds American House.
Kirby W K, saloon, 201 N Hamilton, h same.
Kirkey Frederick bds 413 N Water.
Kirwin John blacksmith, res Salina.
Kittridge Mrs Charlotte, h 905 N Harrison.
Knight C P (Staley & Co) bds 322 N Water.
Knight Horatio C, salt boiler, bds 608 N Washington.
Knight, saloon, bds 307 S Hamilton.
Knight Willard W, bookkeeper, h 311 Madison.
Kolb Mrs Barbara, 601 N Webster.
Kopke Gustav, mason, h 1112 Cass.

Kraus Fritz, carp, bds Meyer's Hall.
Krauss Theodore, physician, 110 N Water, h 105 N Fayette.
Kreutzmann Carl, saloon, 102 N Water, h Hamilton.
Kritzmann Charles, carp, h 505 S Hamilton.
Krogmann Peter H, boots and shoes, 114 S Water, h same.
Krott F, cabinet maker, bds American House.
Krouse Augustus, saloon, 414 S Water, h same.
Kruimern Frederick, lab, h 811 Lyon.
Kuhl Christopher, bakery, 211 N Water, h same.
Kull Conrad, (Mack, Schmid & K) h 1006 S Hamilton.
Kull Jacob, lab, bds 301 Mackinaw.
Kundinger & Frederick (M K & F F) meat market, 216 S Water.
Kundinger M, teamster, h 404 N Hamilton.
Kundinger Michael, (K & Frederick) h 216 S Water.

L

Lacy Albert D, watchmaker, h 802 Monroe.
Lacy, carp, h 510 Throop.
Lafuer Angeline, h 413 N Water.
Lamorandier T, h 208 S Webster.
Lane Peter, engineer, h 607 N Washington.
Lang Hiram J, bds 111 Adams.
Lang William, tailor, h 1004 Cass.
Lapp Angus J, lab, h 1009 S Water.
Larned Francis, wagon maker, h 407 S Hamilton.
Larrabee William, propr Webster House, 401 N Washington.
Lawner Francis, carriage manuf, h 105 Mackinaw.
Lawrence & Dibble, (Miss E L & Mrs J B D) millinery and dress making, 216 N Water.
Lawrence H K, carp, h Fayette.
Lawrence William, lab, bds 809 S Hamilton.
Leech Rev John, Rector St John's Church, h 305 Franklin.
Leasia Francis A, dry goods and groceries, 326 N Water, h 409 Jefferson.
Leavitt W D, salt and lumber manuf, h 601 N Fayette.
Lebuf Joseph, lab.
Lee Joseph, boiler maker, h Court.
Lee Newton D, (L & Northrop) h 108 S Webster.
Lee & Northrop, (N D L & G J N) physicians, 205 N Water.
Lee William, carp, h 908 Cass.
Lefeber Moses, lab, h 812 Clinton.
Legros Joseph, Jr, lab, bds 705 N Water.
Legros, Joseph, Sen, lab, h 705 N Water.
Leidley George, boarding house, 109 Mackinaw.
Leline Powell, (Riese & L) bds Hamilton.
Lemmer Michael, lab, h 1112 Mackinaw.

Leonard Charles, blacksmith, bds 409 S Water.
Leonard John, lab, h 712 Throop.
Leopold John, lab, h 201 N Harrison.
Letke Charles, lab, h 605 Mackinaw.
Lewis Daniel, h 905 S Washington.
Lewis Thomas, sawyer, bds 704 S Water.
Liebental William, carp, bds Meyer's Hall.
Liebert Ignatus, painter, h 412 Cross Road.
Linderman & Churchill, (J W L & J C) meat market 310 N Water.
Linderman Joel W, (L & Churchill) h 405 N Hamilton.
Little Charles D, h 1009 S Washington.
Little William steamboat captain, h 103 Adams.
Lockwood N S, (Swift, L & Leavitt) res Cincinnati.
Long John, (Frazee & L) h 908 Franklin.
Lossing Horace, millwright, h 407 N Webster.
Love John, lab, bds 709 N Water.
Loveridge Alpheus, bds 804 N Hamilton.
Loveridge Stephen, painter, 106 Clinton, h 804 N Hamilton.
Lowry William, carp, res Salina.
Loxley John E, (Cook & L) bds 122 S Water.
Lyon Gideon A, Captain U S A, h 409 Madison.

M

McArdle Edward, saloon, 319 N Water, h same.
McCardle Barney, farmer, h 704 N Fayette.
McCarty Louis, lab, bds 413 N Water.
McCloud David, watchman, h 803 N Harrison.
McCoy A G, carp, bds 409 S Water.
McCullough John, lab, h 306 S Granger.
McCurdy George, carp, bds 811 Cass.
McCurdey Iney, carp, h 811 Cass.
McDonald C, tinsmith, bds 509 Jefferson.
McDonald William, drayman, h 411 Cross Road.
McElgen Charles, lab, bds American House.
McFarland Patrick, lab, bds 709 N Water.
McGregor James, boiler maker, 716 S Water, h 1301 S Water.
McHenry Nelson, carp, h 1109 Court.
McKay John, sawyer, h 704 N Hamilton.
McKenzie Alex, lab, h 606 S Bond.
McKim James, machinist, h Hamilton.
McKinnon John, livery stable, 311 N Water, h 701 N Washington.
McLean Robert, carp, h 1307 S Washington.
McPhee Wm, tailor, bds American House.
McQueen Robert, book keeper, h 403 N Harrison.

McRath William, boot & shoe manuf, 205 S Water, h Cass.
Mabray Joseph, (col'd), barber, 304 S Water, h same.
Mack Christian, (M, Schmid & Kull,) 1001 S Hamilton, res Ann Arbor.
Mack, Schmid & Kull, (C M, F S & C K), salt manufy, 1001 S Hamilton.
Mager Frederick, bakery, bds 316 S Water.
Major George, shoemaker, bds E Sag.
Maunion Frank, engineer, h 705 N Granger.
Manning Joseph G, jobber, h 511 Jefferson.
Manning William, bds 511 Jefferson.
Marlow ——, lab, h N Water near bridge.
Marr Patrick, mason, bds 411 Madison.
Marrow J & Co, (J M & Wm Green), clothing, 117 N Water.
Marrow John, (M & Co), bds Exchange Hotel.
Marshall John, lab, h 808 Jefferson.
Martin Elizabeth, Mrs, h 111 Van Buren.
Martin Jule, lab, h 911 N Bond.
Matthews Conrad, lab, h 912 Jackson.
May John, lab, bds 203 Stephens.
Maybury Joseph, (col'd), barber, h 107 Cass.
Mayett F, lab, bds American House.
Menton John, wagon maker, bds American House.
Merrill Edward T, captain propellor, h 1302 S Washington.
Merrill G H, salt manuf, h 312 Jackson.
Merrill Thomas, lumberman, h 1208 S Washington.
Meserve Samuel, (Miles, Smith & Co), bds 1104 Court.
Methodist Episcopal Church, Rev. A. R. Bartlett pastor, 108 S Washington.
Meyer Chas, propr of Meyers Hall, 504 S Harrison.
Meyer John, lab, h 1003 N Porter.
Michener John, carp, h Court.
Miesler Mathias, mason, h 1012 Mackinaw.
Miles Labon, (M, Smith & Co), h 1104 Court.
Miles, Smith & Co, (Labon Miles, Chas. B. Smith & Samuel Meserve,) crockery & glassware, 216 N Water.
Miller Ames, saloon, 302 S Water, h same.
Miller August, carp, h 406 S Granger.
Miller, Braley & Co, (H M, A F R B & Wm M Miller), bankers 120 N Water.
Miller C C, (Miller & Norton), h 207 Cass.
Miller & Harrington, (H M & D H), grocers, 121 N Water.
Miller Harvey, (Miller, Braley & Co), bds 306 N Washington.
Miller Henry, (M & Harrington) h 406 S Granger.
Miller Hiram L, h 405 S Washington.
Miller Henry, grocer, h 105 S Granger.
Miller Henry D, h 304 S Hamilton.

Miller John C, carp, bds 302 S Water.
Miller Joseph, lab, h 511 Mackinaw.
Miller Lewis, carp, bds Court.
Miller Norman, h 604 S Washington.
Miller & Norton, (C C M & D R N), sash & blind manufs, 404 N Water.
Miller Norman L, h 602 S Washington.
Miller Wm M, lawyer, 205 Jefferson, h 306 N Washington.
Milligan George, carp, bds 807 N Water.
Mills Theodore, express agt, bds 204 N Hamilton.
Milz Guido, clerk American Express Co's office, h 204 N Hamilton.
Miner ———, carp, h 407 N Granger.
Minton John, wagon maker, bds American House
Mitchell D F, physician, h 811 Court.
Mitchell H T, clerk, bds Washington House.
Mitchell Theodore, grocer, bds 111 Adams.
MOLL WM, Post master, h 703 N Webster.
Monroe Milo, carp, bds Water.
Moore James, lab, bds 709 N Water.
Moore John, lawyer, 805 N Washington, h same.
Moore Joseph, carp, h 909 N Harrison.
MOORES OTTO H G, grocery, 317 S Water, h same.
Moreau Theodore, engineer, h 507 N Water.
Morgan Isaac D, gardner, h 512 Miller.
Moro William, cooper, bds Meyer's Hall.
Morris Geo H, carp, h 404 S Granger.
Morris John, lab, bds American House.
Morris Simeon, teamster, h 809 S Harrison.
Morrison Duncan, lab, bds E Sag.
Morse L A, tinsmith, h 412 Franklin.
Mould Thomas, gunsmith, bds 623 N Water.
Moye Augustus, (A E & C Moye), h 109 N Hamilton.
Moye Bros, (A E & C M), meat market, 111 Franklin.
Moye Charles, (A & C Moye), h 109 N Hamilton.
Moye Edward, (A E & C Moye), h 109 N Hamilton.
Mulligne J J, teamster, h 501 N Granger.
Munch Frederick, cabinet maker, h 404 S Webster.
Mundy Chas, lab, bds Cross Roads.
Munson Jerome, teamster, h 1408 S Washington.
Munson L F, h 1402 S Washington.
Munson Nelson, teamster, h 505 N Granger.
Murphy John, blacksmith, 112 Mackinaw, h 705 S Harrison.
Myers John M, lab, bds 709 N Water.
Myre John, lab, h 705 N Porter.

N

Nason Stephen L, spile driver, bds 623 N Water.
Nathan George, machinist, h Hamilton.
Nathan N & Co, (N N, A Smith & M Mendelson) clothing, 115 S Water.
Nester Thomas, lumberman, h 308 N Hamilton.
Newart Francis, lab, h 411 Lyon.
Newell E C, (N & St John) h 507 Ames.
Newell & St John, (E C N & E St J) books and stationery, 107 S Water.
Newman Orrin, ship carpenter, h 507 N Granger.
Newman Theodore, shoemaker, 306 S Oakley.
Newton Henry, lumberman, h 1302 S Fayette.
Nichol William, blacksmith, bds 305 S Hamilton.
Nole David, carp, bds 1407 S Hamilton.
Northrop George J, (Lee & N) bds 108 S Webster.
Northrop Harvey, blacksmith, h 610 S Bond.
Norton D R, (Miller & N) h 509 Jefferson.
Norton James, carp, h 603 Throop.
Nosband John, ship carpenter, h 1308 N Hamilton.

O

Odd Fellow's Hall, 302 N Hamilton.
O'Donnel P, lab, bds 609 Stephens.
Ogden Wellington, sailor, h 211 Cass.
Olds Charles, shingle jointer, bds Court.
Olds William, shingle sawyer h Court.
O'Neal Lawrence, tailor, h 206 S Water.
O'Neal Mrs Lawrence, milliner and dressmaker, 206 S Water, h same,
O'Neill David, museum, 208 S Water, bds Washington House.
O'Neill William, clerk, bds Washington House.
Opfergelt Christian, h 1108 S Washington.
OPFERGELT PHILIP, (O & Wagener) 314 S Water, bds S Washington.
OPFERGELT & WAGENER (P O & L W) harness makers, 314 S Water.
Orr Alexander, lab, h 405 Jackson.
Osborne John P, lab, h 807 N Porter.
Osborne Robert, lab, h 805 N Porter.
Ostrander Robert, blacksmith, bds 611 Adams.
Otto Frederick, shoemaker, h Adams.
Otto Michael, lab, bds 701 N Washington.
Oxengeld Jacob, lab, h 411 Stephens.

P

Paine A B, h 209 Court.
Paine Asa H, deputy U S Marshal, h 301 N Washington.
Paine Thomas, caulker, h 912 Monroe.
Paine V A, lumber manuf, 815 S Water, h 209 Court.
Palm Frederick, lab, h 1206 Van Buren.
Palmer C M, printer, h 506 N Washington.
Palmer J S, clerk, h 108 N Washington.
Palmer Mrs Louisa, 506 N Washington.
Palmer Smith, book keeper. h 108 N Washington.
Pallett George, cigarmaker, bds 409 Throop.
Pallett Mrs A, h 409 Throop.
Parker Catharine, Mrs, h 907 N Fayette.
Parker Henry, lab, bds 912 Adams.
Parks James, lab, h 811 Van Buren.
Parmelee Morris R, clerk, bds Dunbar House.
Purmort Racine, book keeper, bds 201 N Washington.
Parsons A A, (P & Bro), 124 S Water, bds 803 N Hamilton.
Parsons & Bro, (A A & J P, jr,) real estate agents, 124 S Water.
Parsons Isaac jr, (P & Bro), 124 S Water bds 803 N Hamilton.
Partonfelter Andrew, shoemaker, h 609 Adams.
Patridge Gilbert, ship carp, h 607 S Granger.
Parry Phillip, clerk, h 401 S Water.
Patterson Edward, lab, h 105 Emerson.
Paxton Erastus, book keeper, bds 411 Madison.
PEARSON JAMES H, (A W Wright & Co), res Chicago.
Pecor Nelson, lab, bds 111 Adams.
Peisterfield Christopher, tinsmith.
Penoyer James N & Co, (Jas N P & Jay Smith), drugs & medicines, 324 N Water.
Penoyer James N, (J N P & Co, bds 606 N Washington.
Perkins Sanford S, bridgetender, 311 Jackson.
Perkins Wm, carp, h 707 N Harrison.
Pesenecker Michael, saloon, 109 N Water, h 105 S Porter.
Pier William, fruit stand, h 109 S Water.
Pierce Richard, lab, h 712 Clinton.
Phillips Hugh, fireman, h 601 N Bond.
Phinney C, (Gilmore P & Co), res Portland Me.
Plessner Michael, physician, 205 N Water.
Plessner Robert, lab, bds 110 & 112 N Water.
Pluss William, h 812 Williams.
Porterfield Robert, lab, h 1206 N Hamilton.
Post Office, 103 S Water.
Potter F R, bank clerk, bds Washington.
Powell Riley, sawyer, h 603 S Hamilton.
Powers E H, lawyer, h 605 N Washington.

Presbyterian Church, J W Hough pastor, 501 Court.
Prieur J, lumberman, h 609 Stephens.
Purdy Gabriel, lab, h 708 N Fayette.
Purdy John M, broom maker, h 707 N Fayette.
Purvis E P, book keeper, bds 111 Adams.

Q

Quackenbush Jesse H, Sheriff, 102 S Washington, res Salina.

R

Ramsey James, carp.
Randall Charles, blacksmith, h 403 N Granger.
Randall George H, bookkeeper, h 606 S Harrison.
Rathbone G, lab, bds 809 S Hamilton.
Rathbone W H. lab, bds 809 S Hamilton.
Raymond F, (R & Twitchell) h 508 Adams.
Raymond & Twitchell, (F R & J S T) books and stationery, 112 Court.
Redman Michael, h 401 N Hamilton.
Reimer Joseph, lab, h 508 S Granger.
Reimer Michael, lab, h 702 S Porter.
Remmele I, carp, h 505 S Harrison.
Rhines David, cooper, bds 408 N Hamilton.
Rice Bernhard, confectioner, 209 S Water, h same.
Rice N B, physician, bds Webster House.
Rice Nicholas, meat market, 1003 S Washington, h 1001 S Washington.
Rich Bacchus, lab, h 606 N Granger.
Rich Richard, lab, h 912 Adams.
Richards Frederick, engineer, h 607 S Granger.
Richardson James, painter, h 506 S Porter.
RICHARDSON JOHN W, harness maker, 323 N Water, h 502 N Hamilton.
Richardson John. painter, h 308 S Granger.
Richman Charles H, h 206 N Wasington.
Richter August, carp, h 1304 Cass.
Riese Conrad, lab, h 711 Throop.
Riese Frederick, lab, h 711 Throop.
Riese Emil, clothing, h 306 S Harrison.
Riese Herman (R & Leline) h 609 S Hamilton.
Riese & Leline, (H R & P L) carriage manufy, 110 Mackinaw.
Ripley Eliakim C, lumberman, h 201 N Washington.
Ritter Andrew, h 1112 Van Buren.
Riverside Seminary, Miss Elizabeth Fitts, Priucipal, 102 S Washington.
Robinson Joseph H, lumberman, h 610 S Webster.

Robinson W, teamster, bds 809 S Hamilton.
Roche James, lab, h 802 Van Buren.
Rockwith F A, physician, 108 N Water, h 1301 S Washington.
Roeser Otto, Judge of Probate, h 305 S Harrison.
Romike Herman, grocer, h 301 Mackinaw, h same.
Roney Thomas, sawyer, bds near Forest Valley Works.
Rose Frederick W, grocer, 109 Cass, h 1206 Cass.
Rose John, brewer, h 709 N Fayette.
Roth Frederick, lab, h 1003 Cass.
Rouse Amos, lumber inspector, bds Exchange Hotel.
Rungstein Frederick, lab, h 901 Mackinaw.
Rupp George, saloon, 217 N Water, h same.
Rupp John L, lab.
Rust Amasa, lumberman, 102 S Water, h 507 Adams.
Rust, Eaton & Co, (A R, E Rust) James Hay, D L C Faton, George L Burrows and A S Gaylord, 102 S Water.
Rust Ezra, (R & Hay) h 206 S Harrison.
Rust & Hay, (E R & J H) lumbermen, 102 S Water.

S

Safford Truman, lab, h 302 S Mason.
Saginaw County jail, Thomas L Kennedy, jailor, 312 Court.
Saginaw Iron works, Hildreth & Kinsey, 402 N Water.
Sampson G A, engineer, bds Exchange Hotel.
Samuels Benjamin, bridge tender, h 906 S Harrison.
Sanborn John, lumber inspector, h 801 N Webster.
Sarsfield David, lab, h 709 Madison.
Sauder John, tobacconist, bds American House.
Saunders A W, saloon, 208 S Water, h same.
Saunders Edwin, city treas, h 305 N Webster.
Saunders Edwin, clerk, h 305 N Webster.
Saunders James, lab, h 412 Wayne.
Saunders John, tinsmith, bds 509 Cross Road.
Saunders William, gardner, h 301 N Granger.
Savage M W, sawyer, h 1315 S Water.
Sawser J W, harness maker, bds 111 Adams.
Sayers Thomas, carp, h 701 N Granger.
Schagelmyer, ——, tobacconist, h 306 S Hamilton.
Shefnecker Joseph, boarding house, 623 N Water.
Scheib Albert, clerk, h 509 N Fayette.
Scheib Charles, clerk, bds 509 N Fayette.
Scheurmann Emiel, tobacconist, 115 N Water, h same.
Schick Geo, boots & shoes, 314 S Hamilton, h same.
Schmeider John, drayman, h 1101 Mackinaw.
Schmid Frederick, (Mack, S & Kull), 1001 S Hamilton, residence Ann Arbor.

Schmidt George, county clerk, h 612 Mackinaw.
Schneider John, blacksmith, 512 S Water, h 401 Williams.
Schoen John, teamster, h 911 Mackinaw.
Scholtz Joseph, carp 307 N Webster.
Scott Mrs Ann, h 321 N Water.
Scott William, bds 321 N Water.
Schulz George, lab, h 107 N Water.
Schultz George G, boots & shoes, 105 Cass.
Schultz Robert apprentice, bds 105 Cass.
Seeney Robert, cooper, h 405 N Granger.
Seiger William, lab, bds Meyers Hall.
Seigler John, watchmaker, h 812 Monroe.
Sevallie William, lab.
Seyffardt Gustav, lab, h 1108 Adams.
Seyffardt William, (S & Achard), 312 S Water, h 107 N Fayette.
Seyffardt & Achard, (Wm S & Wm A), hardware, 312 S Water.
Sharp Thomas, lab, bds 409 S Water.
Sharrow Louis lab, bds 1213 S Water.
Shaver Barnum, fireman, h 811 N Water.
Shaw C, lab, h 403 N Webster.
Shaw Joseph E, President Tittabawassee boom Company.
Sheffield George Painter, bds 623 N Water.
Shellhaus Joseph, cooper, h 512 Monroe.
Sheltraw Geo, lab, bds 602 Miller.
Sheltraw Smith, lab, h 701 Throop.
Sheridan Peter, lab.
Shimmons Edward R, builder, h 502 Cross Road.
Shimmons Thomas, carp, h 709 N Porter.
Shipe William, lab, h 603 Stephens.
Short Edwin, wagon maker, h 912 Mackinaw.
Shultheiss John, clerk, bds Mackinaw
Siebel Adolph, bakery, 111 N Water, h same.
Sigert Geo, lab, h 704 Throop.
Simon Frederick, (Saloon and Billiards,) 126 S Water, h same.
Simonson John B, teamster, h 706 N. Hamilton.
Simonson G I, bds 706, N Hamilton.
Simpson John G, farmer, h 205, Adams.
Slenou Tolbert, blacksmith, bds 202 Jackson.
Slink John P, lab, h 306 N Water.
Smart James C, farmer, bds Dunbar House.
Smith Archibald, lab, h 507 Williams.
SMITH CHAS B, (Miles & S,) h 312 Ames.
Smith George, lab, bds Dunbar House.
Smith Isaac N, physician, h 501 N Hamilton.
Smith Jay, (J N Penoyer & Co,) h 305 S Washington.
SMITH & MOLL, (J S & Wm M,) druggists, 101 S Water,
Smith Mrs R, h 511 Cass.

CROCKERY, CARPETS AND CUTLERY

ARE SOLD AT

ELLIOTT & HARRISON'S

WHOLESALE & RETAIL STORE in East Saginaw, at prices that have always

GIVEN

Perfect satisfaction, and we intend to deal with our patrons in

A WAY

that shall continue to please them. We have a great variety of articles to which we call your attention. Drop in and examine our stock,

ELLIOTT & HARRISON'S

HOUSE-FURNISHING EMPORIUM!

South Water Street,

EAST SAGINAW MICH.

DUNBAR HOTEL,

G. J. BRINK, Proprietor.

This House has recently been refitted and refurnished. A good Stable in rear of Hotel.

Nos. 404 and 406 South Water St.,

SAGINAW CITY.

NEWELL & ST. JOHN,

Wholesale and Retail Dealers in

School Books, all kinds of Stationery, Blank Books, Arnold's Genuine Inks, Pens, Pencils, &c.

We also keep constantly on hand, a large stock of

Wall Paper and Borders, Window Shades, Patent Fixtures. Tassels, Cords, &c.

No. 107, S. Water St.

SAGINAW CITY, MICH.

Smith Thomas, lumberman, h 312 Stephens,
Smyth William E, jeweler, 202 S Water, h same.
Smyth William E jr, watch maker, bds 202 S Water.
Southwick S A, bartender, bds 201 N Hamilton.
Sova Louis, h 107 Mackinaw.
Souvy Antoine, saloon, 412 S Water, h same.
Spiller Joseph G, Supt. Salt Works, h 707 N Webster.
Squires Josiah, teamster, h 811 Adams.
Staley & Co, (W R S & C P Knight,) saloon, 322 N Water.
Staley W R, (Staley & Co,) h 322 N Water.
Stampfig Frederick, lab, h 1002 Van Buren.
Staples James, lab, h 305 N Fayette.
Staples Robert, h 505 N Fayette.
STARK G. R. (Andre & S) h 701 S Washington.
STARK H J, (Andre & S,) h 704 N Webster.
Starkweather E F, teamster, 810 S Harrison.
Steinbauer John, teamster, h 304 S Webster.
Stegal Lemuel, (col'd,) teamster, h 308 Williams.
Stenger ———, lab, h 1303 Cass.
Stengel John, carp, h 304 S Webster.
Sternhauger William, carp, h 707 S Bond.
Stewart Erastus, lumberman, h 806 Mackinaw.
Stewart George, lumberman, bds 1312 S Water.
Stickney Charles, h 811 Franklin.
Stickney Joseph, lab, h 901 Monroe.
Stickney Oliver, lab, h 801 Madison.
St John Elijah, books and stationery, rooms 121 N Water.
Stolz Louis, wagon maker, bds Hamilton.
Stone Mrs M, boarding house, 606 N Washington.
Storch, William, farmer, h 1308 Cass.
Straup Edward, barber, bds American Hotel.
Streeb George, dry goods and groceries, 213 N Water, h same.
Stroebel John, lab, h 301 N Webster.
Stroebel Ulrich, teamster, h 711 Ames.
Strouse Geo, tailor, h 911 N Harrison.
Strouse Mrs Catharine, h 512 Clinton.
Struve Christian, lab, bds 604 S Granger.
Struve Joachim, lab, h 604 S Granger.
Stucker Mathias, sawyer, h 708 N Hamilton.
Sutherland John H, sawyer, 101 Court, h 409 N Fayette.
Surroun John, tinsmith, h 308 S Mason.
Sutton George W, book keeper, h 702 Court.
Sutton J & Co, (Jonathan S & Joseph S,) grocers, 308 N Water.
Sutton Jonathan, (J S & Co,) h 405 N Hamilton.
Sutton Joseph, (J S & Co,) bds 405 N Hamilton.
Sutton Wm J, clerk, bds 405 N Hamilton.
Swarthout David, carp, h 405 N Hamilton.

SWEET WILLIAM H, lawyer, 108 S Water, h 901 N Hamilton
Swift, Lockwood & Leavitt, (A S, N S L & W D L,) lumber salt manfy, 1401 S Water.
Syfardt Henry, lab.

T

Talon Thomas, sailor, h 612 Miller.
Taylor Joseph, carp, h 909 N Fayette.
Taylor Willaim H, h 312 Jackson.
Tenneson James, lab, h 514 S Water.
Terry James G, (D H Jerome & Co) h 408 N Washington.
Tittabawassee Boom Company, Joseph E Shaw, President, Joseph A Whittier, Secretary, Abel A Brockway, Treasurer, 307 S Water.
Thayer Julius, lab,
Thomas James E, carp, h 411 Jefferson.
Thomas Robert, (cold) barber, bds 107 Cass.
Thomas William, lab, bds 623 N Water.
Thompson Henry, lumberman, h 1010 S Washington.
Thurston William, carp, h 707 N Hamilton.
Toombs James, carp, h 312 Ames.
Towel William, lab.
Townsend Charles, lumberman, h 810 Monroe.
Trakat & Ippel (J H T & G I) grocers, 105 Jefferson.
Trakat J H (T & Ippel) h 105 Jefferson.
Trakat Leopold, architect, h 504 S Fayette.
Trommer John, hats and caps, 113 N Water, h same.
Trower Patrick, lab.
Turner Alfred, carp, bds 807 N Water.
Turner Charles, steamboat captain, h 308 S Harrison.
Turner William, sawyer, h 611 Adams.
Turver Edwin, mason, h 906 Adams.
Tuttle W H, millwright, h 206 S Fayette.
Twitchell James S, (Raymond & T) 102 Court, h 805 Webster.

U

Union School House, L H Birdseye, Principal, 511 Court.
U S Telegraph office, William Dunbar, operator 103 Court.
Utter Charles, engineer, h 807 S Webster.

V

Van Laun, George D, lab, bds 908 Cass.
Van Wey William, lumberman, h 303 S Washington.
Van Wey A G, lumberman, 121 N Water.
Van Zile Gilbert, lab, h 804 S Fayette.

Valentine Samuel, wagon maker, bds 304 S Hamilton.
Vance Henry, bds 103 Adams.
Vanderheyden Rev R, Pastor Catholic Church, h 604 N Washington.
Vansa John, lab, bds 1213 S Water.
Vogt Jacob, groceries and feed, 318 N Water, h 306 Adams.
Vondet Alexander, ship carpenter, h 520 N Water.
Vorster A clerk, 312 S Water.

W

Wade L W, bookkeeper. bds 707 N Washington.
WAGENER LOUIS, (Opfergelt & W) bds 708 Ames.
Wagener, Robert F, lab, h 708 Ames.
Waldbauer George, bakery, 316 S Water, h same.
Waldbauer Louis, baker, h 306 S Hamilton.
Walker, T A, (col'd) barber, 107 N Water, h 512 Franklin.
Walker Robert, carp, bds 509 Cross Road.
Walker Walter, (col'd) barber, bds 512 Franklin.
Wallace Colon bds 610 Adams.
Wallace & Jose, (S W & W J) shingle manufy, 404 N Water.
Wallace Richard, drover, bds Exchange Hotel.
Wallace Stephen, (W & Jose) h 610 Adams.
Wallace Stephen J, lab, h 610 Adams.
Wapler Charles H, fancy turning shop, 1010 S Hamilton h same.
Ward William, engineer, h 612 Ames.
Warehouse for Ward's line of steamers, 401 and 403 S Water, D H Jerome & Co, agents.
Waterman John, lumber manuf, h 306 N Hamilton.
Watkins Robert, bookkeeper, bds Exchange Hotel.
Watson Charles, lab, bds American House.
Webster House, William Larrabee, prpor 401 N Washington.
Webster Samuel H, salt and lumber manuf, bds 201 N Washington.
Weggel John, carp, h 205 N Harrison.
Weiss John, lab, h 905 Lyon.
Weiss John, tinner, bds 905 Lyon.
Welch John, lab, h 1004 Court.
Wells W C, cabinet maker, bds Cass.
Wendell Ahasuerus, h 309 Williams.
Werner Ferdinand, gardner, h 1307 Cass.
Wesener Hugo, clerk, h corner Hamilton and Adams.
Weston John, tinner, h 511 Cross Road.
Weston Mrs R, h 703 Stevens.
Wheeler, engineer, bds Dunbar House.
Wheelock Louis, h 603 N Hamilton.
White John B, physician, 112 Court, h 508 Adams.

F

White Michael lab, h 1003 Mackinaw.
White Samuel, lumberman, bds Exchange Hotel.
Whitman F X, shoemaker, h 1009 Court.
WHITMAN GEORGE B, commission lumber dealer, 205 N Water, h 707 N Washington.
Whitman J C, lumber inspector, 205 N Water, h 706 Monroe.
Whitney Daniel G, salt manuf, 511 N Water, h 608 N Washton
Whittier Joseph A, secretary Tittabawassee Boom Company, res East Saginaw.
Wickham James, cabinet maker, bds Jefferson.
Wider Frederic, paper hanger, 411 S Water, bds 409 S Water.
Wider Charles, tanner, 801 S Water, h 902 S Washington.
Wilhelm John H, carp, h 403 N Hamilton.
Wiley Robert, wagon maker, 103 Mackinaw, h 111 Mackinaw.
Wiley William, lab, bds 1103 Court.
Will D, student, bds 907 N Hamilton.
WILLIAMS G F, & BROS, (G F, S B, & Wm W) lumber manuf, 517 S Water.
WILLIAMS GEORGE F, (G F W & Bros) bds 209 Mackinaw.
Williams S B, (G F W & Bros) h S end S Washington
Williams William, (G F W & Bros) h 209 Mackinaw.
Williamson Christopher, saloon, 420 S Water.
Wilson Elias, brick maker, bds Exchange Hotel.
Wilson Hiram, blacksmith, h 707 N Water.
Wilson Isaac, lab, bds 409 Jefferson.
Wilson J M, h 612 Ames.
Wilson John, cooper, h 806 S Harrison.
Wilson John M, h 401 N Granger.
Wing William, carp, bds 412 Clinton.
Winkler George M, boots and shoes, 406 N Hamilton, h same.
Winkler John, shoemaker, h 1000 Adams.
Winguth Gustave, shoemaker.
Winn W G, (col'd) barber, bds Franklin.
Wollenweber Mathew, cigar maker, bds American Hotel.
Woodruff F P, h 302 N Fayette.
Woolweaver John, lab, h 524 N Water.
Woodward M T, carp, bds Webster House.
WRIGHT A W & Co, (A W W & J H Pearson) lumber manuf, office 602 N Water, mill 702 N Water.
WRIGHT AMI W, (A W W & Co) h 503 N Washington.
Wright Thomas, cabinet maker, h 404 N Water.
Wright William H, millwright h 709 N Water.
Wurts Alexander, sailor, h 206 N Water.
Wurts Mrs A, hair braider, 206 N Water, h same.
Wurtzel & Kampfert, (W W & F K) meat market, 318 S Water.
Wurtzel William, (W & Kampfert) h 106 Van Buren.
Wyckham James, cabinet maker, bds 312 Ames.

JULIUS BROUSSEAU,

Attorney and Counsellor at Law,

And Solicitor in Chancery,

Prompt attention paid to collecting Debts and securing Demands, and other Business entrusted to his care.

Office in Bauer's Block, No. 108 S. Water St. 2d floor,

SAGINAW CITY.

Dr. D. M. BENNETT,

HOMŒPATHIC

PHYSICIAN & SURGEON

No. 102, S. Water St., Bauer's Block,

SAGINAW CITY, MICH.

Millinery and Dress Making!!

MISS. E. L. LAWRENCE & Co.,

Dealers in

MILLINERY & FANCY GOODS

Work done in the latest and most approved styles.

No. 216, N. Water St.,

CITY OF SAGINAW, MICH.

MISS. E. L. LAWRENCE. MRS. E. M. DIBBLE.

WILLIAM E. SMYTH,

DEALER IN

Watches, Clocks, Silver & Plated Ware, Jewelry, &c.

Watch cleaning and repairing done in the best manner, on the shortest notice.

No. 202, South Water Street,

SAGINAW CITY, MICH.

Y

Yost Charles N L, teamster, h 802 Clinton.
Yost William, shoemaker, h 306 S Hamilton.
Young Henry J, cooper, h 403 N Water.
Young John, farmer, h 805 S Fayette.
Young W, lab, bds 809 S Hamilton.

Z

Zagelmeyer & Baurick, (L Z & L B) saloon, 306 S Water.
Zagelmeyer Edward, tobacconist, 408 S Water.
Zagelmeyer Louis, (Z & Baurick) h 306 S Water.
Ziegler John C, watch repairer, 110 N Water.
Zivi Joseph, (Hart & Z) 104 S Water.
Zschoerner G T, grocer, 102 N Water, h same.
Zuck John N, lab, h 506 N Hamilton.

BUSINESS DIRECTORY.

Agents—Insurance.

GAYLORD & HANCHETT, 205 Court.
Grout G K, 205 Jefferson.
Sutherland John H, 102 Court.

Artists, Ambrotype & Photograph.

ARMSTRONG W A, 101 S Water.

Bakers & Confectioners.

Kuhl Christopher, 211 N Water.
Rice Bernhard, 209 N Water.
Siebel Adolph, 111 N Water.
Waldbauer George, 316 S Water.

Banks and Bankers.

Burrows George L, 205 Court.
Miller, Braley & Co, 120 N Water.

Barbers.

Mabray Joseph, 304 S Water.
Walker T A, 107 S Water.

Blacksmiths.

Fish F L P, 508 S Water.
Hollister Major W, 506 S Water.
Murphy John, 112 Mackinaw.
Schneider John N, 512 S Water.

Boiler Makers.

Gregor James, 716 S Water.

Booksellers & Stationers.

Newell & St John, 107 S Water.
Raymond & Twitchell, 112 Court.

Boots & Shoes.

Andre P C & Co, 106 N Water.
Emendorfer F B, 123 N Water.
Felcher & Green, 311 S Water.
Ganspauer John, 215 N Water.
Krogmann Peter H, 114 S Water.
McRath William, 205 S Water.
Schick George, 314 S Hamilton.
Schultz George G, 103 Cass.
Winkler Geo W, 406 N Hamilton.

Butchers.

Kundinger & Frederick, 216 S Water.
Linderman & Churchill, 310 N Water.
Moye Bros, 111 Franklin.
Rice Nicholas, 1003 S Washington.
Rupp George, 219 N Water.
Wurtzel & Kampfert, 316 S Water.

Carriage Manufacturers.

Bostick Austin, 110 and 112 Van Buren.
Fish F L, 510 S Water.
Lawner Francis, 105 Mackinaw.
Riese & Leline, 110 Mackinaw.

Cigars & Tobacco Manufacturers & Dealers.

Frost N M, 205 S Water.
Scheurmann Emiel, 115 N Water.
Zagelmeyer Edward, 408 S Washington.

Clothing—Manufacturers & Dealers.

Bernhard Henry, 301 S Water.
Carpenter Wm A, 105 S Water.
Hart & Zivi, 104 S Water.
Marrow J & Co, 117 N Water.
Nathan N & Co, 115 S Water.

Crockery, China and Glass Ware.

MILES & SMITH, 216 N Water.

Dentists.

Baker E L, 314 S Water.
Beehler Reinhard, 121 N Water.
Hubbell L, 121 N Water.

Drugs and Medicines—Dealers in.

Epting Emil, 110 and 112 N Water.
Penoyer James N & Co, 324 N Water.
Smith & Moll, 101 S Water.

Dry Goods—Dealers in.

GEER BENJAMIN, 106 S Water.
Hudson J A, 201 N Water.
Leasia Francis A, 326 N Water.
Streeb George, 213 N Water.

Flour and Feed.

Gale J M, 213 S Water.

Foundries and Machine Shops.

HILDRETH & KINSEY, cor Water and Williams.

Furniture—Manufacturers & Dealers.

Andre & Adams, 117 S Water.
Andrews & Merrill, 602 S Water.
Fisher Andrew, 601 N Water.
Hilliard E G, 402 N Water.
HAWKINS J S, 218 and 220 N Water.

Groceries and Provisions—Dealers.

Adams G, 113 S Water.
Adams J F, 203 N Water.
Barck Edward, 214 S Water.
Bauer Peter, 104 N Water.
Bennett Joseph, 401 N Water.
Fish B P & W S, 309 S Water.
Grabner Adam, 108 Court.
Grover J C, 501 S Water.
Herrig Bernhard, 205 N Water.
Miller & Harrington, 121 N Water.
Moores Otto H G, 317 S Water.
Romike Herman, 301 Mackinaw.
Rose Frederick W, 109 Cass.
Sutton J & Co, 308 N. Water.
Trakat & Ippel, 105 Jefferson.
Vogt Jacob, 318 N Water.
Zschoerner ——, 102 N Water.

Gunsmiths.

Hawker William, 208 N Water.

Hair Braiders.

Wurts Mrs A, 206 N Water.

Hardware, Stoves and Tinware—Dealers in.

Cook & Loxley, 122 S Water.
JEROME D H & Co, 401 and 403 S Water.
Seyffardt & Achard, 312 S Water.

Harness, Saddles and Trunks.

OPFERGELT & WAGONER, 314 S Water.
RICHARDSON JOHN W, 323 N Water.

Hats and Caps.

Trommer John, 113 N Water.

Hotels.

American Hotel, —— S Hamilton.
Dunbar House, 404 and 406 S Water.
Exchange Hotel, 301 N Water.
TAYLOR HOUSE, cor Court and Hamilton.
Webster House, 401, N Washington.

Lawyers.

BROUSSEAU JULIUS, 108 S Water.
CLARK JAMES W, 205 N Water.
CROSS LESTER, 108 S Water.
EATON F L, 205 N Water.
GAYLORD & HANCHETT, 205 Court.
Miller & Cook, 205 Jefferson.
Moore John, 805 N Washington.
Sutherland John H, 102 Court.
SWEET WILLIAM H, 108 S Water.

Livery.

Jerome Timothy, 222 S Water.
McKINNON JOHN, 311 N Water.

Lumber—Inspectors, Manufacturers and Dealers.

Briggs E, 205 N Water.
Burnham Joseph T, 205 N Water.
Butman & Rust, 205 N Water.
Chapman N H & Co, 205 N Water.

Heather & Allison, 105 S Water.
Paine V A, 815 S Water.
Rust, Eaton & Co, 102 S Water.
Rust & Hay, 102 S Water.
WHITMAN GEORGE B, 205 N Water.
Whitman J C, 205 N Water.
Wright A W & Co, 702 N Water.

Milliners and Dressmakers.

Franke Mrs Lena, 119 N Water.
Lawrence & Dibble, 216 N Water.
O'Neal Mrs Ellen, 206 S Water.

Newspapers.

SAGINAW VALLEY HERALD, Bertram & Gardiner props, 108 N Water.

Physicians.

BENNETT D M, 102 S Water.
Brown P L, 112 Court.
Curtis Chester, 121 N Water.
Franke Louis, 119 N Water.
Jerome J H, 205 N Washington.
Kraus Theodore, 106 N Fayette.
Lee & Northrop, 205 N Water.
Plessner Michael, 205 N Water.
Smith I N, 501 N Hamilton.
White John B, 112 Court.

Planing Mills and Sash and Door Manuf.

Miller & Norton, 404 N Water.

Shingle Manufacturers.

Wallace Jose, 404 N Water.

Stave Manufacturers.

Gilmore, Phinney & Co, 511 N Water.

Watchmakers and Jewelers.

Ackley Frank C, 102 S Water.
Lacy A D, 120 S Water.
Raymond & Twitchell.
Smyth William E, 202 S Water.
Ziegler John C, 110 N Water.

FLORENCE DIRECTORY.

Akins John T, capeuter and joiner.
Babcock & Co, meat market.
Babcock Frederick, (B & Co.)
Barbier Francis, saloon.
Bearinger James, saw filer.
Beinig John, lab.
Bellman Michael, (Babcock & Co.)
Blackmond Francis (Lyons & B.)
Bliss, Sailor & Grant, lumber manfy.
Brown Elisha, saloon.
Buckley William, lab.
Charboneau Francis, boarding house.
Cochrane William J, cooper.
Croll Elias, lab.
Cronk George, (Devenport & C.)
Cusson John, lab.
Devenport & Co, groceries and provisions.
Devenport George, (D & Co.)
Dygart Norman, lab.
Fisher Christopher, lab.
Fisher John, lab.
Gilbert U S.
Gleeck Adam, lab.
Hamilton John, carpenter.
Hoerner John, lumber manuf.
Hubert Joseph, lab.
Ireton Mrs Susanah.
Kay Robert, lab.
Kelly James, lumber manuf.
Lemons William, sawyer.
Lewis T J, sash maker.
Liby Henry, millwright.
Long John, lab.
Lyons & Blackmond, boots and shoes.

Lyons Stephen M, (L & Sluckbier.)
Lyons & Sluckbier, saloon.
Lyons W A, (L & Blackmond.)
Lyons William, carpenter.
McCracken James, lab.
McGraft, Newcomb, sawyer.
Meads William, sawyer.
Mericle James, boarding house.
Merrill & Whittier, lumber manufy.
Murray Michael, lab.
Myers, Nichola, boarding house.
O'Hara John, lab.
Perkins Geo D, engineer.
Pine Michael, sawyer.
Read William M, engineer.
Reading D L, boarding house.
Rhodes, Oscar, engineer.
Rose Frank, lab.
Ross F F
Shaw J E (S & Williams.)
Shaw & Williams, lumber manufy.
Shellhaus George, cooper.
Smitz Michael, cooper.
Starkweather Edward, engineer.
Stokey Charles, cooper.
Sluckbier J, (Lyons & S.)
Taylor William, shingle manufy.
Townsend Jacob, cooper.
Townsend Peter, lab.
Tuhrame, James, (Babcock & Co.)
Waldron George, lab.
Wallace William, carpenter and joiner.
Whittier Joseph A, (Merrill & W.)
Wight Joseph, fireman.
Williams Charles M, (Shaw & W.)
Williams James, machinist.
Workman John, carpenter.
Wray George, teamster.
Wurts John, cooper.

HISTORY OF CARROLLTON.

The village bearing this name is situated on the west bank of the Saginaw River, a little more than one mile below the bridge at East Saginaw, on what has long been known as the Peter Riley Reservation, a fine tract with good high land on the river, with no bayou or marsh in the rear, and had for a long time been the camping ground of the Indian in his annual visit to the trading post of Saginaw.

The discovery of salt in the Valley caused this desirable location to be bought, and during '60 and '61 five companies were formed to operate at this point. In the summer of 1862 a village plat was made by Messrs. Curtis, Ward & Gillett, who were then owners of the larger part of the Reservation; since which time the Village has had a steady healthy growth, until in February 1866, when the eastern portion of the town of Saginaw, including the village of Carrollton, was detached from the Town of Saginaw and erected into a new town by the name of Carrollton. A Post office was established at this village April 1864, bearing the name of the village, and the present Post Master, C. E. Gillett, was appointed to the office.

A Presbyterian Society has been organized at this place and the Rev. M. Gelston is the Pastor.

The coming season it is the intention to build a Union School House of brick, in the center of appropriate grounds.

TOWNSHIP OFFICERS.—Supervisor, Charles E. Gillett; Town Clerk, Archibald Bierd; Treasurer, Martin Stoker; School Inspectors, Charles E. Gillett, Michael Ulrich; Commissioners of Highways, William Garrett, Alexander McBratnie, John Diendorffer; Justices of the Peace, Frederic S. C. Ross, Reuben Crowell, E. F. Gould; Constables, Nicholas Meyers, Patrick Madden, Adelbert H. Babcock, John Linder.

CARROLLTON DIRECTORY.

Abbs John, cooper, res Carrollton Ave.
Abbs Robert, stave and barrel manufy, Gillett & Co's Dock.
Allison J P, Agent Carrollton Mills Co.
Ames John, clerk, Chicago Salt Co.
Arndt August F, blacksmith and wagon maker.
Babcock A H, drover, bds H Babcock's.
Babcock Henry, boarding house, Washington.
Ballentine H A & Co, Chicago Salt Works.
Barnes Elisha, salt packer, bds E McGinnis'.
Best James, salt boiler.
Bierd Archibald, Township Clerk, h Carrollton Ave.
Birid William, salt works, bds A Birid's.
Birid Joseph, salt works, bds A Birid's.
Brennan Mrs Margaret, h Washington.
Brink Leander, Supt Orange Co Salt Co, h Carrollton Ave.
Brown Morris E, drover, bds H Babcock's.
Brown Peter, boatman, h Carrollton Ave.
Bun Jehu, foreman Orange Co Salt Co.
Bunton Chas, foreman Chicago Salt Co, h Washington.
Bunton Edward, lab, h Carrollton Ave.
Burdick D D, butcher, Carrollton Ave.
Cook William, lab.
Courtney Daniel, salt boiler, res Zilwaukee.
Crawfor James, carp, h cor Maple and Washington.
Crowell Reuben, phys, (Harrington & Co,) res Carrollton Ave.
Dailing Cyrus R, lab, h Carrollton Ave.
Dailing William, carp, bds C R Dailing's.
Delude Moses, cooper, h Main.
Delude Paul, cooper, bds M Delude.
Devanny Patrick, lab, h Washington.
Dewey John, mason, bds E McGinnis'.
Dolon Chas, lab, h Carrollton Ave.
Doyle Patrick, lab, h Washington.
Empire Barrel Co, C E Gillett Pres.
Empire Salt Co, Wm P Letchworth Pres, res Buffalo.
Fenno H C, foreman Webster Mill, h Water.
Flannigan Thomas J, Carrollton House, Maple.
Flynn Arthur, lab, bds Carrollton House.
Garrett Wm, cooper, h Maple.
Geary Thos, boatman, h Carrollton Ave.
Gilbert U S, Supt Chicago Salt and Lumber Co, h Main.
GILLETT CHAS E, real estate and ins agt, bds Dr Crowell's.
Gould Erastus F, saw and stave mill, h Main.
Gould Gardner D, bds E F Gould's.

Gould John, bds E F Gould.
Hardy George, carpenter, h Carrollton Ave.
Harrington F & Co, merchants, (F H & R Crowell,) cor Carrollton Ave and Maple.
Harrington Frank, (F H & Co,) bds Dr Crowell's.
Haskins Thos W, lab, h Washington.
Jerome, Hale & Campbell, lumber mills.
Judson Joseph, lab, Orange Co Works.
Kramer Peter, merchant, Carrollton Ave.
Lewis David, foreman Chicago Salt Co, h Carrollton Ave.
Lincoln Ira B, lab, h Main.
Lincoln Oscar S, lab, h Main.
McCaudand Thos, lab, h Carrollton Ave.
McGuinnis Edward, lab, h Carrollton Ave.
McKinney James, engineer, h Carrollton Ave.
McNicoll David, engineer, Saginaw Valley Salt Co.
Madden Patrick, restaurant, Carrollton Ave.
Mann Eugene D, engineer, h Carrollton Ave.
Martin Peter, lab, h Maple.
Moffatt Ishmael, lab, h Carlton Ave.
Montgomery Jas, cooper, h Carrollton Ave.
Murphy Lawrence, lab. bds E McGinnis'.
O'Grady Patrick, lab, Saginaw Valley Salt Co.
Palmer Joseph, lab, bds E McGinnis'.
Perry George, capt scow.
Perry Noah, foreman Carrollton Mill Salt Works.
Perry Stephen, engineer, h Washington.
Pinkham Nathan J, boarding house, Carrollton Mills Co.
Ried Alexander, Supt Empire Salt Co, h Water.
Reed Edward L, lab, bds Mrs O Reed.
Reed Geo W, foreman, h Carrollton Ave.
Reed Mrs O, h Maple.
Reed William M, salt boiler, bds Mrs O Reed's.
Saginaw Valley Salt Co, D Stewart Pres, res Detroit.
Scott Isaac, engineer, C Salt Co.
Scott Wm, farmer, h Nursery Farm.
Spay John, salt boiler, h Zilwaukee St.
Stewart Alexander, engineer, Chicago Salt Works.
Stewart William, engineer, Empire Salt Co, h Carrollton Ave.
Taggart Samuel, cooper, h Carrollton Ave.
Teufel Fritz, foreman cooper shop Orange Co Salt Co, h Washington.
Ure James, Supt Sag Valley Salt Co, h Carrollton Ave.
Webster S H, saw mill and salt works.
Welch Alonzo F, carp h Maple.
Willson George, engineer, bds Pinkhams.
Withey Charles, salt boiler, h Washington.

HISTORY OF EAST SAGINAW.

Coming here from Detroit, strangers find little to admire in the suburbs of the city, that surround the depot at the foot of Franklin street—they have been hurried over miles of well-tilled land, and great stretches of timber; past lakes and streams, and low hills; fields ornamented with farm products; great farm houses and little pioneer cottages; piles of lumber, shingles and staves;—past these they have been carried, and are glad to hear the shrill whistle of the locomotive as it dashes in at the station. Here we meet our stranger friends, as the citizens of East Saginaw are always glad to do, and show them about the City.

Let us while our companions are finding seats in the comfortable street cars, just glance at our surroundings. Close at hand are the usual unattractive out-buildings connected with the Rail Road station. Before us is a better class of houses rising higher as the distance increases towards the business center of the City. A few prominent structures rise above the rest; at our right the masts and cordage of vessels in the river are in full view; away at our left and partially behind us, the original forest trees stand in quiet dignity; before us, the clean dry walks lined with young shade trees invite our steps down Franklin street. We will decline the tempting promenade, for the Conductor's whistle calls us to the street car. The ready Jehu gives the signal to his waiting team and we sweep around a curve from Franklin street into the center of Washington avenue, and move on through the busy street. Lining our route and along the parallel avenues are many fine dwellings, fresh with paint and wearing a pleasant, home look. Of course, we will get out at Genesee street and stop, if you please, at the

BANCROFT, whose towering hight and imposing appearance cannot fail to attract the attention of every visitor to the Valley, or we will partake of the "good cheer" at the EVERETT, whose massive architecture to be admired needs only to be seen.—Having rested and otherwise recuperated nature for the occasion, let us set about learning something of this anomaly, a substantial city in almost a wilderness. We have seen in the oil regions of Pennsylvania cities springing up like mushrooms, and with little more permanance or vitality in them; we have seen great cities planted in the rich mining districts of our far-western territories; and we have seen speculators' cities of only paper existence; but this is indeed an anomaly, a substantial city containing over eight thousand inhabitants – a city built of the most enduring material, and in a rich and costly style of architecture, set down in the midst of a lumbering region where the undisturbed stumps of the original forest trees, and even some of the trees themselves ornament the suburbs and *sentinel* the corporate boundaries. Here are no signs of an ephemeral existence; these structures that we admire have not come up like Jonah's gourd to be overturned by the breath of an east wind—to be abandoned when the pioneer company finds a dry well; or to be forsaken when word comes that a richer lode has been discovered in a neighboring gulch! Nothing looks that way in these streets, and the eager enquiry as to what is the foundation of all this apparent prosperity, is answered by the assurance that Saginaw Lumber, Saginaw Salt, and Fish from the Saginaw waters have each a world-wide reputation and a correspondingly extensive sale.

We may get some idea of the extent of the city of East Saginaw by viewing it from the roof of one of the highest buildings, though we must bear in mind, that only a dozen years ago all the region within the scope of our vision was almost untrodden by the first pioneers of civilization. Prominent in the plain that stretches away on every side are the public school buildings of the city, erected and operating under a free school system. They are ornaments of which the citizens of East Saginaw are justly proud, and the Central structure is as fine an edifice for its use as can be found in the west. The spires of a half dozen churches point their worshiping congregations heavenward. Within the circle of our vision we can count forty-eight chimneys and smoke stacks indicating as many manufactories of lumber, salt, shingles, staves, &c. The Saginaw river, stirred by the incessant turmoil of the busy tugs, flows steadily on in its northerly course. Great vessels and small ones lie at their docks discharging or receiving freights. The frequent screams of the tug whistles drown the busy clangor of the nearest mills, and silence the rumbling of the various street cars. The great *draw* in the city bridge swings at the summons of an approaching tug that pulls after it a heavily laden lake vessel. The scene on the river docks and in the streets is metropolitan. Looking away to the horizon the sky seems to settle down to the fringe of forest trees that environs the landscape. Within the circle on the banks of the river, are the thrifty groups of SALINA and SAGINAW CITY, and these are joined by street Rail Roads as well as by river communication with this city. Three fine bridges span the broad river within our view and serve to accomodate the continual travel from shore to shore. In the busy streets almost any cosmopolitan sojourner can find a fellow citizen. Here are representatives from the four quarters of the globe, and from the "islands of the sea;" yet the everlasting omnipresent Yankee is in the ascendancy, and will ever be so. The aboriginal tenants come in from their camps, not many miles distant, to look upon the growing power of their pale-faced successors, and tread with noiseless steps the thoroughfares which have grown up from their former hunting trails. The squaw carries her grim papoose along where it can look on the wooden image of its paternal progenitor that holds out a bunch of Havanas, in front of some tobacco store. But these aborigines are destined to stop but a little longer in the vicinity. The encroachments of lumbermen, salt makers, and settlers must soon drive them from their scanty foot-hold, to give room for the march of improvement which is making the valley teem with life and genuine prosperity. Having taken as it were a "birds' eye glance" at the city, let us go back to its early history.

The City of East Saginaw lies on the east bank of the Saginaw River, about sixteen miles from its mouth. The original name was Tic-wa-ba-ka-ning meaning the "Butternut Place." The substantial city of to-day with its eight thousand inhabitants, busily engaged in the transaction of a great variety of business, has little resemblance to the wild lot that was plotted in 1850 and then known as the "Hoyt Plot." This Plot comprised all that portion of the present city north of Hoyt street. At that date (1850) the only buildings were a small cottage located about two blocks south of where the Bancroft House now stands, which served the double purpose of church and school house; a board shanty on the present site of the Bancroft house; and a log house standing near the Bridge in the middle of what now is Genesee street, and was occupied by Leon Sney, an Indian interpreter and trader. In the fall of the same year a frame dwelling house was erected by C. W. Grant on Water street, north of Genesee, which he still occupies as a residence.

George Allison was one of the earliest settlers, having come here in 1850, and in June of the same year C. W. Grant, W. F. Glasby, Lester Wheeler and Adoniram Dann arrived. The latter gentleman opened the first boarding house, in the building now known as the "Valley City Hotel" on Water street, erected by W. F. Glasby; who was a carpenter. In 1850 Alfred M. Hoyt and C. W. Grant erected a saw mill, known as the "Blue mill," (from the color of the paint used), for the purpose of sawing plank to be used in the construction of a plank road between East Saginaw and Flint. Mr. Hoyt's first effort in establishing himself here, was to open the most practicable routes of travel, to invite emigration to his projected city; and the result has proved the wisdom of his course, as it has also exceeded his most sanguine expectations. The capacity of the "Blue Mill" was twenty-five hundred thousand feet per annum.

Some time in 1850 there also arrived in the village a blacksmith, named Fred. A. Koehler, and a shoemaker named Seth Willey, who found a demand for their productions and helped to increase the general prosperity of the place. The locality now began to have a name abroad and the accessions to the population were from this date rapid. The village was in the town of Buena Vista and the first election was held at the house of Curtis Emerson.

At this election C. Emerson was made Supervisor and C. W. Grant, Town Clerk; they having each received *Five Votes* being the whole number cast. In 1851 a lawyer arrived by the cognomen of Hunt who "stuck out his shingle" and commenced the practice of law. The same year a Baptist preacher held regular service in the little cottage before-mentioned, where an Episcopal clergyman from Saginaw City had occasionally officiated the year previous. A school was also established the same year on what is now called Washington street, near the corner of Genesee, on the site of the Bancroft. The structure was built of rough boards—the enterprise of C. W. Grant—and the school was taught by Miss Carrie Ingersoll. There was mail communication from Flint to Saginaw City twice a week, the mail being carried on horseback, and from Saginaw City here in a basket, carried by a footman. The first Post Office was established in a wooden building opposite the Bancroft House where Henry Marks' store now stands; and Alfred M. Hoyt was the first Post Master. The mail was carried, as before stated, from Saginaw City by Mr. M. B. Hess; and sometimes he could carry it all in his coat pocket; very frequently the mail matter would not exceed four letters a week. Mr. Hoyt was succeeded in the Post Office by Morgan L. Gage, and he, again, in time, by Moses B. Hess.

J. T. Caulkins was the first to engage in the Grocery business. He purchased a lot near the corner of Washington and Genesee streets for the sum of fifty dollars, and erected a building thereon suitable for a grocery store, in which he carried on his business. He did not, however, remain long. In 1851 he sold his building and lot to M. B. Hess for $600. Some idea of the advance in the value of real estate may be obtained by the assurance that this lot, first purchased by Mr. Caulkins for $50 would to-day find ready sale for $12,000, exclusive of buildings. The first store was kept by Alfred M. Hoyt and James Little, son of Hon. Norman Little. Their building was a frame structure, known as the "Blue Store," located on the lot now occupied by Livingston & Co., corner of Genesee and Water streets.—Messrs. Hoyt & Little kept a general stock of Dry Goods, Groceries, Crockery, Boots and Shoes, and the nameless et ceteras that go to make up the assortment in a country store. They found it necessary in their business to employ an interpreter to facilitate their traffic with the Indians. The "Blue Store" was afterwards enlarged and re-modeled in 1851, by N. Blackmar, and called the Irving House. Menzo C. Stevens became the landlord and kept a good hotel as his patrons were free to testify.—The Irving house was sometime afterwards destroyed by fire.

In the fall of 1851 a store was opened by W. L. P. Little & Co. in a two story wooden building on the river bank, where Bliss, Janes & Co. now do business. Their sales the first year amounted to ninety thousand dollars, and afterwards increased to two hundred and fifty thousand dollars. This store furnished goods for a circuit of country one hundred miles in extent. The store was afterwards destroyed by fire. A ferry was established in 1851 by E. N. Davenport, consisting of a scow or flat boat propelled across the river by a rope and poles. The same year a public school building was erected on the corner of Hoyt and Jefferson streets, at a cost of $15,000. The Union school system was adopted; and in this the proprietors of the town exhibited their usual good judgment, making the expense of education a charge upon the property of the people at large. Several auxiliary schools were organized and suitable buildings erected as the growth of the city called for them. In 1852, a flouring mill was erected on the present site of the Mayflower mills at a cost of $30,000, by Jesse Hoyt. The following year the Galaher mill (saw mill) was erected; and the next year the

Holland mill, also a lumber mill, was built by T. Whitney.— Messrs. Durfey & Atwater erected a mill the same year. The old Blue mill having been burned down, Messrs. Davison and Whitney constructed one on its site sometime in 1854, and in the succeeding year another mill was built by Wm. F. Glasby. The City (flouring) mills on Genesee street were erected in 1860. The present proprietor is J. S. Stevens.

The first church edifice was erected on Washington street, in 1854, by the Methodist Episcopal Society. The Lutheran Church was built the same year. The German Methodist Society next erected a church on Warren street, in 1855. The same year the Congregational Society built their church on Washington street. The Catholic church was erected in 1864. The Protestant Episcopal, in 1865.

Up to 1864 the river had been crossed by means of a clumsy ferry, but during this year a stock company was organized by the citizens of East Saginaw, and a bridge built from the foot of Genesee street, at a cost of $20,000. The plan is according to Brown's patent and it is a fine looking as well as substantial structure. Its length is a little more than 700 feet and it is furnished with the requisite *draw* to accommodate the larger class of vessels navigating the river. About one mile further up the river, at the foot of Bristol street. a second bridge was built in the following year by the citizens of Saginaw.

Alfred M. Hoyt erected the first dock and ware-house. The first boat was a stern wheel steamer named the Buena Vista, and was commanded by Capt. Addison Mowry. The steamers "Magnet" and "Reindeer' were afterwards built by Jesse Hoyt. The first sail vessel was built by the same gentleman and called the "Jesse Hoyt."

The first Banking house was established by Col. W. L. P. Little, in 1855, in a small wooden building on the site of what is now the Exchange Block on Genesee street. Another Banking house was opened in 1863, by Fay, Bliss & Co., under the title of the "Valley Bank." The First National Bank was organized in 1865 with a capital of $100,000 ; J. T. Judd, President, and C. K. Robinson Cashier. Col. W. L. P. Little converted his establishment into a National Bank January 1st, 1866, with a capital of $200,000 under the name of the "Merchants' National Bank." The Banking House of C. K. Robinson & Co., was established in January, 1866. The fact that so large a banking capital is required speaks well for the business transactions of the city.

The U. S. Land office was removed from Flint to this city in 1857 through the influence of Moses B. Hess who became the first Register, and Wm. L. P. Little the first Receiver. By an Act of the Legislature, Feb. 13th, 1855, East Saginaw became an incorporated village. The first election under the village charter occurred in April, 1855, at which Mr. Norman Little was chosen President, and Mr. Chas. B. Mott, Recorder.

The need of a better class of hotels was early felt, and in 1860 the Bancroft House, one of the most princely establishments in the State, was built at a cost of $90,000. It was constructed on a plan so much in advance of its surroundings that the project seemed unwarranted and extravagant, but the growth and prosperity of the young city was so rapid that the vast structure had soon to be enlarged, and this enlargement had to be repeated, so that at this date it is a mammoth structure, and justly entitled to the high reputation it bears. The first proprietor was Henry Hobbs, who succeeded in establishing the reputation of keeping the best hotel in Michigan. Mr. Henry Hobbs was succeeded by G. W. Wesley, the present proprietor, who fully sustains the reputation gained by his predecessor. The further growth of the city soon demanded another large hotel and in 1863 the "Everett House" was erected at a cost of $41,000. This building, though vast in its proportions, soon had to be enlarged to accommodate the increased wants of the traveling community, and stands a splendid monument to the enterprise of its projector and builder, Mr. Crouse, of Hartland, Mich. The present proprietors of the "Everett" are Smith & Crouse, who have gained an enviable reputation among the traveling public as *caterers* to their wants. In 1859 the village of East Saginaw having become of sufficient age and growth, was allowed by an act of the Legislature to throw off her village garments and assume the more dignified and commanding *costume* of a city. The first election occurred under the new city charter, in the spring of 1859, at which Col. Wm. L. P. Little was honored with being chosen the first Mayor. His administration was a very successful one, and marked with rapid strides of City improvement. The Mayor of the City at this writing, is Mr. Dwight G. Holland, who was elected but a few days since.

The largest Livery establishment in the State is located on the corner of Washington and Johnson streets in this City, whose business manager is A. W. Gates, Esq.; it is owned by Messrs. Burrill, Morris and Gates, doing business under the name of A. W. Gates & Co. Mr. Burriil lives in Detroit and Mr. Morris in Pontiac. Their stable is a large brick structure and an ornament to the city. The company are proprietors of all the various stage lines from the city. Mr. Gates the manager is an energetic business man and much thought of for his good qualities of head and heart.

Morgan L. Gage was the first to enter into the business of harness making in this city. The first death occurred in 1852; caused by drowning. A German, whose name we are unable to give, fell from his boat while crossing the river and sunk immediately. His body was not recovered until several days after, when it was found at a point several rods above the place where he fell in, which singular circumstance would indicate an undercurrent in the river. The first *birth* occurred in 1850, which made Mr. Seymour Ensign the happy father of a male child.

Up to December, 1862, the city had no railroad communication with the outside world, and the absolute need of greater facilities for the winter transportation of merchandize, lumber &c., as well as the desire of the citizens for a rapid and comfortable means of tarvel led to the construction of the Flint and Perre Marquette Rail Road; the eastern branch of which, from Flint to East Saginaw, was completed at the date above mentioned. The completion of this branch of the road gave the citizens of East Saginaw direct communication with the various railroad lines centering at Detroit. H. C. Potter was its first Superintendent, and has ever since conducted the affairs of the road with ability and to the entire satisfaction of its patrons. The following statement will convey a more correct idea of the road and its management.

Flint and Pere Marquette Railway.

The proposed route would extend westward from Flint, Genesee county, to Pere Marquette, in Mason county, on Lake Michigan. Distance 172½ miles.

Congress passed an act, June 3, 1856, granting every alternate section of land, designated by odd numbers, then belonging to the United States, for six miles in width, on each side of the located line. The deficiency, if any, was to be made up from the odd numbered sections outside of the six miles, and within fifteen miles of the line.

The entire grant amounts to 662,400 acres. There has been already certified, by the Secretary of the Interior, under this grant, and as pertaining to it, 543,829 acres of land. Of this amount the Company have acquired title to 153,600 acres. The construction of seven miles more will give the title to 76,800 acres additional, and the construction of each and every twenty miles thereafter, will give title to the like additional number of acres, until the whole grant is absorbed.

The last Congress, (1864,) passed a joint resolution, extending the time for the completion of the road, five years from the expiration of the first period named, which will give to June, 1871.

STATEMENT OF EARNINGS.

Year.	No. of Passengers.	Passenger Receipts.	Freight Receipts.	Total Earnings.
1862	28,798	$19,254 15	$12,510 22	$31,764 37
1863	68,753	53,033 35	43,954 69	96,988 04
1864	93,733	71,011 09	43,342 68	114,353 77
1865	108,958	93,309 62	70,524 22	163,833 84

TOTAL SHIPMENTS FROM ALL STATIONS ON F. & P. M. RAILWAY, 1865.

STATIONS.	Lumber Ft.	No. of Staves.	No. of Shingles.	Prod'ts of Animals.	Bbls of Flour.	Agr'ral Prod'ts.	Md'se, lbs	Bbls. Salt.
E. Saginaw,	243,500	7,200	3,997	61,652	263	152,204	3,549,337	22,267
Bridgeport,	1,292,000	118,800	1,644	36	1	950	35,702	3,167
Pine Run,	6,867,000	166,500	8,588	605	72	200	194,611	1
Mt. Morris.	2,880,500	449,000	5,349	66,857	149	364,033	44,710	
Flint.	674,200	18,000		1,181,167	15,313	9,012,582	7,242,244	23
	11,957,200	759,500	19,578,000	1,310,317	15,798	9,524,969	11,066,604	25,458

Memoirs.

Alfred M. Hoyt. In writing the History of East Saginaw one great link in the chain would be wanting were we to neglect a special mention of Mr. Alfred M. Hoyt. To him and Norman Little (of whom we have spoken elsewhere) the city is under a weighty obligation for its present success. His sojourn among us was of short duration, he having staid only four years, returning again to New York ; but in that short space of time by his indomitable perseverance, caused a city to spring up out of the wilderness. He is a son of James M. Hoyt and a brother of Jesse Hoyt. At the time of his fathers' purchase of property in Saginaw, in 1850, he came here to manage the same, and in connection with Norman Little had the superintendence of its growth and prosperity for four years. He erected many fine buildings, opened roads, and did many other things for the material advancement of the place. He represented Saginaw County in the State Legislature in the year 1852, and was the first Postmaster appointed in East Saginaw. In 1854 becoming tired of the arduous duties of a pioneer, he relinquished his entire interest in the "embryo city" to his brother Jesse, which consisted of the whole of the original City as first laid out—called the "Hoyt Plot"—for a sum of money which now would be insufficient to purchase a single block of ground therein.—He was a high minded, whole souled gentleman, liberal to a fault. He is now a successful commission merchant in the City of New York and is one of the firm of Jesse Hoyt & Co. Long may he live to enjoy the richest blessings of Providence.

Col. W. L. P. LITTLE was one of the earliest settlers in this City, and has occupied a prominent position since his arrival.—He is closely identified with the rapid growth of the City, having in conjunction with Jesse Hoyt, Esq., built several very fine brick structures, and contributed in various ways to its general prosperity.

He was born in Avon, New York, in 1814, and first visited this Valley in 1834, on business for his father who owned a tract of timber land in the vicinity of Saginaw City. He came to view the land and pay taxes thereon. His stay although comparatively a short one, was sufficient for him to form a very favorable impression, in regard to the nature and future prospects of the country, for in 1836 we find him permanently located in Saginaw City, in the employment of the "Saginaw City Co." This Company made the first improvements in that City, in the erection of substantial buildings, &c. The Webster House was built by them, which at that early day, was considered a very superior structure, both in architectural design and finish, and the ample spaciousness of its numerous apartments. Mr. Little remained in their employment until 1840, when he commenced the mercantile business, in that city. His uniform gentlemanly bearing and close application to business secured him a large and lucrative trade, which he continued until 1851. He then removed to East Saginaw and entered into partnership with Jesse Hoyt in a general mercantile business. Their store was consumed by fire on the 5th of July 1854, when they "wound up" their mercantile business and commenced a banking institution under the name of Wm. L. P. Little & Co. This they continued until Jan. 1st 1866, when the Merchants' National Bank of East Saginaw was established, with Wm. L. P. Little as President. Mr. Little had the honor of being chosen first Mayor of the City of East Saginaw, which office he filled with credit to himself and to the entire satisfaction of his constituents. He is a man of strong physical endurance, genial and affable in his manners, with a kind and generous disposition.

WM. F. GLASBY, an early settler in East Saginaw, is one of her most prominent and influential citizens. He was formerly from Livingston County, New York, and first made his appearance in East Saginaw in 1850. He was the first master mechanic that settled here. He was a shrewd, active intelligent man, and made several investments in real estate at an early day, that have since made him wealthy. He was very influential in causing the erection of the three Bridges that span the Saginaw at this point, and is one of the heaviest stock holders in them. He held the office of Mayor during the year 1863. Mr. Glasby is a man of sterling worth and integrity, and much esteemed by his fellow-citizens.

In writing the memoir of CURTIS EMERSON, Esq., a seeming contradiction appears as compared with statements given in our Local History of East Saginaw regarding the first settlers.—This is easily reconciled from the fact that the village as well as the City, as originally laid out, comprised only that part known as "Hoyt's Plot," and in writing the early history we have confined ourselves to those limits.

"Emerson's addition" on which Mr. Emerson first located, was afterwards incorporated in the City boundaries.

Curtis Emerson was born in Norwich, Vermont, 4th February 1810, and came to Michigan in 1836. In 1846 he located himself in Saginaw City, and commenced the lumber business.—The following year he moved to the East side of the River and permanently located himself in a building which was already erected, at the foot of what now is known as Bristol street.—There were only two houses, one boarding house, a saw mill, one barn and a black smith shop on the east side of the river at this point, at that time, and they were all deserted; not a living being disturbed the solitude. Mr. Emerson commenced getting out logs and sawing them into boards.. The following year he converted the blacksmith shop into a store, which he connected with his lumbering business. This store was situated on the bank of the river, also at the foot of Bristol street. The few residents here, at that time, were a hardy and jovial little band, who were perfectly happy in each other's company at their evening gatherings. Mr. Emerson's house was the place of resort, and many a convivial meeting was held in the "*Halls of the Montezumas.*" This time-honored structure was burned during the last winter, and all that remains of its classical halls is a heap of charred ruins. Mr. Emerson finding a ferry necessary to his own business, as well as to accommodate the public, for this purpose built a steam boat 74 feet in length, and named her the "Great Eastern." This ferry was continued until 1864, when the bridge was built, rendering it useless. Mr. Emerson is a kind hearted, public-spirited man, strictly honorable in all his dealings, and although at times a little too fond of a social glass, he may be termed a noble and true-hearted gentleman.

Charles W. Grant was also one of the earliest pioneers, and perhaps the first actual settler in East Saginaw. He was born in Chenango County, New York, in 1818. In 1849 he came to what is now East Saginaw. He was elected to the office of Sheriff of Saginaw County in 1855. The year previous he had been appointed Deputy U. S. Marshal, which office he held for five years. In 1857 he was re-elected Sheriff and served till 1859. Mr. Grant has been largely engaged in the lumber business since his first residence in the Valley, and is one of the leading men of the City.

Mr. Moses B. Hess, whose name finds frequent mention in these annals, is so intimately connected with the early history of the city, that we cannot forbear making this further mention of him. He was born in Verona, Oneida County, New York in 1825, and emigrated to Livingston County, Michigan, in 1837.

After spending several years in Brighton and in Lansing, (in the latter place he held the office of Post Master and also State Librarian for eight years,) he removed, in December, 1850, to East Saginaw, and engaged with A. M. Hoyt & Co. as book keeper and cashier. He afterwards engaged in the Grocery business with O. P. Burt and his brother G. G. Hess, in a building on Water street, on the site lately occupied by the Saginaw Valley Bank. Mr. Hess continued in this business only one year, and then opened a drug store on Genesee street, where J. T. Caulkins first commenced the Grocery business, continued in the Drug business eight years. When Mr. Hess first engaged in business here, what is now covered with buildings was an almost undisturbed forest, and he has frequently stood in his store door and shot squirrels, as they leaped from limb to limb on the original forest trees. But few families then resided here, and these formed a neighborhood of social beings who were happy in a frequent interchange of good feeling.—Mr. Hess filled many offices of public trust, national, state and municipal, and only retired from public life in 1861. He has since been engaged in the care of his large property accumulated by careful industry, energy, and the rapid rise in the value of real estate. Mr. Hess is a public spirited man, and has done much for the city in the erection of public buildings and in other material contributions to its general prosperity.—He has frequently exhibited a remarkable energy in overcoming the adverse fortunes that have assailed him. In disposition Mr. Hess is genial and affable, and his hand is ever open to those who are less fortunate in the possession of worldly goods than himself. Mr. G. G. Hess, brother of Moses B. Hess, died in 1861. He was intimately associated with his brother in all the early history of the city, as well as in business enterprises, and was highly esteemed in life for integrity of character; and in his death was deeply lamented.

Another of the early settlers was Alexander English.—He came here from Lansing, April 8th, 1851. His entire worldly possessions consisted of a team and wagon and one extra horse. He worked a farm, the first year after his arrival, for Alfred M. Hoyt. In 1853 he purchased the lime kiln on the river bank just below the Mayflower mills, on Water street, and continued the manufacture of lime until the present year. He quite recently sold the lime kiln property to Messrs. Fish and Holland for $21,000. In 1865 Mr. English purchased the steamer "L. G. Mason," of which he is still the owner, a passengerer boat, that plies between this city and Bay City. Mr. English is a prudent business man and has arisen from comparative poverty to opulence, through his own industry and perseverance.

There are four iron foundries in the city, and these are among the most prosperous branches of business carried on. Warner & Eastman conduct one of these; G. W. Merrill one; Wicks Brothers another, and a new one in course of completion will soon be in operation.

There are two newspaper offices, one issuing a weekly, the other a daily and a weekly paper. They are both well edited and creditable sheets, named respectively: "The East Saginaw Courier," and "Saginaw Enterprise."

SKETCHES OF THE PRESS.

Messrs. Mason & Williamson, from Conneautville, Pa., started the "Saginaw Enterprise," a weekly newspaper, in the Spring of 1853. The paper was printed on a sheet 22x32 inches. The next year Mason sold out to Williamson, and returned to Pennsylvania. Williamson retained the office one year, during a portion of which time he suspended the publication of the Enterprise. Mr. Perry Joslin came to East Saginaw in August, 1856, and in October of the same year purchased the office of Mr. Williamson for $1,000. Mr. Joslin conducted the paper alone until January 1864, when he sold a half interest in it to Mr. Francis Parth for $1,400. In May, 1861, while Mr. Joslin carried on the business, he was burned out and suffered considerable loss, as well by the fire as in the removal of the office fixtures, but his paper continued to appear regularly, though published for a few weeks on a half sheet. Messrs. Joslin & Parth conducted the office until July 1865, when Col. C. V. DeLand became a partner and the value of the office was increased from $8,000 to $12,000. In September of the same year they began the issue of a Daily paper; and the Weekly was enlarged to a 26x39 inch sheet. January 1st 1866 the office was made a stock concern under the State laws, with a capital of $25,000. and Mr. Joslin continued in charge of the paper, at this time the Daily issue was enlarged to the same dimensions as the Weekly. The office is at present supplied with an Ericson Hot Air Engine, a Hoe drum cylinder press, machine and hand presses and a good supply of Job type, both English and German, and issues a well printed sheet, daily and weekly The office is located on the corner of Water and Tuscola streets, in a two story brick building constructed for its present use.

In July, 1859, the *Courier* was established by Geo. F. Lewis, running one hand press, with a moderate stock of job, in addition to newspaper material. In September, 1861, job material and press sold to Mr. Joslin, of the *Enterprise*, upon a "give and take" offer—both proprietors being convinced that there was not enough job printing in the city then for two establishments —and only the newspaper ran for the year following.

In September, 1863, the job printing materials of the *Courier* were replenished, in August, 1863, the paper was enlarged and Major E. W. Lyon became a partner with Mr. Lewis in the establishment, which at this date runs two machine and three hand presses, and in addition to its newspaper material, has a complete and elegant assortment of job type, cuts, borders and apparatus.

The *Courier* establishment has been set up—we mean the material—six times since its first appearance, in six different buildings, and is now located in the 2d story of Grant Block, Washington street, occupying a room 22x80 feet in extent; eligibly situated and judiciously arranged for the management of its extensive business.

c†

We have sketched the local history of East Saginaw, and given an idea of its rapid transition from an untraversed wilderness to a populous city. The future of East Saginaw, is even brighter, if we may judge the future by the past, than its age would lead us to suppose. The position of the city as an inland port, yet so located as not only to command inland trade, but also commercial intercourse by water with the rest of the State, and with all the important Lake ports, makes it a city of whose future it is difficult to conceive. The immense lumbering interests of the surrounding country, that find here their central depot; the exhaustless salines that underlie the whole valley; the extensive fisheries that just begin to engage the attention of the people; these are among the profitable sources of wealth that tend to make of East Saginaw a populous town. Her ample river, into which the largest class of Lake vessels may enter, gives to the city a very desirable mode of access to the outside world. Vessels may load at her wharve, and discharge their cargoes at the docks in Liverpool or Havre, and *Vice Versa.*— The only limit to the course of commerce in this direction is the capacity of the Welland Canal. Any vessel which can pass the Welland locks, can load and unload alternately at East Saginaw and at foreign ports. The rapidly increasing demand for the various indigenous products of the locality, must make for the Valley a widely known fame, and the future of East Saginaw can hardly be less grand and enduring than that of the most favored city on our inland waters. Who shall paint the young giant that grows from a wilderness to a great city in a dozen years? Who shall sketch it at his easel when another decade sweeps by? We may look for a development of vitality here that shall outstrip the most sanguine imaginings of its own sanguine people within the next half-score of years.

Churches and Societies.

ST. PAUL'S CHURCH.

St. Paul's Church, East Saginaw, (Protestant Episcopal), was organized under the ministry of Rev. Z. Spaulding, February 2d, 1864, with not more than two or three communicants.—The succeeding Clergymen were Rev. Edward Mayer, 1858–9, Rev. G. B. Engle, 1859–60, Rev. Henry Banwell, 1860–61, Rev. D. E. Brown, 1861-64, Rev. Wm. Paret, present Rector.

The growth of the Church may be seen from the number of communicants reported at different times. In 1857, there were five, in 1859, eight, and also in 1860 eight; in 1862 twenty-five, 1864, fifty, and in 1865 one hundred.

The Sunday school now numbers 22 Teachers and 160 Scholars; having a library of 320 volumes.

The Church building, on the north-east corner of Lapeer, and Warren streets—not yet quite finished—was begun in October, 1864. It is of wood, in Gothic style; 40 feet by 103, with deep Apsidal Chancel; cost $17,000, including furnaces and furniture; seating about 400 persons.

The lot on which the Church stands was a gift from Mr. Hoyt.

CONGREGATIONAL CHURCH.

In the Spring of 1857, Rev. W. C. Smith, then of Lapeer, was induced to visit East Saginaw with a view to the formation of a new Church. The movement met with so favorable a response that the services of Mr. Smith were secured for a year, begining the first Sabbath in May.

Buena Vista Hall, then just opened, was used as the place of worship, being furnished for this purpose, free of charge, by the owner, Mr. Jesse Hoyt, of New York.

The Congregation commenced and continued to be large. On the first Sabbath in June, a Sunday school was organized by the election of Chester B. Jones. Superintendent. In a short time the school numbered 154 scholars and teachers, with a well-selected library of about 600 volumes.

On Wednesday, the 8th day of September, 1857, the first Congregational Society was organized by the adoption of articles of association and the election of Trustees.

The preliminary steps towards the organization of a Church were taken at several meetings convened for the purpose; first of which was held Sept. 18, at which it was first decided by a vote of 18 to 4, that the Congregational form of Church Government should be adopted, after which articles of faith, a *covenant*, and sundry regulations were agreed upon.

On the 7th of October, an Ecclesiastical council convened by letters missive, assembled in Buena Vista Hall, by which the preliminary proceedings were approved, and the Church publicly recognized. Twenty-two persons united in the organization by letter, and four on profession of their faith. Since then 124 persons have been received to membership, of whom 40 were by profession; 42 have been removed by death or dismission to other Churches, leaving a present membership of 126.

The Sunday school has largely increased, having a present enrollment of 325 and an average attendance of 250; with a library of 500 volumes.

On the first Sabbath in February, 1861, the Congregation removed from the Hall into the new Church edifice, corner of Washington and German streets, which had been built, including lot, at an expense of about $3,500, which is still in use.

A movement is now on foot to build a new House of Worship, to cost $35,000, on lots purchased by the Society on the corner of Jefferson and Hayden streets.

The pastoral office becoming vacant on the resignation of the Rev. W. C. Smith, it was filled by a call to Rev. J. G. W. Cowles of Mansfield, Ohio, who entered upon his ministry with the Church, on the second Sabbath in May, 1865, and was installed pastor, by an Ecclesiastical Council, Sept. 6th 1865.

METHODIST EPISCOPAL CHURCH.

The Methodist Episcopal Church of East Saginaw was organized in 1852, with six members. Rev A. C. Shaw was its first pastor; he remained here two years. Rev. G. S. Clements, jr., succeeded him, and remained two years. He was succeeded by Rev. G. N. Belknap, one year; Rev. Curtis Mosher, two years; Rev. H. N. Brown, two years; Rev. H. O. Parker, two years; Rev. G. W. Warren, one year; Rev. R. R. Richards, one year. Rev. B. S. Taylor is pastor, at this date.

The present membership of the Church is one hundred and thirty-one (131). The church building was erected in 1852, and is located on the corner of German and Washington streets. The property is valued at ten thousand dollars. The Society has recently sold this building, and are preparing to erect a new Church on Jefferson street, at a cost of $40,000, the structure to be of brick, in Gothic style. The number of Sabbath school scholars connected with this church is 206; volumes in library 500.

FIRST BAPTIST CHURCH OF EAST SAGINAW.

This Church was organized with a constituent membership of 15, May 13, 1858. Recognized by a council of sister Churches, August 14, 1858. The Church was supplied about six months by Rev. Samuel Cornelius, now at Ann Arbor. Rev. J. S. Goodman, settled with the Church in November, 1859, and continued as Pastor until Nov. 1863. In the same month letters mission were granted to about twenty Members, living in Saginaw City, for the purpose of organizing a Church in that place.

In October, 1864, the present Pastor, Rev. A. L. Morehouse, settled with the Church.

The present membership is 84.

The Sabbath school numbers 150; two Bible classes; fifteen Teachers. A Sabbath school library of about 300 vols.

A central and desirable site for a new edifice has been secured on the corner of Jefferson and German streets.

MASONIC.

There is one lodge in East Saginaw. It was the first one formed in the Valley and is called "Saginaw Lodge No. 77,"—A Dispensation was granted by the Grand Lodge of Michigan to Moses B. Hess as W. M., David Hughes as S. W. and Jas. A. Large as J. W., with S. C. Munson, S. C. Beach, Absalom F. Hayden and David F. Hess as Charter Members, to open a lodge at East Saginaw, and the first meeting was held at the present Masonic Hall on 23d of June 1855. No work was done until the 30th and 31st of July 1855, when by the assistance of R. W. Bela Cogshall, the then G. V. and Lecturer, the E. A. degree was conferred on Hon. Norman Little, Wm. L. P. Little, Wm. L. Webber and Chas. B. Mott in the order here named. A Charter was granted by the Grand Lodge at its annual session in Jan. 1856, and on the 27th of Feb. 1856 an election for officers under the charter was held, by which Jos. A. Large was chosen as W. M., W. L. Webber as S. W. and Chas W. Grant as J. W., and on the same day R. W. Horace S. Roberts, Deputy Grand Master, assisted by R. W. John B. Hamilton J. G. W. and others dedicated and constituted the Lodge and all its officers.

Since that time the Lodge has been presided over by the following officers for the years ending Dec. 27th, 1857 to 1864:

1857,	W. L. Webber, W. M.,	S. W. Yawkey, S. W.,	George J. Dorr, J. W.
1858	" " " " "	C. M. Curtis, " "	J. S. Estabrook " "
1859	W. J. Bartow " "	J. J. Wheeler " "	C. B. Jones " "
1860	W. L. Webber " "	Jas. F. Brown " "	A. S. Gaylord " "
1861	W. J. Bartow " "	A. S. Gaylord " "	C. B. Mott " "
1862	" " " " "	J. W. Toms " "	J. S. Estabrook " "
1863	" " " " "	" " " " "	W. L. Webber " "
1864	" " " " "	Mark Hodgson " "	Geo. C. Sanborn " "

The three last named have since been twice re-elected and still hold the same offices.

Since the formation of the Lodge there have been initiated 97 persons. The degree of Master Mason has been conferred upon 88. Died 10; admitted from other Lodges 40. The present number of Members is 76. Most of those who have been dismissed left for the purpose of aiding in the formation of new lodges, of which there have been formed, one at Bay City, one at Saginaw City, one at Salina and one at Vassar.

There is much interest now manifested in the prosperity of the Lodge, and its condition is as prosperous as can be desired. Their Hall is 32x50 feet, is lighted with gas and comfortably furnished. The Regular Communications are held on the Tuesday on or next preceding each full moon.

Saginaw Valley Chapter, No. 31, Royal Arch Masons, was chartered Jan. 12, 1864. The first officers named in the charter were W. L. Webber, H. P., Chas. B. Mott, K. and S. W. Yawkey, S.

The following is a list of names of charter members:

W. L. Webber, W. J. Bartow, E. W. Lyon, Chas. B. Mott, L. S. Lenheim, Ezra Rust, George W. Merrill, Judson C. Lowell, Chas. E. Gillett, Geo. F. Lewis, John J. Wheeler, Robert H. Weideman, Addison P. Brewer, Moses B. Hess, Sam'l W. Yawkey, Jno. S. Estabrook, Irving M. Smith, Wm. Hodson, and Chas. W. Grant.

The first meeting of the Chapter was held Feb. 4th, 1864, at which time an election was held. Chas. B. Mott, on account of the condition of his health declined to be elected as King. The officers elected were,—

William L. Webber, - -	H. P.
Judson C. Lowell, - - -	K.
S. W. Yawkey, - - - -	S.
W. J. Bartow, - - -	C. H.
Chas. E. Gillett, - - - -	P. S.
John S. Estabrook, - - -	R. A. C.
E. W. Lyon, - - - -	M. 3d Veil.
Geo. F. Lewis, - - -	M. 2d Veil.
Fred. E. Hoyt, - - - -	M. 1st Veil.

The Chapter was constituted and the officers installed on the 20th day of April, 1864, by Francis Darrow, of Pontiac, R. E. D. H. P., assisted by Stillman Blanchard, R. E. G. V. and L., and a large number of companions from Pontiac and Flint.

At the election held Dec. 4th, 1854, the same officers were re-elected.

The present officers are,

W. L. Webber,	H. P.
W. J. Bartow,	K.
Geo. C. Sanborn,	S.
E. W. Lyon,	C. H.
Irving M. Smith,	P. S.
Geo. C. Warner,	R. A. C.
S. Keeler,	M. 3d. Veil.
C. F. Johnson,	M. 2d Veil.
F. E. Hoyt,	M. 1st Veil.

The present number of members is 56. The regular meetings are held on the first Thursday in every month.

ODD FELLOWS.

O-Saw-Wa-Bon Lodge, No. 14, meets in Odd Fellows Hall, Buena Vista Block, every Friday evening. J. H. McFarlin, N. G., T. E. Doughty, V. G., J. M. Luther, R. S., C. H. Burton, P. S., W. F. Glasby, S.

This Lodge was instituted June 2d, 1855, by Hon. Wm. M. Fenton, Grand Master of the Order in the State of Michigan, with the following named gentlemen as charter members, viz: Jay S. Curtis, Charles B. Mott, Martin Smith, W. L. P. Little, J. H. McFarlin, A. Ferguson, S. B. Knapp, Thomas M. Birdsall. Chas. B. Mott, Esq., was installed N. G., A. Ferguson, V. G.

Owing to the very limited number of business men in the then small town, this Lodge did not meet with its merited success, and after struggling for nearly two years its members ceased to meet as Odd Fellows.

June 2d, 1865, just ten years from its first organization, the Lodge was re-instituted, installing Jay. S. Curtis, N. G.; A. Ferguson, R. S.; C. H. Burton, P. S.; W. F. Glasby, S.; and now ranks with the first lodges in the State of Michigan, having one hundred of the first class business men of the City as members.

Odd Fellowship, although of ancient origin, was introduced into this country about 30 years ago ; and already, we number the fraternity by tens of thousands. During the lapse of time its blessings have been everywhere acknowledged and commended. The sick have been relieved, the destitute comforted, the widow made happy, and the orphan educated.—Wherever our Order flourishes, it will be found that the virtues of benevolence, economy and harmony are cultivated. A member of the Order can always count on "troops of friends," who will never leave him in adversity or affliction. Wheresoever he goes, he is surrounded by brethren, who at a word will hasten to do him good. The chronicles of our Order contain numerous illustrations of the beneficence of the institution. Many virtuous but indigent families have been saved from despair and crime by the munificent charity of our Lodges. This charity is in deed secret, and therefore more grateful efficient. No sense of mortification is attendant on relief furnished by the Lodge. The benefit is a *right* not a *boon.* No matter how long the recipient of our good offices has been an invalid, the relief given is never grudgingly bestowed It is as much a duty to receive as it is a duty to give. We expect no gratitude for our favors ; for every member of the Lodge has an undisputed right to demand them. Such mutual giving and taking preserves a man's soul in independence. An Odd Fellow takes but his own when he receives anything from the Lodge; for his own contributions have constituted the fund he draws from. He must be worthy, however. No invalid through intemperance or immorality can participate in our bounty. The dissipated man, if known to be such, can never enter among us ; but should any unworthy individual be introduced, by successful fraud, into the Fraternity, he will soon be taught that his own inventions will return to plague him.

We cannot undertake to exhibit, at this time, all the peculiar excellencies of our Order Initiation into the mysteries will in due season, display before the candidate the beautiful uses of Odd Fellowship.

An Encampment was instituted in this City, May 10th, 1866, called the Valley Encampment.

Valley Encampment, No. 20, I. O. O. F., meets in Odd Fellows Hall on the 1st and 3d Wednesday of each month. Charter members, J. S. Curtis, C. H. Burton, A. Ferguson, T. E. Doughty, W. H. Southwick, J. M. Luther, J. H. McFarlin.

Officers: J. H. McFarlin, C. P.; J. S. Curtis, H. P.; T. E. Doughty, S. W.; A. Ferguson, S.; C. H. Burton, P.: J. M. Luther, J. W.,

GOOD TEMPLARS.

A lodge of this order was instituted in East Saginaw on the 24th of Nov., 1865, with twenty-four members. The first set of officers were as follows:

Rev. B. S. Taylor, W. C. T.	Dr. O. L. Mason, W. C.
Miss Jane Smith, W. V. T.	Wm. Wiley, P. W. C. T.
D. W. Perkins, Esq., W. S.	Miss Amanda Allen, W. A. S.
C. B. Jones, W. T.	Cornelius Wilson, W. M.
W. H. Burrill, W. F. S.	Miss M. Coggswell, W. D. M.
Miss Anna West, W. I. G.	Capt. O. P. Davison, W. O. G.

Now, after an existence of a little less than five months, the membership of the lodge numbers one hundred and fifty-six, (156) among these several who were formerly addicted to intemperance.

YOUNG MEN'S ASSOCIATION.

The preliminary movement which resulted in the formation of the Young Men's Association of East Saginaw, was the organization of a Lecture Association. This is its brief history:

Monday, October 7th, 1864, a few gentlemen met at the Bancroft House to devise the best way for securing a few good lectures the coming winter. A communication from the Secretary of the Associated Western Literary Societies, Geo. Andrews, Esq., and a letter from H. C. Potter, Esq., who was unavoidably absent, were read.

Chas. B. Mott was called to the chair and J. J. Wheeler was appointed Secretary. On motion, J. J. Wheeler, I. M. Smith and H. M. Flagler were appointed a committee to ascertain and report the best method of obtaining the desired object, and the meeting adjourned to meet at the same place, on Wednesday evening, the 19th.

At the adjonrned meeting, the committee reported and their report was, with a few slight amendments adopted. This report provided for a future permanent Literary Society, and for securing a course of lectures, H. C. Potter, I. M. Smith, and H. M. Flagler being appointed a committee to obtain subscribers thereto. A sufficient number of subscribers were obtained and a course of lectures had at Irving Hall. Irving M. Smith was Secretary of the Association, George K. Newcombe, Treasurer.

At a meeting of the Lecture Association held at the office of Webber & Smith, Friday evening, August 18, 1865, Dr. H. C. Potter being called to the chair and Geo. F. Lewis chosen Secretary, Irving M. Smith, Chairman of committee previously appointed, submitted Articles of Association for the organization of the "YOUNG MEN'S ASSOCIATION OF EAST SAGINAW" in conformity with a recent Act of the Legislature authorizing the incorporation of Societies for Literary and Scientific purposes, which were, on motion adopted, signed by the members present, Messrs. H. C. Potter, Wm. L. Webber, Samuel W. Yawkey, Calvin D. Bliss, G. B. Boardman, Geo. K. Newcombe, Irving M. Smith, C. K. Robinson, L. C. Storrs, G. C. Warner, Geo. F. Lewis, C. H. Gage, W. J. Bartow, Geo. W. Morley, S. J. Reynolds, T. E. Morris and E. W. Morley, properly acknowledged and copies thereof transmitted to the Secretary of State, and County Clerk of Saginaw County.

These Articles provide that the corporation thus formed shall continue for the full period of thirty years from and after the date thereof. Its object to be the promotion of literary and scientific pursuits. The affairs of the Association are managed by a board of sixteen Directors, elected annually by ballot on the second Tuesday in March.

The preliminary organization being effected, the following members were elected as the first BOARD OF DIRECTORS:

President, Dr. H. C. Potter; *1st Vice President*, Geo. K. Newcombe; *2d Vice President*, Irving M. Smith; *Treasurer*, L. C Storrs; *Recording Secretary*, Geo. F. Lewis; *Corresponding Secretary*, G. B. Boardman; W. L. Webber, Geo. C. Warner, C. H. Gage, S. W. Yawkey.

A course of lectures was provided for the winter of 1855–6, and at the election of officers in March, 1866, the Association made choice of the present efficient Board of Directors.

President, Chauncy H. Gage; *1st Vice President*, William J. Bartow; *2d Vice President*, Charles Ten Eyck; *Treasurer*, L. C. Storrs; *Recording Secretary*, Myron A. Johnson; *Corresponding Secretary*, Irving M. Smith; Noah C. Richardson, John S. Estabrook, George W. Morley, Thos. E. Morris, DeWitt C. Gage, M. H. Gallaher, Chas T. Wickes, D. S. Hall, B. J. Brown, E. W. Lyon.

The Association now numbers something over one hundred active members. Its condition and management give hopeful assurance that it will soon become one of the most creditable institutions of its class in the North-west.

SAGINAW CO. AGRICULTURAL SOCIETY.

Pursuant to call, a meeting for the organization of a County Agricultural Society was held at Buena Vista Hall, East Saginaw, Saturday, P. M., March 24th. The call having been read, on motion, Wm. McBratnie was called to the chair and Geo. F. Lewis chosen Secretary.

A committee was appointed consisting of W. L. Webber, M. W. Quackenbush, C. McBratnie, Wm. M. Smith, John Wiltse, Who reported a constitution, which was adopted.

The following officers were elected:

President, Barney H. York; *Vice Presidents*, Geo. F. VeinFleet, Wm. M. Smith, Wm. McBratnie, W. J. Bartow; *Secretary*, Geo. F. Lewis: *Treasurer*, Thomas L. Jackson.

Members of Executive Committee—John Wiltse, Wellington R. Burt, John G. Hubinger, Andrew Crofoot, Andrew Goetz, N. S. Beach, Robert Ure.

NEPTUNE BOAT CLUB

Was organized in the summer of 1859, its leading members at the outset being S. R. Kirby, Jas. F. Brown, F. A. Koehler, J. E. and J. H. Mershon, F. N. Bridgeman, George Scram, Z. W. Wright and others whose names we have not been able to obtain. A fine six oared barge, the "*Neptune*," length 45 feet, beam 3 feet 9 inches, Capt S. R. Kirby, designer; M. S. Filkins, builder, was built for the Club the first year of its organization, and is still in excellent condition, with this are sets of spruce and ash oars and other requisite appurtenances. A new four-oared boat will be added this season to the property of the Club who have a commodious house therefor near the Mayflower Mills.

Officers of the Club: *President*, Geo. F. Lewis; *Secretary* and *Treasurer*, Myron A. Johnson; *Coxswain*, Douglas Hoyt, *1st Ass't Coxswain*, Chas. H. Wilkins; *2d Ass't*, Fred. E. Hoyt.

FIRE DEPARTMENT.

This city boasts of a well organized Fire Department, consisting of one second class Rotary Steamer, of the Seneca Falls manufacture, with a Hose cart and fifteen hundred feet of rubber hose; together with a large span of horses always in readiness to attach at a moments warning. Also one independent hand Engine, owned by the Company manning it; and two other hand Engines owned by the City, also a Hook & Ladder Truck, with a full supply of ladders and hooks. One of their Engines are manned wholly by Germans. There is no better organized and disciplined Fire Department in the West, than in East Saginaw; the noble boys in "red" being always ready, and willing, to render efficient service.

THE COLORED DEBATING SOCIETY.

The Association was organized February, 1866, and is composed of both male and female members, and its object is the moral and intellectual improvement of its members. The meetings are held weekly, and consists of exercises in debating questions and declamation. Lewis Reno, Pres't., Washington Foot, Vice Pres't. G. J. Goodridge, Recording Secretary, Wm. Goodridge, Corresponding Secretary, W. Q. Atwood, Treasurer.

☞ To say anything in addition to what we have already said, in praise of the Bancroft House, or its gentlemanly proprietor, Mr. G W. Wesley, would be superfluous. We will only add, that in connection with the Bancroft Mr. Wesley has one of the finest BILLIARD ROOMS in the State, supplied with four tables of the most approved manufacture. And his room being spacious and admirably lighted and ventilated, renders it a very inviting resort to lovers of the "cue." Mr. Ryan, his gentlemanly attendant, is always watchful to render every attention to his patrons.

See card, outside front cover.

FREY BROTHERS, dealers in Books and Stationery, commenced business on Water street, East Saginaw, in 1862. On the first of February, 1866, Mr. Henry W. Wickleim became a member of the firm, changing its name to J. F. Frey & Co. Their business becoming increased they found it necessary to remove to their present large and commodious store in the Crouse Block, on Genesee street, which occurred about two months since.—Their stock is very rich and varied, consisting of almost every kind of books and a large assortment of stationery, &c., &c.—Their prices are very low; indeed as low as the same articles could be purchased for at retail in the eastern market. "Quick sales and small profits," is the plan upon which they work, which will ultimately prove a great success. Call and examine their rich and splendid assortment of Books and Stationery—See card, page 49.

MR. B. B. BUCKHOUT as an enterprising business man is worthy especial notice in our pages. He came here from Central New York in 1853, and engaged with Col. W. L. P. Little as clerk for one year; at the expiration of which time he entered into a partnership with Messrs. Beach & Morris, in a general merchandizing business. This partnership was dissolved after the continuance of one year, by mutual consent; and the stock on hand was divided among the partners, equally. Mr. Buckhout took the Hardware portion of the stock and opened a general

Hardware store, which he has continued ever since, and we are glad to say with success. His store is located at No. 124, north Water street, and is supplied with a full assortment, from cellar to garret. Mr. Buckhout is a pleasant and agreeable man to do business with, and has a *host* of friends in the Valley. Long may he wave. See card, page 51.

JAS. S. DELAND, commenced business in company with Mr. H. H. Woodruff in September, 1865, under the firm of H. H. Woodruff & Co., carrying on the Grocery and Provision business. In Febuary, 1865, H. H. Woodruff, relinquished his interest to his partner, who still continues the business. His store is large and capacious, being eighty feet in depth and twenty feet wide, well stocked with a fresh supply of Groceries and provisions. During the short time he has been in business, he has acquired a large patronage, by honest dealing and adhering to the principle of "quick sales and small profits." His store is located in a central part of town, at No. 224, South Washington street. See card, page 53.

M. H. ALLARDT, ever since his arrival in East Saginaw has been closely identified with the interests of the City, holding some office of trust, the greater part of the time. The first knowledge we have of his early history is in the "*Plaindealer* office;" at Cleveland, Ohio, where he learned the Printer's trade. He afterwards published the first German paper in Michigan, at Detroit. He afterwards returned to Cleveland and entered the Cleveland law school, where he graduated in 1861. In the spring of 1862 he came to East Saginaw and opened a law office. He was elected City Clerk the same year, and proved a very efficient member of the Council. In the Spring of 1864 he was elected Alderman of the 2d Ward, and in 1866 he was re-elected; which office he now holds. He received the Agency for several first class Insurance Companies and has been engaged quite extensively in that business. He lately purchased Mr. W. H. Southwick's interest in the Tobacco store in the Irving Block on Genesee street, which business, together with his Insurance business, he is now engaged in. Mr. Allardt is a very clear minded, intelligent, and candid man; a useful member of society, and much esteemed for his many good qualities. See card, page 55.

Messrs. ELLIOTT & HARRISON came to East Saginaw in January, 1866, and opened a Crockery and general house furnishing store in the Empire Block on South Water street. This firm are pioneers in the Valley in keeping Carpets, Oil Cloths, Cutlery, Plated goods and all the other articles, useful, convenient and ornamental in the way of housekeeping supplies. The generous patronage extended to the firm has led them to increase their facilities for supplying the demands of the public both at Wholesale and Retail, until their store has assumed an extent and variety difficult to be surpassed. These gentlemen, both, have had a long experience in their busines, and just previous to their settling here, were citizens of Binghamton, New York. From a personal acquaintance, we can recommend them as fair and square dealers. Call and see their stock.

See card, page 59.

CHARLES H. SMITH & Co., manufacturers and dealers in Boots, Shoes, Rubbers and Boot Pacs, in the Empire Block, on South Water street, in this City, are formerly from Binghamton, New York, and are gentlemen worthy the confidence and patronage of the citizens of the Valley. They keep a very extensive assortment; and manufacture the best kind of work, as we can personally attest, having tried them. Their store is spacious and well lighted; and customers dealing with them will be politely treated and fairly dealt with. Give them a call. See card, page 61.

In March, 1865, MR. MARSHALL G. SMITH became proprietor of the "EVERETT HOUSE," bringing with him the experience of eight years as a landlord; and if what "everybody" says can be relied upon, he "knows how to keep a hotel." In January, 1866, Mr. G. H. Crouse, son of Robert Crouse—who owns and built the house—became associated with Mr. Smith in the management of the business. The *Table d' Hote* is well supplied with all the delicacies of the season, and a stranger stopping with them is made to "feel at home." They have a fine set of billiard tables connected with the establishment for those having a fancy for that kind of recreation. In all its appointments the Everett House is one of the most complete and desirable hotels in the west. See card, outside, back cover.

The Dry Goods store of WILLIAM BARIE situate on Genesee street deserves especial mention. Mr. Barie is an old resident of East Saginaw and has literally "grown with its growth and strengthened with its strength." He commenced business here in 1859 carrying on a variety store such as is usually kept in country towns, until 1862, when he made the Dry Goods Trade his speciality. His store is well located and filled with the choicest selection of goods that can be purchased in New York market. He is gentlemanly in his manners and always glad to show his goods. Give him a call.—See Advertisement page 88.

STEVENS, POOL & Co., are extensive dealers in Dry Goods, Fancy Goods, Notions, Lumberman's goods, &c., and now permanently occupy their new store recently fitted up for them in the Everett Block on Genesee street. They first commenced business on Water street in the spring of 1865, and built up for themselves an enviable reputation as dealers, and a large and lucrative patronage. Their present location is one of the finest in the city and their store a perfect model, being finished off in the most exquisite style, unsurpassed in any place west of New York. They have a full and well selected stock, and their prices are really very low. The following are the gentlemen who compose the firm: J: R. Stevens, B. F. Pool and J. T. Barnham, who are well and favorably known.

Among the largest and best business establishments in the Saginaw Valley may be mentioned that of Messrs. LENHEIM & IDDINGS, Manufacturers, and wholesale and retail dealers in Boots, Shoes, and Leather, at No. 211, Genesee street. Mr.

Lenheim was the first to engage in the Boot & Shoe trade, exclusively, in this city. His business was established on Water street in 1862, in the store now occupied by H. Duncan, where he continued until January, 1865. His business becoming so increased he found it necessary to remove to the store adjoining, which was double the capacity, and gave him a better opportunity of displaying his immense stock of goods, and increase his facilities for manufacturing. His store was noted for being the place where good bargains could be obtained in boots and shoes. On the 5th of March, 1865, Richard M. Iddings became a member of the firm, at which time they removed to the store now occupied by them, No. 211, Genesee street, Everett Block, which is more roomy than the one just vacated, and is a better location for business. Their stock is complete, and their custom work warranted to give entire satisfaction. See their cards, pages 72 and 112.

The firm of J. R. Livingston & Co., is composed of J. R. Livingston and R. J. Tappan, the latter well known as the late gentlemanly and obliging Clerk at the Bancroft House. These gentlemen both possess rare qualities as business men, uniting with a pleasing and gentlemanly manner, the strictest integrity and honesty of dealing. Their store is located at No. 102 Genesee, corner of Water streets, and has lately been enlarged, re-fitted and re-painted; so that now it presents a most attractive appearance. Their stock is *rich* and *elegant*, comprising as large a variety, as can be found in the Valley. Such men are sure to succeed; and they have our best wishes.

See their Advertisment page 74.

John O'Brien, has been in business in this city for seven years past, and may almost be considered as one of the pioneers.— His store is located on Genesee street east of Cass, and keeps a full assortment of Family Groceries; which he sells very cheap for cash. Mr. O'Brien has secured many friends and a good trade by fair dealing and gentlemanly deportment. Give him a call. See his advertising, page 86.

H. N. DOTY who for three years past has been engaged in the Grocery business at No. 101 Lapeer corner Jefferson streets, is a fair and honest dealer, and keeps a good assortment of Family Groceries. His store is neatly kept and customers are treated politely. We hazard nothing in saying that persons once dealing with him, will be sure to deal with him again. See card, page 89.

W. I. HOWARD doing business with his brother, on Washington street, as Grocerymen, is an old resident of the City, having been engaged in trade here for more than eight years. His assortment of groceries is full and fresh. His long and favorable acquaintance with our citizens renders it unnecessary for us to speak of his honesty and fair dealing, as he already enjoys that enviable reputation. May success attend them. See card, page 55.

W. N. GRAY, Merchant Tailor, and wholesale and retail dealer in Mens, Youths, and Boys READY MADE CLOTHING, may be classed among our best business men. He commenced business in this City in March, 1864, on Water street, and continued there until 1865. In September, of the same year he removed to his present location, No. 119 Genesee street, opposite the Bancroft House. His store is elegantly fitted up and furnished with the choicest selection of goods for Men's wear.

Mr. Edward Morris (late with Cullin, of Broadway, New York), as a Cutter enjoys an enviable reputation and always gives entire satisfaction to customers. Mr. Gray makes custom trading his *speciality*, having his Fashion Patterns gotten up in New York especially for him, he is enabled to furnish garments in the very latest Paris and New York styles. His custom room over his store occupies the whole space from front to rear, where may be seen a splendid stock of English, French and American Cassimeres, French coatings, vestings, &c., really worth inspection. Mr. Gray is a man correct in his business dealings, and advertises liberally, which ever brings pecuniary success. See card, page 44.

The Iron Foundry buildings occupied by WICKES BROTHERS, on North Water street, was erected by H. W. Wood & Co., formerly of Flint, in July 1860. The firm of H. W. Wood & Co., was composed at that time of H. W. Wood and H. D. & E. N. Wickes, who carried on business successfully until July, 1865, at which time the senior partner withdrew his interest and H. D. & E. N. Wickes continued the business under the name and style of WICKES BROTHERS. The main building, is a substantial wood structure one story high, one hundred and eighty feet in length by forty-four feet in width, which, together with other smaller buildings connected with it, occupies *four* full Lots, making a frontage on north Water street of one hundred and twenty feet extending back two hundred and forty feet to North Washington street. This enterprising firm keeps steadily employed twenty-two men, and do all kinds of jobs in their line, such as Stationary Engines, all kinds of mill geering and machinery, also salt well machinery, and all kinds of iron and brass castings. They are also the sole manufacturers of the popular "Michigan Board Machine and siding mill." Their stock of *patterns* and the facilities for manufacturing are as complete as any establishment north of Detroit. They are both practical mechanics, *working* with their men, and have by honest dealing and industry won an enviable reputation and a good business. See card, page 45.

HUGH WALLACE carries on the Saddle, Harness and Trunk making business, No. 302, Genesee street, nearly opposite the Everett House. He commenced the harness and saddle making business in company with his brother, in 1861, and although he has met with severe losses by fire and otherwise, he has manfully struggled against his adverse fortunes and has succeeded in accumulating a small property. He purchased his brother's interest in 1865, and continues the business with good success. He does his work well, and gives good satisfaction. His foreman, John Franklin, ranks among the first mechanics in the trade. Give him a call. See his card page 89.

M. H. GALLAHER came to East Saginaw, June, 1862, and engaged in the Insurance business with C. B. Mott, taking general charge of the office business up to the time of Mr. Mott's decease, which occurred May 14th, 1865. In July following he was appointed the Agent for the Companies formerly represented by Mr. Mott, and by careful management and close application he has largely increased his business. He represents a number of the oldest and most reliable Insurance Companies in the Union. By his straight-forward manner of doing business he has won the confidence and esteem of the business men of the Valley.—We be-speak for him an increased patronage.

Messrs. EDWARD AIKIN, & L. H. BABCOCK commenced the Crockery and glass ware business in this city two years ago on Washington street, where they carried on an extensive trade.—About a year ago, L. H. Babcock relinquished his interest in the business to James Stinson. They removed to their present location, No. 209 Genesee street, Everett Block, in March last. Their new store is well lighted and roomy, being twenty-three feet in width by eighty feet in length, and three stories high; containing as large, and as rich a stock as can be found west of Buffalo. Their goods are arranged in the most tasty style, displaying their splendid assortment to the greatest advantage imaginable. It is a sight really worth seeing, even if no attention is had of purchasing. They are both gentlemen of pleasing manners and are always happy to exhibit their wares.—Country merchants will find every advantage that Eastern markets afford, and their interest at all times carefully guarded.

The Jewelry store of S. T. LEGGETT, located at No. 106, South Washington street, in this city, is particularly worthy of mention. The variety and richness of his stock, is not excelled outside of Detroit, and his gentlemanly mode of dealing elicits the commendations of all those who have business transactions with him. He first commenced business in this city in the year 1862, in the store at present occupied by H. C. Silsbee; on Water street, and continued there until February, 1866, when he removed to his present location. His store, in pcint of finish and design, is faultless, being a perfect *model* in *artistic display*. Those wishing their watches repaired, will find in him, a mechanic of superior skill. See his card page 114.

RICHARD LUSTER, commenced business on the north-east corner Genesee and Cass streets, in 1863, carrying on the Grocery and Provision trade. He keeps everything in his line, which he sells either at whole-sale or retail. As a dealer Mr. Lester is accommodating, gentlemanly and honest. His store is centrally located and neatly kept. Give him a call. See card, page 116.

HENRY MARKS, dealer in Hats, Caps, Furs, ready made clothing and Gent's furnishing goods, at No. 115 Genesee street, has been in trade here for eleven years past. With a small capital and a large amount of enterprise at the outset, he has succeeded in accumulating a nice little property. He purchased of Chas. Allen, Esq., the lot upon which his store is erected, about nine years ago, and about two years since he erected the fine looking building he now occupies. Mr. Marks, as a dealer, stands well in the community. See page 92.

W. H. SOUTHWICK, dealer in Tobacco and Segars, and Leather Belting in connection with William Ward, at No. 107 Genesee street, first settled in East Saginaw in 1865. He came from Rochester, N Y., and engaged in the business of Lumber Inspector in this place. He continued in the business until 1862, at which time he was appointed Assistant U. S. Assessor for this district. In 1862 he was elected one of the Aldermen of the City to represent the 3d Ward; the duties of which office he discharged with credit. In 1864 he became interested with M. H. Allardt in the Tobacco and Segar business in the Irving Block, which he continued till Feb. 1866, when he sold back his interest to his partner. In April, the same year, he formed a partnership with Mr. Wm. Ward in transacting the leather belting and tobacco and segar business, at No. 107 Genesee st., which, together with his duties as U. S. Assessor he now continues. Their stock is large and their facilities for giving good bargains is very great. Those wishing a supply of leather belting or anything in their line would do well to call on them.—See their Advertisement on fly leaf.

IMPROVEMENT – SALT MAKING BY THE "CHAPIN SYSTEM."—The "Chapin system of Salt making" has now reached a point where it can constantly demand the earnest attention and investigation of "salt men" and business men generally. There are four "Blocks" in successful operation on this plan already, and another one in the course of completion,— one in SAGINAW City, by the Saginaw City Salt Manufacturing Company, in which Messrs Barnard & Binder are the principal stock owners, one in the city of ST. CLAIR,— two in ZILWAUKIE, and one in progress of erection in Bay City. The Blocks at Zilwaukie operated by the Western Salt Company in which the Messrs. DRIGGS are interested, have an evaporating surface of about 2,700 square feet each. They are somewhat larger than that of Messrs. Barnard and Binder, and are producing a correspondingly larger amount of Salt, with a consumption of fuel of about one cord of wood in the manufacture of ten barrels of salt. The Block of Messrs. Barnard & Binder is situated directly on the Saginaw river and three-fourths of a mile above Saginaw City. The dimensions of the building itself is 40 feet in width by 140 in length, having several compartments 10 feet wide extending 116 feet in length of the building on either side for the reception of the salt previous to packing.

In the central portion of the building occupying the entire length and breadth between the "bins," is a large vat, shaped like the letter V; in the front end of which is a huge "fire box," five and a half feet in diameter, and 11 feet in length, from which extends a flue in half-circular form four feet in diameter communicating with the smokestack at the rear end of the building. On this vat rests a large graining pan extending over the entire top, on each side of which is a draining board three feet in width.

In the process of manufacture, this vat is filled from the tanks or reservoirs in the rear of the block by means of pump logs, which empty the brine into a "boiling box" communicating with the vat, and resting directly over the furnace. In passing through this boiling box and along the flue to the rear, from whence the pan is fed, the brine is heated to the point of saturation and all the impurities are precipitated to the bottom of the vat, and from thence are drawn off about once in a season, through an orifice under the fire box. The "bitter water" whenever it collects, is drawn off through a similar orifice at a level with the graining pan.

It is estimated that this block is yielding an average of about sixty barrels of salt per diem, with a consumption of from five to six cords of wood or seven cords of pine slabs. One man only is employed on a "tower," decreasing the expense for labor from the ordinary, full one-half.

We can say from actual observation that the appearance of the salt manufactured at this block indicates a much purer and finer quality than that made by the old method, indeed a salt that "cannot be beat." It is claimed, and we believe correctly, that many of the impurities which, in the ordinary process of kettle boiling, are crystalized *with the salt*, and precipitated before they reach the pan, where in this operation the crystalization takes place, thus leaving the salt perfectly pure. The evidences are that a salt purer in quality and clearer, can be made by this than by the old process. and made at a reduction in cost of at least one-third. In this view of the case, its general introduction is greatly to be hoped for, as a matter of public as well as private interest and benefit. See page 88.

Boyd & Booth, successors to Geo. C., Sanborn; have had a large experience in the Grocery and Provision business. They have a full supply of everything in their line. Purchasers will find them gentlemen, fair and upright Dealers. We wish them the success their merits deserve. See card, page 76.

We would call especial attention to the advertisement of G. Fred. Lewis, dealer in Stationery, at No. 103, South Washington street, opposite the Bancroft House. His store is neatly kept and well supplied with every variety of Stationery, at very low prices. His assistant Mr. A FERGUSON, carries on in connection with this store a general Rail Road Ticket Agency and Telegraph office, and can furnish tickets over all the popular Roads east and west. Mr. Ferguson is a man of character, having been established in this city a number of years, and has secured many friends by his manly and gentlemanly course of conduct. We recommend him unqualifiedly to the patronage of the public. See advertisement, pages following Indian and Pioneer History.

Attention is called to the advertisement of J. C. WHALEN & SON, wholesale and retail dealers in Groceries & Provisions, at No. 222, South Washington street. They have a large and convenient store and their stock is fresh and well assorted. Purchasers will find it to their advantage to give them a call. See their advertising, page 86.

S. & J MAUTNER, whose advertisement will be found in this book, are well located being in the Bliss Block, No, 204 Genesee, and have a well selected stock of goods. Those in want of Ready Made Clothing can here find a choice to select from.

H. R. PROCTOR, dealer in Watches, Jewelry, Silver ware &c., is located at No 123 Genesee corner of Washington, under the sign of the CITY CLOCK, one of the most prominent situations in the City. His store is well stocked and tastefully arranged, presenting a gorgeous display of the richest and most dazzling articles of jewelry and silver ware. He is a public spirited man and as such should receive a liberal patronage. He erected the transparent dial clock over his store at his own individual cost, and keeps the same in running order both night and day for the accommodation of the public. He is gentlemanly and corteous in all his transactions, and being a first class workman in his trade, perfect satisfaction can be relied upon. His advertisement will be found in our book on page 100.

The advertisement of Messrs. GILLETT & GAMBLE, Attorneys and Counselors at Law and Insurance Agents, will be found on

Page 82. They are gentleman of ability in their practice, and business entrusted to them will be faithfully attended to. See card, page 82.

Messrs. Barnum & White, late of Buffalo, New York, have opened a Wholesale and Retail Grocery and Provision store on Water street, in the store recently occupied by L. S. Lenheim as a boot and shoe store. They have a fresh supply of everything in their line, purchased since the decline in prices, which they are enabled to offer to consumers and dealers at a very low figure. They are young men, pleasant and agreeable in their manners, and always pleased to show their goods; call and see them.

Messrs. Wiggins & Clark, carry on the Merchant Tailoring business exclusively. They do not deal in "ready made clothing" except their own manufacture. They purchased their stock of cloths, cassimeres, vestings, &c. &c, since the recent decline in prices, for which they paid cash; consequently are enabled to furnish goods at a very low figure. Mr. Clark has had sixteen years experience in his business in Cleveland, O., and vicinity, and will personally attend to the cutting and fitting department. They are both pleasant and obliging men and will give entire satisfaction to those patronizing them. See their card.

Pioneer Foundry.—The Iron works in this city lately belonging to Messrs. Warner & Eastmen; since purchased by Messrs. J. H. Hill & George Morris, were established in 1854 by Messrs. Warner, Eastman & Chandlers, who managed the same for several years. Afterwards the Messrs. Chandlers sold their interest to Mr. Shaw, and the firm was changed to Warner, Eastman & Shaw. Mr. Shaw after a time withdrew his interest from the concern, leaving the business in the hands of Messrs. Warner & Eastman, who continued the same until April, 1866, when they sold to Messrs. Hill & Morris, the present proprietors. The first steam engine manufactured in Saginaw Valley, which is the one now used in driving the machinery connected with the foundry and planing mill attached, was built at this foundry, by Mr. Morris, who was the superintendent of the works, and is as reliable and serviceable a piece of machinery as was ever turned out from any works. Mr. Morris is an "old hand at the bellows," having had from fifteen to twenty years experience in the Foundry business. With this ample experience and superior facilities in the way of machinery, they are prepared to fill orders for the manufacture of machinery, mill gearing, &c. &c., in the shortest possible time. They employ a large number of men in their works, and also have connected with the Foundry, a Planing mill where they manufacture siding and flooring. The Messrs. Hill & Morris are both prudent business men full of the "go-ahead" spirit, so requisite in this business. Their success is a foregone conclusion.

EAST SAGINAW DIRECTORY.

ABBREVIATIONS.—For ab., read *above*; bds., *boards*; bet., *between*; carp., *carpenter;* cor., *corner;* col'd *colored;* E., *East;* h., *house;* lab., *laborer;* manuf., *manufacturer;* manufy., *manufactory;* N., *north*; propr., *proprietor;* res., *residence;* S., *south*.

The word *Street* is implied.

A

Abbey E W, business agt (E Sag Enterprise) bds 424 Johnson
Abbott Thomas, carpenter, h 1523 Genesee
Abbs Robert, cooper, 501 N Water h Carrollton.
Abbs Thomas, cooper, h 310 N Rockwell.
Abel Azel, foreman planing mill, h 419 S Warren.
Abraham John, laborer, h 319 N Fifth.
Actheridge G, clothing, h 107 S Fourth.
Adgeman Martin, bds 307 James.
Agertz Christ, carpenter, h 125 N Clay.
Ahlers Henry, printer, bds 303 S Washington.
Ahrns John, laborer, h 421 N Third.
Aikin Edwin, (Aikin & Stinson) h 401 S Jefferson.
AIKIN & STINSON (E Aikin & I Stinson,)Crockery dealers 209 Genesee.
ALLARDT M H, Insurance agt & Tobacconist, 112 Genesee, h 110 S Fourth.
Allbee H J, h 502 N Washington.
Allen Robert, laborer, bds N Water, near McLane's mills.
Allen Samuel, carpenter, h 519 N Warren.
Allen Wm, carpenter, h 1409 Genesee.
Allington David K, machinist, h 314 S Jefferson.
Alsner William, laborer, h 811 Millard.
Altman Kidan, laborer, h near E Sag salt works.
American Express Co, L W Tisdale agt, 116 S Washington.
American Hotel, (Chas B Stever propr) 113 N Cass.
Ames L, laborer, bds Lapeer.
Amos Henry, (col'd,) waiter Bancroft House.
Anderson Charles, watchman, F & P M R R, h 708 N Jefferson.

Anderson James, laborer, h 602 N Water.
Angest August, laborer, bds 1,117 S Water.
Angest Mrs Janette, washer woman, h 412 Tuscola.
Anglie Patrick, peddler, bds 724 N Washington.
Anschutz C, laborer, h east end Tuscola.
Arndt August, Blacksmith, bds 305 N Cass.
Arnold George, ship carpenter; h 309 N Cass.
Arnold Mrs Mary A, h 116 N Webster.
Arnold Thomas, machinist, h 709 S Washington.
Ashley Frederick, clerk bds Bancroft House.
Ashman, Miss C school teacher, res Salina.
Ausman Henry, h 502 N Fifth.
Austin David M, drayman, h 404 Potter.
Avery S, lumberman, h 523 Carroll.
Axford Charles J, engineer, h 121 N Franklin.

B

Bachant Charles G, painter, 203 N Jefferson h 419 Maple.
Bailey M T, lumberman, h 321 S Washington.
Bailey Thomas, moulder, h 1211 S Water.
BAKER JAS J, wagon maker, 320 Genesee, bds 319 S Warren.
Baker John, blacksmith, h 224 N Fourth.
Baker Joseph, h 205 S Rockwell.
Baker Valentine, carriage maker, h Genesee.
Baker William, carriage maker, h 319 S Warren,
Baker William carriage maker, h 323 S Webster.
Balcom John, carpenter, h 416 Emerson.
Baldwin Albert, foreman, (C & E Ten Eyck) h 410 N Fourth.
Ballentine H A, salt manuf, bds Bancroft House.
Ball Frank N, clerk, bds 301 S Water.
Ball H J, grocer, 223 S Washington, h 301 S Water.
BANCROFT HOUSE, G W Wesley propr, 118 Genesee cor Washington.
Banford Andrew, carpenter, h 517 N Jefferson.
Banford A W, clerk, bds 517 N Jefferson.
Banford Oliver, cooper, bds 517 N Jefferson.
Baptist Church, (Henry L Morehouse pastor,) 114 S Jefferson.
Baptist Church, 607, William.
Barclay Spencer, (Barclay & Tyler) bds Everett House.
Barclay & Tyler, (S B & J T) meat market 304 Genesee.
Bardstetter K, shoemaker, h Johnson.
Barie William, dry goods 203 Genesee h 106 N Clay.
Barkham Robert W, miller h 115 N Warren.
Barkler S, laborer, h 108 Tenth.
Barney Chauncey, ship carpenter, bds 309 N Cass.
BARNUM GEORGE G. (B & White,) 122 N Water bds Bancroft House.

J. F. FREY & CO.,

DEALERS IN

Fancy and Staple Stationery,

SCHOOL BOOKS,

Blank Books of all Descriptions, Drawing Paper, Tracing Cloth,

PAPER HANGINGS,

TOYS AND FANCY GOODS,

And a variety of other Goods too numerous to mention.

Everett House Block, No. 113, Genesee Street.

J. F. FREY, H. W. WICKLEIN.

F. JOS. HERB,

WATCHMAKER & JEWELER.

Watches, Clocks, Jewelry, and Spectacles,

Every article warranted as represented.

Repaired on short notice.

Watches, Clocks, Jewelry, &c., &c.,

All Articles at the Lowest Cash Price.

Everett House Block, No. 113, Genesee Street.

No. 101 and 103 S. Washington St., Bliss Block, 2d floor.

Barrider, Augustus, clerk, bds 1117 S Water.
Barry Miss Kate, with S Watson & Co, bds 411 S Washington.
BARNUM & WHITE, (Geo G B & Chas H W,) 122 N Water.
Bartow J H, machinist, bds 1121, S Water.
Bartow W J, Supt E S St R W, h 516 N Washington.
Basinger Joseph, laborer, h Hoyt.
Bates Henry, laborer, h 123 N Fifth.
Baum Adam, meat market, 524 Genesee h 518 German.
Baum Martin, boots & shoes 401 Genesee, h 111 N Warren.
Baumgarten Amand, grocer, 902 Genesee, h same.
Baxter W J, lumberman, 104 N Washington.
Bays John, h 114 N Rockwell.
Bead J R, machinist. bds Lapeer.
Beam Patrick, boiler maker, h Mason.
Beangeter John, bds 103 S Warren.
Beard George R, ornamental painter, h cor Warren & Genesee.
Beatiner Mathias, teamster h 219 S Sixth.
Beauchaw John, laborer bds Jefferson.
Bechrow George, laborer, h 210 N Webster.
Beckbissinger John, baker, 124 N Jefferson, h same.
Bedet Louis, carpenter & joiner, bds Monitor House.
Begle Charles W, carpenter & joiner, h 920 S Webster.
Begrow John, carpenter, h 125 N Clay.
Bell A P, teamster, h 410 N Warren.
Bell John, laborer, h 407 Fitzhugh.
Bell Miss C, school teacher, bds Washington.
Bell Robert, (freight agent F & P M R R) h 601 S Jefferson.
Bellevue Hotel, Riegel & Bloedon propr, 602 German.
Belknap John, printer, bds Steckert's hotel.
Bennett D C, physician, 101 Genesee, h 302 Hayden.
Bennett George, carpenter, h 708 Emerson.
Benedict Hiram W, agt H C L & Co, bds 423 N Washington.
Benstien Herman, laborer, bds 313 Genesee.
Bertran G, (pastor G. E. M. church) 115 N Warren h same.
Besch Joseph, mason, h 315 N Third.
Best Charles, Boarding House, 502 N Water.
Betzner Egnetz, saloon, 120 N Franklin, h same.
Bezner Benj, boarding house, 1025 S Water.
Beesley Robt, (col'd) waiter Bancroft House.
Bickel George, meat market, 123 Lapeer, h same.
Bidlien John, laborer, h 301 Wadsworth.
Bigardus Hamilton, h 1012 Emerson.
Billings John W, clerk, bds N Warren.
Binder Chas H, carpenter h 1024 James.
Binder Wm, stave dealer, 510 S Water, res Sag City.
Bingham Alonzo L, school teacher, h 703 S Jefferson.
Bingham Martin, clerk bds 703 S Jefferson.

Birch John G, engineer, h 620 S Warren.
Birch Joseph, carpenter, h 218 N Warren.
BIRDSALL ALBERT, blacksmith, 320 Genesee, h 305 N Cass.
Birmingame Cline, painter h Warren.
Birnell Augustus, hostler, bds Everett House.
Bissell Albert G, druggist 109 Genesee, h Park Auenue.
Bisner John, h 218 N Warren.
Blackmer Merritt, lumberman, h 407 S Warren.
Blair John, foreman (Carlisle & Co.'s tannery,) h Deerfield road.
Blankherd Herman, clerk, bds 505 N Jefferson.
Blankherd William, clerk bds 505 N Jefferson.
Blanketz Wm, clerk, bds Jefferson.
Bleir Solomon, clothing 123 S Washington, h same.
BLISS CALVIN D, (C D Bliss & Co,) 106 N Washington, h 316 N Jefferson.
BLISS C D & Co, auctioneers, 106 N Washington.
Bliss, Janes, & Co dry goods & groceries 102 and 104 S Water.
Bliss Mrs H A, (B & Pettibone) 107 N Washington.
Bliss & Pettibone, (H A B & M A P,) 107 N Washington.
Bliss S B, (B, Janes & Co,) h 316 N Water.
Bliss Wallace W, clerk, h 304 N Jefferson.
Bloomer Alfred B, engineer, h 708 N Warren.
Block John, laborer, h 609 Maple.
Blœdon Edward (Riegle & B.) 602 German.
Blum John, laborer, h 219 S Fourth.
Blyben William, h 516 S Jefferson.
Boardman George, (Cross & B,) h 1005 S Washington
Bochar John, Mason, h 604 N Fourth.
Bode August, Yankee notions, 106 Lapeer, h same.
Boehm George, cooper, bds 117 S Webster.
Bogardus Hamilton, laborer, h Emerson.
Bola David, cooper, bds 224 Cornelia.
Borgert D, laborer, h 1519 Johnson.
Borgert Frederick, carpenter, h 120 N Fifth.
Borgert Henry (B & Rimers) h 202 Wadsworth.
Borgert & Rimers, tailors, 113 Genesee.
Bortmann Adolph, carpenter, h 102 N Third.
Bostian Christ, laborer, h 224 James.
Booth James H, (Boyd & Booth) bds Everett House.
Bottcher Charles, sailor, h 825 Tuscola.
Bothwell James, baker, h E end Tuscola.
Bounter Charles, spile driver, h 614 N Washington.
Bowyer William C, tailor, h 323 First.
Boyden Mrs E L, milliner, 127 N Washington.
Boyden W A, h 127 N Washington.
Boyd & Booth, (R B, & Jas H B,) grocers, 101 Genesee.
Boyd Robert, (B & Booth,) 101 Genesee.

Braden Casper, carpenter, h 301 S Washington.
Bradley John F, photographer, bds 523 Fitzhugh.
Bradshaw William C, laborer, h 302 N Third.
Brady James, cooper, bds Monitor House.
Brady James B, billiard room, 405 Genesee.
Braman Michael, laborer, h 224 Elm.
Branstetter C. shoemaker, h 1024 Johnson.
Bray Andrew, lumberman, h 411 S Washington.
Brennan Michael laborer, h 218 Elm.
Brewer A P, surveyor, h 319 S Washington.
Bridgeman George & Co, gas fitters, 113 S Water.
Bridgeman George (G B & Co,) h 224 N Jefferson.
Brimner John, Prop'r Sherman House 131 S Water.
Britton H W, carpenter and joiner, h 225 Maple.
Brookmire John, lab h N Washington, near E Sag Salt Works.
Brooks Horatio, coffee and spice mills, 123 N Water.
Brooks Tracy C. h 1410 Genesee.
Broski G, clerk, h 104 S Jefferson.
Broughton Charles, mason, h 602 Thompson.
Broughton John, baker and confectioner, 129 S Washington, h same.
Brown A B, clerk, bds 401 S Jefferson.
Brown Archy, lumberman, bds Everett House.
Brown Benjamin, bds 408 Millard.
BROWN B J, (B Hall & James,) 103 S Washington, bds cor Wells and Park Avenue.
Brown George O, bar tender, bds 112 N Franklin.
BROWN, HALL & JAMES, (B J B, J H. & T M J,) insurance agents and lawyers, 103 S Washington.
Brown Henry H, tailor, h 602 S Jefferson.
Brown James F, Cashier Merchant's National Bank, h 324 N Washington.
Brown Joseph L, carp, bds Maple.
Brown Michael, (col'd) carpenter and joiner, 221 S Franklin, h 216 N Fifth.
Brown Mrs. Nancy, teacher select school, 117 N Jefferson, bds 214 N Cass.
Brown Patrick, lab, h N Washington, near E Sag salt works.
Brown R D, jeweler, bds 408 Millard.
Browne William, insurance agent, 102 Genesee, h 823 Emerson.
Brucker Charles H, hotel and saloon, 405 Genesee, h same.
Brunn Andrew, laborer, h 216 S Third.
Bruske Edward, tailor h 202 N Third.
Bruske Edward, tinsmith; bds 824 Genesee.
Bruske Gotlieb, 824 Genesee, h same.
Bruske Gustavus, clerk, bds 824 Genesee.
Buchanan Irwin, builder, h 315 N Third.

Buchner Isaac, stave dealer, h 325 Wadsworth.
BUCKHOUT B B, hardware, 124 N Water, h 226 N Wash'n.
Buffalo salt Co, F Wildman sup't, 1131 S Water.
Buikel John, Bakery, 119 S Franklin, h same.
Bullard Albert F. (Shaw B & Co,) bds Bancroft House.
Bullock Charles L, bds 701 N Jefferson.
Bullock Ephraim K, prop'r Bullock's Hotel, 701 N Jefferson.
Bullock James, h 419 Astor.
Bundy J F, lumberman, h 224 S Jefferson.
Burr Washington, teamster, h 207 Wells.
Burrill Harvey D, salt manuf, h 423 N Jefferson.
Burdick Jessie A, engineer Valley City fire engine, 205, N Water, h same.
Burger Ernst, machinist, bds 509 Lapeer.
Burger Joseph, boots and shoes, h 106 S Webster.
Burnham J T, (Stevens, P & Co,) residence Saginaw City.
Burns Edward, shoemaker, 914 Genesee.
Burtch E, Blacksmith, 624 N Water, h 605 Carroll.
Burtch Ransom, blacksmith, bds Franklin.
Burtch William, carpenter, bds 605 Carroll.
Burtless M, Farmer, h 113 N Fifth.
Burton Charles H, book-keeper, bds 409 S Jefferson.
Burton Harvey, brewer, (J Erd & Co,) h 1001 S Water.
Burt Brothers, (O P & Edwin B,) real estate dealers, 107 N Washington.
Burt Edwin, (Burt Brothers,) h 619 S Jefferson.
Burtt John E, (B & Loomis,) 319 Genesee, h 1521 Genesee.
Burt Joseph lumberman, h 235 N Washington.
BURTT & LOOMIS, (J E B & R H L,) painters, 319 Genesee.
Burt Miss E, school teacher, bds 511 S Jefferson.
Burt O P, (Burt Bros,) residence Buffalo.
Burt Wellington R, lumberman, h 511 S Jefferson.
Burwick Frederick, laborer, bds 202 N Franklin.
Buss Eugene, Clerk, bds Steckert's hotel.
Bussey Jerome, porter Everett House.
Bussinger, Joseph, laborer, h 306 Wells.
Button & Sturtevant, lawyers, 325 Genesee.
Button William H, (B & Sturtevant,) 325 Genesee bds 606 S Webster.
Butler Daniel, laborer, bds 110 N Jefferson.
Byrne Edward, shoe maker, h Genesee.
Byrer B, laborer, h 1723 Johnson.

C

Caldwell Thomas, carp, h 1020 Emerson.
Caley A C, paying teller Merchant's Nat'l Bank, bds Bancroft.

Caley F H, book keeper Merchants' Nat'l Bank, bds Bancroft.
Calpaine Christ, lab, h 519 First.
Cambell Alexander, carp, h 115 N Clay.
CAMERON JAMES G, carriage maker, 206 and 208 N Franklin, h 415 N Franklin.
Cameron J C, lumber dealer, bds Bancroft.
Campau Joseph, farmer, h 1119 S Washington.
Campbell Thomas C, carp, h Genesee.
Camp Charles H, lawyer, 105 N Washington, 2d floor, h 1017 S Washington.
Cannon James, porter, Bancroft.
Carband, painter, bds Jefferson.
Carey George, lab, bds 624 Hoyt.
Carey Harrison, (Sears & Co,) residence Saginaw City.
Carlisle F W, (C & Co,) leather dealer, 128 N Water, h 521 Miller.
Carman Henry, blacksmith, h 218 S Third.
Carmichael Henry, lab, bds 914, Genesee.
Carr John, horse farrier, h 309 First.
Carroll Thomas, saloon, 117 Lapeer, h same.
Carson Thomas, carp, bds 316 N Franklin.
Carter A B, clerk, bds Washington.
Carter George, builder, h 325 S Water.
Casey & Chute, (F G C & B C,) propr's St Nicholas Restaurant, 101 S Washington, cor Genesee.
Casey F G, (Casey & Chute,) bds St. Nicholas Restaurant 202 Genesee.
Casey Patrick, lab, h 623 N Franklin.
Cashin P, clerk, bds cor Lapeer and Clay.
Cassidy George, saloon, 209 S Washington.
Catholic Church 601 Hoyt.
CATLIN E S, (C & Sanborn,) 122 N Water, h 601 Caroll.
CATLIN & SANBORN, lumber dealers, 122 N Water.
Caughell D, lumber inspector, h 908 Johnson.
Chadima Frank, lab, h 202 N Fourth.
Chambers W C, bds Everett House.
Champagne A E, saloon, 119 S Water. h 111 Hayden.
Champagne John, waterman h 413 S Water.
Champlin O H P, music store, 317 Genesee, h 408 N Washington.
Chandler John, machinist, bds 324 Astor.
Chapin G P, clerk, h 608 N Washington.
Chapin Nathan, h 713 S Warren.
Cheesbro B F, musician, h 301 S Webster.
Cheesbro Frederick, carp, bds 301 S Webster.
Cheesbro Frederick, carp, bds 812 Tuscola.
Cheesbro F, teamster, bds Genesee.
Cheesbro John, planer h 812 Tuscola.

Cheesbro John, lab, h Genesee.
Cheney Henry H, gunsmith, 108 N Jefferson, h same.
Chisholm Archibald, ship carpenter, h 309 N Cass.
Choate C B, (Shaw, Reynolds & Co,) h 417 Carroll.
Cholet A, Clerk, h 630 Hoyt.
Cholet Augustus, bar tender, h 636 Hoyt.
Cholet George, [C & Hurteau] 125 S Water, res Syracuse.
Cholet & Hurteau, (George C & Zoel H,) bowling saloon, 125 S Water.
Christopherson Godfrey, butcher, bds Carroll.
Chute B, [Casey & Chute,] bds 202 Genesee.
Cieliton James, lab, h 216 N Fourth.
City Lime Works, Holland & Fish prop'rs, 512 N Water.
Clark A, carp, h 124 Martha.
Clark A E & J, blacksmiths, 115 German.
Clark Alexander, [A E & J C,] h German.
Clark C A, conductor street car, h 311 S Cherry.
Clark C H, carpenter, h 816 Brady.
Clark David, drayman, h 108 S Clay.
Clark E H, Carp, h Maple.
Clark Elmer, clerk, bds Seventh. East end.
Clark Henry D, [Wiggins & Co,] h 609 Jefferson.
Clark Jacob T, lab, bds 618 N Washington.
Clark James carp, h 325 N Franklin.
Clark John, (A E & J C,) h 812 S Jefferson.
CLARK & LOVELAND, lawyers, 105 N Washington.
Clark N S, teller first National Bank, 114 S Washington, bds Bancroft House.
Clark L A, Cashier First National Bank, 114 S Washington, h 612 N Warren.
CLARK W A, (C & Loveland,) residence Saginaw City.
Clark W S. bank clerk, bds Bancroft.
Clay & Lester, (S G C & H S L,) 112 Genesee.
Clay S G, [C & Lester,] barber, h 615 S Water.
Claydon Walter, lab, bds 908 S Jefferson.
Cleary Courtlandt C, carriage maker, h 1539 Genesee.
Clifton W. lab, h 417 S Water.
Cliperton William, h 408 Park.
Clough Lester, lab, bds near R R shop.
Clure Michael, lab, h N Washington, near E Sag salt works.
Coates W H, [C H Smith & Co,] bds Bancroft.
Cook Edward, lab, h 214 William.
Cooper George, mason, h 216 N Sixth.
Cooper Mrs. Mary, h 324 S Washington.
Cochrane John, bds 113 N Cass.
Cochrane W J, carpenter & joiner, h 818 Emerson.
Code James, lab, h 321 First.

Cogswell Don A, lumber inspector, h 715 Genesee.
Coig Archibald, carpenter, h 211 N Cass.
Collins H T, [L C Storrs & Co.] h Park Avenue.
Collins Thomas, lab, bds 724 N Washington.
Colbrath Charles C, printer, bds S Washington,
Cole C, saloon, h 307 S Water.
Colfax Jonathan, bridge toll collector, h 206 Maple.
Colfax William, propr skating park, h 419 Park.
COMMERCIAL IRON WORKS, 524 N Water, Wickes Bros proprietors.
Common Council Room, 104 Genesee.
Conconon Rodger, lab, bds 221 S Franklin.
Conday Joseph, teamster, h 325 N Franklin.
Congregational Church, John G W Cowles Pastor, 202 S Washington.
Conrad George, bar tender, bds 117 S Water.
Contee William, (col'd) waiter, Bancroft.
Coppelt John, saloon, 121 S Water, h Hayden.
Corbin James, Capt. tug boat *Star* h 701 S Webster.
Cornwell James, machinist, bds S Washington.
Corser B W, millwright, h 217 Maple.
Courtier J F, lab, bds 207 S Water.
Cowherd William, machinist, bds S Washington.
Cowles Rev John G W, Pastor Congregational Church, h 313 S Washington.
Coyla John, sailor, bds 625 N Franklin.
Crabbe George, (C H Smith & Co,) h 211 Hayden.
Craig Martin, teamster, bds 708 N Warren.
Cramlich Mathias, lab, bds S Washington, in the grove.
Crane Joseph, porter, h Carroll.
Cresswell Abner, machinist, h 519 N Washington.
Cristy John, lab, h 704 James.
Crocker George, stage driver, bds Saginaw Valley House.
Crocker Mrs Lucy, h 813 S Water.
Croll John, lab, h 607 Tuscola.
Crossen Hugh, mason, h 221 N Cass.
Cross & Boardman, (G F C & G B B,) grocers, 115 N Water.
Cross George F, (C & Boardman,) h 310 S Washington.
Cross John, lab, h 108 Eighth.
Cross Lester E, clerk, bds 318 N Cass.
Cross Lorenzo, lab, h 312 N Franklin.
CROUSE GEO H, (Smith & C,) Everett House
Cruttenden Will H, watch maker, bds Everett House.
Cullinan Thomas, lab, h 1113 Fitzhugh.
Cummings Luther E, lumberman, h 707 N Jefferson.
Curtis Clark, hardware, h 225 Carroll.
Curtis C M, (C M & F A Curtis,) h 501 N Washington.

Curtis C M & F A, stove dealers, 115 S Water.
Curtis F A, (C M & F A C,) h 232 N Washington.
Curtis Jacob. cooper, h 621 Johnson.
Curtis Jay S, physician, h 132 N Washington.
Cuthberth James, lab, h 607 Maple.

D

Dagener William, wood chopper, h 1003 Lapeer.
Daniels John S, engineer, h 821 Johnson.
Daniels Spencer M, laborer, bds 821 Johnson.
Danker C, laborer, h 206 N Webster.
Darmstaetter Lewis, Brewer, S Washington in the grove.
David Moses, Boarding House, 207 S Water.
Davidson John C, painter, h 605 S Webster.
Davidson Robert, laborer, bds 1612 Genesee.
Davison George, chair maker, h 410 Maple.
Davison Oliver, turner, 125 S Cass, h 412 Maple.
Davis Charles F, printer, bds 602 N Franklin.
Davis Cornelius, painter, h 706 Park.
Davis Orin R, steam boat engineer, bds 801 Lapeer.
Davis William M, h 602 N Franklin.
Dawson James C, cabinet maker, bds 924 Emerson.
Dawson John, cabinet maker, h 924 Emerson.
Dawston Peter, (col'd) waiter, Bancroft.
Decker —— drayman, h 1413 Genesee.
DeForest W H, clerk, bds 525 N Franklin.
Deguire Frederick, laborer, h 713 Maple.
Deickmann Charles, clerk, bds 123 N Washington.
Deiter S J, machinist, h 520 N Water.
Deitrich John, apprentice, bds N Washington.
DELAND C V, h 405 S Washington.
DELAND JAMES S, Grocer, 224 S Washington, bds 405 S Washington.
DeLand Mrs Rachael, school teacher, res Salina.
Delavergene Louis, carpenter, h 302 Park.
Dembois F W, saloon, h 801 Genesee.
Densmore William, h 212 Astor.
Deering James (Deering & Sons) h 210 S Webster.
Deering James, jr, (Deering & Sons) bds 210 S Webster.
Deering James, engineer, h 304 N Fifth.
Deering James, (Gallaher, Mead, and Deering,) h Johnson.
Deering Jonathan, (Deering & Sons) bds 210 S Webster.
Deering & Sons, Dry Goods, 402 Genesee.
Deering William, (Deering & Sons,) bds 210 S Webster.
Derby Benj, merchant, h 502 Carroll.
Derby John h 319 N Jefferson.

Derby John P, h 510 Fitzhugh.
Derby Louis, (col'd) laborer, h 404 N Warren.
Derosier Louis, laborer, h 829 S Water.
Derry Thomas, engineer, h 425 Fitzhugh.
Devil Frederick, cooper, h N Jefferson.
Devine Thomas, salt boiler, h N Washington, near East Saginaw salt works.
Dewaisark George, laborer, h 102 Ninth.
Deyhly David, farmer, h 504 Lapeer.
Dickinson Samuel J, clerk, h 625 S Jefferson.
Dieckmann Frederick, gardner, h 425 First.
Dieckson William S, carpenter & joiner, h near east end Tuscola.
Dietz William G, builder, h 319 S Jefferson.
Dillingham John B, (Wisner & D,) h 611 Thompson.
Dingman George, horse farrier, h 613 N Jefferson.
Ditties Frederick, laborer, h 521 First.
Ditties Phillip, clerk, bds 521 First.
Dixon Albert, jeweler, h 807 Lapeer.
Dobson Mrs Ann, h 1416 Genesee.
Dollar George, mason, h 820 Hoyt.
Doll Temple E, bds 416 N Jefferson.
Dolan John, saloon, N Washington, near E Sag salt works.
Donlan John, sailor, bds 1231 S Water.
Donner Charles, fireman, h 216 German.
Doty H N, groceries & provisions, 101 Lapeer, h 828 Hoyt.
Doughty Charles, (T E Doughty & Co.,) h 216 Maple.
Doughty T E & Co, jewelry and books 110 Genesee.
Doughty T E (T E Doughty & Co) h 307 N Jefferson.
Downs Seth, wheelwright, 808 S Washington, h 812 S Washington.
Doyle Phillip, laborer, h N Washington, near E Sag salt works.
Draper Calvin D, capenter, h 1523 Genesee.
Dreher Peter, h 1218 Fitzhugh.
Driggs H C, Salt and Land Office; 102 N Washington, bds Bancroft.
Driggs Wm L, U. S Land office, 102 N Washington, bds Bancroft House.
Duncan David, carpenter, h 1559 Genesee.
Duncan H R, clothing, 108 N Water, h 610 S Washington.
DUNK ALFRED A, Druggist, 201 Genesee. bds Bancroft.
Dunlap Alexander, saloon, 1117 S Water, h same.
Dunn James, engineer; h 210 N Fifth.
Dunn Jeremiah, tailor, bds 219 S Water.
Dunn John, engineer, bds 210 N Fifth.
Dunn Patrick, laborer, bds 210 N Fifth.
Duquette Edward, laborer, h 602 N Water.
Durand William, sash and blind maker, bds 701 Carroll.

A. A. DUNK,

Prescription Druggist

AND

DEALER IN

Drugs and Medicines,

Perfumery, Brushes,

And Druggists Fancy Articles generally.

Physicians Prescriptions and Family Recipes prepared at all hours, day and night.

SIGN OF THE GOLDEN MORTAR,

No. 102, North Washington, cor. Genesee,

EAST SAGINAW.

☞BROWN & JAMES, Attorneys and Land Agents,

Durkee E, laborer, bds 119 Cornelia.
Durkee George W, farmer, h S Washington, S of Bayou.
Durkee Seymour, rule maker, h 921 Emerson.
Dutton Chauncy S, stave dealer, 325 Genesee, h 311 N Cass.
Dwan John, laborer, h N Washington, near E Sag salt works.
Dwille G, laborer, bds 624 Hoyt.

E

Eakins Miss J, milliner and dress maker, h 115 N Fifth.
Earls Archibald, lumberman, h 932 S Washington.
Eastman & Brooks, agts Excelsior coffee and spice mills, 123 S Water.
Eastman Henry N, (E & Brooks,) h 307 S Washington.
Eastman L H, machinist, (Warner & E,) h 210 Hoyt.
Easton, Capt steam tug, h 1569 Genesee.
Easton Roderick, musician, h 1304 Genesee.
East Saginaw City Lime Works, 510 N Water.
EAST SAGINAW COURIER OFFICE, G. F. Lewis proprietor, 224 S Washington.
EAST SAGINAW DAILY AND WEEKLY ENTERPRISE Co, Perry Joslin editor and prop'r, 201 N Water.
East Saginaw Gas Light Co, J L Ketchum Vice President and Treasurer, 113 S Water.
East Saginaw Gas Works, 423 S Water.
East Saginaw Street Railway, W J Bartow Supt, office 716 N Washington.
Eaton Benjamin, boiler maker, h 1221 Mason.
Eckert Christ, cabinet maker, 916 Genesee.
Eckert Ernst, cabinet maker, 916 Genesee.
Eddy Charles K, lumberman, h 417 S Washington.
Eddy Edward, lumberman, h 416 N Jefferson.
Eddy Romulus A, tinsmith, h 324 N Jefferson.
Eden J, lab, h 609 N Jefferson.
Edget Henry S, insurance agent, h 310 N Cass.
Edinger William, painter, h 1011 Johnson.
Edmondson J S, (Agent S & F Foster') h N Washington.
Eggert Henry, lab, h 208 N Third.
Eldridge Milford, sailor. h 411 Park.
Elliott Alfred, lighterman, h 110 Elm.
Elliott Alfred, waterman, h 912 S Washington.
ELLIOTT & HARRISON, (L R E & H L H,) crockery, 114 S Water.
Elliott Josiah, capt tug boat, h 414 N Water.
ELLIOTT L R, (E & Harrison,) bds Everett House.
Ellis David, carp, h 904 S Warren.
Ellis Henry, carp, bds 904 S Warren.

Ellsworth A L, agent F & P M R R, h 419 Carroll.
Ellsworth Lewis C, clerk, bds 419 Carroll.
Ellsworth Norton, bds 419 Carroll.
Elsifer George, teamster, bds 324 N Franklin.
Elsifer John H, spile driver, h 324 N Franklin.
Elsifer Miss A C, school teacher, bds 324 N Franklin.
Elwardt Joseph, tailor, h 214 N Rockwell.
Elwell Clark, carp and joiner, h 202 S Jefferson.
Emerson Byron, painter, bds 705 S Warren.
Emerson Curtis, h 1001 S Washington.
Emerson Richard, painter, h 705 S Warren.
Emo Michael, lab, h 621 N Franklin.
Engel George H, (Swilling & Co,) h 125 Lapeer.
England James, Cooper, h 302 N Rockwell.
England Thomas, apprentice, bds 302 N Rockwell.
English Alexander, lime burner, h 514 N Water.
Episcopal Church, cor Lapeer and Warren.
Erd John & Co, brewers, 917 S Water.
Erd John, (Erd John & Co,) h 919 S Water.
Erwin William, lab, h 933 S Washington.
Eschenbach Kasper, prop'r Farmers Hotel 605 Genesee.
Estabrook J S, lumber dealer, h 318 N Washington.
Estabrook & Mason, lumber dealers, 101 S Washington.
Etheridge Josiah, clerk, h Fourth.
Etzdorff August, carp and joiner, bds Genesee.
EVERETT HOUSE, Smith & Crouse propr's, 219 Genesee.
Everts John H, bar tender, bds 1117 S Water.
Eview Christ, lab, h 113 N Clay.
Evo John, Lab, bds 1119 S Washington.
Excell Charles, carp, h Beecher.
Excelsior Coffee and Spice Mills, Eastman & Brooks agents, 123 S Water.
Eymer Andrew, grocer, 109 Lapeer, h same.

F

Fairchild Reuben, sawyer, h 613 James.
Fall Stephen, laborer, h 905 Lapeer.
Farmer George, miller, h 212 S Third.
Farmer James, cooper, bds Monitor House.
Farmer John, carriage maker, 113 S Franklin, bds 2113 Maple.
Farmer Richard, lumberman, h 2113 Maple.
Farnsworth A, physician, 102 Genesee, 2d floor, h 302 N Jefferson.
Farrand H C, physician 125 N Washington, h 411 S Warren.
Farwell Samuel, R R director, bds 1304 S Jefferson.
Fassett David C, clerk, bds Everett House.

Fay Conrad, clerk, h 917 Lapeer.
Fay B M, Pres't, Sag Valley Bank, res Sag City.
Feck Jerome, lighterman, h 109 Hayden.
Feiger Frederick, cooper, bds Johnson.
Feige E, cabinet maker, h 111 S Web ter.
Feige Frederick F, cabinet maker, h 118 S Clay.
Feige George, cabinet maker, bds 111 S Webster.
Feige Henry, clerk, bds, Sherman House.
Feige Reinhardt, lock smith, 417 Genesee, h 125 S Third.
Ferguson A, manager W U Telegraph Co., bds Everett.
Fettig Donat, teamster, bds S Washington, in grove.
Final William, lumberman, h 1317 Genesee.
Finkerton John, joiner, h 310 N Third.
Fink Ernest, carpenter, 319 S Water.
First National Bank, E T Judd Pres't. J L Ketchum Vice Pres't, L A Clark Cashier, 114 S Washington.
Fisher Frederick, shoemaker, h 108 N Fourth.
Fisher Jacob, saloon, h 416 S Warren.
Fisher Jeremiah, builder, h 512 N Washington.
Fish W W, dry goods, 103 Genesee, bds Bancroft.
Fittinger Herman, vinegar manuf, h 1325 Tuscola.
Fitzgerald Edwin, laborer, h 524 N Rockwell,
Fitzgerald L, carpenter, bds 406 N Jefferson.
Fitzgerald William, spile driver, h 406 N Jefferson.
Flagler Henry M, salt manuf, (F & York), h 718 S Washington.
Flanders George A, (Thompson & Flanders), bds Everett House.
Flegle Charles H, teamster, h 903 Lapeer.
Flwelling James, carpenter, h 1002 Emerson.
Floyd Richard, boiler maker, h Warren.
Fogelsanger Emanuel, laborer, h 401 Millard.
Fogelsanger Emanuel, miller h 419 S Cass.
Foley Thomas R, painter, h 429 S Warren.
Forey Thomas, laborer, bds 219 S Water.
Forin Thomas, laborer, bds 1231 S Water.
Forrest Daniel, shoemaker, h 109 S Fifth.
Forsyth C, cabinet maker, bds 708 N Jefferson.
Forsyth James, cabinet maker, bds 708 N Jefferson.
Fosmire, John A, h 314 N Third.
Fosmire William H, bds 314 N Third.
Foster S A, machinist, h 519 N Washington.
Fournier Peter, laborer, h 1023 S Water.
Fox G B, h 103 S Wells.
Fox Lucien H, (Perkins & F), 101 Genesee, h Cherry.
Foot Washington, (col'd), plasterer, h 405 N Webster.
Frank George, book keeper, bds 224 S Webster.
Frank Henry, mason, h 412 N Rockwell.
Frank John, butcher, h S Water.

Frank John, butcher, bds 705 German.
Frank John, tanner, h 705 German.
Franklin John, harness maker, bds S Washington.
Frazier Patrick, h 1121 S Water.
Freedman H, teacher of the Jews, h 105 S Clay.
Freeman Michael, engineer city mills, h 414 S Washington.
Freight Depot, (F & P M R R), R Bell agt, 801 N Washington.
Freman Nathan, laborer, h N Water, near McLane's mill.
French Mrs Mary A, (col'd), washer woman, h 316 N Warren.
Fretta Henry, laborer, h 308 N Franklin.
Frey J. F & Co, (J F F & H H W), books & stationery, 213 Genesee.
Frey John F, (Frey & Co), h 104 Jefferson.
Frey Julius T, book binder, 213 Genesee, h 119 N Webster.
Frey Simon, teamster, h 611 N Franklin.
Fricke Charles, cigar maker, bds German.
Fritz John, cigar maker, 125 N Jefferson, h same.
Fritz Frederick, laborer, h 205 S Fourth.
Frizelle Charles S, (F & Bro), 119 Genesee.
Frizelle Bros, (C S S, & F F), drugs, 119 Genesee.
Frizelle Seymour F, (F & Bro), bds Bancroft House.
Frost Weston, h 802 S Washington.
Fughman Henry, tanner, h plank road.
Fust Jacob, laborer, h 410 N Rockwell.

G

GAGE CHAUNCEY H, (G & Lewis), bds 829 S Washington.
Gage D W C, lawyer, h 1103 S Water.
Gage G B, apprentice, bds 829 S Washington.
GAGE & LEWIS, (C H G, & W A L), lawyers, 101 Genesee.
Gage Mrs Abigal, h 1107 S Water.
Gage Morgan L, saddler, h 829 S Washington.
Gallaher John, (G, Mead & Deering), h 1218 S Jefferson.
Gallaher M H, insurance agt, 101 S Washington, h Park avenue.
Galinfell Frank, laborer, h 223 N Cass.
Gamble James, (Gillett & G), bds 511 S Jefferson.
Ganshaw Frederick, patern maker, res Sag City.
Gansman Henry, shoemaker, bds 316 S Webster.
Gardner Charles, farmer, h 1218 S Jefferson.
Gardner F F, salt manuf, h 210 S Warren.
Gardner Fritz, shoemaker, h 924 S Webster.
GARRIGUES Dr. S S, (Wadsworth & Co), h 235 N Washington.
Garrison Charles O, lumberman, h 704 N Franklin.
Gartner Frederick G, saloon, 313 Genesee, h same.
Gartner Fritz, saloon, h 315 Elm.
Garvey James, laborer, h 211 N Cass.

LENHEIM & IDDINGS,

SUCCESSORS TO L. S. LENHEIM,

Manufacturers of and Wholesale Dealers in

BOOTS, SHOES & LEATHER,

Call and examine our Stock before purchasing elsewhere. Our motto is "quick sales and small profits."

No. 211, Genesee Street, Everett Block.

STOP! STOP!! STOP!!!

AT

FRANK JOHNSON'S

AND YOU WILL FIND A COMPLETE STOCK OF

Groceries & Provisions,

Which are sold at the lowest cash price.

No. 306, Genesee Street.

☞BROWN & JAMES, Attorneys and Land Agents,

Garvey Philip, laborer, h 211 William.
Garvey Thomas, bds 1211 William.
Garvin Miss M A, dress maker, 204 N Washington.
Gates A W, (A W Gates & Co), h 211 N Washington.
Gates A W & Co, livery & stage office, 201 N Washington.
Gaven Dominick, laborer, h 221 S Franklin.
Geable John, watch maker, bds Johnson.
Gehlert John J, tinsmith, 401 Genesee, h cor Cass and Genesee.
Geisler Peter, carpenter and joiner, h 104 S Jefferson.
Gelinas Alexander, carpenter, h 410 N Franklin.
Gelinas O, cabinet maker, 109 S Franklin, h 410 S Franklin.
Germain Edward, jr, carpenter, bds 321 N Third.
Germain Edward, sen, carpenter, h 321 N Third.
Germain Thomas, builder, 411 Tuscola, h 201 N Jefferson.
German Dancing Hall, 202 N Third.
German English school, C Watz principal, 110 N Third.
German Hall Turning Society, 102 N Third.
German Methodist Church, 115 N Warren.
Gerow Joseph, saloon, 209 Millard, h same.
Geztner John, laborer, h 313 First.
Gibb John, carpenter, h east of N Sixth, near Tuscola.
Gibel John, clerk, bds 1024 Johnson.
Gibson Mrs J, (col'd), dress maker, h 1217 Johnson.
Gibson Robert, harness maker, bds with Mrs. Packer.
Gies George H, printer, bds Tuscola, with Mr. Joslin.
Gilbert Martin, lumberman, bds Bancroft House.
Giles John, engineer, h 601 N Fourth.
Gillett & Gamble, lawyers, 204 Genesee 2d floor.
Gillett William (G & Gamble) bds 705 S Jefferson.
Gillett Miss M C, school teacher, bds Washington.
Gilmore Geo F, bds 803 William.
Gilmore Patrick, lab, h 420 N Fifth.
Gilmore Robert, bds 424 Fitzhugh.
Giseman John, mason, h 115 S Sixth.
Glasby Wm F, bridge builder, h 407 S Water.
Glassar G, lab, h 621 Maple.
Gleason Authur, (E H G & Son,) bds Everett House.
Gleason E H (E H G & Son,) h 412 Carroll.
Gleason E H & Son, grocers, 107 N Washington.
Glenz Charles, shoemaker, h 511 Lapeer.
Glover Henry H, painter, h 617 S Webster.
Glover Justice J, lawyer, h 701 Fitzhugh.
Glover O L, house and sign painter, 208 N Water, h 201 S Fifth.
Gochal William, h 305 S Water.
Goddard Ezra G, civil engineer & surveyor, 101 Genesee, h 509 Thompson.
Godley William, livery stable, h 511 Genesee.

Goeschell Edward. (H & E Goeschell) h 1417 Genesee.
Goeschell Hermann, (G, H & E G), h 509 Lapeer.
Goeschell H & E, grocers, 908 Genesee.
Goeschell Louis, clerk, bds 1417 Genesee.
Gohret George M, lab, h Genesee.
Golden George, machinist, h Warren.
Goldie Wm F, clerk, bds Webster.
Goldie Adam, book keeper, h 215 S Webster.
Good Henry, machinist, h 609 Carroll.
Goodell A E, bakery, 131 N Washington, bds Everett House.
Gooding C E, clerk, h 322 N Cass.
Gooding Duncan W, h 322 N Cass.
Gooding & Hawkins, forwarding & commission merchants, 123 and 125 N Water.
Goodridge Brothers, (G J & W G), photographers, 103 N Washington, 3d floor.
Goodridge, G J, (G & Brother), 103 N Washington.
Goodridge Wallace, (G & Bro), bds 321 Genesee.
Goppelt John, h 407 Hayden.
Gordon Thomas, sailor, h 415 S Warren.
Goss George, lab. h 409 S Washington.
Gothrie Calvin, foreman saw mill, h 1101 S Jefferson.
Goulding Geo W, machinist, bds 319 N Warren.
Gould O A, lumberman, h 218 S Washington.
Gouthery Calvin, sawyer, h 1017 S Jefferson.
Gradt Leonard, photographer, bds 502 N Water.
Graham William, bar keeper, bds Sag Valley Hotel.
Grant Chas W, lumberman, bds Everett House.
Grant William, mason, bds 212 Millard.
Graswieser Joseph, laborer, S Washington, back of B S Works.
Graves Miss H E, tailoress, bds 511 Genesee.
Gravier Edwin, saloon, 202 N Washington, h 213 N Washington.
Grayge Charles, sailor, h 623 Maple.
Gray John, laborer, h 309 S Water.
Gray William N, clothing, 121 Genesee, h Washington.
Great Western R R Ticket Agency, A Ferguson agt, 103 S Washington.
Green Daniel, laborer, h 116 N Fourth.
Green James, lab, h N Washington, near E Sag Salt Works.
Green Patrick, lab, h N Washington, near E Sag Salt Works.
Green R H, moulder, h 406 Maple.
Green Richard, moulder, h 916 Emerson.
Gregory William, carpenter, h 221 N Cass.
Gridley G W, (Haskins & G), bds Mason.
Griese Charles, barber, bds First.
Griffin B, printer, bds 219 S Water.

Griffis Miss Sarah, boarding house, 712 S Washington.
Grinnell Mrs M P, boarding house 423 N Washington.
Grinnell Sebastian, lab, h near E Sag Salt Works.
Griwi Henry, lab, h 206 S Fourth.
Grove William W, lab, h 720 N Franklin.
Grover John W, bds 121 N Franklin.
Grubbe James, blacksmith, bds 214 N Cass.
Gunther Ephraim, teacher, h 219 S Third.
Guiler George W, carpenter & joiner, h 501 Wells.
Guyer John, cabinet maker, bds Genesee.

H

Haas, Andrew, boiler maker, h James,
Haag, Joseph, lab, h 121 N Cass.
Haben John, lab, h 315 S Warren.
Haddesley William, carp, h 208 N Cherry.
Hade Frederick, butcher, bds 308 S Webster.
Haight John, h 122 S Clay.
Haike Philip, carp and joiner, h 106 S Rockwell.
Hale F T, foreman Shaw R & Co, h 320 S Washington.
Hale Henry, tinsmith, h 320 S Washington.
Hales Lewis, Gardner, h Webster.
Hall D S, physician, 125 N Washington, h 218 N Water.
Hall Henry, lab, h 110 N Rockwell.
HALL JOHNATHAN, (Brown, H & James,) h 812 Hoyt.
Hall L C, book keeper, (with D F Rose,) 101 Genesee, h First.
Hall Mrs C, h 324 Astor.
Hall Mrs J, dress maker, bds Everett House.
Hall Oscar, h 406 S Warren.
Hall Thomas, lab, h 322 N Third.
Hallock Fred M, (Stoddard & H,) bds Bancroft.
Hallock H H, clerk bds Everett.
Hames James H, carpenter and Joiner, h 217 Maple.
Hames John, painter, h 210 German.
Hamill James B, h 311 S Jefferson.
Hamilton Charles, book keeper, bds N Washington.
Hamilton Samuel, bar keeper, bds Bancroft.
Hammell Mrs W, h 317 S Water.
Hammond Clarence W, clerk bds Everett House.
Hammond Mrs E G, milliner and dress maker, 109 S Washington, h same.
Hand Mrs Ellen, grocery, 114 N Cass, h same.
Hansel Mathias, lab, h 1002 Tuscola.
Harber Alexander, carpenter and Joiner, h 308 N Franklin.
Harder James, Farmer, bds 1002 S Jefferson.
Harden James, watchman, W & Eastman, h Mason.
Harkness W K, salt manuf, h 614 S Washington.

Hayden Frederick, lab, h 213 N Cass.
Harnden Mrs Clara, seamstress, h 1007 Lapeer.
Harney George, (Town & H,) h 101 S Washington.
Harnish Frederick, segar maker h 122 S Fourth.
Huron Log Booming Co, E Eddy Pres't, J L Ketchum Treas. 113 S Water,
Harris Charles, teamster, h 702 N Warren.
Harris James, prop'r Monitor House, 623 N Washington.
Harris J B, clerk, bds 623 N Washington.
Harris John, clothing, h 115 Lapeer.
HARRISON H L, (Elliott & H,) bds Everett House.
Hart John, carpenter, h 224 Cornelia.
Harteau Zoel, (Cholet & H,) 125 S Water, bds William.
Hartigan Edward, cooper, h N Washington, near East Saginaw salt works.
Hartigan Patrick, carpenter, h 821 Emerson.
Hartman John, cabinet maker, bds Genesee.
Haskell E W, sailor, bds 502 S water.
Haskel S V, clerk, bds 112 N Washington.
Haskins Horace R, (H & Guiley,) h 602 Mason.
Haskins & Guiley, machinists, 516 Mason.
Hatch Alva, carpenter and joiner, h 612 N Washington.
Hathaway Horace, h 901 S Washington.
Hatt John, lab, h N East end Tuscola.
Hatton Wm W, street commissioner, h 913 Hoyt.
Haufner John, lab, h 422 N Fourth.
Haumbarger Charles, carpenter, h 608 Lapeer.
Hawkins Charles, lab, h 623 N Franklin.
Hawkins Wesley, (Gooding & H,) bds Everett House.
Hawkins William, shoemaker, h East of N Sixth near Tuscola.
Hayden Charles, lab, bds 407 S Warren.
Hayden John, lumber inspector, h 424 N Fifth.
Hayden Miss L A, school teacher, bds Washington.
Hay George, blacksmith, 210 Tuscola, bds 123 N Washington.
Hayslop John, lab, bds 625 N Franklin.
Hazard Rowland, machinist, bds 712 S Washington.
Hazard Thomas, foreman A W Gates & Co, h 210 S Washington.
Hedley William, lab, h N Washington, near E Sag salt works.
Heidecker Frederick, (Moye, H & Weiss,) bds Webster.
Heineman Charles, upholsterer, h Lapeer.
Heinlein George, tailor, h 501 N Fifth.
Heinlein Henry, merchant tailor, 409 Genesee, h 403 Lapeer.
Heinlein Wolfgang, brewer, h 407 McKrosky.
Held George, blacksmith, h 703 Tuscola.
Heller A, upholsterer, h 1703 Johnson.
Heminger O, carpenter, h 413 N Second.
Henckley James A, U S revenue office, h 803 William.

EAST SAGINAW
Steam Boiler Works.

THOS. STEELE,
MANUFACTURER OF

High and Low

Pressure Boilers,

In rear of Eagle Foundry, No. 112 Mason St.
EAST SAGINAW, MICH.

Locomotive and Tubular Boilers, and all other description of

BOILER WORK,

Also, Sheet Iron Breeching and Smoke Pipe made to any dimensions.

Work done as cheap as can be obtained at any point West.

Refer to all Steamboat men and Mill owners on Saginaw River.

☞BROWN & JAMES, Attorneys and Land Agents,

Hendrick John, lab, h 615 Maple,
Hennings Christopher, watchman Wickes Bros.
Hennings John, lab, h 120 N Webster.
Henry Robert, carpenter, h 313 N Second.
Henselman John, tinsmith, 701 German, h, same.
Hepinstall Miss, school teacher, 511 Millard, bds Hoyt.
Herbage Daniel, painter, bds 708 N Jefferson.
Herbert Frederick, book keeper, h 209 Hoyt.
Herb Francis J, jeweler, 213 Genesee, h 219 S Webster.
Hergarty Patrick, lab, h 306 Cornelia,
Herpel Ernst, furniture, 115 N Jefferson, h same.
Herring F W, physician, 816 Genesee, h same.
Herring Henry P, (Wheeler & H,), 101 Genesee, res Sag City.
Herteau Zoel, bowling saloon, bds 111 Hayden.
Hess D F, tailor, h 212 N Washington.
Hess M B, office 2 Arcade Block, N Washington, bds Bancroft.
Hesse B, physician, h 813 William.
Hesse Wm, lab, h 1802 Johnson.
Heston L, propr Saginaw Valley hotel, 116 N Water.
Hibernia Hotel, O'Brien Martin propr, 724 N Washington.
Hickey John, lab, bds 219 S Water.
Hickey S, carp & joiner, h 907 Johnson.
Hicks D C, sawyer, h 1024 S Jefferson.
Hicks G W, (col'd, upholsterer, 236 S Washington, h Franklin.
Hicks Joseph, lab, bds 218 N Third.
Higgins Thomas, lab, bds Saginaw Valley House.
Hilborn Henry, cook, h 407 Fitzhugh.
Hilliard Jackson M, grocer, h 305 Lapeer.
Hilliard J H, saloon, 105 N Washington, h 515 Fitzhugh.
Hill George W, baker, bds Sherman House.
Hill James H, (H & Morris), h 405 S Jefferson.
Hill Louis, lab, h 308 N Franklin.
Hill & Morris, (J H H & Geo M), proprs pioneer iron works 901 S Water.
Hill S B, lumberman, h 310 S Jefferson.
Hineman Charles, upholsterer, h 110 N Warren.
Hodgson Mark, engineer, h 614 S Jefferson.
Hodson William, lumberman, h 317 N Jefferson.
Hodson Thomas, sash and door maker, h 214 N Fourth.
Hœrner Charles, (G H & Co), h 212 N Third.
Hœrner Geo & Co, (Geo & Chas H), grocers, 627 Hoyt.
Hœrner George (H & Co), h 212 N Third.
Hoffman Ernst, lab, h 602 Thompson.
Hoffman Henry, tanner, h 1565 Genesee.
Hoisington Geo, lab, h 1020 James.
Holden Peter, lab, h 102 Tenth.
Holland D G, (F W Carlisle & Co), h 402 N Water.

Holland & Derby, (D G H & B P D), proprs E Sag lime works, 510 N Water.
Holmes Charles A, insurance agt, office 3 Hess Block, h 221 S Fourth.
Holmes Mrs M, h 417 S Water.
Holmes Thomas, devil, Courier office, bds 417 S Water.
Holst Henry, lab, h 613 N Franklin.
Holtz Daniel, carp, h 616 N Washington.
Holtz John, lab, h 616 N Washington.
Holyede Frederick, shoemaker, 703 German, bds 701 German.
Honner Frank, lab, h 219 N Webster.
Horton Henry D, lab, h 920 Emerson.
Hosey William, saddler, bds 411 S Washington.
Hotchkiss W H. tinsmith, bds Warren street.
Hough E A. grocer, 104 N Washington, h 314 S Warren.
Hough J J, clerk, bds 309 S Webster.
Hough Mrs Mary A, h 309 S Webster.
Houlahan James, lab, bds 324 N Fourth.
Houlahan Michael; lab, h 324 N Fourth.
Houlahan Phillip, lab, bds 324 N Fourth.
Houlahan Thomas, lab, bds, 324 N Fourth.
Hould Ohesime H, lab, bds Sag Valley Hotel.
Hover Mrs. C, h 412 First.
Hovey L B, harness maker, 206 N Washington, h 806 Lapeer.
Hovey Luscius D, student, bds 806 Lapeer.
Howard & Brother, (W J & P L H), grocers, 125 N Washington.
Howard Daniel F, joiner, h 404 First.
Howard John, (col'd), waiter Bancroft.
Howard Porter L, (H & Bro), bds 201 N Franklin.
Howard W I, (H & Brother), h 201 N Franklin.
Howard William, (col'd), waiter, Bancroft.
Hoyt D, assistant cashier Merch'ts National Bank, bds Bancroft.
Hoyt Henry H, lawyer, 101 Genesee bds 618 N Franklin.
Hoyt F E, book keeper Mayflower mill, h 420 N Water.
Hubbard George, carpenter, h 1407, Genesee.
Hubbard Willard A, carp, h 305 Lapeer.
Hubbell Thomas M, boat builder, h 610 N Franklin.
Hubert Frederick, meat market, 114 N Washington, h 117 N Franklin.
Hubert Joseph, butcher, h 117 N Franklin.
Hudson Mrs, h 410 Potter.
Hull W Hooker, (C H Smith & Co), bds 112 Hayden.
Humbler Joseph, saloon, 102 N Cass, bds 423 N Third.
Humes James, carpenter & joiner, h 223 Maple.
Humes John, machinist, h 1212 Mason.
*Humphrey D F, auctioneer, h 410 S Washington.

☞BROWN & JAMES, Attorneys and Land Agents,

Humphrey George, cooper, h 423 Tuscola.
Hunt A D, lumberman, h 207 Lapeer.
Hunt Geo W, mason, h 1531, Genesee.
Hunter A H, lumber inspector, 122 N Water, h 416 N Water.
Hunter A G, clerk, bds 416 N Water.
Huntley Mrs H, h 112 N Fourth.
Hutton Thomas, bds 1513 Genesee.
Hutton Wm, lab, h 1513 Genesee.
Hutzel Joseph, musician, h 516 N Franklin.

I

Iddings R M, (Lenheim & I), bds 315 S Washington.
Ingersoll S M, harness maker, h 116 N Fifth.
Ingleman H, (col'd), lab, h 725 Maple.
Irwin Patrick, bar tender, bds 724 N Washington.
Ivey John, bds Bancroft House.

J

Jaby Joseph, cartman, h 624 S Jefferson.
Jackson A, h 701 S Jefferson.
Jackson A E, grocer, 511 S Washington, h 505 S Washington.
Jackson Andrew, (col'd), lab, h 1203 Johnson.
Jackson Frederick, lab, h 115 S Third.
Jackson James B, h 701 S Jefferson.
Jacob Christian, carp, h 324 N Sixth.
Jahuke Charles, lab, h 211 N Webster.
Jahutt Thomas, carp, h 310 N Fourth.
Jajk John, lab, h 206 N Fourth.
JAMES THOMAS M, (Brown H & James) h cor Wells & Park avenue.
Janes W C, (Bliss, J & Co), h 418 S Washington.
Jarner Moses, h 625 Tuscola.
Jeffers Edward, lumberman, bds 408 Carroll.
Jeffers John, book keeper, bds 408 Carroll.
Jeffers John, hotel propr, 1231 S Water.
Jeffers Michael, comptroller, 102 N Washington, h 408 Carroll.
Jenks L S, clerk, bds N Water.
Jewett Geo W, bds 716 N Franklin.
Jewett Horace W, lumberman, h 716 N Franklin.
Jewett Volney H, clerk, bds 716 N Franklin.
JOB PRINTING, OFFICE, (Lewis & Lyon propr's,) 103 S Washington, 4th floor.
Johnson Benjamin, (col'd), waiter, Bancroft.
Johnson C F, carp, h 423 S Washington.
Johnson Elizabeth, washer woman, bds 215 William.
Johnson Frank, grocer, 306 Genesee, bds Everett House.

J. C. WHALEN & SON,

Wholesale and Retail Dealers in

GROCERIES & PROVISIONS,

No. 222, South Washington Street.

Cash Paid for all kinds of Country Produce.

Our Stock is Fresh and Complete.
Call and examine.

JOHN McKAY'S

SALOON AND RESTAURANT;

ALSO WHOLESALE DEALER IN

Fresh Fish, Oysters and Game,

No. 126, S. Washington St., East Saginaw.

FRED A. KŒHLER,

Carries on the

Blacksmithing Business

In all its branches. Work done with neatness and dispatch.
Special attention given to HORSE-SHOEING and
WAGON IRONING.
No. 212, Tuscola St. near Water,

EAST SAGINAW, MICH.

NARRAGANSETT INSURANCE Co., Providence,

Johnson Ira H, carp, h 513 James.
Johnson James, teamster, h 808 Lapeer.
Johnson J B, clerk, h 109 S Sixth.
Johnson Mark S, lab, h 409 N Webster.
Johnson Miss Aville, dress maker, h Hoyt.
Johnson Miss Louise, school teacher, bds Genesee.
Johnson Myron A, book keeper, bds N Washington.
Johnson Quincy, h 1014 Emerson.
Johnson Wm, moulder, h 616 Miller.
Jones C B, lumber dealer, h 813 S Washington.
Jones C, farmer, bds 625 Maple.
Jones Monroe, cider & vinegar manuf, 424 N Franklin, h same.
Joslin Charles M, lumber inspector, 101 Genesee, bds S Washington.
Joslin Harvey, lawyer, 101 Genesee, h 220 S Webster.
Joslin Perry, editor & manager Daily & Weekly Enterprise, h 207 Tuscola.
Judd E T, Pres't first National Bank, 114 S Washington, h 413 N Jefferson.

K

Katchwits Wm, lab, h 215 N Webster.
Kain Michael, saloon, 620 N Washington, h same.
Kaiser Jacob J, jr, blacksmith, bds 316 S Webster.
Kaiser Jacob, sen, blacksmith, h 211 S Webster.
Kapitan Joseph, cooper.
Kapplinger John, drayman, h 106 N Warren.
Karns James, lab, h 213 S Sixth.
Kaye William, painter, bds 412 German.
Keeler D D, mason, h 209 Cherry.
Keeler F D, ticket agent, bds Everett House.
Keeling, W H, conductor F & P M R R, bds Bancroft.
Kehl Charles, carp, h 1608 Johnson.
Keisler Julius, lab, h 218 N Franklin.
Keisler Julius, lab, h 223 N Cass.
Kelly John, sailor, bds 122 N Cass.
Kencler John, mason, h 107, S Third.
Kennedy Daniel A, lumber dealer, h 525 Miller.
Kennedy M, tailor, 107 N Washington.
Kennedy Miss Annie, bds Bancroft.
Kenzher John, mason, h 107 S Third.
Kern William, carp, h 318 S Jefferson.
Kerr Thomas, lab, bds 524 Potter.
Kerwin M, carp, h 410 N Webster.
Kerwin Patrick, lab, h 123 S Fifth.
Ketchum J L & Co, lumbermen, 113 S Water.

Ketchum J L, (Vice Pres't first national bank, and J L K & Co) h 202 S Jefferson.
Keys Henry, (col'd), lab, h S Washington near B S Works.
Khrone Carl, lab, h 202 Lapeer.
Kilburn Henry, lab, h 411 N Warren.
Killian Charles, tobacconist, 407 Genesee, bds 405 Genesee.
Killian James, blacksmith, bds 405 Genesee.
Killinger Frederick, carp, h 1009 Johnson.
Kilpatrick James, harness maker, bds 623 Hoyt.
Kilpe Louis, mason, h 1021 James.
Kimball Erastus, lab, h 712 Emerson.
Kimball John, grocer, 103 Lapeer, h east of N Sixth near Tuscola.
King Charles, lab, h 1525 Genesee.
King Jacob, lab, h 716 S Washington.
Kingsbury Nelson, teamster, h 203 Wells.
Kinney Patrick, lab, h near E S works.
Kippmuller Adam M, drayman, h 411 James.
Kirckhoff Henry, clerk, h 602 Hoyt.
Kirby Adison, lath sawyer, h 801 S Jefferson.
Kirby Allen, ship carp, h 414 N Washington.
Kirby A R, saw repairer, h 502 Emerson.
Kirby Stephen R, architect, h 223 S Jefferson.
Kirwan William, harness maker.
Kissell C, lab, bds Deerfield road.
Kleinfeld Frances, sawyer, h 211 S Webster.
Klumpp Gottlieb, meat market, 105 Lapeer, h same.
Knapp Lucian, printer, bds Tuscola with Mr. Joslin.
Knapp S B, carp, and joiner, bds 802 S Washington.
Kneppel Charles, farmer, h 817 James.
Knickerbocker Wesley, foreman Buffalo Salt Co, bds 1121 S Water.
Knight Isaac R, lumberman, h 1001 S Water.
Koch L, laborer, h 522 First.
Koch Moses, clothier, 123 Genesee, bds Bancroft House.
Koehler, Emanuel, h 815 James.
Koehler F A, blacksmith, 212 Tuscola, h 214 N Cass.
Koehler Frank, lab, h 801 James.
Koenig Adolph, carp, h 501 Lapeer.
Kohn Caleb, lab, h 805 Maple.
Kohn F, lab, bds 801 Maple.
Korp Jacob, carp, h 216 N Webster.
Koster Adam, lab, h east end Tuscola.
Krekow Amil, baker, bds 107 Lapeer.
Krekow William, bakery, 107 Lapeer h same.
Kreutozberger John, lab, h 1024 S Webster.
Krohn Joseph, lab, h 413 Carroll.

Kroll Jerome P, insurance agt, bds 715 Genesee.
Krouser Herman, carp, h 119 S Third.
Kull Mrs. Caroline, bowling saloon, 709 Genesee, h same.
Kurtzman Lewis, saloon, 504 Lapeer, h same.
Kuster Adam, cooper, bds 828 Lapeer.
Kuster Geo A, lab, h 828 Lapeer.

L

Læaona Frederick, lab, bds 202 N Franklin.
Laird Henry, joiner, h 408 First.
Lambert Aaron, rule maker. h 1303 S Water.
Lambert Oliver, rule maker, h 1303 S Water.
Lambert Levi, cooper, bds 505 N Jefferson.
Lamb John C, engineer, h 901 S Jefferson.
Lamb John, lab, h 105 N Warren.
Land James A, conductor, F & P M R R, h 111 N Sixth.
Land John, saloon & boarding house, 122 N Jefferson.
Langa Guttlixe, saloon, 109 N Jefferson, h same.
Langdon Frederick, lab, h 206 N Rockwell.
Langebar Joseph, lab, h 1625 Johnson.
Lange William, shoemaker, (C H Smith & Co),
Lange William, brewer, bds S Washington, in the grove.
Langlass Charles, carp, h 1006 S Webster.
Langmær Christopher, tailor, h 114 N Rockwell.
Langschwage Frederick, tailor, h 211 S Third.
Lapham Zachariah T, engineer, 809 S Jefferson.
Laprese Edward, painter, bds Water.
Laraway Henry, carp. h 710 N Franklin.
Larkins John, machinist bds Everett House.
Lathrop G A, physician, bds 423 N Washington.
Laughlin Martin, lab, h 524 Potter.
Laughrey Robert, mason, h 710 Emerson.
Launer George, teamster, h 1514 Johnson.
Lavene George, lab, 1309 S Water.
Lavene Moses, lab, h 1309 S Water.
Lavene William, lab, bds 1309 S Water.
Lawrence Joseph, lumber inspector, h N east end Tuscola.
Layer Andrew, clerk, h Clay.
Leadbeater Mrs Helen, h 1231 S Washington.
Leaton John C, law student, bds 722 Hoyt.
Leaton J T, lumberman, h 722 Hoyt.
Leaton Wm C, bds 722 Hoyt.
Ledlie Gilbert W, clerk F & P M R R, bds 423 N Washington.
Lee Charles, lumberman, h 623 S Water.
Lee John, clerk, bds 112 N Washington.
Lee Joseph, boiler maker, h 608 Potter.

Ready-Made Clothing

HENRY MARKS,

The oldest dealer in

READY-MADE CLOTHING,

Hats, Caps, Furs, and

Gents' Furnishing Goods,

IN EAST SAGINAW.

He buys his Goods for Cash and is enabled to sell goods as low as the lowest.

He promises entire satisfaction to his customers. Remember his Store,

No. 115, Genesee Street, opposite the Bancroft House.

☞BROWN & JAMES, Attorneys and Land Agents,

Leesh Diedrick, lab, h 223 N Cass.
Leggett C W, apprentice, bds Everett House.
LEGGETT S T, jeweler, 105 S Washington, bds Bancroft House.
Lehman Paul, grocer, h 401 Lapeer.
Lehman Paul, clerk, bds 401 Lapeer.
Leigh William, carp, h 118 Cornelia.
LENHEIM & IDDINGS, (L S L & R M I), boots & shoes, 211 Genesee.
LENHEIM L S, (L & Iddings) h 624 Hoyt.
Lentz Simon, lab, bds 401 Millard.
Lenz William, clerk, h German.
Leonard J C, agt Chicago Salt & Lumber Co, bds Everett House.
Leonhardt Christopher, saloon, 102 N Cass, h 412 N Webster.
Lepp Peter, barber, bds First.
Leroy M F, city marshal, 104 Genesee, h 315 S Jefferson.
Leroy Milton, carriage maker, h 211 Maple.
Lester Harrison, bar keeper, bds 504 S Water.
Lewis Edwin, apprentice, bds 702 S Washington.
Lewis George, lumberman, h S Washington, south of old coloney road.
Lewis G F, stationer, 103 S Washington, (and Lewis & Lyon), h 616 S Washington.
Lewis James, h 702 S Washington.
Lewis & Lyon, (G F L & E W L), propr's Job Printing office, 103 S Washington, 4th floor.
LEWIS WILLIAM A, (G & Lewis), h 205 Hoyt.
Lewis Wm H, lab, h 1313 S Washington.
Lewitzkee Fritz, lab, h 525 First.
Leyer Andrew, clerk, h 108 N Clay.
Lidday Michael, tanner, h N Washington.
Lido John, lab, h 311 James.
Linderman J C, miller, city mills, h Water cor Thompson.
Lingham Henry, lumberman, h 709 Emerson.
Lipscomb E, millwright, h 208 N Cass.
Lipscomb Mrs A, washer woman, h 614 S Warren.
Lipscomb Nelson, lumberman, h 303 Hoyt.
Lirkey John, harness maker, h 210 N Fourth.
Litchfield E E, clerk, bds Bancroft.
Little M, capt tug traffic, h 801 S Water.
Little William, lab, bds Sag Valley House.
Little William N, h 1125 Carroll.
LITTLE W L P, Pres't Merchant's National Bank, h 306 N Water.
Livermore Samuel, farmer, h 1539 Genesee.
Livermore Seymour, carp, h 1314 Genesee.
Livingston Albert, waiter, bds Sag Valley House.
Livingston Daniel. ferryman, h N Water, near McLeans mill.

Livingston H C & Co, produce commission dealers, Benedict H W, agt, 223 N Water.
LIVINGSTON J R & Co, (J R L & R J T), dry goods 102 Genesee.
LIVINGSTON J R, (J R L & Co), bds Bancroft House.
Lloyd William, butcher, h 301 S Jefferson.
Lockley George, (with M H Gallaher), h 501 S Water.
Lockman Daniel, (col'd) drayman, h 401 Fitzhugh.
Lohmann Paul, grocer, h 513 Lapeer.
Lohrer, Martin, shoemaker, bds Genesee.
Longerman Frederick, lab, h 217 N Fourth.
Loomis Royal, (Burt & L), h 1412 Genesee.
Lophon L, h 923 S Jefferson.
Lopley John, lab, h 305 N Fourth.
Lorke Louis, harness maker, 107 S Cass, h Fourth.
Loundra Lewis, carp, h 616 Thompson.
LOVELAND WM J, (Clark & L), bds 608 N Washington.
Lowder Samuel, machinist, h 613 Maple.
Lull A, lumberman, h 201 N Chestnut.
Lung Frederick, baker, h 701 Lapeer.
LUSTER RICHARD, grocer, 325 Genesee, h 612 Tuscola
Luther J M, supt E S Salt Works, h 610 N Washington.
LYON E W, (Lewis & L), h 303 S Washington.
Lyon Robert, lab, h 603 N Washington.

M

McBeier Richard, grocer, 602 James, h same.
McCane Mrs Mary A, midwife, h 519 N Webster.
McCauly ——, dressmaker, 235 S Washington.
McLean Chester, carp & joiner, 109 S Franklin, h 515 Millard.
McClellan Francis, carp, h 412 German.
McClenen Robert, painter, h N east end Tuscola.
McComb Joseph, carp, bds 709 Maple.
McCormick Archibald, lumberman, bds 723 S Washington.
McCormick James, lumberman, h 723 S Washington.
McDonenall James R, lumberman, bds 118 N Franklin.
McDoneath Mrs L, h 317 N Fourth.
McDonald W F, saloon, bds 113 N Cass.
McDonald William, saloon, 318 Genesee, h same.
McDougall R B, h 317 First.
McEachron Peter, builder, 117 S Cass, h 613 Thompson.
McFadden Robert, lab, h 631 Maple.
McFairish A, lumberman, h 222 N Rockwell.
McFarlin John H, builder, 116 N Jefferson, h 622 Johnson.
McFarlin Peter, carp, h 123 S Fifth.
McFarlin Silas, clerk, bds 622 Johnson.

☞BROWN & JAMES, Attorneys and Land Agents,

McHale M, h 220 N Fifth.
McHale Patrick, shoemaker, h 220 N Fifth.
McIntire Daniel, lab, h N Washington, near E Sag Salt works.
McIntee Patrick, carp, h 518 N Washington.
McKay John, lab, h 1208 Mason.
McKay John, saloon, 126 S Washington, h same.
McKay Mrs Mary H, saloon, 118 N Franklin, h same.
McKee Thomas W, clerk, bds 312 S Warren.
McKenney John, engineer, bds 724 N Washington.
McKenzie Robert, moulder, h 516 Maple.
McKenzie Wm, lab, bds 1223 S Water.
McKinney E W, carp, bds S Washington.
McKnight William A, teller C K R & Co's Bank, bds 110 Hoyt.
McKnight William, bridge tender, (Bristol street bridge), h 110 Hoyt.
McLane C C, lumberman, 105 South Washington, h 520 North Franklin.
McLanes mill, L McLane, propr, N Water, near E S salt works.
Mclane Murdoch, lab, h 315 S Water.
McLane Seth, lumberman, 105 S Washington, h 603 Jefferson.
McLaughlin Elijah, mason, h 820 Hoyt.
McCleary Thompson, carp, h 422 Potter.
McLellon Francis, cabinet maker, 109 S Cass, h same.
McMillan C S, book keeper, (Shaw, Reynolds & Co,) bds Washington.
McMillen John, lab, bds 625 N Franklin.
McSweeney Edward, gardner, h 1202 Genesee.
McSweeney Miles, blacksmith, h Fitzhugh.
McVicar John, mason, bds 412 German.
McWethy F F, h 115 S Webster.
McWethy L D, h 115 S Webster.
MACK JAMES, (Wilkin & Mack), bds Everett House.
Maddigan John; lab, h 216 N Fourth.
Maguire James, lab, h 520 N Water.
Maham Daniel, h 701 S Webster.
Maher John, plasterer, h 519 Wells.
Maier William, lab, h 125 S Franklin.
Major George, shoemaker, bds 221 N Cass.
Major John, lab, h 221 N Cass.
Malcom Warren, lab, h 205 Millard.
Malone Josh C, (col'd), waiter Bancroft.
Maloney John, lab, h 510 Wells.
Maloney M, lab, bds 510 Wells.
Maridelle Horace, harness maker, h Maple.
Mann Frederick, bakery, 402 Potter, h 518 Potter.
Mann H S, bds 803 William.
Mann Thomas, yard man, Bancroft House.

Marcello Charles, lab, h 823 S Water.
MARKS HENRY, clothing, 114 S Water & 115 Genesee.
Marks John, (W Zimmerman & Co), h 105 S Warren.
Marr Benjamin F, cabinet maker, h 925 S Jefferson.
Marrie Sanck, shoemaker, h 854 Lapeer.
Marsky Charles F, (Schwartz & M), h 222 S Third.
Martindale Miss Jennie, milliner, bds Everett House.
Martin Ellen, (col'd) washer woman, h 215 William.
Martin Joseph, brick-layer, h 717 Maple.
Martin Mrs Ellen, (col'd), washer woman, h 107 S Franklin.
Martin Robert, carp, h 224 N Sixth,
Masonic Lodge Room, 104 Genesee, 3d floor.
Mason Edward M, Principal Union School, h 1551 Genesee.
Mason John B, painter, h 1211 Tuscola.
Mason John, h 706 Carroll.
Mason L P, (Estabrook & M), h 215 S Jefferson.
Mason O L, physician, 125 N Washington.
Massbacher Frederick, physician, 101 Lapeer.
Massey Charles, lighterman, h 1031 S Washington.
Masauret T, groceries and provisions, 116 N Washington.
MATHER E G, clerk Bancroft House.
Maurrer George, h 123 S Fourth.
Mautner S & A, clothing, 204 Genesee.
Mayer Frank W, clerk, bds 123 N Washington.
Mayflower mills, W L P Little agt, 424 N Water.
MEAD A P, (Gallaher, M & D), h 307 Hoyt.
MEANY STEPHEN, capt, steamer L G Mason, h 524 N Washington.
Meidlain John, bakery 124 N Franklin, h same.
Meitzer L, peddler, h 119 Lapeer.
Melchers Henry, druggist 102 N Jefferson, bds Lapeer.
Mellville John, cook, h 317 N Second.
Mendell Henry, boiler maker, h 625 Maple.
Mendell Horace, harness maker, h 625 Maple.
Merchants' National Bank, W L P Little Pres't. James Brown, Cashier, 114 Genesee.
Merrill A J, lab, bds 913 S Washington.
Merrill Ezil, carp, h 1612 Genesee.
Merrill Geo C, machinist, h 805 Hoyt.
MERRILL G W, machinist, 1002 S Water, bds 1123 S Water.
Merrill Henry, stage driver, bds Sag Valley House.
Merrill R W, machinist, h 913 S Washington.
Merrill Wm M, sup't Albany City Salt Co, h 618 N Warren.
Mershon Abraham, lab, bds 1209 S Water.
Mershon A H, planing mill, 624 S Water, h 314 N Washington.
Mershon James E, telegraph operator, h 419 N Franklin.
Mershon J H, lumberman, 401 Potter, h 420 N Washington.

☞BROWN & JAMES, Attorneys and Land Agents,

Mershon Joseph, lab, bds 1209 S Water.
Mershon Mathew, stage driver, bds Saginaw Valley House.
Mershon Peter, lab, h 1209 S Water.
Methodist Church, 201 S Washington.
Meyer Charles T. saloon, 308 Potter, h same.
Meyer John G, music teacher, h 516 N Franklin.
Michal Patrick, shoemaker, h 225 N Sixth.
Michigan Salt Co, D K Allington Sup't, 113 S Water.
Mickley Geo. P, (Mosher & M), h 320 Astor.
Mickley Samuel. clerk, bds 320 Astor.
MIDLER A J, (Root & M), bds Everett House.
Middleton Joseph, machinist, bds S Water.
Mier William, teamster, h 301 German.
Millard Charles, shoemaker, bds 316 S Webster.
Millard James, machinist, h 514 Potter.
Miller Albert, carp & joiner, bds 1608 Johnson.
Miller E, carp, bds 1608 Johnson.
Miller H, Justice of the Peace, 101 Genesee, h 1026 S Washington.
Miller John, Boarding House, 601 S Water.
Miller John, lab, bds 207 S Water.
Miller John lab, h 208 S Fifth.
Miller John H. tinner, h 124 N Warren.
Miller Louis, lab, h 407 James.
Miller Richard, carp, bds 316 N Franklin.
Miller R, wagon maker, h 210 S Clay.
Miller Wm F, sailor, bds 625 N Franklin.
Mills John, carp, h 1019 Lapeer.
Milne John S, carp, h 208 Lapeer..
Milner George, lumberman, bds Everett House.
Minnick Mathew, h 415 S Washington.
Mitchell Alexander, jr, clerk, bds 702 Thompson.
Mitchell Alexander, sen, grocer, 233 S Washington, h 702 Thompson.
Mitchell Charles H, clerk, bds Everett House.
Mitchell George A, lumberman, bds 707 N Jefferson.
Mittermeir Elizabeth, h 807 William.
Mœller F J & Co, real estate agency, 402 Genesee.
Mœller F J, (Mœller F J & Co), h 909 Lapeer.
Moilas George, lab, h 104 Seventh.
Moilas Henry, lab, h 220 N Webster.
Moilas James, lab, bds 220 N Webster.
Moilas John, lab, bds 220 N Webster.
Moilas William, lab, bds 220 N Webster.
Molco Charles, lab, h 202 N Franklin.
Monitor House, James Harris propr, 623 N Washington.
Monroe William, lab, h 210 N Franklin.

☞HALL & JAMES, General Insurance Agents,

Montgomery George W, lab, bds 712 S Washington.
Montgomery William, clerk, h 512 Maple.
Montgomery William, grocer, h 512 Maple.
Montonye Robert, turner, h 1602 Johnson.
Moore Frederick, carp, h 1024 S Warren.
Moore V R, clerk, bds 423 N Washington.
Moore William, lab, h 622 Thompson.
Moreau James, ship caulker, bds 308 Potter.
Morehouse Rev Henry L, Pastor Baptist Church, bds 109 S Jefferson.
Morey Horace, grocer. bds Metropolitan Hotel.
Morey Samuel, grocer, h 407 Millard.
Morgan M, shoemaker, 117 N Jefferson, h same.
Morgan Richard R, farmer, h 214 Seventh.
Morgan William W, moulder, h 522 Maple.
Moriarty Michael, lab, h 612 S Franklin.
Morley Bros, (G W, C H & E W M,) hardware dealers, 110 & 112 S Water.
Morley C H, (M Bros), h 606 N Warren.
Morley E W, (M Bros), bds Bancroft.
Morley G W, (M Bros), bds Bancroft.
Morley M, lab, h 814 Lapeer.
Moross Columbus V, architect and builder, h 607 Lapeer.
Morris Edward, tailor, h 423 N Washington.
Morris George, (Hill & Morris). h 512 Thompson.
Morris M B, lumberman, h 207 Maple.
Morris T E, clerk, bds 423 N Washington.
Morris Wm E, tinsmith, h 101 S Jefferson.
Morrison Geo, saloon, 114 N Franklin, h same.
Morrison J S, Boarding House, 213 S Water.
Morrison Miss E J, milliner, 108 N Washington, h same,
Morrisy Michael, tailor, h 608 S Jefferson.
Morse N B, lumberman, h 207 Maple.
Morse Oscar F, clerk, bds 207 Maple.
Morsheetz John H, boiler maker, 209 S Rockwell, h Third.
Mosher Mickley, (T R M & G P M), grocers, 323 Genesee.
Mosher T B, bds Bancroft.
Mosher Thomas R, (M & Mickley,) h 525 N Jefferson.
Mosher Adelbert Z, Printer, bds Everett House.
Moss Thomas, contractor, h 317 Park.
Moulton G E, bds Bancroft.
Mower Brothers, (M C & T D M), ice dealers, 1223 S Water.
Mower M C, (M & Bros), h 624 Hoyt.
Mower T D, (M & Bros), h Bristol.
Moye Albert, (M H & Weiss), h 812 Tuscola.
Moye Hidecker & Wiess, meat market, 625 Hoyt.
Mumford P, h 408 Millard.

Murdock Andrew, sailor, h 907 S Webster.
Murdock David, sailor, bds 502 N Water.
Murdock John lab, h 302 German.
Murdock Peter, capt vessel, bds 416 N Water.
Murdock Samuel, sailor, bds 502 N Water.
Murphy F J, lumber dealer, 104 N Washington.
Murray Andrew, teamster, h 811 Millard,
Murray Patrick, lab, bds 104 Seventh.

N

Nagle P W, (N & Willard), h 123 S Sixth.
Nagle & Willard, (P W N & J C W), grocers, 113 N Water.
Nash Thomas, carp & joiner, h 924 S Jefferson.
Naterd Frederick, lab, h 312 S Warren.
Nay O W, book keeper, bds 723 S Water.
Neal W J, meat market, 624 N Washington, bds Carroll.
Nelson David, butcher, bds American Hotel.
Nelson Julius, sailor, h 515 S Jefferson.
Nelty Frank, (N & Page) h 636 Hoyt.
Nelty & Page, (F N & L P), carriage makers and blacksmiths, 307 Tuscola.
Nerreter John, saloon & billiards, 319 Genesee, h Washington.
Nevin Benard, tailor, h 313 S Cherry.
NEWCOMBE GEO K, (Spencer & N), h 423 S Jefferson.
Newman W, cigar maker, 102 N Jefferson, h 205 S Rockwell.
Newton Alfred, law student, bds 608 N Washington.
Newton A R, clerk, (E Sag Salt Works) bds 608 N Washington.
Newton Edward, machinist, bds 608 N Washington.
Newton Henry, clerk, bds 608 N Washington.
Newton L F, drayman, h 624 S Warren.
Newton Silas, sawyer, h 602 Thompson.
Nichodemus Jacob, bar keeper, h 225 S Webster.
Nichodemus Peter, saloon 403 Genesee, h 225 S Webster.
Nicholas Mrs. Mary, ladies hair dresser, 321 Genesse,
Nicholson Miss E, milliner, 108 N Washington, h same.
Nichols D K, clerk, bds Bancroft.
Nichols Frederick, harness maker, h 202 Lapeer.
Nichols John, carp & joiner, h 915 Johnson.
Nichol Robert, lab, h 603 N Washington.
Nichol Wm, lab, bds 603 N Washington.
NIEDERSTADT A G, boots & shoes, 214 S Washington h same.
Niederstadt John, boiler maker, h 910 S Warren.
Niederstadt G, clerk, h 309 S Webster.
Nienstadt Charles, h 110 N Clay.
Noel B, painter, 206 N Franklin, h 215 N Jefferson.

Noland John, lab, h 705 Lapeer.
Nolan Thomas, lab, h 1015 S Water.
Nolan William, carp, h 705 Maple.
Northrop Geo, book keeper, bds 118 N Cass.
Nothen John, lab, h 424 Fitzhugh.
Nugent John, millwright, 1223 S Washington.
Nuoff George, lab, h 111 S Fourth.
Nye Caleb, lab, h 816 Lapeer.
Nye Charles, engineer, h 1222 Johnson.

O

O'Brien C, painter, h 330 S Webster.
O'Brien George, lab, h 615 Millard.
O'Brien James, waiter, bds 123 S Washington.
O'BRIEN JOHN, groceries & provisions 404 Genesee, h 307 Lapeer.
O'Brien Martin, propr Hibernia Hotel, 724 N Washington.
O'Brien Patrick, lab, h 405 N Fifth.
O'Brien Timothy, lab, h 625 Wells.
O'Donnell Daniel, propr Canada House, 625 N Franklin.
O'Donnell James, saloon, h 618 N Washington.
O'Donnell Michael, cooper, bds 403 Fitzhugh.
O'Donnell Michael, bar tender, bds 618 N Washington.
O'Horo Francis, lab, bds 1231 S Water.
O'Neil William, blacksmith, h 318 Park.
Oakliff Martin, porter, Bancroft.
Ohda John, lab, h 212 S Fifth.
Ohland Frederick, lab, bds 210 N Rockwell.
Oland Henry, lab, bds 210 N Rockwell.
Oland Joseph, lab, bds 210 N Rockwell.
Oldfield A N, train dispatcher, bds Everett House.
Olds William, soap & candle manuf, 207 S Franklin, h 622 S Webster.
Ormsby R J, mason, h 418 Fitzhugh.
Ortman Charles, lumberman, bds 110 S Fourth.
Osborn John, stave dealer, h 314 N Cass.
Osborne N, physician, 207 Genesee, h cor Hoyt & Jefferson.
Osmon Henry, carp, h 421 N Second.
Osmond William, organ builder, h 108 S Chestnut.
Otish Thomas, lab, h N Water near Garrisons mill.
Otto August, clerk, bds German.
Otto Frank, tobacconist, 301 Genesee, h German.
Overton J, carp, h 312 Park.
Owens Henry G, clerk, bds Washington.
Owen J M, pattern maker, h 618 S Franklin.
Owsten John G, engineer, h 401 Johnson.

P

Packhem Charles, blacksmith, bds 214 N Cass.
Paddock Alexander, lawyer, h N Water.
Page C H, tinsmith, bds American Hotel.
Page Joseph, carriage maker, bds Warren.
Page Lewis L, (Nelty & P), bds 636 Hoyt.
Page Mrs Carrie A, saleswoman, bds Everett House.
Palm Christ, mason, h 119 N Warren.
Palm Frederick, carp, h 124 N Warren.
Palmer James, cooper, bds 423 Tuscola.
Palmer P, teamster, h 122 N Franklin.
Panitzsch Edward, furrier, h 507 Lapeer.
Panitzsch Mrs Ernstina, dressmaker, h 507 Lapeer.
Parquet Joseph, saloon, 217 S Water.
PARET REV WM, rector St P's E Church, h 306 S Jefferson.
Parker William, teamster, bds 720 N Franklin.
Parkhust Curtis, clerk, bds 132 N Washington.
Park Dexter, book keeper, h 503 S Water
Parks Edwin, tinsmith, h 610 S Webster.
Parlim Mrs Mary E, physician, bds 101 S Jefferson.
Parsons Augustus, carriage maker, h 1206 Mason.
Parsons William, builder, h 813 Emerson.
Parth Francis, Printer, bds 207 Tuscola.
Partridge A, lab, h 306 Wells.
Passolt Henry, potash manuf, h 1224 S Washington.
Patte Henry, lab, h 207 S Fourth.
Patterson Francis, carp, bds 901 S Jefferson.
Patterson Wm, clerk, bds Sherman House.
Paull E H, Receiving Teller Merchant's National Bank, bds Bancroft.
Paull William, lab, bds Saginaw Valley House.
Pearson C G, ship carp, bds Monitor House.
Pearson James, teamster, h 119 Cornelia.
Pearson James, h 701 Carroll.
Peck Benjamin, teamster, h 306 N Third.
Peer James, blacksmith, h 618 S Warren.
Pelton Daniel, clerk, h 219 S Fourth.
Pendergast G, painter, bds 120 N Jefferson.
Pendergast John A, painter, 105 S Cass, h 120 N Jefferson.
Pendle George, brick layer, bds 214 S Washington.
Pendle Henry, brick layer, bds 214 S Washington.
Penfield E P & H L, dry goods, 106 Genesee.
Penfield, E P, (E P & H L P), h 415 N Washington.
Penfield H L, (E P & H L P), bds 423 N Washington.
Penny Aaron R, salt manuf, h 422 S Jefferson.
Perkins Daniel, (P & Fox), bds 608 N Washington.

PIONEER IRON WORKS,

EAST SAGINAW, MICH.

HILL & MORRIS,

MANUFACTURERS OF

STEAM Machinery,

STEAM Engines,

Gang, Circular and Mulay Saw Mills,

OF MOST IMPROVED STYLE,

Tools and Fixtures for Salt Manufacturers, Steam Boats, &c.,
All kinds of Iron and Brass Castings made to order.
Wrought Iron Forging, Jobbing and Repairing
done in the best manner.
Also, Dressing Lumber, and Manufacturing Flooring and
Siding to order.

J. H. HILL, GEO. MORRIS.

J. H. HILL,

DEALER IN

REAL ESTATE,

PARTICULARLY PINE LANDS.

I have large tracts of Pine Land on the Cass, Pine, Tobacco, Cedar, Tittabawassee, Swan, Sauble and Devil Rivers; also, on Cheboygan and Thunder Bay, which I will sell at moderate rates.

EAST SAGINAW, MICH.

☞HALL & JAMES, General Insurance Agents,

PERKIS & FOX, (D W P & L H F), Insurance Agents, 101 Genesee.
Perry Charles C, lumber inspector, h 115 N Third.
Perry C N, lumber inspector, h 609 S Water.
Perry Peter, lab, bds 720 N Franklin.
Perry William, teamster, h 120 N Fourth.
Peters Charles, Printer, bds 202 N Franklin.
Peters Charles, lab, h 405 Johnson.
Peters William, lab, h 216 S Webster.
Peterson Charles, (col'd) drayman, h 520 N Warren.
Peterson Jerry, (col'd) waiter Bancroft House.
Pettibone Mrs M A, (Bliss & P), 107 N Washington.
Phillips A J, lumberman, h 606 S Webster.
Pie William, lab, bds 324 N Fourth.
Piler Charles, carriage maker, h 108 N Rockwell.
Pinnett Mrs Catharine, h 303 James.
Pioneer Engine House, J L Brown Foreman, 401 S Water.
PLESSNER HENRY, agt Mt Hope Nurseries, 125 N Washington, h 807 Lapeer.
Plessner Miss Ida, school teacher, bds 807 Lapeer.
Plicker John, lab, h 401 James.
Plicker Nicholas, clerk, h 401 James.
Pollock William, blacksmith, h 612 S Franklin.
Ponschœn Henry, tailor, h 1601 Johnson.
Pool B F, (Stevens P & Co), h 318 N Cass.
Porter William, lab, h 903 S Jefferson.
Post Charles & Co, lumber dealers, 402 Genesee.
Post Daniel, lab, h N Water.
Post Office, D C Gage P M, 321 Genesee.
Post Samuel, clerk, h 307 S Jefferson.
Post S N, machinist, h N Washington.
Porterfield T J, lumberman, bds Bancroft.
Potter Benjamin, clerk, bds American Hotel.
Potter H C, supt F & P M R R, h 1304 S Jefferson.
Powers E H, lawyer, 207 Genesee, res Sag City.
Prall David J, (P & Duncan), h 316 Park.
Prall & Duncan, (D J P & D A D), furniture manuf, 121 N Jefferson.
Pratt H A, h 811 S Jefferson.
Pratt H, carp, h 316 Hayden.
Pratt Homer, bds 316 Hayden.
Pratt Rollin, carp, bds 316 Hayden.
Pratt Scott, engineer, bds 811 S Jefferson.
Prengnetz John, lab, h 913 Tuscola.
Proctor H R, jeweler, 125 Genesee, bds Bancroft House.
Puckel William, carp, h 305 S Webster.
Purcell William, carp, h 305 S Webster.

BROWN & JAMES, Attorneys and Land Agents,

Purryea Henry, lab, h 820 Lapeer.
Purcing A C, engineer, h 225 Maple.

Q

Quelch John, porter, h Potter.
Quinn O J, spile driver, h 607 S Washington.
Quinn John, peddler, bds 412 German.

R

Rachel Joseph, carp, h 504 N Rockwell.
Rademacher Frederick, machinist, bds Carroll.
Rademacher H, machinist, h Carroll.
Rahan Michael, lab, h 710 Miller.
Ramsey Andrew, blacksmith, bds 625 N Franklin.
Randall George, (R & Son), bds 416 S Jefferson.
Randall Herman) (R & Son), h 416 S Jefferson.
Randall James T, photographer, 325 Genesee, h 523 Fitzhugh.
Randall & Son, (H & G R), blacksmiths, 109 Mason.
Randolph Wm Henry, baker, h 212 N Washington.
Rankin Austin L, h 613 S Jefferson.
Rason Charles, lab, h N Washington, near E Sag salt works
Rathbone D G, clerk, bds 701 Fitzhugh.
Raupp Nicholas jr, brewer, 123 N Warren, h same.
Raupp Nicholas, sen, saloon, 124 N Jefferson.
Raupp Timmas, butcher, bds 312 Genesee.
Raymond Lewis, h 209 Miller.
Reach Charles, carp, h 704 Tuscola.
Reardon John, Boarding House, 209 S Water.
Reardon William, lab, 212 William.
Redson Alexander, farmer, h S Washington, south of old coloney road.
Redson Jonathan, farmer, h 1002 S Jefferson.
Redson Mrs Margaret, h 708 Thompson.
Reed John, machinist, bds Monitor House.
Reetz August, saloon, h 116 S Fourth.
Reeve D B, news dealer, 321 Genesee, h 412 S Washington.
Reichle Anthony, carriage trimmer, h 425 Carroll.
Reichelle Frederick, butcher, bds 105 Lapeer.
Reigel & Blœdon, proprs Bellevue Hotel, 602 German.
Reigel Gustav, (R & B), 602 German.
Reikenbach Henry, lab, h 402 Wadsworth.
Renega F W, lab, h 1215 S Water.
Reno Joseph, lab, bds 913 Hoyt.
Rescue Engine House, 316 German.
Reynolds S J, (Shaw, R & Co), h 525 N Franklin.
Reynolds Robert, lab, h N Washington, near E Sag salt works.

Reynolds John, painter, h 224 N Fourth.
Reyno Abraham, (col'd), barber, 111 Genesee, h same.
Reyno Louis, (col'd) barber Everett House, h 214 Maple.
Richardson Samuel, lab, h 611 Millard.
Richardson Noah C, with Boyd & Booth, 101 Genesee, h Jefferson.
Richmond Jacob, h 215 S Fifth,
Richardson William, machinist, bds 609 Carroll.
Ricker Geo. M, ship carp, h 801 Lapeer.
Richardson Ira, lumberman, bds 416 N Jefferson.
Richmond Jacob, cabinet maker, 115 N Jefferson, h Third.
Rice J D, agt Grover & Baker's sewing machines. 130 S Washington, bds Sherman House.
Richardson William, apprentice, bds Carroll.
Riker Ephraim, grocer & fish dealer, h 624 S Washington.
Rikert James, Printer, bds Jefferson.
Riley George, moulder, h 1209 S Water.
Riley James, boiler maker, h 725 Maple,
Riley John, moulder, h 1209 S Water.
Riley Joseph, carp, bds 612 S Franklin.
Riley Patrick, lab, h 616 S Warren.
Riley William, painter, 324 Genesee, h 125 N Cass.
Rimers Wm, (Bogert & R), 113 Genesee.
Ringer William, bar tender, bds 302 Potter.
Ripley H C, salt & land office, bds Bancroft.
Ripley L G, clerk, bds Jefferson.
Riselay Charles, engineer, h N Water, near Garrisons mills.
Ritchell Wence, clerk, bds cor Cass & Rockwell.
Ritter William, tailor, 321 Genesee, h same.
Robertson John, moulder, bds 404 Potter.
Robertson J P, clerk, bds 523 Fitzhugh.
Robel M, rag peddler, h 203 S Wells.
Robinson Charles K, lawyer and banker, h 401 S Washington.
Robinson C K & Co, bankers, 204 Genesee.
Robinson D J, lumberman, h 623 Johnson.
Robinson James, butcher, bds 402 S Warren.
Robinson Silas D, carp, bds 502 N Water.
Robinson Thomas, teamster, 623 N Franklin.
Robinson Wm, (col'd), waiter Bancroft.
Rockey Peter, lab, h 221 S Fifth.
RODERICK JAMES, bowling saloon, 312 Genesee, h 325 N Washington.
Rogers Miss Annie, dressmaker, bds Hoyt.
Rohl Frederick, lab, h N Washington, near E Sag salt works.
Romp, Frederick, cooper, h 308 N Rockwell.
ROOT & MIDLER, (A M R & A J M), liquor dealers, 127 N Water.

BROWN & JAMES, Attorneys and Land Agents,

ROOT A M, (R & Midler), h 225 S Washington.
Roper William, stave dealer, 402 Genesee, bds American.
Rosaland Chirst, lab, h 202 N Rockwell.
Roseland Charles, clerk, bds 202 N Rockwell.
Rose D F, lumber dealer, 101 Genesee, h 201 S Jefferson.
Rose Julius K, h 424 N Washington.
Ross B B, physician, 103 N Washington, h 523 S Jefferson.
Roth B, lab, h 112 Cornelia.
Rouse Jacob, h 217 S Third.
Rudd Albert, teamster, bds 802 Lapeer.
Rudd Anson, farmer, B 802 Lapeer.
Rudd Bryant, teamster, bds 802 Lapeer.
Rulph Ann, (col'd), washer woman, bds 205 William.
Rump Frederick, cooper, h Johnson.
Rust A, (J F Rust & Co), h 524 S Jefferson.
Rust David W, (J F Rust & Co), bds 524 S Jefferson.
Rust J F & Co, (J F, D W & A R), lumberman 101 Genesee.
Rust John F, (J F R & Co), h 323 S Jefferson.
Russell Elias, yard man Bancroft.
Rutheford John, lab, h 321 First.
Ruth Miss Annie, (col'd) washer woman, 107 S Franklin.
Ryan James, bds 413 Astor.
Ryan John, lab, h 401 Cornelia.
Ryan John, ass't bar keeper, Bancroft House.
Ryan Patrick, plasterer, h 413 Astor.
Ryan Thomas H, stewart, Bancroft House.
Rye John, blacksmith, h 121 N Fifth.

S

Sager George, lab, h 913 Lapeer.
Saginaw Valley Bank, B M Fay Pres't, T P Sheldon Cashier, 101 S Washington.
Saginaw Valley Com'l School, W R Tillinghast Principal, 101 Lapeer.
Saginaw Valley Hotel, L Heston propr, 116 N Water.
Salspaugh Amos, (col'd), barber, bds 111 Genesee.
Sanborn Geo C, grocer, h 417 S Jefferson.
Sanborn J A, (Catlin & S), 122 N Water, res Sag City.
Sasse Richard, lab, bds 1231 S Water.
Sauter Philip, cabinet maker, h Clay.
Saylor Thomas, lumberman, 102 N Washington, bds Everett House.
Schacker Henry, carp, bds 119 N Webster.
Shacker R, carp, h 217 N Rockwell.
Schauder Louis, saloon, h 709 Genesee.
Schlatterer Christopher, lighterman, h 709 German.

Schmelser Nicholas, grocer, h 1113 S Water.
Schmidt Adolph, shoemaker, h 314 S Webster.
Schmidt C, brush maker, h 706 James.
Schmidt Edward, shoemaker, h 314 S Webster.
Schmitz Michael, cooper, h 925 Lapeer.
Schmidt John, lab, h 117 N Webster.
Schmidt John N, lab, h 118 N Warren.
Schmidt John S, lab, h near E Sag salt works.
Schmitz Anthony, (Chas Post & Co, & F J M & Co), h 124 N Rockwell.
Schmitz Christ, lab, h 420 N Fifth.
Schmitz Loren, brush maker, h 1001 Lapeer.
Schnautz Edward, gunsmith, h 822 Genesee.
Schnell John G, propr, Farmers Hotel, 904 Genesee.
Schoeb Gabriel, shoemaker, 918 Genesee, h 1012 Johnson.
Scholl John, lab, h 222 N Third.
Scholz Otto, clerk, bds Third.
Schooley M, lab, h 216 William.
School House, 605 Fitzhugh.
Schomaker John, blacksmith, bds 210 N Warren.
Schott Peter, peddler, bds 401 Johnson.
Schott Mark, peddler, bds 401 Johnson.
Schott Samuel, peddler, h 401 Johnson.
Schotts George, lab, h 1013 Fitzhugh.
Schouder Philip, carp, h 119 N Clay.
Schroeder Charles, shoemaker, h 212 S Fifth.
Schroeder C, shoemaker, h 205 S Rockwell.
Schroeder Mrs L, h 111 S Third.
Schramm Charles, lab, h 210 N Cass.
Schramm Charles, miller, h 210 N Cass.
Schultz John, blacksmith, 206 N Cass, h 202 N Cass.
Schupp A, forwarding, 229 N Water.
Schupp Augustus, grocer, 205 Genesee, h 801 S Washington.
Schurpen Mrs, h 116 Elm.
Schwahn John P, bar keeper, bds 123 S Washington.
Schwarn Conrad, h 112 N Webster.
Schwartz Henry, (S & Marskey) h 217 N Washington.
Schwartz & Marskey, (Henry S & Chas M), furniture, 411 Genesee.
Schyler John, lab, h 311 James.
Scott David, lab, h N Water, near Garrison's mill.
Scott George B, boatman, h 104 Lapeer.
Scott William, farmer, h 224 N Fourth.
Seemann Joseph, Printer, bds Bancroft.
Sears & Carey, (W B S & Carey), surveyors,, 101 Genesee.
Sears F P & Co, lumbermen, 1131 S Water.
Sears F P, (F P S & Co), h 216 N Washington.

☞BROWN & JAMES, Attorneys and Land Agents,

Sears W B, (S & Carey) h 302 S Washington.
Seed James, clerk, bds 408 S Warren.
Seed Mrs J C, h 408 S Warren.
Seeley John, blacksmith, bds 308 Potter.
Seward Frederick, lab, h 816 German.
Sewer Fred, lab, bds 606 Lapeer.
Seymour Alfred, bds 1314 Genesee.
Seymour Joseph, teamster, h 607 N Franklin.
Seymour Martin, carpenter, h 222 N Jefferson.
Shane Mrs Catharine, 119 S Washington.
Shane M A, carp & joiner, h 225 James.
Sharp William F, with Boyd & Booth, 101 Genesee.
SHAW, BULLARD & CO, (C F S & Bullard), wholesale grocers, 123 & 125 N Water.
SHAW CHARLES F, (S, Bullard & Co), bds Bancroft House.
Shaw H L, (T E Doughty & Co), h 510 N Jefferson.
Shaw Humphrey, stave dealer, 602 S Water, h 603 S Water.
Shaw J E, lumber dealer, Bds Bancroft.
SHAW, REYNOLDS & CO, (S S S, J R & C B C), hardware, 104 Genesee, & 109 S Water.
Shea Dennis, lab, bds 1231 S Water.
Shea Edward, ship carp, h 302 German.
Sheehan Timothy, lab, bds 724 N Washington.
Sheehy P, carp, h near plank road.
Shefferman John, butcher, bds 711 Genesee.
Sheldon T P, cashier Sag Valley Bank, h 726 Hoyt.
Sheridan Thomas, lab, h 201 S Sixth.
Sherlock Hugh, ship carp. bds 724 N Washington.
Sherman George, lab, bds 913 Hoyt.
Sherman Horace, lab, bds 913 Hoyt.
Sherman House, John Brimner, propr, 131 S Water.
Shirley E A, sawyer, h near Chapin's mill.
Silsbee H C, furniture, 108 S Water, bds Bancroft House.
Simet Michael, lab, h 218 N Fourth.
Simmons Henry, bar tender, bds Everett House.
Simmons S, druggist, h 105 N Fourth.
Skating Park, (L P Mason, S V Haskell & I B Johnson propr's.
Skinner George, carp, bds 323 First.
Slade Luther, lab, h S Washington, S of the bayou.
Slater Joseph, saloon, 110 N Jefferson, h same.
Slayton Miss Elvira, dressmaker, bds Everett House.
Smalley William, lab, h 312 N Franklin.
Smalley William, teamster, h 405 N Warren.
Smith Alfred, stage driver, bds Sag Valley House.
Smith A R, engineer, h 601 N Fourth.
Smith Charles H & Co, boots & shoes, 116 S Water.
Smith Charles H, (C H S & Co). h 112 Hayden.

CITY BOWLING

SALOON.

The undersigned having, at great expense, fitted up two

FIRST CLASS ALLEYS

In Moses Hess' building, 312 Genesee St.,

Would respectfully solicit the patronage of the public. This game is cosidnered a most healthy and beneficial amusement, and those visiting our Alley will meet with gentlemanly treatment and low charges.

JAMES RODERICK.

East Saginaw, May 1, 1866.

Smith Charles, printer, bds 505 N Webster.
Smith Charles, moulder, h 1218 Mason.
Smith Cornelius, moulder, h 1218 Mason.
SMITH & CROUSE, (M G S & Geo H C), proprs Everett House, 219 Genesee.
Smith B, engineer, h 302 Elm.
Smith Edmund B, salt manuf, h 1032 S Washington.
Smith Henry A, dentist, 325 Genesee, h same.
SMITH IRVING M, (Webber & S), bds Bancroft House.
Smith James, teamster, bds 122 N Franklin.
Smith James M, teamster, h 1408 Genesee.
Smith J M, lawyer, bds Bancroft.
Smith John H, harness maker, h 217 S Rockwell.
Smith Joseph, caulker, h 122 N Cass.
Smith Joseph, ship carp, h 421 N Webster.
Smith Martin, capt, h 512 N Water.
SMITH M G, (S & Crouse), Everett House.
Smith Miss Jennie, bds Bancroft.
Smith Mrs E A, h 505 N Webster.
Smith Peter, lab, bds 401 Millard.
Smith Robert I, sawyer, h 419 Second.
Smith William D, teamster, h 319 S Cherry.
Smith Wm E, saloon, 112 N Franklin, h same.
Smith William, teamster, bds 122 N Franklin.
Snyder Luther, engineer, h 509 Millard.
Solomon C, butcher, h 220 N Warren.
Sommar John, bds 501 James.
Sommar Joseph, lab, h 501 James.
Sondok John, lab, h 941 Lapeer.
Sonner Isidor, carp, h 1009 Lapeer.
Sopulthess Casper, lab, h 904 Carroll.
Southwick Bronson, clerk, bds 416 N Franklin.
SOUTHWICK WM H, (Ward & S) Ass't U S Assessor, h 416 N Franklin.
Sovay F S, boarding house,, 201 S Water.
Soyer George, ale & liquors, 104 N Washington, h 715 S Warren.
Spangler Fleming, artisian well borer. h 302 N Washington.
Spencer C C, clerk, bds 229 S Washington.
Spencer J A, carp, bds 309 S Washington.
Spencer M B, lab, h 310 S Warren.
SPENCER & NEWCOMBE,)T B S & Geo K N), sash and blind manufy, 206 N Jefferson.
SPENCER THOMAS B, (S & Newcombe), h 229 S Washington.
Spinney A B, physician, 325 Genesee, h 301 Cherry.
Spring Frank, lab, h 709 Maple.

C. D. BLISS & CO.,

Auction & Commission Merchants.

Crouse Block, N. Washington.

(*The oldest established Auction House in Northern Michigan.*)
Consignments of Dry Goods, Clothing, Books, Furniture, Yankee Notions, &c., respectfully solicited. Sales attended to in any part of the County or Valley.

☞A General Stock of FURNITURE constantly on hand.

E. W. WIGGINS,

Real Estate Broker,

LAND AND TAX AGENT,

Office, No. 107, Genesee Street, opposite Irving Hall,

EAST SAGINAW, MICH.

ELLWANGER & BARRY,

Mt. Hope Nurseries,

ROCHESTER, N. Y.

These Nurseries are the most extensive in the UNITED STATES covering over 500 Acres, embracing the cultivation of all desirable HARDY FRUITS, ORNAMENTAL SHRUBS, ROSES, EVERGREENS, PLANTS, etc., etc.

Orders Received by **HENRY PLESSNER**, *Agent.*
No. 125, North Water Street.

EAST SAGINAW.

☞BROWN & JAMES, Attorneys and Land Agents,

Spring Mrs M, h 504 S Water.
St Mary Abram, shoemaker, h 211 Millard.
St Mary Joseph, lab, h 211 Millard,
St Nicholas Restaurant, (Casey, F G & Co), proprs, basement Bliss Block.
Stauber Jacob, saloon, 117 S Water, h same.
Starker D F, clerk, bds 801 S Water.
Starkweather Edward O, engineer, h 608 S Washington.
Statts William, engineer, h 206 N Fifth.
Steamon Mrs Nancy, h 217 Elm.
Stearns Mrs C E, school teacher, bds 103 Wells.
Stearns Wm H, Marble dealer, 107 S Cass, h 211 N Warren.
Stecker Geo, gardner Bancroft House.
Steckert George, farmer, h N Washington.
Steckert Jacob, propr Steckert's Hotel, 123 N Washington.
Steckert's Hotel, Jacob Steckert propr, 123 N Washington.
Steele Henry S, h 619 Maple.
STEELE THOMAS, boiler maker, 112 Mason, h 402 Maple.
Steinman Charles, shoemaker, bds Genesee.
Steinhagen Christopher, clerk, h 107 S Webster.
Stevens John, baggageman F & P M R R, h 604 N Washington.
STEVENS J R, (S, Pool & Co), bds 112 N Washington.
STEVENS J S & Co, City flouring mills, 308 Genesee.
STEVENS J S, (J S Stevens & Co), bds Bancroft.
Stevens M C, boarding house, 112 N Washington.
STEVENS POOL & Co, (J K S, B F P & J L B), dry goods, 207 Genesee.
Steve John, lab, h 201 S Clay.
Stever C, bds 608 Thompson.
Stever Charles B, propr American Hotel, 113 N Cass.
Scever R T, (Tucker & S), h 608 Thompson.
Stewart Alexander, lab, h 611 N Washington
Stewart John N, Capt propeller Star, h 513 Thompson.
Stewart O, saloon, 302 Potter, h same.
STINSON JAMES, (Aikin & S) h 601 Thompson.
Stirks Simon, sailor, bds 1555 Genesee.
Stocklayer Henry, lab, h 629 Maple.
Stoddard Fred A, (S & Hallock), bds Bancroft.
STODDARD & HALLOCK, clothing, 109 N Washington.
Stoddard Samuel, mason, h 625 Miller.
Stolz Frederick, butcher, h 210 N Warren.
Stolz John, butcher, h 210 N Warren.
Storch John, h 108 S Clay.
Storch L, shoemaker, h S Washington, back of Sutton's salt works.
Storrs L C & Co, grocers, 106 S Water.
Storrs L C, (L C S & Co), h 231 S Water.

Story Frank, carp, bds 316 N Franklin.
Stover Hiram H, foreman saw mill, h 425 S Warren.
Strasburg August, propr Washington Hotel, 103 S Warren.
Straw Charles, clerk, bds S Washington.
Sturtevant Ethan A, (Button & S), bds 523 S Jefferson.
Sturtevant & Button, (E A S & W H B), lawyers, 325 Genesee.
Styler A, conductor E Sag S Railway, bds 720 N Franklin.
Sullivan David, lab, h S Washington, S of the grove.
Summerfield Charles, clerk, bds St Nicholas saloon.
Sommers John, fireman, h 113 S Rockwell.
Sumner Christ, lab, h 306 N Fourth.
Sunberry Charles, lab, h 218 N Cass.
Sutherland George, lab, h 518 N Webster.
Sutton P A, h 301 Lapeer.
Sweeney M, blacksmith, h 402 N Fourth.
Sweeny William, (col'd) barber, bds 111 Genesee.
Schwenk George, carp, h 805 William.
Sweet James, carp & joiner, bds S Washington.
Sweet W T, lumberman, h 514 N Jefferson.
Swift John, sash & blind maker, h 304 N Cass.
Swilling Charles C, (S & Engle), h 125 Lapeer.
Swilling & Co, (Chas S & G H Engle), saloon,) 125 Lapeer.

T

Talbot Richard, contractor, h 224 S Webster.
TAPPEN R J, (J R Livingston & Co). bds Bancroft.
Tarter Peter, tailor, h 401 Johnson.
Taylor A, h 401 S Warren.
Taylor Alonzo, cooper, h 602 William.
Taylor Col J R, (J R T & Co,), h 707 S Washington.
Taylor, J R & Co, real estate brokers & auctioneers, 103 S Washington.
Taylor L, cooper, bds 403 Fitzhugh.
Teakle Joseph, stove dealer, 225 S Washington, h 601 Thompson.
Tebo Christopher, foreman, G C Warner & Co, h 301 Mason.
Techenten Charles, drayman, h 606 Lapeer.
Temoster John, lab, h 213 N Rockwell.
Ten Eyck C & E shingle and stave manufy, 705 N Water.
Ten Eyck Charles, (C & E Ten Eyck), h 1111 S Washington.
Ten Eyck Egbert (C & E T), bds 624 Fitzhugh.
Thede Marcus, blacksmith, h 120 S Fourth.
Thieme Franz lab, h 802 Millard,
Tholl John N, meat market, 311 Genesee, h 711 Genesee.
Thomas John, lab, h 103 S Third.
Thomas Robert, (col'd) waiter Bancroft.
Thomas Sampson W, lab, h 611 Millard.

THOMPSON B M, (T & Flanders,) h 710 Hoyt.
Thompson Edward, lab, h 811 S Water.
THOMPSON & FLANDERS, lawyers, 204 Genesee.
Thompson Frank, lab, bds 720 N Franklin.
Thompson George, teamster, h 621 S Webster.
Thompson John, physician, 116 N Washington, h N Jefferson.
Thompson Orange S, supt plank road, h 504 N Franklin.
Throop John, mason, h 423 N Third.
Tisdale Freeman, carp, bds Monitor House.
Tibbitts George W, clerk, F & P M R R, bds 423 N Washington.
Tisdale L W, agt American Express Co, 116 S Washington, h 308 N Jefferson.
Topping & Hosmer, (O T & J J H), produce dealers, 202 N Water.
Topping Orlando, (T & Hosmer) bds Steckert's Hotel.
Topping William, carp, h 219 N Sixth.
Torrey Mrs A, h 12'0 S Jefferson.
Town & Harney, (S R T & G H) saloon, 102 N Washington.
Town S R (T & Harney) 102 N Washington.
Town Richard S, bar tender, 102 N Washington.
Townsend Charles, lumberman, h 323 N Jefferson.
Travedic Henry, sash & door maker, bds 610 S Warren.
Travedic Richard; lab, h 610 S Warren.
Travers John, shoemaker, h 108 S Fifth.
Trippe S, ship builder, bds Everett House.
Tucker & Steaver, (T T & R T S) Exchange billiard rooms & saloon 113 Genesee.
Tucker Thompson, (T & Stever), h 216 Hoyt.
Teufel Frederick, cooper, 505 N Jefferson.
Tuhy Martin, carp, h 415 Astor.
Turner S W, physician, 202 N Water, h 310 N Franklin.
Twaits James W. lumber inspector, h 618 S Jefferson.
Tyler A W, boarding house, 424 Johnson.
Tyler J, (Barclay & Tyler) bds Everett House.

U

Ufer Charles, carver & joiner, h 113 N Jefferson.
Union Dining Saloon, Town & Harney propr's, 102 N Washington,
Union School, 120 S Clay.
Uppendahl Frederick, shoemaker, 108 N Cass, h same.
U S Custom House, H Joslin deputy collector, 101 Genesee.

V

Valentine Henry D, lab, h 1307 S Water.
Valentine J C, book keeper, h 611 S Webster.

Valley Benjamin, teamster, h 119 Cornelia.
Valley Charles, lab, h 117 Cornelia.
Valley City Steam Fire Engine, Jesse A Burdock, foreman 205 N Water.
Valley Frank, teamster, h 1125 S Warren.
Van Buskirk Melvin, lab, bds 403 Fitzhugh.
Vanderhoof William C, sash & door maker, 109 S Franklin.
Van Duren A, physician, 325 Genesee, h 824 Johnson.
Van Norman John D, h 111 N Clay.
Van Norman Mrs E, h 208 German.
Van Norman R, lab, bds, 111 N Clay.
Vanwert Mrs M, tailoress, h 510 Hayden.
Van Wray, G V W, toll house, 1624 Genesee, h same.
Varey Thomas C, carp, h 220 N Sixth.
Vassar & Sanilac plank road Co, J L Ketchum Treas, M L Gage supt 113 S Water.
Vaughn A S, dry goods, 107 N Water, bds Bancroft House.
Volusin Bude, carp, h 216 Emerson.
Von Daniels Charles, physician, 125 N Warren, h same.
Von Daniels Ernest, bds 125 N Warren.
Voorheis J E, builder, h S Washington, S of grove.
Vrets R B, engineer, bds N Washington, near E Sag salt works.

W

WADSWORTH & Co. druggists, 317 Genesee.
WadsworthOrry H, (Wadsworth & Co) h 202 S Jefferson.
Wagner G, fisherman, bds 218 N Third.
Wagener John, lab, h 110 S Webster.
Wagener William, fisherman, h 218 N Third.
Wainwright John & Co, produce commission merchants, 623 N Water.
Wainwright John, (W & Co), h 817 Emerson.
Wakefield Levi S, steam boat carp, h 302 Lapeer.
Walker William, h 318 S Webster.
Wallace Hugh, harness maker, 302 Genesee, h 623 Hoyt.
Wallace John, lab, bds 110 N Jefferson.
Wallace John, lab, bds 122 N Jefferson.
Waller Henry, carp & joiner, h 402 Wells.
Walsh Patrick, lab, h 124 Cornelia.
Walsh Thomas H, bds Everett House.
Waltz Charles, brewer, h 816 S Washington.
Walz Daniel, lab, h 1013 Lapeer.
Ward John, coat room clerk, Bancroft House.
Ward Patrick, lab, h 922 Johnson.
WARD & SOUTHWICK, (Wm Ward & W H S)tobacco, cigars and leather belting, 107 Genesee.

WARD WM, (W & Southwick), h 408 S Washington.
Wardell James, ship carp, h 827 S Washington·
Wardell Mrs Matilda, drssemaker, h 827 S Washington.
Warner George C & Co, (Geo C W, & W H W & L H F) lumberman, 802 S Water.
Warner George C, (G C W & Co), h 602 S Washington.
Warner W H, (G C W & Co), h 506 S Washington.
Washington Hotel, (August Strasburg, propr), 103 S Warren.
Wasserman Christopher, tailor bds Chestnut.
Wasserman Frederick, second hand clothing, 104 N Cass, h Chestnut.
Watson G H, gas fitter, (G Bridgeman & Co) h Genesee.
Watson James, carp & joiner, h 209 S Sixth.
Watson Seymour, lumberman, bds Everett House.
Watson S & Co, millinery & dress-making, 209 Genesee.
Watz Chas, lab, h S Washington.
Watz Constantine, h 113 N Third.
Way Richard, iron forger, h 219 S Washington.
Wear John, lab, h 216 N Franklin.
Weaver Ellis, lumberman, h 215 Hoyt.
WEAVER JAMES A, (Weaver & Wilkin) h 306 S Washington.
WEAVER & WILKIN, (J A W & F G W), boots & shoes. 108 Genesee.
Webber Carl, shoemaker, h 805 Genesee.
Webber Christian, bds 805 Genesee.
Webber James S, h 109 S Jefferson.
WEBBER & SMITH, (W L W & I M S), lawyers 102 N Washington.
WEBBER WILLIAM L, (W & Smith), h 236 N Washington.
Wegst Adam, cooper, h 311 N Third.
WEIDEMANN ROBERT H, lumberman. 101 Genesee, h 723 S Washington.
Weincke Andrew, harness maker, bds 707 Genesee.
Weincke John, harness maker, 707 Genesee, h same.
Weiss Charles E, (Moye, H & W), h 306 S Webster.
Weist Joseph A, h 102 N Fourth.
Weitenmeller Richard, lab, h 844 Lapeer.
Wells S, cooper, h 403 Fitzhugh.
Wells Simon, saloon, 112 N Jefferson, h same.
Welms Frederick, lab, h 224 N Franklin.
Welsh David, (W Wright & Co), bds 523 N Franklin.
Welsh James, lab, h N Washington, near E Sag salt works.
Welsh Thomas, (W Wright & Co), bds 523 N Franklin.
Welsh Wright & Co, (D & T W, & F W) grocers, 606 N Washington.
Welton F E, clerk American Express Co, bds American Hotel.

Thomas D. Germain,

BUILDER.

No. 411, Tuscola Street,

EAST SAGINAW, MICH.

I am prepared to contract for the building of wood or brick

PUBLIC BUILDINGS,

PRIVATE RESIDENCES,

BUSINESS BLOCKS, &c.

AND GIVE SATISFACTION.

A. W. GATES & CO.,

Livery and Sale Stables,

No. 201, N. Washington St., cor. Tuscola,

EAST SAGINAW, MICH.

OLIVER P. BURT. EDWIN BURT.

BURT & BROTHER,

DEALERS IN

LUMBER

ALSO IN PINE AND FARMING LANDS.

Office in Arcade Block, Corner of Washington and Genesee Streets.

HALL & JAMES, General Insurance Agents,

Wenks Joseph, clerk, bds 1320 Genesee, h same.
Wenks Louis, grocery, 1320 Genesee, h same.
Wentz John, lab, bds 218 N Third.
Wermer William,, saloon, 405 and 407 Lapeer.
Werschky Gustavus, cabinet maker, h 207 S Clay.
WESLEY CHARLES T, clerk, bds Bancroft House.
WESLEY G W, propr Bancroft House, 118 Genesee, corner Washington.
Western Union Telegraph Co, A Ferguson manager, 103 S Washington.
West Albert, (col'd), cook, Bancroft House.
West Alfred, cook, h 207 N Jefferson.
West Alonzo, (col'd) waiter Bancroft House.
West G J, boarding house, 309 S Washington.
West John, (J W & Co), h 420 S Warren.
West Richard, butcher, h 318 S Washington.
West William C, butcher, bds 402 S Warren.
West William, lab, h 608 Potter.
Wetz Charles, lab, h 221 N Fourth.
WHALEN F F, (W & Son,,) bds 617 Hoyt.
WHALEN J C, (W & Son), h 617 Hoyt.
WHALEN & SON, (J C & F F W), grocers, 222 S Washington.
Whealmaker H, moulder, h 825 Carroll.
Wheaton Henry, carp, h 602 S Warren.
Wheeler C, ship carp, h 408 N Warren.
Wheeler & Herring, lawyers, 101 Genesee.
Wheeler John J, (W & Herring), h 624 Fitzhugh.
Wheeler M M, physician, 127 N Washington, bds Everett House.
WHIPPLE P, dentist, 101 Genesee, H 115 S Jefferson.
WHITE CHARLES H, (Barnum & W), bds Bancroft House.
White E B, driver American Express wagon, bds American Hotel.
White I H, saloon 502 S Water, h same.
White Orlando, Printer, bds Franklin.
White R W, contractor, h 109 N Clay.
WHITING L C, dentist, 104 Genesee, h 320 S Webster.
Whiting Nelson, painter, bds American Hotel.
Whitman Geo B, lumber dealer, 104 N Washington.
Whitney Silas, express messenger, h 412 S Jefferson.
Whitney Wm A, Printer, bds Everett House.
Whitney Wm F, lumberman, bds Bancroft.
Whittier J A, lumberman, h 220 N Water.
Whitz Jacob, lab, h 1120 Tuscola.
WICKES BROTHERS, (H D & E N W,) propr's Commercial iron works, 524 N Water.
WICKES C T, book keeper bds 512 N Water.
WICKES E N (Wickes Bros), bds 512 N Water.

WICKS H D (Wicks Bros), h 312 N Jefferson.
WICKLEIN HENRY W, (Frey & Co), bds Everett House.
WIGGINS & CLARK, (Geo B W & H D C), merchant tailors, 110 S Franklin.
WIGGINS EDWARD W, real estate agt. 107 Genesee, h 1125 S Jefferson.
Wiggins Geo B, lumberman, bds Everett House.
Wightman B H, engineer, h near east Sag salt works.
Wight H, book keeper Merchants' Nat'l Bank h 418 N Water.
Wight John A, carp, h 601 James.
Wilcox George Franklin, engineer, h 1307 S Water.
Wilcox Geo W, engineer, h 1307 S Water.
Wilcox Wm Charles, bds 1307 S Water.
Wildman Frederick S, supt Buffalo salt Co, h 301 Lapeer.
Wildman Henry, boiler maker, h 112 Cornelia.
Wildman Robert, farmer, h 112 Cornelia.
Wilkes Elias, mason, h 1504 Genesee.
WILKIN FRANK G, merchant tailor, (W & Mack), 105 Genesee bds 306 S Washington.
WILKIN & MACK, (Frank G W & James M), hats, caps and furs, 108 Genesee.
Wilkinson Anthony M, bar tender, bds 625 N Franklin.
Willard J C, (Nagle & Willard), h 316 N Franklin.
Willard James, machinist.
Williams Harvey, fisherman, h 723 S Water.
Williams Henry, engineer, h N Washington, near E Sag salt works.
Williams John, lumberman, bds 303 Hoyt.
Williams Robert N, conductor, h 425 N Jefferson.
Williamson John, mason, h 212 Millard.
Willis William, lumberman, h 1555 Genesee.
Wilson R N, baggageman, h N Jefferson.
Windman Robert, boiler maker, bds Maple.
Winfrey Thomas, (col'd), drayman, h 302 N Warren.
Wing Harvey, waiter, bds 102 N Washington.
Winkler John, drayman h 113 N Webster.
Winn Isaac L, carp, bds 504 Lapeer.
Wisner C W, (W & Dillingham), h 614 Thompson.
Wisner & Dillingham, lawyers, 102 N Washington.
Withelm Solomon, brewer, h 317 S Warren.
Wlprt Frederick, carriage maker, h 105 S Clay.
Witz John, lab, h East of N Sixth, near Tuscola.
Witz R, lab, h 1401 Tuscola.
Wolhforth Henry, machinest, h Lapeer.
Wolke John H, lab, E Sag salt works.
Wood A B, h 216 N Washington.
Wood Richard, messenger, W U Telegraph Co, bds Everett House.

Woodard Francis H, engineer, h 603 Third.
Woodruff Albert, machinist, bds 324 Astor.
Woodruff Henry, h 503 S Jefferson.
Woodruff H H, bds 503 S Jefferson.
Wray John, salt boiler, h N Washington, near E Sag salt works.
Wrege Charles, carp, h 101 S Rockwell.
Wrege Fritz, carp, h 122 N Clay.
Wrege John, carp, h 101 S Rockwell.
Wren Richard, h N Washington.
Wright Archibald, baker, bds 123 N Washington.
Wright E B, groceries & provisions, 204 N Water, h 425 Johnson.
Wright F, (Welsh, W, & Co), h 523 N Franklin.
Wurtz B F, clerk, bds 931 Lapeer.
Wurtz E W, lab, city mills, h 931 Lapeer.
Wurtz George, brewer, bds S Washington, in the grove.
Wurtz John, lab, bds 931 Lapeer.
Wyckoff John, turner, h 1013 S Washington.
Wylie James M, carp, h 408 N Fourth.
Wylie Robert, carp, h 408 N Fourth.
Wylie William, carp, bds 408 N Fourth.

Y

Yager John, lab, h 1802 Johnson.
Yawkey, S W, commission lumber dealer, 102 Genesee, h 708 S Washington.
YAWKEY, W C, commission lumber dealer 701 Genesee, bds 112 N Washington.
Yeager Henry, lab, bds 110 N Jefferson.
Yonkey William, clerk, bds 109 Lapeer.
York B H, salt manuf, (Flagler & Y), h 1102 S Washington.
Yorke Marcus, blacksmith, bds 316 N Franklin.
Yorkey Philip, teamster, h 117 S Rockwell.
Youst Anthony, shoemaker, h east end Tuscola.
Yungmann Herman, barber, 319 Genesee, h 306 S Clay.

Z

Zarnko Frederick, lab, h 309 N Fifth.
Zeim Augustus, carp, bds, 324 N Sixth.
Zeigen Casper, tailor, bds Lapeer.
Ziegner Frederick, brewer, h 117 S Webster.
ZIMMERMAN WM & CO, liquor dealers, 211 N Water.
ZIMMERMAN WM, (Wm Z & Co) h 307 James.
Zwerke A, clerk, bds 223 N Webster.
Zwerk John, carriage maker, h 123 N Webster.
Zwerk William, clerk, bds 123 N Webster.

☞BROWN & JAMES, Attorneys and Land Agents,

Home Insurance Company,

OFFICE, 135 BROADWAY.

New York, January 30th, 1866.

The undersigned take pleasure in presenting the usual Semi-Annual Statement, from which it appears that notwithstanding the fiery trial of the past year, during which the Company has paid losses to the amount of $1,637,852 36, *without omitting the usual semi-annual dividends, "The Home," with its capital of* Two Millions *intact, and a net surplus of* $1,444,957 90, *continues to offer, to all who seek* Reliable Insurance, *inducements surpassed by no other Company.*

CHAS. J. MARTIN, Pres't.
A. F. WILLMARTH, Vice-President.

JOHN McGEE, Sec'y.
J. H. WASHBURN, Ass't-Sec'y.

DIRECTORS.

GEO. C. COLLINS	of Geo. C. Collins & Co.
DANFORD N. BARNEY	Pres. of Wells, Fargo & Co.'s Express.
LUCIUS HOPKINS	of Hopkins, Dwight & Trowbridge.
THOMAS MESSENGER	of T. & H. Messenger.
WILLIAM H. MELLEN	late Claflin, Mellen & Co.
HOMER MORGAN	
LEVI P. STONE	late Stone, Starr & Co.
JAMES HUMPHREY	late Barney, Humphrey & Butler.
GEO. PEARCE	of Geo. Pearce & Co.
WARD A. WORK	of Ward A. Work & Son.
JAMES LOW	of Low, Harriman & Durfee.
ISAAC H. FROTHINGHAM	President Union Trust Company.
CHARLES A. BULKLEY	of Bulkley & Co.
GEO. D. MORGAN	late of E. D. Morgan & Co.
OLIVER E. WOOD	of O. E. Wood & Co.
ALFRED S. BARNES	of A. S. Barnes & Co.
GEORGE BLISS	of George Bliss & Co.
ROE LOCKWOOD	late R. Lockwood & Son.
LEVI P. MORTON	of L. P. Morton & Co.
CURTIS NOBLE	of Noble & Douglass.
J. B. HUTCHINSON	of J. C. Howe & Co., Boston.
CHARLES P. BALDWIN	of Baldwin, Starr & Co.
AMOS T. DWIGHT	of Hopkins, Dwight & Trowbridge.
HENRY A. HURLBUT	late Swift, Hurlbut & Co.
JESSE HOYT	of Jesse Hoyt & Co.
WILLIAM STURGIS	late Sturgis, Shaw & Co.
JOHN R. FORD	late Ford Rubber Co.
GEORGE T. STEDMAN	of Stedman, Carlisle & Shaw, Cincinnati
SIDNEY MASON	late Mason & Thompson.
DAVID I. BOYD	of Boyd, Brothers & Co., Albany.
CHARLES J. MARTIN	President.
ARTHUR F. WILLMARTH	Vice-President.
F. H. COSSITT	of Cossitt, Hill & Co., Memphis.
WILLIAM R. FOSDICK	President St. Nicholas National Bank.
LEWIS ROBERTS	of L. Roberts & Co.
S. B. CALDWELL	of Caldwell & Morris.
A. J. WILLS	of Thomson & Wills
WM. H. TOWNSEND	of Henrys, Smith & Townsend.
WILLIAM CLAFLIN	of Wm. Claflin & Co., Boston.
P. C. VAN SCHAICK	of Van Schaick & Edwards.
THOMAS T. BUCKLEY	of Buckley, Sheldon & Co.
JAMES S. STURGES	of Sturges & Co.
OLIVER S. CARTER	of Carter & Hawley.
HENRY M. TABER	of C. C. & H. M. Taber.

HOME

Insurance Company of New-York,

OFFICE, No. 135 BROADWAY.

CASH CAPITAL, - - - - -	$2,000,000 00
ASSETS, 1st January, 1866, -	3,598,674 14
LIABILITIES, - - - - - -	153,746 24

ABSTRACT OF THE

TWENTY-FIFTH SEMI-ANNUAL STATEMENT,

Showing the condition of the Company on the 1st day of Jan. 1866.

ASSETS.

Cash, Balance in Bank....	$50,744 49
Bonds and Mortgages, being first lien on Real Estate......	1,196,892 50
Loans on Stocks, payable on demand	97,392 08
United States Stocks, (market value)	1,350,834 00
State and Municipal Stocks and Bonds, (market value)....	405,425 00
Bank Stocks, (market value,).......	113,550 00
Interest due on 1st January, 1866	27,431 16
Balance in hands of Agents and in course of transmission	173,010 51
Bills Receivable, (for Premiums on Inland Risks, &c,)....	43,153 45
Government Stamps on hand............	110 00
Other Property, Miscellaneous Items....	13,505 13
Premiums due and uncollected on Policies issued at Office (Fire, Inland and Marine)	43,141 88
Steamer Magnet and Wrecking Apparatus	83,483 94
Total,....	$3,598,674 14

LIABILITIES.

Claims for Losses Outstanding on 1st January, 1866.. ..	152,946 24
Due Stockholders on account Dividend....	800 00

CHAS. J. MARTIN, President.
A. F. WILLMARTH, Vice-President.

JOHN McGEE, Secretary.
J. H. WASHBURN, Ass't-Secretary.
D. A. HEALD, General Agent.

BUSINESS DIRECTORY.

Agents—Insurance.

ALLARDT M H, 112 Genesee.
BROWN, HALL, & JAMES, 103 S Washington.
BROWNE WILL, 102 Genesee.
GALLAHER M H, 103 S Washington.
Holmes Charles A, 103 N Washington.
PERKINS & FOX, 103 Genesee.

Artists, Ambrotype & Photograph.

GOODRIDGE BROTHERS, 104 N Washington.
Randall James T. 325 Genesee.
Roberts William, 108 N Washington.

Auction & Commission Merchants.

BLISS C D & Co, 106 N Washington.

Architects & Builders.

Dietz William G, cor Cass & German.
GERMAIN THOMAS, 411 Tuscola.
McEachron P, 117 S Cass.
McFarlin John H, 116 N Jefferson.
Moross Columbus V, 607 Lapeer.

Bakers & Confectioners.

Beckbissinger John, 124 N Jefferson.
Broughton John, 129 S Washington.
GOODELL A E & Co, 131 N Washington.
Krekow William, 107 Lapeer.
Mann Frederick, 402 Potter.
Meidlain John, 124 N Franklin.

Banks and Bankers.

First National Bank, 114 S Washington.
Merchants' National Bank, 114 Genesee.
Robinson C K & Co, 204 Genesee, cor Washington.
Saginaw Valley Bank, 101 S Washington.

Barbers & Hairdressers.

Clay & Lester, 112 Genesee.
Reyno Abraham, 111 Genesee.
Reyno Louis, Everett House.
Yungmann Herman, 319 Genesee.

Blacksmiths.

Clark A E & J, 115 German.
Birdsall Albert, 320 Genesee.
Burtch E, 624 N Water.
Hay George, 210 Tuscola.
KOEHLER F A, 112 Tuscola.
Randall & Son, 109 Mason.
Schultz John, 206 N Cass.

Book Binders.

FREY ALBERT H, 213 Genesee.

Booksellers & Stationers.

Doughty T E & Co, 110 Genesee.
FREY & Co, 213 Genesee.
LEWIS G F, 103 S Washington.

Boots & Shoes.

Baum Martin 401 Genesee.
LENHEIM & IDDINGS, 211 Genesee.
NIEDERSTADT A E, 214 S Washington.
Schoch Gabriel, 916 Genesee.
SMITH CHARLES H & Co, 116 S Water.
WEAVER & WILKIN, 108 Genesee.

Butchers.

Barclay & Tyler, 804 Genesee.
Baum Adam, 524 Genesee.
Bickel George, 123 Lapeer.
Hubert Frederick, 114 N Washington.
Klumpp Gottlieb, 101 Lapeer.
Moye, Hidecker & Wiess, 625 Hoyt.
Neal W J, 624 N Washington.
Tholl John M, 311 Genesee.
West J & Co, 127 S Washington.

Carriage Manufacturers.

Baker James 320 Genesee.
Cameron James G, 206 & 208 N Franklin.
Nelty & Page, 207 Tuscola.

Civil Engineers & Surveyors.

Goddard Ezra, 101 Genesee.
Sears & Carey 101 Genesee.

Cigars & Tobacco Manufacturers & Dealers

ALLARDT M H, 112 Genesee.
Killian Charles, 407 Genesee.
WARD & SOUTHWICK, 107 Genesee.

Clothing—Manufacturers & Dealers.

Blier Solomon, 123 S Washington.
Duncan H R, 108 N Water.
GRAY WILLIAM N, 121 Genesee.
Heinlien Henry, 409 Genesee.
KOCH MOSES, 123 Genesee.
MARKS HENRY, 111 S Water & 115 Genesee.
MAUTNER S & A, 204 Genesee.
Mercer J C, 110 N Water.
Stoddard & Hallock, 109 N Washington.
WIGGINS & CLARK, 110 S Franklin.
WILKIN FRANK G, 105 Genesee.

Crockery, China and Glass Ware.

AIKIN & STINSON, 209 Genesee.
ELLIOTT & HARRISON 114 S Water.

Dentists.

SMITH HENRY A. 325 Genesee.
WHIPPLE P, 101 Genesee.
WHITING L C. 104 Genesee.

Drugs and Medicines—Dealers in.

Bissell Albert G, 109 Genesee.
DUNK ALFRED A, 201 Genesee.
Frizelle Brothers 119 Genesee.
Melchers Henry, 102 N Jefferson.
WADSWORTH & CO, 317 Genesee.

Dry Goods—Dealers in.

BARIE WILLIAM, 203 Genesee.
Bliss, Janes & Co, 102 & 104 S Water.
DEERING & SON, 402 Genesee.
Fish Wilber W, 103 Genesee.
LIVINGSTON J R & CO, 102 Genesee, cor Water.
PENFIELD E P & H L, 106 Genesee.
Stevens, Pool & Co, 207 Genesee.
Vaughn A S, 107 N Water.

Flour Manufacturers.

Mayflower Mills, 424 N Water.
STEVENS J S, city mills, 308 Genesee.

Forwarding & Commission Merchants.

Gooding & Hawkins, 127 & 129 N Water.
Schupp A, 229 N Water.

Foundries and Machine Shops.

Haskins & Gridley 516 Mason.
HILL & MORRIS, 901 S Water.
MERRILL G W, 1002 S Water.
WICKES BROTHERS, 534 N Water.

Furniture—Manufacturers & Dealers.

Herpel Ernst, 115 N Jefferson.
Hicks G W, 236 S Washington.
McLellon Frances 109, S Cass.
Prall & Duncan, 119 N Jefferson.
Richmond Jacob, 115 N Jefferson.
Swartz & Marskey, 411 Genesee.
Silsbee H C, 108 S Water.

Groceries and Provisions—Dealers.

BARNUM & WHITE, 122 N Water.
Ball H J, 223 S Washington.
Baumgarten Amand, 902 Genesee.
Bliss Janes & Co, 102 & 104 S Water.
BOYD & BOOTH, 101 Genesee.
DeLAND JAMES S. 224 S Washington.
DOTY H N, 101 Lapeer.
Eymer Andrew, 109 Lapeer.
Foster S & F, 101 N Water.
Goeschell H & F, 908 Genesee.
Gleason & Son, 107 N Washington.
Hœrner George & Co, 627 Hoyt.
HOUGH E A, 104 N Washington.
HOWARD W I & Bro, 125 N Washington.
Jackson A E, 511 S Washington.
JOHNSON FRANK, 306 Genesee.
Kimball John, 103 Lapeer.
LUSTER RICHARD, 325 Genesee.
Massuret T, 116 N Washington.
McBeier Richard, 602 James.
Mitchell Alexander, 223 S Washington.

Mosher & Mickley, 323 Genesee.
Nagle & Willard, 113 N Water.
O'BRIEN JOHN, 404 Genesee.
Schmelser Nicholas.
SCHUPP AUGUSTUS, 205 Genesee.
SHAW, BULLARD & Co, 123 & 125 N Water.
Storrs L C & Co, 106 S Water.
STRAW CHARLES, 115 N Water.
Welsh, Wright & Co, 606 N Washington.
Wenks Louis, 1320 Genesee.
WHALEN & SON, 222 S Washington.
Wright E B, 204 N Water.

Gunsmiths.

Cheney Henry H, 108 N Jefferson.

Hardware, Stoves and Tinware—Manuf's and Dealers.

BUCKHOUT B B, 124 N Water.
Curtis C M & F A, 115 S Water.
Gehlert John J, 401 Genesee.
Henselman John, 701 German.
MORLEY BROS, 110 & 112 S Water.
SHAW, REYNOLDS & Co, 104 Genesee & 109 S Water.

Harness, Saddles and Trunks.

Hovey L B, 206 N Washington.
Lorke Louis, 107 S Cass.
WALLACE HUGH, 302 Genesee.
Weincke John, 707 Genesee.

Hats, Caps and Furs—Dealers in.

MARKS HENRY, 115 Genesee.
WILKIN & MACK, 108 Genesee.

Hotels.

American Hotel, 113 N Cass.
BANCROFT HOUSE, 118 & 120 Genesee.
Bellevue House, 602 German.
Canada House, 625 N Franklin.
EVERETT HOUSE, 219 Genesee.
Farmers Hotel, 904 Genesee.
Hibernia Hotel, 724 N Washington.
Jeffers Hotel, 1231 S Water.
Monitor House, 623 N Washington.
Saginaw Valley House, 116 N Water.
Sherman House, 131 S Water.
Washington Hotel, 103 S Warren.

Justices of the Peace.

Jeffers Michael, 103 N Washington.
Maurer George, 112 Genesee.
Miller Hezekiah, 101 Genesee.
PERKINS DANIEL W, 101 Genesee.

Lawyers.

BROWN & JAMES, 103 S Washington.
Button & Sturtevant, 325 Genesee.
Camp Charles H, 105 N Washington.
CLARK & LOVELAND, 105 N Washington.
GAGE & LEWIS, 101 S Washington.
GILLETT & GAMBLE, 204 Genesee.
Hoyt Henry H, 101 Genesee.
Joslin Harvey 101 Genesee.
PERKINS DANIEL W, 101 Genesee.
Powers E H, 207 Genesee.
THOMPSON & FLANDERS, 205 Genesee.
WEBBER & SMITH, 102 N Washington.
Wheeler & Herring, 101 Genesee.
Wisner & Dillingham, 102 N Washington.

Leather Belting.

WARD & SOUTHWICK, 107 Genesee.

Liquor Dealers—Wholesale.

ROOT & MIDLER, 131 N Water.
ZIMMERMAN W & CO, 221 N Water.

Livery.

GATES A W & CO, 201 N Water.

Lumber—Inspectors, Manufacturers and Dealers.

BURT & BRO, 107 N Washington.
CATLIN & SANBORN, 122 N Water.
Estabrook & Mason, 101 S Washington.
Hayden John, h 424 Fifth.
Hunter A H 122, N Water.
Jones C B, 120 S Water.
McLane C C, 105 S Washington.
McLane Seth 105 S Washington.
Perry C N & Sons, 107 N Washington.
Post Charles & Co, 402 Genesee.
ROSE D F, 101 N Water.

Rust John F & Co, 101 N Washington.
Sears F P & Co, 1131 S Water.
Shaw J E, bds Bancroft.
WEIDEMANN ROBERT H, 101 Genesee.
Whitman George B, 103 N Washington.
Yawkey Samuel W, 102 Genesee.
YAWKEY WM C & CO, 101 Genesee.

Marble Dealers.

Stearns William H, 107 S Cass.

Milliners and Dressmakers.

Bliss & Pettibone, 107 N Washington.
Boyden Mrs E L, 127 N Washington.
Hammond Mrs E G, 109 S Washington.

Morrison Miss E J, 108 N Washington.
Nicholson Miss E, 108 N Washington.
Watson S & Co, 209 Genesee.

Music Dealers.

Champlin O H 317 Genesee.

News Dealers.

REEVES D B & CO, 321 Genesee.

Newspapers.

EAST SAGINAW COURIER, (Weekly), 224 S Washington.
EAST SAGINAW ENTERPRISE, (Daily & Weekly,) 202 N Water.

Painters, Paper Hangers and Glaziers.

Banchant Charles G, 203 N Jefferson.
BURT & LOOMIS, 319 Genesee.
Glover O L, 208 N Water.
NOEL B, 206 N Franklin.
PENDERGAST JOHN A, 105 S Cass.
Riley William, 324 Genesee.

Physicians.

Bennett D C, 101 Genesee.
Farnsworth A, 102 Geensee.
Hall D S, 125 N Washington.
Herring F W, 816 Genesee.
Hesse B, 813 William.
Mason O L, 125 N Washington.

Massbacher Frederick, 101 Lapeer.
Osborne N, 207 Genesee.
Ross D B, 103 N Washington.
SPINNEY A B, 325 Genesee.
Thompson John, 116 N Washington.
Turner S W, 202 N Water.
Vandusen A, 325 Genesee.
Von Daniels Charles, 125 N Warren.
WHEELER M M, 127 N Washington.

Planing Mills and Sash and Door Manuf.

GALLAHER, MEAD & DEERING, 211 Hayden.
Mershon A H, 624 S Water.
SPENCER & NEWCOMBE, 206 N Jefferson.

Real Estate—Agents and Dealers.

BROWN, HALL & JAMES, 103 S Washington.
BURT & BROTHER, 107 N Washington.
HESS M B, 105 N Washington, Hess Block.
Moeller F S & Co, 402 Genesee.
TAYLOR J R & CO, 103 S Washington.
WIGGINS EDWARD W, 107 Genesee.

Stave Dealers.

Binder Wm, 510 S Water.
Curtis C M & F A, 115 S Water.
Dutton Chauncy S, 325 Genesee.
Roper William, 402 Genesee.
Shaw Humphrey, 602 S Water.
Ten Eyck C & E, 705 N Water.

Watchmakers and Jewelers.

Doughty T E & Co, 110 Genesee.
HERB F JOS, 213 Genesee.
LEGGETT S T, 105 S Washington.
PROCTOR H R, 125 Genesee.

SALINA DIRECTORY.

ABBREVIATIONS.—For ab., read *above*; bds., *boards*; bet., *between* carp., *carpenter;* cor., *corner;* col'd *colored;* E., *East* h., *house;* lab., *laborer;* manuf., *manufacturer;* manufy., *manufactory;* N. *north*; propr., *proprietor;* res., *residence;* S., *south.*

The word *Street* is implied.

A

Adams Peter, lab, bds Miller.
Alexander House, McHenry & Cole, proprs, Mackinaw.
Allen L E, lab, h Morris.
Allen S T, (A & Sutherland), h Washington.
Allen & Sutherland, salt and lumber manufs.
Allison James S, carp, h Morris.
Ann Arbor salt and lumber manuf, (Sutherland, Bennett, Chapin and Gallaher) proprs.
Ashman Jehudi, ship carp, h Miller.
Ashman William, lab, h Centre.
Baker William L, engineer, h Miller.
Bankfield Joseph, lab, h Miller.
Barley John, lab, h Mackinaw.
Barney Daniel, lab, h Mackinaw.
Barridge Geo W, carp, h Mackinaw.
Barton Daniel, lab, h Centre.
Bastedo John, lab, bds Mackinaw.
Beach Laban, carp, h Miller.
Bebee C R, clerk, bds Mackinaw.
Bebee L P & Co, (L P B & O D Bellinger,) grocers, Mackinaw.
Becker Mathia, saloon, Miller, h same.
Bellinger O D, (Bebee & B), h Mackinaw.
Bessette Joseph, lab, h Randolph.
Biddlecomb, Mrs F E, h Rust.
Blight John, lab, h Randolph.
Bortle S H, carp, h Hess.
Botsford P V M, lawyer, Mackinaw.
Bowles Thomas, lab, h Mackinaw.

Boyd James O, lab, h Centre.
Bradley & Burrows, (H H B & F B), grocers, Mackinaw.
Bradley H H, (B & Burrows h, Mackinaw, h same.
Briggs Jonathan, cooper, h Randolph.
Broughton Joseph, teamster, h Randolph.
Brown Geo, lawyer, bds Alexander House.
Brown Isaac, lab, h Miller.
Bronner Jacob, lab, h Miller.
Buckley James, wagon maker, bds Mackinaw.
Buckley Michael, wagon maker, bds Mackinaw.
Buckley Patrick, carriage manufactory, Mackinaw, h same.
Bundy & Lowman, lumber manuf.
Burrows F, (Bradley & B), h Mackinaw.
Burts John C. lab, h Mackinaw.
Callahan Jerry, lab, h Eaton,
Campbell Andrew, carp, h Mackinaw.
Carmel Charles, lab, h Mackinaw.
Carriage manufactory, Patrick Buckley propr, Mackinaw.
Carter Perry, cooper, h Washington.
Carter Perry, salt manuf, h Washington.
Caswell J A, saloon, Mackinaw, h same.
Chase Henry, lab, h Centre.
Choven H, engineer, h Miller.
Churchill John, (Rogers & C,) bds Washington.
Clark Levi, lab, h William.
Cline Peter, sawyer, h Mackinaw.
Cobb Mrs K M, dressmaker, Washington, h same.
Cobleigh William, engineer, h Miller.
Cole A B, (McHenry & C,) propr, Alexander House,
Coleman Joseph E, sawyer, h Mackinaw.
Collins Richard, saloon, Washington h same.
Coogen James, cooper, bds Salina House.
Coogen Michael, cooper, bds Salina House.
Crane Rev R H, pastor Methodist Church, h Randolph.
Crosgrave William, lab, bds Mackinaw.
Curtis A C, painter, h William.
Curtis Alfred, painter, h William.
Danley Jacob, lab, bds Salina House.
Dates John, lab, h Mackinaw.
Davis Geo L, carp, h Mackinaw.
DeLand M P, h Miller.
Denton, A J, lab, h Miller.
Dodge I F, lab, h Hess.
Donahue John, engineer, h Rust.
Durkee Robert, carp, h William.
Eaton William, teamster, bds Salina House.
Eavetrough, pump & pump-log manufy, Charles A Mann propr.

Eglow John, blacksmith, h Mackinaw.
Ellis William, furniture, Washington.
Eshelman ——, lab, bds Alexander House.
Fitch Jacob, bds Salina House.
Flagler & York, salt manuf.
Fraser Homer, lab, h William.
Gaffney James, lab, h Miller.
Gallagher Wm, (Hess & G), druggists, h Mackinaw.
Gilbert Lyman. lab, h Miller.
Gravel Adolphus, lab, h Miller.
Griggs E L, clerk, bds Salina House.
Griggs L S, clothing Mackinaw, bds Alexander House.
Grohmann Alois, clerk, Salina House.
Grohmann Anthony bds Salina House.
Hall J J, carp, h Hess.
Hall Job, blacksmith, bds Alexander House.
Haskness & Co, (W K H & J O'Donnell), dry goods & groceries, Washington.
Harkness W K, (H & O'Donnell), Washington res East Saginaw.
Haven William, bar tender, h Hess.
Henry Edward, lab, bds Alexander House.
Henry James, engineer, h Miller.
Hess Charles (H & Gallagher,) druggist Washington bds Mackinaw.
Hess & Gallagher, (Chas H & Wm G), druggists, Washington.
Hess Peter, farmer, h Mackinaw.
Hickey Eugene, lab, h Miller.
Hilson T M, sailor, h William.
Hinman D W, salt manuf, h Mackinaw.
Holt Isaac, sawyer, h Hess.
Honeywell Mrs J A, h Miller.
Horton Hugh A, carp, h Hess.
Hosmer J J, grocer, h Mackinaw.
Houlahan Richard, lab, h Mackinaw.
Hewes William, boarding house, Miller.
Hubbard Theron T, physician, Washington.
Humphrey John C, carp, h Hess.
Hunter David, salt boiler, h William.
Hunter Jeremiah, carp, h Centre.
Hurlbert John, carp, h Miller.
Hutchinson Daniel, caulker, bds National House.
Hutchinson Wm, caulker, bds National House.
Ingledew John, lumber manuf, h Washington.
Inglehart Mrs Caroline, h Miller.
Irwin & Co, salt manuf.
Jackson Andrew, teamster, h William.

James Alexander, cooper, bds Miller.
Jamison Thomas, butcher, h Gallagher.
Jerroy Joseph, lab, bds National Hotel.
Kirwin John, blacksmith, h Mackinaw.
Kirwin Wm, harnessmaker, bds Mackinaw.
Knapp E R, physician, Mackinaw, h William.
Knight Frank, lab, bds Mackinaw.
Kriby John, grocer, h Mackinaw.
Leasia A B, lab, h Hess.
Leasia C F, meat market.
Lettis Isaac, boarding house, Randolph.
Lindley John, carp, h Hess.
Linton A millwright, h Mackinaw.
Linton Stewart S, carp, h Mackinaw.
Loomis John, lab, h Miller.
Lowry W W, cabinet maker, h Miller.
Lucas William, groceries, boots & shoes, Washington.
Lucas William, shoemaker, h Miller.
Luck Charles, shoemaker.
Luck Fritz, carp.
Luck John, carp, h Miller.
Lumber manufy, Bundy & Lowman.
Lyness R H, stave maker, h Miller.
McBride Hugh, lab, h Centre.
McDonald J R, lab, h Mackinaw.
McHenry & Cole, (J Mc & A B C), proprietors Alexander House Mackinaw.
McHenry J, (McHenry & Bro), h Mackinaw.
McHenry J & M A, saloon, Washington.
McHenry J, (McH & Cole), proprs Alexander House.
McHenry M A, (McHenry & Bro), bds Alexander House.
McGuire James, lab, bds Salina House.
McGunn P A, saloon, Mackinaw, h same.
McIntyre D, Justice Peace, Mackinaw, h Hess.
McMaster James A, groceries, Centre, h same.
Mann Chas A, propr Salina House.
Martindale E A, lawyer, h Hess.
Maxam H L, fireman, h Centre.
Maxam Lewis, lab, h Miller.
Merritt William, lab, h Mackinaw.
Methodist Episcopal Church, (Rev R H Crane pastor), Hess.
Millet Frank, engineer, h Centre.
Milligan Samuel, teamster, h Morris.
Mills P, teamster, h Miller.
Monfore Newton, lab, bds National Hotel.
Moses Willard, hoopmaker, bds Salina House.
Moal Charles, lab, h Miller.

Mowbray John, brewer, h Miller.
Mowbray Wm, brewery, Miller, h same.
National House, Walter Conrad propr, Mackinaw.
Needham James, lab, h Hess.
Needham Thomas, lab, h Hess.
Needham Wm H, lab, h Hess.
Newell Philo, carp, h Washington.
Nimmons William, foreman salt block, h Mackinaw.
Nye N B & Co, salt manufy, Miller.
O'Donnell John, (Harkness & O), bds Salina House.
Oversby William, lab, h Miller.
Oudden Patrick, lab.
Parker Thomas, watchman, Miller.
Peek J A, carp, h Miller.
Penner Joseph, lab, bds Alexander House.
Peterson John, lab, bds Miller.
Philips Chas H, engineer, bds National House.
Quick Abraham R, lab, h Hess.
Quackenbush Jesse H (Sheriff) h Hess.
Quackenbush M W, h William.
Randall N A, clerk, h Washington.
Reynolds Benjamin, lab, h Miller.
Reynolds Peter, bds Miller.
Reynolds Sheldon, sailor, bds Miller.
Reynolds Silas, farmer, h Miller.
Reynolds W, physician, Mackinaw, bds Washington.
Rice William H, lab, h Centre.
Rogers Alva, (R & Churchill), meat market, Washington.
Rogers & Churchill, (A R & J C), meat market, Washington.
Rose Wm, butcher, h Mackinaw.
Russell Isaac, h Mackinaw.
Rust John F, (J F R & J Ingledew), salt and lumber manufs Rust.
Ryan John, lab, h Miller.
Salina House, Chas A Mann propr.
Salt & lumber manuf, John F Rust & Co props, Rust.
Salt manufy, Carter Perry propr.
Salt manuf, Flagler & York proprs.
Salt manufy, W K Harkness propr.
Salt manufy, Irwin & Co. proprs.
Salt manufy, Welsh & Hinman proprs.
Sash & blind manufy, M W Scott propr, Mackinaw.
Sauder Henry, lab, h Morris.
Sawyer Burton F, clerk, bds Washington.
Schlayel August, lab, bds Salina House.
Schoonover Thomas, Insurance agt, h Hess.
Schultz Theodore, lab, h Miller.

Scott M W, sash & blind mauufy, Mackinaw, h same.
Shirley Thos A, lab, h Miller.
Shunhite Charles, lab, h Morris.
Sikes A P, mason, h Miller.
Simpson Jas, brewer, h Miller.
Simpson John, engineer, h Hess.
Smith A C, farmer, h Centre.
Smith Barthuell, cooper, h Mackinaw.
Smith W C, saloon Mackinaw.
Somers Geo, bds Washington.
Soper William, lab, bds Mackinaw.
Spaulding Charles, saloon, Washington, h same.
Spitzer John, teamster, bds Salina House.
Springer John G, carp, h Randolph.
Stanton L H, butcher, bds Washington.
Stevens T D, hoopmaker, bds Salina House.
Stewart Charles, shoemaker, h Miller.
Stillwell T W, cooper, h Hess.
Stotts Joseph R, carp, h Miller.
Strickland Mrs Elizabeth, h Washington.
Sutherland C, (A & S), salt and lumber manuf, h Mackinaw.
Swarthout Cornelius N, engineer, bds Salina House.
Swarthout Rufus, lab, bds Salina House.
Taggart A S, school teacher, h Hess.
Taggart James, lab, h Rust.
Tansley Mrs Silence, saloon, h same.
Taylor Thomas jr, lab, bds Mackinaw.
Terry Arthur W, mason, h Washington.
Thatcher Erastus, dry goods & groceries, Washington.
Thompson James, lab, h Miller.
Thompson Robert, lab, h Miller.
Thompson Thomas, lab, h Miller.
Townsend William A, teamster, h Miller.
Towson Henry, lab, h Miller.
Tyler Mrs A, millinery, Mackinaw, h same.
Vandermark A G, cooper, h Randolph.
Van Seyke Wm, carp, h Hess.
Van Tifflin Edward, teamster, h Miller.
Veasia Viger, lab, h Rust.
Vincent Moses, carp, h Washington.
Vochner Mrs S, bakery, Centre.
Walker John, lab, h Miller.
Wallace Edmund, saloon, Randolph, h same.
Walter Conrad, propr National House Mackinaw.
Walters William, salt boiler, h William.
Watson George, lab, h Hess.
Welsh & Henman, salt manufs.

West A J, lumber insp, h Hess.
Williams Henry, blacksmith, h Mackinaw.
Williams Henry, blacksmith, Miller, h Mackinaw.
Wilson John, teamster, bds Salina House.
Wilson James, cooper, h Miller.
Wilson Richard, lab, h Miller.
Wise Jacob F, lab, h Centre.
Worden John P, ostler Salina House.
Youmans Henry, mill foreman, Miller, h Mackinaw.
Young George, lab, bds Salina House.

BRIDGEPORT CENTER.

Chandler, W.
Foster, J. B.
Foster, Alanson.
Foster, Henry.
Hodgman, L.
Hill, George.
Jackson, Jehiel,
Jackson, Lyman.
Lull, C. A.
Massner, Christopher.
Miner, George.
Osborn, M.
Pettibone, D. A.
Whitney, Ira.

HISTORY OF BAY CITY.

Bay City, in the county of Bay and State of Michigan, is situated on the right and east bank of Saginaw River, and about four miles from its mouth. It is in Township fourteen, North Range five East principal meridian; in latitude forty-three and a half, nearly north, and in longitude eighty-four, west.

The ground on which it stands is from twelve to twenty, and in places, thirty feet above the surface of the river; which, at this point, from its nearness to the Bay and from its breadth, as well as from the peculiar conformation of the country above, maintains very nearly an even stage of water; seldom varying from its accustomed height more than from two to four feet—the chief rise and fall being regulated by the stage of water in the lakes. The ground on which the city stands is admirably adapted to the demands of a large place. It is firm in structure—being composed of compact clay and loam—high enough for all the purposes of drainage and for cellars, and yet not rising into hills nor sinking into gullies, so as to necessitate expensive grading; allowing the easy moving of heavy materials and of buildings, such as the requirements of a growing city call for.

In early days the land was *wet* in the first months of the year, as in the forests adjacent it sometimes still is; not because it lacked a sufficient height for good drainage, but from the compact nature of the subsoil forbidding the easy escape of the water beneath. Any lands, even the highest, are liable to be wet from the same cause. This difficulty is in process of remedy precisely as fast as the country is settled, cleared and brought under culture.

EARLY HISTORY.

The State of Michigan, in common with all the Northwest, was originally in possession of the Indian tribes. But in 1819, Gen. Riley, for many years Postmaster in the city of Schenectady, N. Y., and who had been a trader among the Chippewa Indians, obtained from the chiefs of that tribe a section of land for his son, John Riley, born of an Indian mother. This section of land was that on which Bay City is built, and was styled "the John Riley Reserve."

A few white settlers began to come into the Saginaw Valley as early as 1828. The valley had in fact been visited in 1792, by the grandfather of Medor Trombley, in pursuit of furs, who perished in the following manner: He made a musk-rat spear for an Indian. One spear only created a demand for another by another Indian. The second spear was an improvement upon the first, which fact excited the ill blood of the owner of the inferior article, and in the confab growing out of it Trombley was stabbed in the back. He was able nevertheless to retreat to his boat. He started for Detroit, but did not reach it; being knocked overboard by the boom of his small craft and drowned in Lake Huron.

Capt. Joseph F. Marsac, of French descent, and till 1838, when he removed to Lower Saginaw, a resident of Hamtramack, near Detroit, also made occasional trips to the Saginaw Valley, and in 1819 he was present at a treaty-making between Gen. Cass, for the Government, and the Indians.

Hon. Eleazer Jewett came to the valley in 1828, and was followed in 1829–30 by Gardiner and Ephraim Williams, all of whom settled at or near Saginaw. The next settlers in the valley were Hon. Albert Miller and James McCormick, deceased; both of whom settled finally in what is now Portsmouth, and Hon. —— Ure; all previous to 1832. James Fraser came in 1834, and settled at first on a farm upon the Tittabawassee.— Previous to 1835 he was followed by Medor and Joseph Trombley, and between that and 1838, by Cromwell Barney, Thomas Rogers and Hon. Sidney S. Campbell.

At Bay City the first white settlers were Leon Trombley and one Mesho, both of French extraction, and who emigrated here from Detroit in 1832. Trombley was an appointee of the Government, to instruct the Indians in agriculture ; but from defective education himself in the agricultural art, he was not of great service in that behalf to the red men. He did however possess some knowledge of the principles of barter, and so proceeded to build a log house for the joint purposes of residence and trader, and being supplied with goods by the American Fur Company, he carried on a traffic in furs for some years. His store and residence stood near the present site of the law office of Hon. James Birney, on Water street, and was the first building erected in Bay City.

He was joined in the following year by two nephews, already mentioned, Medor and Joseph Trombley, who engaged in the same business and who are still living ; one at Bangor and one at Portsmouth.

In the latter part of the same year Benjamin Cushway was sent here by the U S. Government as blacksmith for the Indians ; which occupation he followed for twenty years, until removed with the tribe to Isabella ; whence afterward he went to Saginaw City to reside, where he is still living. About the year 1835, Benway Trombley, Leon Trombley Jr., John Trudell and Louis Trombley, joined the settlement here.

Until the year 1836, therefore, the place was occupied as a mere trading post, and little was thought of any immediate endeavors in the way of a town. But the spirit of speculation had been rising for some years in the country at large, and that saw cities wherever there were rivers, and great value in lands wherever situated and however uncultivated. In that year therefore, a company was formed at Detroit, for the improvement of a town site on the lower Saginaw. The members of it were Stevens T. Mason, F. H. Stevens, Electus Backus, Horace Hallock, Henry R. Schoolcraft, John Hurlbut, Andrew T.

McReynolds, H. K. Sanger and Phineas Dow, of that city, and James Fraser of Saginaw.

The company was styled "The Saginaw Bay Company." It proceeded to purchase of John Riley, with the sanction of the U. S. Government, the tract of land known as Riley's Reservation, and on which Bay City now stands.

In the year following, or 1837, having laid out a town, the company proceeded to construct a store house and dock, at the foot of Center Street, and also a small building on Fifth Street, which was used as their office.

Their intention was to proceed at once to build up a village.— But like a great many intentions of that time, it was upset by causes out of their reach. The financial revulsion, commencing in 1836 and continuing to operate for some years, overtook their endeavor before it had assumed any very tangible shape or reached any considerable results, and forced them to abandon it. The company was dissolved and the parties removed to different parts of the country. Afterwards Hon. James G. Birney, Daniel H. Fitzhugh and James Fraser, purchased the interest of the old company and proceeded to realize something of their designs.

As already narrated Medor Trombley emigrated to this valley in 1835. He settled in Portsmouth, and built a log house near where the Center House now stands, and began trade with the Indians. His first trip to the valley was on foot, following an Indian trail from Detroit to Saginaw, and driving at the same time some cattle. From Saginaw to this point he came on a raft down the river. He then returned for his cattle which had been left at Saginaw, and swam them across the river at the "Lone Tree," now called "The Elbow." After two year's trade in company with his brother Joseph, he proceeded to erect a frame house, which is still standing, and which has the honor of being the first frame building erected in the valley. The lumber of which it was constructed was brought from Detroit for that purpose upon a vessel of twenty-eight tons burthen called the *Savage*.

It is now known as the Center House in Portsmouth. For a long time it was called the "Big House," and in the year 1840 was purchased by James McCormick, remodeled, finished and occupied by him until his death, some years after. This vessel above named, called the *Savage*, seems to have been the first of any size that ever visited this region. It was a schooner, and each of its arrivals at Lower Saginaw was announced by the American Fur Company's agents, by the firing of a cannon.

BOUNDARIES AND POLITICAL HISTORY.

This entire region until 1843, was included in the Township of Saginaw. At that time the Township of Hampton, including Lower Saginaw, now Bay City, and belonging to the County of Saginaw was organized. At first and for some years, the name "Lower Saginaw" designated all the white settlement in this immediate region.

The first township meeting for the Town of Hampton, County of Saginaw, took place in the year 1843, and was held at the house of Sidney S. Campbell, in the building now known as the Globe Hotel, on the corner of Fifth and Water Streets, Bay City. This was the first framed dwelling built in Bay City proper.—The lots on which the building was erected had been given to Mr. Campbell, by the Saginaw Bay Company, as an inducement for him to settle in the town. Previously to this, the Company had erected a block house intended for a dwelling, but used as a boarding house.

The election at this time was for a Supervisor. Hon. James G. Birney and S. S. Campbell, were the candidates; Mr. Campbell receiving seven votes, and Mr. Birney six, Mr. C. was declared elected.

The County of Bay was organized in 1857. The act of organization was entitied "an act to organize the County of Arenac and parts of other counties, by the name of Bay County," and was approved February 17, 1857.

The first election for county officers was held on the 9th day of June, 1857. The whole number of votes cast for Sheriff was

106; of which Nathan Simons received the entire number.—For County Clerk, Elijah S. Catlin also received the whole, 106. For County Treasurer there seems to have been some competition; James Watson received 100 votes, J. H. Little. James Hutchinson and Pero Roy each received one vote; from which it is safe to conclude that neither of these three were considered as elected. For Judge of Probate, S. S. Campbell, received the orthodox number, 106. For Prosecuting Attorney, Chester H. Freeman received 107; one voter it is supposed being able to remain only for that one vote. For Register of Deeds, Theodore M. Bligh, 106. For Circuit Court Commissioner, Stephen K. Wright was chosen, and for County Surveyor, James J. McCormick.

The first meeting of the Board of Supervisors for Bay County was held at the house of Judge Campbell, on the 10th of August, 1858. The Board consisted of two members; George W. Smock, from the Town of Williams, and S. S. Campbell, from the town of Hampton; these two townships being at that time, the only ones organized in the county.

The Circuit Court held its first session after the organization of the county, on the 6th day of April, 1859, in a building rented of the late James Fraser, where it is still held.

PERMANENT SETTLEMENTS.

On the first day of March, 1838, Mr. S. S. Campbell arrived at Lower Saginaw. He found here Cromwell Barney, living with his family in a small log house where the store of Munger & Co. now stands. Mr. Barney was then engaged in building a house for Mr. Campbell, upon the ground at present covered by the Globe Hotel, which house was so far completed as to be occupied by Mr. C. and his family the same year.

Mr. Campbell killed a large buck on the following day—the second of March—on the opposite side of the river. This was the last of his race for a long while; for Mr. C. states that he did not see another deer nor the track of one for five years.—The previous winter having been attended with a good deal of snow, which became crusted over, the wolves and Indian hunters chased them down and nearly exterminated the race · the crust not being sufficiently strong to bear up the deer, while the wolf dog, and hunter upon his snow shoes, could glide along over it with ease. The wolves in those years are described as being amazingly plenty, but have been all the while gradually thinning out in all the lower and centre portions of the State.—The month of March in that year—1838—is described by Mr. Campbell as being as warm as is usual for the month of June

During the following winter, that of 1838–9, Gen. Rosseau, well known at present for the part he has taken in the late war, was engaged with his uncle, Dr. Rosseau, in the performance of a surveying contract with the General Government; their work being the subdivision of the townships in this vicinity.

Other surveying was done by Louis Clawson, whose arrival was in the spring of 1839, with a Government contract to survey the whole territory from Au Sauble to Thunder Bay. In the following year, Mr. E. Jewett made a survey of the Prairie Road; now Woodside Avenue.

On the 19th of July, 1839, Stephen Wolverton, of Erie, Pennsylvania, whose name the "Wolverton House" now bears, arrived, commissioned to build a Light House at the mouth of the river. He came on a small vessel, commanded by Capt. Stiles. The Light House was commenced but not finished by him. The work was completed by Capt. Levi Johnson, of Cleveland, O., whose arrival was in the year following, or May 14th, 1840.—During the same year, Thomas Rogers, who had been living since 1838, at Portsmouth, removed to Lower Saginaw, where he resided till 1852, when he died of cholera; that disease then prevailing in the settlement. His family still remain in the place. Mr. Rogers was by trade a blacksmith. Other arrivals that year were Seth Willey, who now resides at East Saginaw; Capt. B. F. Pierce, who engaged in building fish boats and in fishing, and who still resides upon the west side of the river; Capt. John S. Wilson, whose arrival was upon the 28th of May, and also Capt. Robert McNiff, who came upon a small vessel of eight or ten tons burthen, named the *Daniel Cooper*.

During the year 1841, the place was visited by the brig *Ramsey Crooks*, Capt. David Stanard; but whether the vessel brought freight or passengers is not stated. The year, nevertheless, was signalized by the arrival of a number of emigrants. Among them are James Busby, and Frederick Durr; the latter a single man, but not averse it seems to matrimony. Nor was he alone of that mind, for a Miss Clark, a damsel of suitable years, engaged in the honorable pursuit of instilling useful knowledge into the youthful mind, was of the same way of thinking, and became Mrs. Durr, "for better or worse." This was the first marrying among exclusively white people in Lower Saginaw. Who performed the needful ceremony is not stated. Probably the marriage fee was absorbed by some magistrate, for there is no mention here of any Protestant clergyman, till after that time.

There was not only a beginning made in the way of matrimony thus early, but the other memorable experiences of humanity, such as being born and dying, were also inaugurated.— The first death was that of Nathaniel B. Burnet, who came here from Pine River, on the western shore of Saginaw Bay, where he had been building a saw mill. His disease is not given. He was buried without funeral ceremonies, in what has been known since that time as the Potter's Field. Not long after Mrs. Durr deceased, and these were the only deaths in the settlement for a number of years.

The first white child born was Elizabeth Barney, daughter of Cromwell Barney, who is, if still living, and will please to excuse an allusion to a lady's age, some twenty-five years old. The second birth was that of Edward M. Campbell, son of Hon. S. S. Campbell.

Other arrivals that year, were the family of Nathan Pierce, and Hon. James G. Birney and family. Mr. Birney came from Detroit to this place, and it is well recollected by the country at large in connection with his candidacy for the Presidency of the United States in 1844, that the place of his residence was Lower

Saginaw, Michigan. Mr. James J. McCormick also made his residence here in 1841.

In the following year, 1842, Frederick Backus came in with a respectable stock of goods, and commenced a general trade.

The growth of the place from 1842 to 1848 was but slow.—Most of the residents were without large means, and suffered often the privations which attend frontier settlements. As a sample of the scale of operations in those days, it is related that Mr. Henry Benson, in the year 1846, living then upon the farm of Mr. Campbell, upon the Cass River, cut and hauled 184 feet of timber, running measure, and floated it down the river, selling it for $5 52 to pay the rent of the said farm. Mr. B. is now a stockholder in the First National Bank.

The same timber was sold by Mr. Campbell to Hon. James G. Birney, and was used by him in building the house on Water Street, now occupied by James Shearer. Mr. Birney resided in this house after its erection, during his stay in the place. It is still among the best dwelling houses in the city.

In the year 1848, settlers began once more to arrive with greater frequency. Curtis Munger and Edwin Park began the business of cooperage and fishing, and as the place was beginning to grow from the lumber trade, they extended their business to include a grocery establishment, large enough for a commencement, it being 14x16 feet, and containing a sufficiency of usables for all present demands. In 1852 they built the store upon the river bank now occupied by Munger & Co. In 1857, A. S. Munger arrived from Elkhart, Ind., and the firm launched into a general mercantile business.

Mr. H. C. Munger served three years as President of the Common Council of Bay City, after its incorporation as a village and before it became a city.

In October, 1848, J. B. and B. B. Hart, took up their residence in the place, and about the same time S. S. Barclay and Douglas Sayles. C. C. C. Chilson arrived on the 15th of March, of the same year; and the next month John H. Yawkey, who was followed a little later by J. T. Calkins and S. J. Clemens.

These last two engaged in trade in a small way upon Water Street. Capt. John Cline, of the brig *E. H. Scott*, arrived in July, 1849. At the close of the year the following persons arrived, viz: Alex. McKay, J. S. Barclay, H. McEwen, and Capt. A. S. Pearsons and wife. The year 1850 and '51 were marked by the arrival of a number of settlers. During the first of these years the arrivals were S. Presly, Clark Moulthrop, Capt. Geo. Carpenter, Col. Henry Raymond, Alex. McEwen, James Watson and Thomas Whitney. This latter person built the first mill in Bangor, in the year 1854. In the year 1851, the professions of Law and Medicine sent on their representatives, although previously to this the settlement had enjoyed the medical services of a lady, who had gained a knowledge of the healing art, of her father,, who was a physician, viz: Mrs. Thomas Rogers.

But this year Dr. Geo. E Smith commenced medical practice; and Mr. James L. S. Fox hung out his shingle, to indicate his willingness to do the legal for all parties determined on lawful quarrel.

Hon. James G. Birney, who arrived some years previously, was a lawyer, but did not engage in practice. Mr. Fox was soon joined in the profession by Wm. L. Sherman, Esq., and thus a proper antagonism was instituted, such as render law suits interesting and "profitable."

The highly necessary and respectable craft which builds integumenial covering for men, got itself represented here in the person of Edward Williamson, about the same time; who began at once to ply the shears and the needle. Men of various crafts and professions followed. Hobart Alvord, C. Munger, Martin Watrous; and then John Drake and two others, who at once purchased a mill site on the opposite side of the river, of Hon. James G. Birney, and erected a mill thereon in the following year.

Mr. C. E. Jennison had arrived the year before, or in 1850, and had commenced business with James Fraser, in a building not far from where the Fraser House now stands. He was from Danville, Penn. After a year and a half he bought out

Mr. Fraser's interest and prosecuted business by himself. He was joined afterwards by his brother, H. W. Jennison, and in 1855, their store as at present occupied was built, as also those now in use by Binder & Co., and by S. Wilkin & Co.

Among the early traders were F. W. Backus, who carried on the business at the foot of Center Street, in a building somewhat "old"—though when it became such is not quite certain—and which belonged to Mr. Watrous. Wm. Pomeroy & Co., also commenced trade very early. They were succeeded or joined by J. B. and B. B. Hart; all near the foot of Center Street. Then came James Fraser, who was followed by Calkins and Clemens, and then by J. H. Little, and Williamson, who carried on their business on Water Street, near where the brick store of Mr. Lord now stands. Others who engaged in business about the same time, were Hiram O. McEwen, B. B. Hart, James Mason, E. B. Ferris & Co., and Dr. Geo. E. Smith, who united the grocery business with his medical practice.

The first brick building in the place was a dwelling house, erected by Thomas W. Watkins, on the corner of Washington and Center Streets. T. C. Phillips erected the second brick dwelling, situate on corner of Adams and Tenth Streets.—Subsequent to this a brick store had been built on South Water Street, adjoining the Fraser House. Afterwards the County Office Building was erected, at the corner of Center and Jefferson. Others, which the late James Fraser built, were a brick block on Water Street, also the new hotel which bears his name.

LUMBER AND MILLS.

The first interest which called people into this valley was that which pioneers all our western land, viz; trade with the aborigones. For the purposes of this traffic, the forests are explored and the rivers are threaded. Reports are thus carried to the older parts of the country, of the features and resources of the new. That the Saginaw River was belted by pine timber in unlimited quantities, would naturally be known at an early day, and the traders would after a while be succeeded by the choppers. Consequently after a few years from the time of the French pioneers another set of men began to think of saw logs and mills. The upper streams which flow into and make the Saginaw are convenient for floating down the logs, but it is an economy to make the logs into boards where they can easily be transferred to vessels for shipment. Consequently the lower Saginaw was fixed on at an early day as the suitable place for mills, and steps were taken to erect them.

The first mill in this region was undertaken at Kaw-kaw-lin, by Fraser and Barney, as early as 1844. Hopkins, Pomeroy and Fraser, commenced one soon after at Lower Saginaw; which was the first one in the place. Catlin and Fraser built one soon after, as did also Campbell and McCormick; and about the same time was built the Stanton Mill, now owned by H. M. Bradley and brother.

There are now in the place thirty mills for the manufacture of lumber, and three for the making of shingles; all running by steam, and a part of them joined also in the making of salt.

The Bridge.—This was built by a stock company in 1864–5. It was opened to the public in April, 1865. It is 1,864 feet long; of Brown's patent; and was built by W. F. Glasby, at a cost of $35,000. The capital stock is $50,000. C. W. Gibson is Secretary and Treasurer.

First National Bank of Bay City, was organized Janunry 15, 1864, with a capital of $50,000; which was increased in September, 1865, to $100,000. Its officers are C. W. Gibson, President, and Harvey J. Clark, Cashier.

The Bank deals largely in domestic and foreign exchange.—It has done a good business, and made liberal dividends to its stockholders.

It was the successor of the banking firm of C. W. Gibson & Co.; who commenced business in the then village, in March, 1863, in a room ten by twelve, in the Union House, corner of Third and Water Streets.

City Railway.—The Railway was organized in February, 1865. The track to Portsmouth was laid in the summer and fall of 1865, and the cars commenced running in November, of that year. Its officers are M. Butman, President, Wm. McEwen, Treasurer, N. B. Bradley, Secretary, and James Fraser, deceased, W. McEwen, Geo. Campbell, M. Butman and N. B. Bradley, Directors.

CIVIL HISTORY.

The place was known as Lower Saginaw, until 1857. It was then changed by an act of the Legislature, which provided, "That the name of the village of Lower Saginaw, in the Township of Hampton, and the State of Michigan, be and the same is hereby changed to *Bay City*. The act was approved Feb. 10, 1857, and was to take effect immediately. Bay City was incorporated as a village in February, 1859. In this act the village comprised all the territory of the settlement of Portsmouth. In 1865–6, the village of Bay City became "a city," exclusive of Portsmouth, and its first charter election took place on the second of April, 1865. N. B. Bradley, Esq., was the first Mayor. He was succeeded by His Honor, Jas. Watson, who was elected April 2, 1866.

The city comprises a territory of three square miles, and has an estimated population of about 5,000.

James Fraser.—A history of the first thirty years of the settlement of the Saginaw Valley, without mention of James Fraser, would be eminently like the play of Hamlet with the part of Hamlet left out. To borrow a cant phrase of the day, it might be said of him, more than of any other one man, that for a great part of the period above referred to, "he ran the machine." In the earlier days no one did so much towards bringing the advantages of the region before the public, and in inducing the influx of population and capital.

If in the end his efforts were crowned with the possesion of great wealth, it cannot be denied that it was the legitimate result of honorable enterprise directed by uncommon sagacity and force of character; and that in its acquisition, he was the instrument, and always the cheerful and willing one, of contributing very largely to the success and comfort of many others.

The biographer who could have caught and combined the story of James Fraser's life, as it frequently fell from his lips in his own racy and graphic language in moments of free social intercourse, might have given the world a most amusing and certainly not uninstructive book. To the student of human nature it would have presented some new and interesting combination of the threads and colors which enter into the warp and woof of life. It is, however, no part of our purpose to attempt anything of the kind. If we can succeed in presenting an outline which can be recognized, our object will have been attained.

James Fraser was as might be guessed from his name a native of the North of Scotland. He was born in extremely humble circumstances and had no advantages of education or fortune beyond what his own energy, wholly unaided, secured him.—It was no part of his manly nature in the day of his wealth and prosperity, to forget his origin, or to exact forgetfulness from others; on the contrary the contrast between the commencement and the close of his career was to him neither a source of pride and boast, as it is to some self-made men, nor of shame and concealment as perhaps more frequently occurs. He treated the matter sensibly and rationally, speaking of the scenes of his early youth when he had occasion to illustrate the topic of conversation with neither reserve nor ostentation, and very generally with the design and effect of "setting the table in a roar." His friends might sometimes be amused to hear of his having waded bare legged through the snow to carry a message for a ha-penny—or his taking daily a brick of turf under his arm as a contribution to the fire of the village school. But his reminisences of Scotland were not all of this humble type. The writer has frequently heard him refer to the fact, that he was on board the vessel with his great countryman, Sir Walter Scott, while performing a voyage among the islands of the Scottish coast to take notes for the location of his novel "The Pirate."

Mr. Fraser's emigration to this country occurred in the year 1829; he did not come a penniless adventurer but brought some $10,000 over with him which he had managed to accumulate in Scotland, and as he used to describe it, felt on landing, as if he could buy the whole northwest. This pleasant delusion was speedily dissipated by his losing the whole amount in unlucky speculations of his own and of a friend and partner.

Finding it necessary to begin again, he entered upon a small business in the city of Detroit and with such success that in two or three years time he had recovered his losses, and had acquired such experience in the new field of operations as to render loss in the future less probable. He now bethought himself of carrying into execution a plan he had long meditated of becoming a land-owner and a breeder of stock—principally horses.—Having visited the Saginaw country and become satisfied of its natural advantages he purchased an extensive farm on the banks of the Tittabawassee, about five miles above Saginaw city, and in the year 1834, when there was not probably a dozen white people residing within the limits of what was the Saginaw country moved upon it, with his family. He was not destined, however, to make his fortune out of breed mares and Durham bulls.—That he would have had a measure of success in that line is almost certain for the word fail was not in his lexicon, but the speculation in lands which at that time broke out over the entire west, opened a shorter road to the attainment of wealth; though throughout his life he never lost his fondness for cattle, particularly horses, of which he was always a kind but sometimes a severely exacting master. Into the new movement he entered largely but with such prudence that the revulsion of 1837 which prostrated perhaps nine out of every ten who were deeply engaged in western speculations, did not seriously affect him. His opportunities were of course great and his keen eye had detected in advance the principle points of value in the Valley. He was early a large proprietor in the site of Saginaw City, and bought and sold the "reserve" on which

Carrollton was laid out, but his principal and always favorite enterprise was building up a town at the mouth of the river.

He was a member and the leading spirit of the Saginaw Bay Company which purchased the site on which Bay City now stands but which was then called Lower Saginaw. In many of these enterprises he had been able to associate with himself men of large wealth and high respectability who reposed great confidence in his judgement and integrity. After the great commercial colapse of 1837, Mr. Fraser turned his attention to the manufacture of lumber which speedily became and now remains the great interest of the valley. In pursuit of this business in the year 1845 he founded the large lumbering establishment at Kawkawlin, and remained in this trade with great success as one of the heaviest operators of the Northwest until 1857, when by good luck or sound judgement he went out of it, just in time to avoid the disasters of that memorable year. From this time forth he devoted himself mainly to the management of his estate which had grown to be large. The discovery of salt in 1860 added so much to the value and reputation of Saginaw property, that it will ever be regarded as one of the principal historical events of the Valley. Of course Mr. Fraser shared largely in the interest thus awakened and participated greatly in the profits which thereby accrued to the fortunate holders of desirable lots. He contributed handsomely to the developement of this manufacture in Bay County, and was one of the principal stockholders and up to the time of his death, the President of Bay City Salt Manufacturing Company, among the first which went into operation.

In his intercourse with the world Mr. Frazer was one of the most genial and pleasant of men. Prompt and ready in speech as in action he was always prepared with an answer and no man who ventured to try conclusions with him in the way of jest or banter ever went away without his change. In his home he was truly hospitable, his house being for a long time head quarters for the strangers who wandered into the valley.

It was, however, in his working faculties that Mr. Fraser stood before most of his fellow men. It is perfectly safe to say that there are few living capable of enduring even for a short time what he passed through as the daily routine of life. At a time when the saddle and canoe were almost the only means of communication, his business required his presence in almost every part of the valley, and often at the head quarters of the State in Detroit. He was then literally ubiquitous. He seemed entirely insensible to fatigue, heat or cold, or anything which stood between him and the object at which he aimed. He more than once rode straight through from Saginaw City to Detroit by the light of a single sun a distance of about ninity-five miles, on some occasions never changing his horse. But this was nothing; arriving at home at nightfall after toils which most men would have considered a warrant for a long rest, and finding a letter or a message which required his presence elsewhere, with scarce a pause, he would spring again into the saddle and no matter how dark, or wet or cold he would plunge into the almost pathless forest with a seeming recklessness but with an instinctive sagacity and force of will and power of endurance that always brought him through and generally "on time."—With the land office at Detroit for the goal and a choice section of land for the prize it is believed that there was never man who beat James Fraser in the race. Often in the dead of night the solitary settler at the Cass crossing would hear a horse thundering at full speed across the bridge and would say next morning that James Fraser had gone in or out as the case might be The first glimpse the writer ever had of him was in the trail between Flint and Cass in 1836. The mud was knee-deep and water was above the mud, but he passed at speed with merely a shout. He was without a hat and covered with soil, his head being bound with a handkerchief. On meeting him afterwards we learned that he had been all night in the woods having lost his way—and afterwards his hat, but he was going to Detroit to enter some land at Lower Saginaw, and his errand brooked no delay. A thousand anecdotes are related to show his extraordinary energy and activity, and any one who ever had the luck to be "put through" by him in the old days would believe almost any thing that could be said on these points without calling witnesses.

As a business man Mr. Fraser was in a class by himself. For a long time his head was his ledger and his hat was his safe, yet with a memory clear and tenacious even to the smallest details, he transacted his affairs with nearly as much exactness if with less red tape than your regularly trained counting house man. When his affairs extended entirely beyond his capacious mental grasp he was forced to employ the usual agencies, but to the last he had a strong tendency to do his own "figuring" in his own short hand way often greatly to the disgust and botheration of his clerks.

Mr. Fraser had two great faults—he made money too fast for some people and did not spend it fast enough for others. Possibly if he had disarmed criticism on both these points he might have ended life as poor as he began it. This was not to be.—Men like James Fraser were born to make their way in the world. Nothing short of solitary confinement ever prevent them from acquiring property and the power which property brings.—That which the thoughtless world calls generosity and which is generally extravagance or shiftlessness is a trait wholly inconsistent with such a character, yet in the scale of usefulness, which stands first, the man who employs, or the man who gives? which is the benefactor, 'he who spreads the spirit of pauperism by indiscriminate alms giving, or he who demands the sweat of industry in exchange for the bread he distributes?

It is not intended to even intimate that the subject of this brief memoir was in the slightest degree niggardly—nothing was farther from the fact. He gave frequently, and often liberally. Few men were less callous to the sight in sound of distress in any form. What is meant is to point out the folly of those who expect inconsistent traits in the same character. The loose grips which lets go, as fast as it grasps produces no result. The man who is always wishing to give generally has nothing to bestow, kindness negatives itself; acquisitiveness should precede benevolence. They do not often unite in the same person. In Mr. Fraser's phrenology acquisitiveness of course predominated, but benevolence was by no means a deficient or inactive organ. The secret of his success was not in his power of retaining but in his tremendous faculty of acquiring.

To say that the death of such a man left a large void in the scene of his toils and triumphs, is a statement for which all will be prepared. He had arrived at quite an advanced age, but there was nothing in his appearance to indicate the approaching close. Those who knew him most intimately, now speak of failure bodily and mental. To the world nothing of the kind was apparent. He had resided for some time in Connecticut, but at his last visit to the valley a week or two before his death, his look was as fresh and joyous and his step to all appearance as elastic as ever. When it was announced that James Fraser was dead, the feling was a sort of incredulity. Men could not at first understand it. Of any other man the story had been plausible, but for him who had defied death in a thousand forms—whose hair-breadth escapes had so long been the theme of those who knew him, for the rough-riding, strong-willed, omnipresent, indomitable James Fraser to lie down and die in his bed, like other men was astonishing. It did not seem the true catastrophe for such a drama. But it was so. The shot which had so often missed him on the wing struck him at length in the nest. He died calmly and peacefully at last, surrounded by his family and by every comfort which wealth and affection could bestow.—Those who were are at his side as the last solemn hour approached, testify that he met it not only with the nerve of a man of courage but with the hope of those who look forward to a high and eternal life of pure happiness beyond the grave.

Hon. Jas. G. Birney.—Mr. Birney's reputation is rather national than local, yet a man who has been of sufficient weight of character to be nominated and supported by any respectable Party of the American people for the Presidency of the United

States, must continue to be an object of interest, in whatever place he should for any time reside.

Mr. Birney was born in Danville, Ky., but removed to Alabama where he spent some years of his life; when he removed to Cincinnati, New York, and afterwards to Detroit, and finally to Lower Saginaw. He arrived here in 1841, and remained here until 1856 or 1857. His residence was here in 1844; when with Henry Clay, and James K. Polk, as his competitors, he performed as the candidate of the Liberty Party the Presidential race. But as he represented an idea which was not then very popular, he was of course defeated. But the Presidency has been held by more than one man inferior to him in talents. and inferior in personal integrity and elevation of character.

He came here to look after and improve the land which he had purchased with the remainder of a property somewhat impaired by the experiences he had gone through in the emancipation of his slaves, and the unfriendly treatment he had met with in consequence, among those who did not wish the "institution" to made unpopular, by such opinions as he held, and by such acts as those opinions were expressed in.

Mr. Birney was a welcome resident here. It is elsewhere stated, that he presided at the first public religious service in the place, and his custom was to maintain such a service during his stay, while his health permitted, and till others took the work off his hands. At these meetings, all persons, without respect to denominational differences, united in worship.

Mr. Birney is remembered with great affection by the old residents here. No matter how much they differed from him upon public questions, all revered him and speak of him now with great respect.

He will be esteemed more fully a hundred years hence than he is to-day.

It may be singular to some that a man who held this relation to the public should have selected his residence in a region so new as Lower Saginaw then was, with so few comforts and advantages as it then afforded. and with so much of positive experience as it at that time involved. But Mr. Birney was led and governed much by ideas. His mind was somewhat of the contemplative sort which relies more upon itself than upon others. He preferred the wilderness to many of the men with whom his experiences had brought him into contact. He could here at least have peace ; and though the forest proffered him but little of occupation, such as previous life fitted him for, still he enjoyed their solitude and passed many comfortable days in what is now Bay City. Mr. Birney's religious connection was with the Presbyterian Church.

James McCormick.—The pioneers of the Saginaw Valley deserve more than a passing notice. It is through their perseverance privations and sufferings, that this beautiful valley is now what it is. We are now enjoying the benefits of their hard labor. Few of the present generation can appreciate what sufferings those pioneers, with their families, passed through.—Weeks and months perhaps without bread. Says an old pioneer, "We were like a band of brothers; if one had any provisions he divided it with his neighbor.

One of the first pioneers of the valley was James McCormick, of Scotch descent, born at Albany, N. Y., May 25th, 1787 ; where he owned a fine farm, and was in affluent circumstances. He lost his property by endorsing for friends. He then collected what few effects he had, left the State, and with his large family, started for the far West. In 1832, he landed in Detroit, where he left his family for a short time, until he could find them a home. Here by the advice of the late John R. Williams, an old townsman, he removed to the Flint where he arrived in August, the same year. At that time the front line of settlement was at Grand Blanc. From there to Flint, he had to cut the brush and trees on each side of the Indian trail to let his wagon, upon which were a few household goods and his family, to pass through. Consequently this was the first wagon brought to Flint. Here he bought a half breed title to 125 acres of land on the north side of Flint River, and east of Saginaw Street; on which he built the second house that was built at Flint.—Here he remained until the spring of 1834, when he sold his title for six hundred dollars, to one Smith, who claimed an Indian title to the same property. He got part of his pay, but the larger part he failed to receive. He then, with his family, removed 30 miles below, farther into the wildernes, and settled on the old Indian Fields, which he rented from the Indians.

Here he pitched a tent, and commenced building a shelter for his family. He remained in this place several years, tilling his land. About this time the small pox broke out among the Indians, and large numbers died of the disease. They could not hunt, consequently they were in a starving condition. He happening to have a large crop that year, furnished them with provisions and kept them from starving. This kindness they never forgot; and in their treaty with the U. S. Government to dispose of their lands, they refused to sell unless subject to a lease they had made with James McCormick of a mile square of land, where he lived, for the term of 99 years, as a recompense for his kindness to them on several occasions in supplying them with food, when they were unable to hunt.

This, Mr. Schoolcraft, the Government Commissioner, refused to do. "Then;" said the chiefs, "We will not sell our land, unless our white brother is provided for, *we will not sign the treaty.*" The treaty was then broken up, and the Indians returned to their homes. (This is one among the many noble instances of Indian gratitude.)

There was not a white man in the country so much honored and respected by the Indians, as the late James McCormick.—He was always opposed to selling them liquor, and was always their protector and friend. Any grievances of theirs were always referred to him, and his decision final; "For," said they, "he never lies to us."

Some time after this Mr. Schoolcraft sent word to the chiefs that he would accede to their proposition, and invited them to another treaty. The Indians assembled again, and were informed by Mr. Schoolcraft that he had made provisions in the treaty, ceding to James McCormick six hundred and forty acres of land, or one square mile. The Indians, with this understanding, signed the treaty, with full confidence that Mr. Schoolcraft had dealt honorably with them. This afterwards proved not to be the fact, as he had left it out of the treaty altogether. The Government afterwards sold the land occupied by Mr. McCormick, to which he thought he had a just title by the treaty, and he was ejected therefrom.

He then moved with his family to Lower Saginaw—now called Bay City and Portsmouth—about the year 1841. Here, with his son, James J., he purchased an interest in the old Portsmouth Mill, the second mill on the Saginaw River. He soon afterwards purchased the building now called the Center House, which was the first framed building built below Saginaw City, and converted it into a dwelling for his family; where he died April 2d, 1846, honored and beloved both by the whites and the Indians. His remains, together with his wife, Ellen, lie in a neighboring cemetery, and it is in contemplation, early the coming season, to erect a monument to this pioneer's memory.

Mr. McCormick left nine children; of whom six were boys, and three girls. The boys were named respectively Robert, Joseph, James J., William R., Archibald and Andrew. Archibald was the first male child born at Flint, and Andrew, the first male child born in the Township of Taymouth, Saginaw County.

To the above account of his life, written by his son, it is proper to state in addition that Mr. McCormick was a man of considerable literary qualifications; and that he left a volume or two of his poems, many of which were published in the newspapers of his day. Some steps have been taken to bring them out in permanent form, but the design has not yet been realized.

Hon. Sidney S. Campbell.—Mr. Campbell was from Oneida County, New York. His town was called Paris. He came to Michigan in 1830, and settled at Pontiac, whence he removed to Cass River Bridge, arriving on the 1st day of March, 1836.

Here he laid out a town and called it Bridgeport; his partner in the business being Mr. G. D. Williams, It was surveyed by Capt. Parks, of Pontiac; a post office was established there, and Mr. Campbell was appointed Postmaster. This being in the days of the great land speculation, lots were wonderfully high in Bridgeport, and Mr. C. sold some three blocks in his town in the woods, for $600. Whether they were "water lots" or not, is not said. As the times changed the estimate of fronter and other town property changed also; and from being very precious, town lots became a poor sort of property, Bridgeport did not grow to the size of Detroit in some years, and if report be true, has not yet quite overtaken the City of the Straits; although it is a very respectable place.

Mr. Campbell came to Lower Saginaw in 1837; had him a house built where the Globe Hotel now stands, and moved into it in April of the same year. He has ever since lived here, and has held various public offices, as appears in our historical sketch of Bay City. He is at present Judge of Probate for Bay County, and has apparently many years of life before him yet. His residence is a pleasant place below the city, and is not included within the city limits.

JOSEPH F. MARSAC.—Capt. Marsac is of French origin, and was born near Detroit, on the 25th of December, 1793. He is consequently seventy-three years of age at this time. He visited the Saginaw region at various times, at an early day, and before settlement in it was thought of.

In November, 1838, he removed to Lower Saginaw, making his trip in the steamboat *Gov. Marcy*, and settled at the place now occupied by James J. McCormick. He afterwards removed to Portsmouth, where he now resides. For some years after his removal here he held office under the Government, as Interpreter and Inspector of the Revenues. He is now a farmer.

Previous to his removal to the Saginaw Valley he had seen considerable of affairs, having been employed at first in the Custom House, at Detroit, for about eleven years; then residing near Baltimore; then at Grosse Point, eight miles from Detroit, on account he says of some trouble with the Indians. He was one of the persons employed in the building of Fort Gratiot, near Port Huron. He went to Malden, to build a fort there; but the Treaty of Ghent having been made the fort was abandoned, and he returned home. He spent a year at Monroe, in hunting; there being a great plenty of game in that region.—Afterwards he visited Chicago, and was engaged with Kinzie and others, in selling goods to the Indians. Chicago then consisted of five houses. This was in 1816. One of his trips for trade was this: He started for the interior on horseback, but sold his horse at Niles—though Niles was not there then either in name or fact—and procuring a row boat, which he loaded with corn for the trade at Chicago, he rowed down the St. Joseph River to its mouth, and into the lake, cruising about the south shore to its head, until he reached Chicago. From Chicago to Detroit his return was on foot, by an Indian trail.—From his farm near Detroit, in 1819, with Gen. Lewis Cass, he visited Saginaw City, called then O-sa-ge-nong, or "home of the Sacs," where a treaty was made. His return to Detroit was in a vessel, and his employment for eleven years was again in the Custom House, Gov. Trowbridge being the officer in chief.

Capt. Marsac is still hale and hearty; speaks several languages; but his native French better than any. In conversation he is inclined to mix them considerably, but is easily understood, and is quite interesting, as well from his varied experiences as the odd bits of knowledge he has managed to pick up.

Hon. Albet Miller.—Now a resident of Portsmouth, emigrated from the State of Vermont, in 1832, and has been a constant inhabitant of the Saginaw Valley from that day to this. His earliest residence was in Saginaw City; where he was engaged for some years in selling goods; but in 1839, he removed to a farm upon the Tittabawassee River; whether attracted to that locality by the beauty of the region, or the beauty of its name, he does not state; but he resided there till the year 1848, when he came to Portsmouth, where he still lives.

As early as 1836 he had surveyed the Town of Portsmouth, intending to make of it a fine city, if possible, along with the other great towns which were taking root all over the western prairies, and along all the rivers of this new world. His town, like the rest, had to wait a little; but it is coming on nevertheless, and will be a place to live in if any is in this valley.

While living at Saginaw City, Mr. Miller was appointed by Governor Mason, in 1835, a Justice of the Peace and Judge of Probate for the County of Saginaw. Michigan, was then a territory; but upon its becoming a State he was elected to the latter office—Judge of Probate for the term of four years—and at the end of his term he was elected again; so that he held the office nine years, and thus earned his title fairly—"Judge Milier"—a title by the way not only of honor, but of convenience, as it serves to distinguish him from the other Millers, very numerous hereabouts, and even from the "Albert Millers," of whom there are more than one.

Judge Miller also served the State as a Member of the Legislature for one term. He sat with that body in 1847, at its last session held in Detroit; at which session some business of considerable importance to the State was transacted.

On his arrival at Portsmouth, in 1818, the place was considerably new. Not two acres of cultivated land existed in the place. It consisted in fact of a few cabins and a little clearing about the mill, then in process of erection. This mill was built by B. K. Hall, Cromwell Barney and Judge Miller. It was the first in the place, and the second upon the Saginaw River. It still runs, though it may have to call in the principle of the Indian's gun for its identity, which though it had a new barrel, stock, lock and ramrod, was the same old gun yet. In 1852, Portsmouth consisted of about one hundred persons. Of these, the cholera, in two weeks, removed nine. Of the society left a number yet remain in the place, Judge Miller among them.

He has frequently held town offices, and is an Elder in the Presbyterian Church at Bay City. He is now in the midst of his days, and will it is hoped remain to be useful many years.

Israel Catlin.—He was born in Chemung, now Schuyler Co., N. Y., in 1814. His chosen trade was that of Joiner, which he prosecuted for several years in his younger days, at Brooklyn; and while there visited Europe as ship's carpenter upon the ship *Hudson*. In 1841 he returned to Chemung, and thence emigrated to Lower Saginaw. His first passage from Saginaw City was made upon a small schooner which happened to be passing. The only post office at that time for the region was at Saginaw City, and the mails were obtained whenever it was practicable; sometimes once in a month, and with great good luck once a week. The country was a dense forest, and the surface was uniformly covered with water to a late period; often till July. The offer of all the region on condition of living upon the land, would not at that time been thought worth acceptance by every young man.

There were then but four dwelling houses in the place. One of these was kept as a public house; but upon his arrival, Mr. C. could get no dinner, from the fact that the establishment possessed nothing eatable to make a dinner of. At the mouth of the Kaw-kaw-lin River, however, at the house of Mr. Harvey Williams, he obtained something in the way of supper. Thence he made his way to Kaw-kaw-lin village, where he assisted in building a mill then in process of erection, by Fraser and Barney. He had the superintendence of this mill for a couple of years, and then took up his residence at Lower Saginaw; where he has survived its different changes of name and incorporation; being at one time its Postmaster; and where he has raised and reared a family. In company with Mr. Fraser he built one of the first mills here, and has ever since been engaged in the manufacturing of lumber. Mr. C. is still in the midst of his years, and bids fair to be useful a long while yet.—He is an influential member of the Episcopal Church, and an honored citizen.

BAY CITY NEWSPAPERS.

The first newspaper published in Bay City, was known as the BAY CITY PRESS. It was Republican in politics, and was only issued for a few weeks, some time in the year 1856. The paper was owned by Mr. P. Joslin, and was edited by the Hon. James Birney. The office was in the old Watson warehouse, which was burned down in the great fire of 1865.

Succeeding it came a Weekly paper, at first called THE PRESS, and afterwards the BAY CITY PRESS AND TIMES. Its publication was commenced in 1859, by the late Wm. Bryce, and was continued until the fall of 1864, when he accepted the position of Quartermaster of the 29th Michigan Infantry, and the paper was discontinued. Originally it was neutral in politics, but shortly previous to the campaign of 1860, it became Republican in its preferences. After the discontinuance of his paper, the printing material was purchased by the "Journal Company," and in October, 1864, a Weekly Republican paper named BAY CITY JOURNAL, with Mr. John Culbert as Editor, made its appearance, and which is continued at the present time by Mr. J. Culbert, he having bought out the other members of the "Journal Co."

In June, 1864, Mr. Wm. T. Kennedy formerly of the Rural New Yorker, of Rochester, New York, commenced issuing a Weekly Democratic paper entitled the BAY CITY SIGNAL, and which is being published at present.

CHURCHES.

The first visitants and settlers to the Saginaw Valley were of the Catholic Church; and received the occasional visits of the members of that faith from 1839 and onward to their settlement here.

The first Protestant religious service of a public character was held at the original school house, which stood upon the ground adjoining James Shearer's mill, it was presided over by Hon. Jas. G. Birney, deceased.

The matter of religious denomination was not yet known ; but people of all sects met and worshipped together. This was in 1841.

It is remembered also, that in this school house, a Temperance meeting was held, and an address delivered by Hon. Gerritt Smith, of Petersboro, N. Y., a name well known in the United States.

The first Protestant Church edifice erected in the place was that now owned by the Methodist denomination. It wasbuilt in 18—, as a Union Church ; and in part paid for by a subscription. But subsequently, the principal portion of the worshippers being Methodists, and desiring a Church of their own, it was relinquished to them upon their assuming the liabilities, consisting of a few hundred dollars which encumbered the property.

Previously to this the Catholic Church had been built; being commenced in the winter of 1850-1 ; and was the first Church edifice in the place. The several denominations are sketched as follows, besides those here enumerated, there are at present two Lutheran Churches; one of them being at present engaged in the erection of a large and fine edifice. There is also a Universalist meeting held in the Court room, though without a formal organization at present.

PROTESTANT EPISCOPAL CHURCH.

The Protestant Episcopal Church, in Bay City, Michigan, begins its history in the FITZHUGH FAMILY. The first of its communicants it will be observed is, Mrs. Wm. D. Fitzhugh, whose husband was leader in Church efforts at first. To the zeal and fidelity of Mr. Israel Catlin, (connected by marriage with the same family), the Parish owes its preservation in the important struggles.

The Family, possessing large real estate in this Valley and devotedly attached to the Church, did in conjunction with Col. Henry Raymond and some of lesser influence, early exert themselves to bring her holy ministrations here ; and have ever since been, in some one or more of its members, her main supports.

The first Protestant Episcopal ordained minister whose services were had at this point, then called Lower Saginaw, was the Rev. (deacon) Joseph Adderly, missionary at Saginaw City. He had no regular services here and came but three times, and those in the fall of 1850.

The Rev. Daniel B. Lyon, missionary to Saginaw City from December 21st, 1851, to July 4th, 1852, came here a few times (perhaps half a dozen), in that interval. The first clergyman to visit the field regularly was the Rev. Voltaire Spalding, who become missionary to this whole region, making Saginaw City his home, on the 22d day of January, 1853. He officiated here on each third Sunday, and received from the flock in support $100 per annum. The connection and arrangement continued until the resignation of his stations, on or about the first of June 1858. About a year after his arrival — on the 4th day of March 1854—the Parish organization took place under the name and title of "Trinity Church, Lower Saginaw, Saginaw County, Michigan." The corporators were, Henry Raymond, Israel Catlin, Daniel Burns, John Drake, Geo. E. Smith, Elijah S. Catlin, Jonathan S. Barclay, Barzillai B. Hart, Henry Young, Curtis Munger, Richard Padley, Henry H. Alvord, H. H. Chapman and Jas. Hays.

Rev. Mr. Spalding presided at the organization, and Col. Henry Raymond was Secretary; Israel Catlin was elected Senior Warden, and Richard Padley Junior Warden; and Curtis Munger, George F. Smith, B. B. Hart, Daniel Burns, J. S. Barclay Henry Raymond, Thomas Carney and Hiram F. Ferris Vestrymen.

By referring to the Register of St. John's Church, Saginaw City, it will be found that there were at the time Mr. Spalding resigned his charge, five communicants belonging to this Church.

From Mr. Spalding's departure in June 1858, to May 1860, the Parish was without a Pastor. Nevertheless, in this interegnum the few churchmen were not idle. On the best of plats allotted by the original Patentees to Church sites and of which Messrs. Chas. Fitzhugh, Israel Catlin and Henry Raymond had taken possession the preceding winter, by depositing lumber and begining a Church, the Parish with very little help from abroad, erected a neat and ecclisological edifice. By the special exertions of Mr. Catlin, this edifice was CONSECRATED to the worship of GOD, THE FATHER, THE SON AND HOLY GHOST, by the Right Rev. Samuel Allen McCoskey on the 5th Thursday after Easter May 10th, 1860.

The Rev. Edward Magee, by an arrangement with the vestry of St. John's Church, Saginaw City, took charge of this fold on Sunday after Ascension, May 20th, 1860, devoting to it alternate Sundays; or half of his time, receiving therefor $300 per annum. This arrangement continued until the 25th of May, 1861, when he resigned his charge of St. John's Church, Saginaw City, and confined his labors wholly to this Parish, till by sickness compelled to leave, on Thursday preceding Advent Sunday, Nov. 18th, 1861. This ministery of a year and a half shows a list of 14 Baptisms, 6 confirmations, 1 marriage, and 2 burials.—The number of communicants belonging to the Church at the time of his resignation, being about twenty, The number of families twenty.

From this time onward to the coming of the Rev. Gilbert B. Hayden, 24th day of November, 1862, (to whom the Parish is indebted for this condensed record of its history), the Parish was again vacant, but for the most of the space, a Sunday school was maintained by the pious exertions of the senior Warden.—In this interval, too, the ladies of the Congregation got up a supper, on the evening of June 25th, 1862, for the benefit of the Church, and realized $72. During his ministry seven were admitted to the sacred Rite of Confirmation—ten communicants were received into the Parish from abroad—making the number of communicants belonging to the Church, at the time of his resignation, August 1st, 1863, about thirty-seven.

On the 25th of September, 1863, the Rev. A. M. Lewis was called to the Rectorship of this Parish and entered upon his duties the 1st of October, 1863. He continued his ministrations for two years, resigning his charge on the last Sunday in Sept.

1865. During his Rectorship the Parish enlarged the church edifice at an expense of $1.200, more than doubling its capacity. He baptized 53 persons, 12 adults and 41 children, presented to the Bishop 26 for confirmation, celebrated 7 marriages and performed 13 burials.

The number of communicants received into the Parish from abroad during his incumbency was twenty-four. At the time of his resignation there were about sixty-five communicants belonging to this Church. On the 19th of January, 1866, the Vestry of this Parish extended a unanimous call to the Rev. Fayette Royce, Rector of Grace Church, Nunda, N. Y., to become their Pastor. He accepted their call on or about the 1st of February, 1866, and entered upon his duties on the 4th day of the following month, being the 3d Sunday in Lent The Congregation having been without a Rector five months. He finds the Parish in a healthy condition—in debt $600, for the enlargement of the Church, and in great need of a Parsonage. The number of communicants belonging to the Church at the time the present Rector assumed charge, as nearly as he can ascertain, were about sixty. A Sunday school has been sustained with more or less success from the time of the organization of the Parish. The average number of pupils being about 25.

FIRST PRESBYTERIAN CHURCH.

The Church was organized on the 4th of September, 1856, under the title of the First Presbyterian Church of Lower Saginaw, by Rev. Lucius J. Root. It consisted at first of only eight members, and worshipped for a time in a public school house; the congregation corresponding in size with the Church.

Hon. Albert Miller, was its first officer, being elected deacon soon after its first organization. Although the Church was Presbyterian in form from the first, it was without a session until June, 1858, when Hon. A. Miller, and Scott W. Sayles were chosen, and ordained as presiding Elders.

Rev. L. J. Root was called to the pastorate, and installed by the Presbytery of Saginaw, on the 17th of November, 1858; and this relation continued until February, 1860, when his dismission took place.

After his removal, Rev. E. J. Stewart became the Stated Supply of the congregation ; entering upon his work in June, 1861, and continuing until September, 1864.

In January, 1863, Messrs. Bazrillei B. Hart, Dr. Geo. E. Smith and James S. Monroe, were elected presiding Elders, and in October, 1863, H. D. Towan was added to the Eldership.

Mr. Sayles died during the year 1864, and Mr. Towan removed from the place in the same year; leaving the session at present, constituted of Hon. A. Miller, Dr. Geo. E. Smith, B. B. Hart and Jas. L. Monroe, with the pastor of the Church.

After its early worship in the school house, as already narrated, the congregation occupied the Court Room, and a public Hall by turns, and increasing somewhat with the growth of the place.—During the year 1861, a Church edifice, somewhat smaller in size than the one at present occupied, was erected ; but in the midst of the celebration of the Lord's Supper within its walls in February, 1862, it took fire, from some defect in its furnace, and was consumed.

The present edifice was immediately undertaken; and by the vigorous exertions of the Minister, Rev. E. J. Stewart, was completed and dedicated, nearly free of debt, on the 25th of December, 1863.

The Church organization has grown from its original eight, to an entire membership of one hundred and twenty-three. Of these, eight have died, and twenty-six dismissed to other connections; leaving as the present membership, eighty-nine.

The present pastor, Rev. J. Ambrose Wight, was called in April, 1865; commenced his labors in May; and was installed as Pastor in November following.

A weekly prayer meeting, and a Sabbath school have always been maintained by the Church. The present Superintendent of the Sunday school is Mr. Jas. L. Monroe, and the school numbers something over one hundred members.

E‡

The present Church edifice is of wood, well built, and seated: and is forty by eighty feet on the ground. It has a tower and spire. It has 72 slips, and is furnished with a singers gallery; beneath which is a large vestibule, used as a lecture and conference room. The Church will seat four hundred persons. It is heated by a furnace. Its position is on Washington street near Tenth, on the highest and pleasantest grounds in the City, and the region around it is in process of filling up with good buildings, with much rapidity.

FIRST BAPTIST CHURCH.

On the 15th day of June, A. D. 1858, the first Baptist Church was organized in what is now Bay County, and consisted of fourteen members, six of whom were residents of Bay City and eight of Portsmouth. The name of the society was the First Baptist Church of Portsmouth and Bay City, and a house of worship was subsequently built, mostly through the efforts and with means furnished by John N. Braddock, who has since gone to his rest. The pulpit was supplied by Rev. S. Handy—"who rests from his labors and his works do follow him." Rev. T. Cornelius now of Ann Arbor, took charge until Sept. 1st, 1861, when Rev. Franklin Johnson became Pastor, and continued for two years, preaching part of that time in Bay City, Sabbath evenings, occupying the County Court Room alternately with the First Presbyterian Society of Bay City, until Feb. 2, 1862, when they expected to have services every evening in the same place, the Presbyterian society having that day taken possession of their house of worship just completed but owing to its destruction by fire that day during the services, the Presbyterians were driven back to their old quarters, and the Baptists then obtained the use of Birney Hall from the Masons, who held and occupied it as a Masonic Hall, which they continued to occupy for Sabbath school, public worship and prayer meetings, until the occupation of their house of worship on Washington Avenue.

February 2d, 1862, the day on which the Presbyterian church was burned, the Baptists of Bay City organized a Sabbath school with less than six scholars.

In the spring of 1863, the late Mr. James Fraser commenced the erection of a beautiful house on lots donated by himself and Dr. D. H. Fitzhugh, on Washington Avenue, which was completed and dedicated the 18th of August. 1863, costing with the furniture nearly $5,000. A church having been formed in Bay City on the 18th of July preceeding, by 27 members who withdrew from the Portsmouth and Bay City Church for that purpose, and the Rev. Franklin Johnson was installed Pastor, who continued until May, 1865, when the health of himself and wife obliged him to remove east. He was succeeded by Rev. S. L. Holman, who remained until October, 1865, since which time the Church has been without a Pastor. They have recently extended a call to the Rev. D. Bennett Patterson, of Staten Island, New York, who enters upon his duties here the first of May next. The Church members at this date, (March, 1866), number 103; and the Sabbath school members about 90.

CATHOLIC CHURCH.

Visits of Catholic Clergymen to Bay County from the year 1829 to 1850, by Rev. M. Kundig, L. Kilroy, P. Kendekens, V. G. Louis Monaghan. Rev. T. Kendekens visited in 1850 Bay City, at that time Lower Saginaw. The present church, (called St. Joseph), was commenced under his directions in the winter 1850-51, on lots No. 9 and 10, block 27, donated by the Company: Mr. J. Birney executed the deed. He made his monthly visits to said place, until August 1852. He was succeeded by Rev. H. T. H. Schutges, the present pastor of Bay City. He attended to Saginaw Valley for a period of ten years. Residing first in Saginaw City. Removed to Bay City in 1855. Under his care St. Joseph Church was finished, and an addition of 14 feet with steeple was made. The church is 72x40, well finished and ornamented. A residence for Pastor was built in 1856. The number of Catholics was small in 1852—about twenty—at present there are at least 200 Catholics.

A Catholic grave yard was donated by James Marsac; the deed executed by Capt. Joseph Marsac, heir of James, about 1840. This grave yard being in the center of the town was sold for the benefit of the Church. Mr. Michael Daily donated a five acre lot for a grave yard, on the west side of the river.—Mr. Wm. D. Fitzhugh of Mt. Morris, N. Y., donated five acres on the east side of the river for a Catholic grave yard.

MASONIC.

In October, 1860, a Dispensation was granted by M. W. Grand Master to Wm. R. McCormick as W. M., Wm. A Bryce, as S. W. and N. B. Bradley as J. W., for the organization of a Lodge of Free and accepted Masons at Bay City, and a charter was granted January 11th, 1861, by the lamented Col H. S. Roberts then M. W. G. M.

At the election held in December prior to the granting of the charter, Wm. A. Bryce was elected Master, serving two years, and who was succeeded by N. B. Bradley, the present Master, this being his 3d year in that office.

The first meetings of the Lodge were held in a small room in rear of Bay City Post office, which was conducted by Wm. A. Bryce, and was located in the upper part of the building formerly occupied by C. R. Jennison, on ground now occupied by the Fraser Hotel Block, from which place they soon after moved into Birney Hall, which was fitted up by them and occupied until 1864, when their present Lodge room was built for them by Mr. Fraser.

The regular meetings are held on Wednesday on or before the full of the moon in each month, weekly meetings are held for work.

The present officers are,

N. B. Bradley, W. M.	Ed. Wood, J D.
H. H. Hatch, S. W.	Isaac Marston, Sec'y.
Geo. C. Frey, J. W.	C. Munger, Treas.
R. J. Carney, S. D.	A. W. Tripp, Tyler.

Present number of members, 71.

Members deceased, H. W. Jennison, Geo. R. Alvord, Chas. Smith and W. A. Bryce.

The following named members have done battle for the Union in the late Rebellion:

Brevet Brig. Gen. B. E. Partridge, who entered the service in the 16th Mich. Inf'ty, as Sergeant.

Col. H. S. Raymond, as Capt. in the 23d Michigan Inf'ty.

Capt. Geo. R. Alvord, as Q. M. Sergeant.

Capt. Jas. G. Birney, now on duty at Salt Lake City, U. T. who entered as private in the 7th Cavalry.

Sergeant Byron C. Bedell.

GOOD TEMPLARS.

Bay City Lodge, No. 109, I. O. G. Templars was organized Nov. 13th, 1860. The Society holds regular meetings every Monday evening. It numbers at present about 100 members.

SCHOOLS.

Schools do not always wait for shool houses, but they do of necessity wait for pupils, and for teachers to instruct them.

There was no school house here till the year 1843–4. But a school, of some five or six pupils, had been taught, by Miss Clark who became Mrs. Drew, some two years after, and until her marriage; matrimony in this instance, as in many others, arresting a good educational enterprise. Miss Clark's school was kept in a private house.

In 1843 a small framed school house was commenced, and completed the next season, at an expense of two hundred dollars.—This building, though humble as to cost and dimensions, was a very useful structure; accommodating not the school alone, but all public, political, moral and religious meetings for several years. In truth it was the public "Hall" of Lower Saginaw.

A Miss Robinson from Flint was the first teacher within its walls. She was succeeded by Carlos Bacon, Rev. T. J. Root and Edward Faring. In 18—, the house upon Adams street at present in use was erected. The other teachers in the Public school, as Principals, have been Wm. Gano, E. B. Deniven and Peter S. Heinordt. It is safe to remark, that with the increase of the place, there has been a correspondent multiplication of pupils attendant upon one Public school.

The present system is that of the Union school; and a very and salutary record of rules for their regulation has been adopted. It is in contemplation to grade the schools, and to make sufficient provision for them as to buildings, at an early day — The city has at present two large buildings, of wood, for their use.

The Globe Hotel, No. 202 North Water Street, is a popular place of resort for all who appreciate good eating and drinking. Meals are served at all hours, upon the European plan. Its present proprietor, Mr. A. N. Rouech, is a model Landlord, and his reputation as a caterer is unimpeached. The Billiard Room, connected with the Hotel, is furnished with all the modern improvements.

Residents of Bay City and other places on the line of water transportation can always find a desirable assortment of Crockery in all its varieties; Carpets, Oilcloths, Mirrors, Cutlery, Plated Goods, Filters, &c., &c., at the House-furnishing Emporium of Elliott & Harrison, South Water Street, East Saginaw. Their Store is situated on the Dock, just above the Bridge, and the River Boats land in the immediate vicinity, making it the most convenient location for the river trade that could be found. Packages and Parcels are delivered on board the Boats, and everything desirable is done for the convenience of customers.— Ho tels and Wholesale Dealers are supplied at liberal prices. Their facilities for supplying the wants of the public are unsurpassed.

J. Z. Newcomb commenced business in July, 1865. His Store, South Water Street, is large and commodious, and well stocked with everything pertaining to the Dry Goods Trade.— Having had a large experience in the Dry Goods Trade in one of the largest cities of Western New York, he fully understands his business, and the interests of his customers will at all times be safely guarded. He is gentlemanly in his manners, and is a fair and square dealer. We bespeak for him an increased patronage.

The Store of Messrs. Cross & Begley, Dealers in Drugs and Medicines, deserves more than a mere passing notice. The proprietors are both Physicians of skill and prominence in their profession; and having had twenty-five years experience in the Drug and Medicine business they may be relied upon with all confidence in putting up prescriptions.

To say their Store is arranged in good taste would not be enough; the design and execution of its interior arrangements would do credit to similar establishments in larger cities.—Its location is central, and the finest one in the city, being in the Fraser Hotel Block, having two fronts, one on Water, and one on Center Street. Doctor Cross, as a surgical operator, ranks among the first in his profession. His recent successful operation in extracting a "fatty tumor" from the back, beneath the shoulder blade, of a young lady of this city, reflects great credit upon him as a surgeon of the first order. Doctor Cross is a graduate of the University of Glasgow, Scotland, and Licentiate of the Medical Board of Upper Canada. They are both reliable gentlemen, and their store is a model one in all its appointments.

The Iron Foundry business of John McDowell was established in 1866, by John Burden, who continued the business until 1862, when John McDowell purchased his interest, and still continues the business. The buildings are large and commodious, and eighteen first class workmen are constantly employed. The proprietor is a practical mechanic, and the fact that he has had 35 years experience, is a sufficient guarantee that he fully understands every branch of his business.

BAY COUNTY OFFICERS.

Sheriff.—Patrick J. Perrott.
County Clerk.—Nathaniel Whittemore.
Register of Deeds.—Bernard Witthauer.
County Treasurer.—Algernon S. Munger.
Judge of Probate.—Sidney S. Campbell.
Prosecuting Attorney.—Luther Beckwith.
Circuit Court Commissioner.—Archibald McDonell.
County Surveyor.—James M. Johnstone.
Coroner.—Oliver H. P. Goodwin.

BAY CITY OFFICERS.

Mayor.—James Watson
Recorder.—William T. Kennedy, Jr.
City Treasurer.—Ernst Frank.
Marshal.—Horace Becker.
Directors of the Poor;—O. H. P. Goodwin, Thomas Carney.
Aldermen—*First Ward.*—Jerome Sweet, Jacob Knoblaugh.
Second Ward.—Jacob H. Little, Henry S. Morris.
Third Ward.—Angus Miller, Phillip Simon.

Justices of the Peace.—Constantine Kinderman, Charles H. Dennison, John McNamara.

BAY CITY DIRECTORY.

ABBREVIATIONS.—For ab., read *above*; bds., *boards*; bet., *between* carp., *carpenter;* cor., *corner;* col'd *colored;* E., *East* h., *house;* lab., *laborer;* manuf., *manufacturer;* manufy., *manufactory;* N. *north*; propr., *proprietor;* res., *residence;* S., *south.*

The word *Street* is implied.

A

Abstract County Records, Bush Benjamin F, 301 N Water.
Adams George, Shoemaker, bds 213 S. Water.
Adams John, Farmer, h east end Twenty-Second.
Adams Manville, laborer, h 1601 S Water.
Adams Frederick, laborer, h 622 Howard.
Alord Joseph, lab h 325 Fraser.
Alvord Hubert, steamboat captain, bds 108 S Monroe.
Alward Joseph, lab, h 420 N Jefferson.
Anderson Alexander, tailor, h 516 N Saginaw.
Andrews Anthony, shoemaker, bds 125 S Water.
Andrus William, sawyer, h 124 Bowery.
Aplin & Bro, (George & Henry H A) Grocers, 117 S Water.
Aplin Ceorge, (Aplin & Bro) h 117 S Water,
Aplin Henry H (Aplin & Bro) h 117 S Water,
Arnold Frederick, bakery, 114 Fifth, h same.
Arnold Godfried, Bakery, 215 S Water, h same.
Arnold John, lab, h 301 S Washington.
Atkins L Q, undertaker 1405 S Water, h same.
Averell Charles M, 510 N Water.
Azherman Christian, Confectioner, h 641 S Washington.

B

Babcock Edward, painter, h 313 S Jackson.
Babo Charles, saloon, 114 Center, h 123 S Jefferson.
Babo P, clerk, bds 501 Fifth.

Babstman George, shoemaker, h 216 S Saginaw.
Bailey George O, clerk, bds 208 Fifth.
Bailey J A, clerk, bds 208 Fifth.
Baker Alfred W, lumber inspector, h 306 S Jefferson.
Baker C, (Smith B & Brown) Park & McDowell's dock near bridge, h Fifth.
Baker H A, ice dealer, bds 514 N Water.
Balanger Alfred, carp, bds 317 S Saginaw.
Ballantine John, lab, h 325 Woodside Avenue.
Bancroft, F A, clerk, bds 503 S Water.
Banerntind Vincent, clerk, bds 808 Centre.
Baptist Church, 118 N Washington.
Barbaw Joseph carp, h 214 S Madison.
Barclay J S, h 325 N Washington.
Barlow Will, clerk, bds 512 N Water.
Barney John, drayman, h Fraser's Second Addition.
Barret Alexander, carp, h 418 Fitzhugh.
Barrett J W, (Brown & B) 1113 Fourth, h 512 Eighth,
Barse C V B, (B & Morris) res Olean, N Y.
BARSE & MORRIS, (C V B B & H S M) hardware, 310 N Water.
Barse M W, clerk, bds 802 Centre.
Bartle James, fisherman, bds 903 Seventh.
Bartlett Lyman, laborer, h 501 Fraser.
Bartley David, carp, Fraser's Second Addition.
Bassett E H, clerk, bds Wolverton House.
Bay City Lodge, No 129, I O G T, 211 N Water.
Bay City Signal, Kennedy William T, Editor and propr, 211 N. Water.
Beach H G, tinner, 203 N Water, h 211 N Washington.
Beattie James, clerk, bds 310 S Madison.
Beattie John, h 310 S Madison.
Beattie N, clerk, bds 310 S Madison.
Becker Horace, propr Barclay House, 202 Third.
Beckwith & Cook, (L B & J R C) lawyers, 301 N Water.
Beckwith Luther, (B & Cook) h Centre.
Beebe E H, sawyer, bds Milliken House.
Bellmore Mrs A, h Fraser's Second Addition.
Bemunder Peter, lab, h 317 N Jackson.
Bennet James S, sailor, h 609 S Jefferson.
Berdikzi Bertold lab, h 602 S Adams.
Bermont John, sawyer, h 617 N Saginaw.
Berthold George, lab, h 209 Howard.
Binder & Co, (W B & C Scheurman) Dry Goods, 211 N Water.
Binder William, (Binder & Co) res Saginaw City.
Birch Miss Esther, teacher, 321 Broadway, bds Portsmouth.
Birney James, lawyer, 217 N Water, h Tenth.

Bligh Samuel. bookkeeper, bds 907 Centre.
Bligh Theodore M, Physician, h 907 Centre.
Bloedon Louis, Furniture, 413 N Water, h 402 S Washington.
Blodget Horace, Engineer, h 613 N Adams.
Bodwin C, lab, h 523 N Madison.
Bootyable Richard, insurance agent, bds 214 S Madison.
Bothe August, clerk, bds Madison.
Boutell Benjamin, sailor, bds 402 N Saginaw.
Boutell D, h 402 N Saginaw.
Boutell Wallace, bds 402 N Saginaw.
Bower William, sawyer, h 516 N Saginaw.
Bowerman David, mason, h s side Seventh.
Bowerman Richard, carp, h s side Seventh.
Bowers W, lab, bds 801 Fraser.
Bradley H M, lumber manuf, 522 S Water, h 101 Howard.
Bradley, N B, lumber and salt manuf, h 1001 S Water.
Brany, John, lab, h 302 Eighteenth.
Brandimore Edward, engineer, h 402 Howard.
Brantigan Frederick, lab, n 308 N Jackson.
Bredester John, lab, h 215 Howard.
Breono George, lab, bds 307 S Water.
Brewster Loren D, bookkeeper, bds 1005 S Water.
Brewster Robert E, lumber inspector, h 1005 S Water.
Brinkmann John, lab, h 911 S Monroe.
Brookhouse Rinhardt, carpenter and joiner, h 319 Broadway.
Brooks G, (B & Stevens) bds Tenth.
Brooks John, (Phillips B & Stevens) bds 612 N Jefferson.
Brooks & Stevens, (G B & J V S) meat market, 208 N Water.
Brown & Barrett, (H J B & J W B) painters, 113 Fourth.
Brown George, carp, bds 402 Tenth.
Brown Isaac, lab, h 407 Fraser.
Brown Harvey J, (B & Barrett) h S Madison.
Brown Henry J, painter, h 421 S Madison.
Brown Joseph lab, h 412 N Jefferson.
Brown J O, telegraph operator, 116 N Water, h 611 S Saginaw.
Brownson William, carp, h 221 S Adams.
Bryce, C O, printer, bds Globe Hotel.
Buck Justice, lab, h 203 Broadway.
Burkhait Michael, teamster, h 211 S Jackson.
Burlington Riley, captain steamer Wave, h 509 N Water.
Burns Barney, teamster, h Fraser's Second Addition.
Burns Daniel, lumberman, h 402 Fourth.
Burns Patrick, lab, h 220 S Van Buren.
Burton William, sailor, h 519 S Adams.
BUSH BENJAMIN F, civil engineer and surveyor, 301 N Water, h 622 S Saginaw.
Byor Adam, lab, h 711 Eleventh.

J. Z. NEWCOMB, Jobber and Retail Dealer in Dry Goods,

C

Cameron C, lumberman, h 301 Bowery.
Campbell George, builder, 308 N Water, bds Wolverton House.
Campbell Hon Sydney S, (Judge Probate,) cor Centre & Jefferson, res, junction Johnson st & Woodside avenue.
Carney Patrick, mason, h 713 Seventh.
Callison David, lab, h 604 S Saginaw.
Carney R J, (Watkins & C)arney, 124 S Water, h 105 N Jefferson.
Carney T & Co, (T C, R J C & J Knoblaugh) sash & blind manufy, 723 S Water.
Carney Thomas, sen, h 204 N Washington.
Carney T, (T Carney & Co), h 107 Eleventh.
Carter Allen, carp & joiner, h 413 S Saginaw.
Carter Robert, carp & joiner, bds 413 S Saginaw.
Carter Thomas, carp & joiner, bds 413 S Saginaw.
Carter William, bds 413 S Saginaw.
Catlin Israel, lumber manuf, h 112 Eighth.
Catholic Church, Rev Henry Skutches pastor, 410 N Washington.
Cathcart & Co, boots & shoes, 105 S Water.
Cathcart W A, (C & Co), bds Wolverton House.
Chamberlain H A, lumber insp, h 503 S Jefferson.
Champine Charles, lab, bds 307 S Water.
Chapman Samuel, (col'd), dyer, bds 314 S Saginaw.
Chapman W R, (col'd), dyer, 314 S Saginaw, h same.
Chrisban Thomas, millwright, h 409 Third.
Christ Henry, cooper, bds 625 N Van Buren.
Christopher T, pattern maker, h 723 S Washington.
Chonel D, salt boiler, h 625 N Van Buren.
Chron Thomas, Lake Captain, h 628 S Saginaw.
Clago Mrs Catherine, h 612 N Washington.
Clark H J, cashier First National Bank, bds 512 N Water.
Clark William, lab. bds Barclay House,
Clemans Isaac T, h 107 N Jefferson.
Clemans L T, manager U S Telegraph, 319 S Water, h 107 N Jefferson.
Close Frederick, lab, h 202 Sixth.
Close G, lab, h 202 Sixth.
Coda Frederick, carp, h 419 N Jefferson.
Coffee Patrick, lab, bds 307 S Water.
Coffrey Thomas, lab, bds 202 Second.
Cokely Richard, lab, h 113 S Saginaw.
Colburn E J, (Jarvis & C), 306 N Water, h Adams.
Colburn J N, (C & Mather,) h 207 S Adams.
Colburn & Mather, (J N C & M N M), painters, 212 Center.

AT

ELLIOTT & HARRISON'S

HOUSE-FURNISHING EMPORIUM,

South Water Street, EAST SAGINAW, MICH.

Crockery, China Ware, Cutlery, Plated

Goods, Mirrors, Mats, Carpets, Oil Cloths, Window Shades,

Lamps, Lanterns, Chamber Setts, Toilet Setts, Clothes

Racks, Coffee Mills, Nut Crackers, Egg Beaters, &c.

ARE SOLD AT

PRICES

THAT DEFY

COMPETITION.

John McDowell,

MANUFACTURER OF

Steam Engines,

OF ALL KINDS,

Salt and Potash Kettles, Mill Gearing of every description, Plows, and all kinds of Brass and Iron Castings made to order.

BAY CITY, MICH.

J. Z. NEWCOMB, Jobber and Retail Dealer in Dry Goods,

Collier John, overseer salt block, bds 521 Fraser.
Collier John, lab, bds 423 Bowery.
Collins Barney, lab, bds 125 S Water.
Collins Frederick, carp, h 225 N Washington.
Collins L F, carp & joiner, h 216 Fourth.
Collins Mrs Margaret, h 217 N Washington.
Collins William, mason, h 313 S Jefferson.
Coleman L S, clerk, bds 512 N Water.
Colver D, (Westover & C), h 225 S Jefferson.
Conner Charles, peddler, h 113 Eleventh.
Conner E O, grocer, h 325 N Washington.
Connley Michael, carp & joiner, h 225 Howard.
Cook J R, (Beckwith & C), h 618 Saginaw.
Cook Philip, basket maker, h 312 N Van Buren.
Corbin Charles F, Justice Peace, 310 N Water, h 402 Ninth.
Corbin Miss C, school teacher, bds 402 Ninth,
Corbin Miss E R, milliner, 115 S Adam, bds same.
Correon J. lime burner, 1802 S Water.
Cotter Michael, lab, h 624 N Jefferson.
Cottrell John, clerk, bds 512 N Water.
Coulter J W, clerk, bds 212 N Washington.
County Office Buildings, cor Center & Jefferson.
Court House 301 N Water.
Courtright Daniel, carp h 309 N Jefferson.
Craig John, lumber insp, h 416 Eighteenth.
Crandell Frank, fancy goods & notions, 107 S Water, h N Water.
Cranage Thomas, book keeper, h 525 N Washington.
Crouse ——, lab, h 710 Eleventh.
Cross & Pegley, (Thomas C & Rowley P,) druggists, 101 S Water cor Center.
Cross Roland A, clerk, bds 312 Center.
Cross Thomas, (C & Pegley), 101 S Water, h 312 Center.
Culbert Alexander, book keeper, bds 313 Seventh.
Culbert John, editor & propr Bay City Journal, 202 Fourth, bds 313 Seventh.
Cummings Alphonso, sawyer, bds 815 S Water.
Cunningham Benard, h 202 N Saginaw.
Cunningham Francis, shoemaker, bds 213 S Water.
Curry Duncan, lab, bds, Montreal House.
Curry Isaac, sawyer, bds 506 N Saginaw.
Curry Richard, clerk, h 320 S Madison.
Curry W H, (Judson & C), 118 N Water, h 702 S Adams.
Curry Wm H, book keeper, h 502 S Adams.
Cusson Edwin, carp, h 415 N Van Buren.
Cusson Joseph, (C & Sweet), h Jefferson,
Cusson & Sweet, (J C & J W S), builders, 215 N Washington.
Cutlar Nathan, teamster, h 116 Second.

The Old Union, The Old Faith, The Old Constitution!

The Bay City Signal,

A large Political, News, and Family Paper, every time Democratic,

And always devoted to the interests of the Saginaw Valley.

ISSUED EACH WEDNESDAY BY

W. T. KENNEDY, Jr.,

TERMS, $2,00 PER ANNUM.

THE BEST ADVERTISING MEDIUM IN THE VALLEY.

Job Work executed neatly, promptly, and cheaply.

J. Z. NEWCOMB, Jobber and Retail Dealer in Dry Goods,

D

Dagan Thomas, saloon, 1802 S Water, h same.
Daly Michael, h 601 N Washington.
Daly William, lab, h Fraser's Second Addition.
Dalson Daniel, lab, h Frasers Second Addition.
Dann A, propr Wolverton House, 321 N Water.
Davidson Alex. machinist, bds Saginaw.
Davidson A, blacksmith, h between Eleventh & Thirteenth.
Davidson Charles S, cooper, h 424 N Madison.
Davison James, blacksmith, 739 S Water, h 307 S Adams.
Davis George, engineer, bds 125 S Water.
Davis John H, lab, bds 622 Howard.
Day Charles D, insurance agt, h 221 S Adam.
DeAigle Joseph U, lab, bds Millikin House.
DeBats Mathew, lab, h 505 Van Buren.
DeCort Bruno, cooper, bds 411 N Van Buren.
DeCort Charles, lab, h 411 N Van Buren.
DeCort Peter, lab, bds 411 N Van Buren.
DeGraw Z W, boarding house, 524 S Water.
DeMary William, lab, h 421 S Madison.
DeMersh L, lab, bds 317 S Saginaw.
DePlanty Francis, sawyer, h Woodside avenue.
DePlanty Joseph, lab, h 1005 Third.
DePlinto Alexander, carp & joiner, h 612 Fraser.
Dewar C, carp & joiner, bds 204 N Washington.
Dewar Richmond, carp, bds Fifth.
Del Charles, farmer, h 316 N Van Buren.
DELZELL & DENNISON, (T A D & E B D), Grocers & ship chandlers, 301 N Water.
DELZELL T A, (D & Dennison.) h 302 N Madison.
DENNISON CHARLES H, lawyer, 309 N Water, bds 512 N Water.
Dennison E B, (Delzell & D), 301 N Water, h Center.
Denny Patrick, lab, bds 307 S Water.
Dexter James H, carp, h 105 Fraser.
Dillan John, lab, bds 624 N Washington.
Dingman William, carp, h 504 Second.
Doan Richard, teamster, h Fraser's Second Addition.
Doughty George, books, stationery and jewelry, 301 N Water, h 305 N Van Buren.
Downs Charles C, clerk, bds 409 S Saginaw.
DOWNS W H, boots, shoes & gents furnishing goods, 300 N Water, h 916 Center.
Drago Joseph, lab, bds 107 Bowery.
Drake John, insurance agt & ass't assessor internal revenue, 116 N Water, h 205 N Adams.

J. Z. NEWCOMB, Jobber and Retail Dealer in Dry Goods,

Duchane John, painter, h 311 S Adams.
Dunbar E L, (Mercer & D), 405 N Water bds Third.
Dumder John, lab, h 319 N Van Buren.

E

Easdale James, moulder, bds S Water.
Eastman Anthony, lab, h 307 Frazer.
Eaton J D, painter, bds 511 S Water.
Eddy Henry, teamster, bds 903 Seventh.
Eddy J W, sawyer, bds 1009 S Water.
Eddy Samuel L, blacksmith, 120 S Water, h 903 Seventh.
Edelmann John G, butcher, h 511 Ninth.
Edgert Jacob, lab, bds 633 S Monroe.
Edmons Isaac, lab, h 107 Fitzhugh.
Eicnemeyer Edward, builder, 309 Sixth, h 115 S Washington.
Emrick Jacob, saloon, 219 S Water, h same.
Englehart Martin, lab, h 507 Ninth.
Episcopal Church, 109 S Washington.
Ernest John, cabinet maker, h 319 N Jefferson.
Evans John, lab, bds 125 S Water.
Evans William, lab, h 609 N Jefferson.

F

Falconer Wm D, clerk, bds Washington.
Fay L, bds 1006 Center.
Fay Wm L, (Gates & F,) h 510 Center.
Feagherly J W, h 207 S Jefferson.
Feiger C, steam boat capt, bds 108 S Monroe.
Felker Amos, carp, h 101 Fraser,
Fenally Patrick, toll gate keeper, h same.
Ferris William, ship carp, h 606 N Washington.
File Ira B, carp, bds 202 Eighth.
Finch Edwin teamster, h 401 S Van Buren.
Fingland James, propr Oswego House, 201 Second.
First National Bank, C W Gibson Pres't, H J Clark, Cashier, 212 N Water.
Fisher Frederick, sawyer, h 109 William.
Fitzhugh Charles C, farmer, h 207 Tenth.
Fitzhugh Henry M, superintendent of Bay City salt works, h Fraser's Addition.
Fitzpatrick John, lab, bds 307 S Water.
Flagaelle Henry, blacksmith, h 317 S Saginaw.
Flagler S, engineer, bds Millikin House.
Fogel John, lab, h 634 S Jackson.
Fordon John A, wagon maker & blacksmith, 116 S Water, h 117 S Adams.

Foster Milo H, builder, 112 S Washington h 703 Fifth.
Fountain Louis, boots & shoes, 111 Fourth, h 520 N Jefferson.
Fowler Edgar, salt manuf, h Fraser's Second Addition.
Fox David, mill wright, h 616 N Adams.
Fox Henry, bar keeper, bds Water.
Fox Joseph S, fireman, h 623 N Jefferson.
Fox Thomas, blacksmith, bds 624 N Washington.
Fox William, pastor Methodist Episcopal Church, h 212 N Washington.
Fox William, propr terrapin restaurant, 101 S Water, h 415 S Water.
Frank Ernst, tobacco & cigars, 206 N Water, h 124 S Van Buren.
Frank John, sawyer, h 121 S Madison.
Frank Thomas, butcher, h 325 Williams.
Fray George C, lumber manuf, h 122 N Washington.
Frazer John, lumber manuf, bds 702 Center.
Freeman Chester H, lawyer, h 313 N Madison.
Freeman Mrs E O, millner, 306 Third, h same.
Freeman S, carp, bds 116 N Saginaw.
Fritz George, lab, h 322 N Van Buren.
Frost Henry, mason, h 411 S Washington.

G

Galey Joseph, moulder, bds S Water.
Gardner Albert, painter, h 617 S Adams.
Garlemean Thomas, carp, h near corner Woodside Avenue and Plank Road.
Garrels H S, lab, h 307 N Washington.
Garrels M, painter, bds 307 N Washington.
Garrett Richard M, shoemaker, h 324 S Monroe.
Garrett T, lab, h 316 S Monroe.
Gates Charles, teamster, h N side Center.
Gates & Fay, (S G M G & W L F) lumber manuf, 202 S Water.
Gates S G M, (G & Fay) h 301 N Washington.
Gawing William, carp, bds 402 Tenth.
German Lutheran Church, 124 S Madison.
German Lutheran Church, 317 S Washington.
Gevaret John, Boarding House, 402 N Jefferson.
German School, 507 Sixth.
GIBSON C W, President First National Bank, 212 N Water, h 1006 Center.
Gibson John, toll bridge clerk, bds 512 N Water.
Glending Edward, machinist, bds 722 S Saginaw.
Goebel Henry, (Zerwis & G) h 202 S Washington.
Golden John, shoemaker, res Wenona.
Goodale H A, physician, h 208 S Washington.

Gooding O H P, ice dealer, h 204 N Jefferson.
Goodrich James, salt well borer, h 602 Howard.
Gorden Henry, lab, h 320 Fitzhugh.
Gorder John G, h 525 S Adams.
Gourley Cornelius, lab, h 205 S Van Buren.
Graffort Frank M, (cold) barber, bds 605 Third.
Graffort William, (cold) barber, 311 N Water, h 605 Third.
Grandy William, sawyer, h 1109 S Water.
Grant Archabel, teamster, h 225 S Adams.
Grant John, sailor, h 409 S Adams.
Green James, engineer, h 402 N Jefferson.
Gregson Moses (Holland & G) h 701 Seventh.
Greul Pavlus, saloon, 419 S Saginaw.
GRIER & McDONELL, (T C G & A McD) lawyers, 308 N Water.
GRIER T C, (G & McDonell) h 509 S Jefferson.
Griffin Simon, lab, h 319 N Jefferson.
Grisoke John, lab, h 308 Tenth.
Griswold Harry, dry goods, 109 S Water, h 202 N Madison.
Griswold Hiram S, physician, h 122 N Washington.
Gresgans Joseph, lab, bds 307 S Water.
Grover E, bds 202 Third.
Gudchinsky Herman, lab, h 715 Third.
Gustin Charles, clerk, bds Center.
Gustin H A, grocer, 317 N Water, h 106 S Jefferson.
Gwilt John, carp, h 314 S Jefferson.

H

Haeber William, saloon, 405 N Van Buren, h same.
Hago Conrad, clerk, h 423 S Washington.
Haggy, —— gunsmith, h Fifth.
Hale Myron H, lab, h 614 Fifth.
Hallock Daniel, teamster, h 218 S Saginaw.
Halsted Joseph, joiner, h 108 S Monroe.
Hamet O F, commission merchant, bds 302 N Saginaw.
Hamilton William, teamster, h 705 Twenty-Second.
Hammond George, stave inspector, h 207 S Madison.
Harding John, h 423 Bowery.
Hargrave E J, millwright, h 1021 S Water.
Hart B B, (Smith & H) h 217 Third.
Hart J B, (H & Monroe) h 401 First.
Hart & Monroe, (J B H & J L M) dry goods and groceries, 405 N Water.
Hartman Edward, lab, h 724 S Saginaw.
Harris J, bookkeeper, bds Globe Hotel.
Hartrauft, carpenter and joiner, bds 204 N Washington.

Harwood John, carp, bds 113 S Saginaw.
Harwood Peter, carp, bds 113 S Saginaw.
HATCH H H, (Marston & H) h 704 Tenth.
Hatfield James, (cold) barber, bds 605 Third.
Haughton Miss Emma, teacher, bds Tenth.
HAWLEY C R & CO, dry goods, 111 S Water.
HAWLEY C R, (C R H & Co) bds 503 S Water.
Hawley Truman, sawyer, bds 524 S Water.
Hayden John, mason, bds Milliken House.
Hebert James, clerk, h 208 N Saginaw.
Heininger John, tinner, bds 213 S Saginaw.
Heinzmann Christopher, lab, h s side Seventh.
Helbig Oscar, (Zouner & H) h 303 S Water.
Helmick George, meat market, 117 Fourth, h 413 Sixth.
Hemma Miss Janette, milliner, 401 Center, h same.
Hemstreet H M, harness maker, 214 Center, bds Adams.
Henderson Alexander, millwright, h 518 S Saginaw.
Henderson James, cooper, bds 424 N Madison.
Hennessey Patrick, bricklayer, h 908 Fifth.
Henenes John, carp, h Fraser's Second Addition.
Herce John, potash manuf, h 907 Fifth.
Herman Charles, h 221 S Saginaw.
Hesler Peter, barkeeper, bds 202 Third.
Hess Henry, h 1002 Center.
Heuman Leonard, grocer, 119 N Water, h Seventh.
Hiesordt P S, Principal Union School, h 220 N Monroe.
Hill George, machinist, bds Washington.
Hill Isaac H, salt manuf, res Woodside.
Hill William, machinist, h 635 S Washington.
Hinman Lenhart, provisions, h s side Seventh.
Himmler John, Pastor Lutheran Church, h 507 Sixth.
Hoag Miss Sarah, milliner, bds 115 S Adams.
Hodgers John, lab, h 203 Howard.
Hogan Miss Delia, dressmaker, bds 116 N Saginaw.
Hoishkush Robert, lab, h 507 Fourth.
Holland & Gregson, (J H & M G) 111 S Adams.
Holland John (H & Gregson) h 301 S Madison.
Hollinger Jacob, clothing, h 215 S Saginaw.
Hoornaert Clemence, lab, bds 402 N Jefferson.
Hoover E H, lumberman, bds 202 Third.
Hotchkiss G W, (H & Mercer) h 935 Third.
Hotchkiss & Mercer (G W H & W M) lumber dealers and inspectors, 405 N Water.
Hough Henry, teamster, h 521 Fraser.
House Gates, teamster, bds 116 Third.
Howard George L, carp, h 701 William.
Howard Henry C, bds 321 Broadway.

Howard John B. sailor, h 321 Broadway.
Howard O C, mason, h 701 William.
Howes Thomas, h 512 N Water.
Hubbard, John L. carp, h 211 S Jackson.
Hubbell Richard, harness maker, bds N Water.
Hubner August, lab, h 211 S Madison.
Huff H B, teamster, h 520 Bowery.
Huffman Frank, tailor, h 201 S Adams.
HUGGINS ANDREW, civil engineer and surveyor, 116 N Water, h 424 S Washington.
Hugh E, joiner, h 306 N Van Buren.
Hughes John, engineer, h 407 Third.
Hugot Armand, sawyer, h 801 S Water.
Hurley Henry, carp, h 815 Fourth.
Hurskers Cornelius, lab, h 1603 Third.
Hutchinson Henry, lumberman, bds 222 N Water.
Hyde John, clerk, h 224 S Monroe.

I

INGHAM ALBERT, engineer, h 625 S Adams.

J

Jackson G R, insp & shipper of lumber, 202 S Water, h 123 N Washington.
Jacob Fernando, clerk, h Washington.
Jarmin George, lab, h 115 William.
Jarvis & Colburn, (M M J & E I C), vegetables and confectionaries, 306 N Water.
Jarvis M M, (J & Colburn), res Portsmouth.
Jay Charles, h 402 Tenth.
Jemerson, Thomas W, lab, h 501 Eighth,
Jennings Edward, lab, h 301 Sixth.
Jennison C E, hardware. 201 N Water, h 217 Center.
Johnson C M, supervisor, h 915 Center.
Johnson A, carp & joiner, h 609 N Jefferson.
Johnson Charles, lab, bds 317 S Saginaw.
Johnson Daniel, carp & joiner, bds Miliken House.
Johnson Frank, boiler maker, bds 302 N Jefferson.
Johnson George, conductor Bay City street cars, h 115 S Adams.
Johnson George H, collector of tolls on bridge, bds Wolverton House.
Johnson Israel, carp, bds Fraser's Second Addition.
Johnson John, lab, h 107 Bowery.
Johnson Joseph, lab, h 618 N Saginaw.
Johnson M, physician, 302 N Jefferson, h same.
JOHNSON C, boiler maker, h 302 N Jefferson.

PHILLIPS & BROOKS,

Wholesole and Retail Dealers in

GROCERIES,

Provisions, Feed, &c.

102, S Water, cor. of Center Street,

BAY CITY, MICH.

☞ Goods delivered free of charge in any part of the city.

THOMAS LUXTON,

Manufacturer and Dealer in

Saddles, Harness, Whips

Trunks, &c.,

All Repairing Neatly and Substantially Done to Order.

No. 115, South Water Street,

BAY CITY.

J. Z. NEWCOMB, Jobber and Retail Dealer in Dry Goods,

Johnson William, lab, h 406 N Van Buren.
Johnston Alexander, lab, h 302 Fourteenth.
Johnston James M, h 302 S Washington.
Jones John, teamster, h S side Seventh.
Jordan Robert P, carp, h 401 S Van Buren.
Joslyn John F, bds 402 Ninth.
JUDSON, JOHNSON & CURREY, (J S J, F J & W H C,) insurance agts, 118 N Water.
JUDSON JOHN S, (J & Curry), h 1115 Center.

K

Kaiser A, (K & Co), h 915 Third,
Kaiser & Co, (A R K & J B Weidemann), meat market, 401 N Water.
Kalie Christopher, lab, h 624 S Jackson.
Kardetzky Berthold, lab, h near Bay City salt works.
Kawrman Louis, lab, h 628 S Jackson.
Keen William, tailor, 114 Centre, h 611 Ninth.
Keidt George, lab, h 420 N Madison.
Keister George; carp, h 224 S Jefferson.
Keith Alfred, engineer, h 223 N Van Buren.
Keith John, h 113 Fourth.
Kelley John, lab, h Fraser's Second Addition.
Kellog Joseph, foreman saw mill, h 302 Sixteenth.
Kelson David, lab, h bet Eleventh & Thirteenth.
KENNEDY WM T, editor and propr Bay City Signal 211, N Water, h 609 N Adams.
Kenny John, lab, h 904 Seventh.
Kenutch G, carp, h 501 William.
Kerry John, blacksmith, h Fraser's Second Addition.
Kiester George carp, h J efferson.
Kilduff John jr, bar keeper, bds 121 S Water.
Kilduff John, (Kilduff & Bro), 121 S Water.
Kilduff John & Michael, saloon, 121 S Water, h same.
Kilduff & O'Conner, (P K & Wm O), grocers, 209 S Water.
Kilduff Michael, (Kilduff & Bro), 121 S Water.
Kilduff P, (K & O'Connor,) h 209 S Water.
Kilduff William, bar keeper, bds 121 S Water.
Kinderman Constantine, physician, 418 N Water.
King Joseph, lab, bds 307 S Water.
Kerser Michael, carp, h 308 N Jackson.
Kleesattel Ambrose, clerk. h 306 N Monroe.
Kline John C, grocer, h 702 Third.
Knapp William, carp, h 424 N Madison.
Knecht Casper, clerk, res Portsmouth.
Knoblauch (T Carney & Co), h 416 N Madison.

Knox John W, clerk, h 506 S Jefferson.
Koch Henry, cooper, 606 Second, h 424 N Madison.
Kothe Frederick, cabinet maker, h Jefferson.
Kunz Joseph, cabinet maker, h 124 S Adam.

L

Labadie Oliver, lab, h 402 Fourteenth.
Labadie Paul, lab, h 107 Bowery.
Labadie Peter, lab, bds 402 Fourteenth.
Lambert John, liquor dealer, h 225 S Saginaw.
Landon H, physician, 308 N Water.
Lang Frederick, lab, h near S end of Madison.
Langade Joseph, lab, bds 301 Fraser.
Lapp George, carp & joiner, bds 125 S Water.
Larkins Michael, engineer, h 318 N Adams.
Lasguine Bruno, lab, h 411 N Madison.
Lawrence George, bds 316 N Washington.
LeMear Louis, lab, h 319 Fraser.
Lemosure Simon, sawyer, bds 121 S Madison.
Leonard James, carp, h 604 Howard.
Lesprenel Louis, lab, h 106 Bowery.
Levendor John, lab, h 424 N Van Buren.
Lewis Charles E, mill wright, h 627 S Washington.
Lewis James J, lumber manuf, h 625 S Van Buren.
Lewis J C, (L & Perkins) h 322 S Washington.
Lewis & Perkins, (J C L & F B P), grocers, 118 Center;
Lieferat Charles, clerk, h Seventh.
Lindsay John, machinist, bds 633 S Water.
Little John H, (Sullivan & L), grocers, 302 Center, h Center.
Littleton Christopher, (col'd), pattern maker, h Washington.
Livingston A, clothing, h 207 S Saginaw.
Lloyd Gordon W, (Jas L & Co), res Detroit.
Locker Robert, clerk, bds Centre.
Lovenstein A, clothing, 120 N Water, h Saginaw.
Longpre & Bro, (Leon & Louis L), 312 N Saginaw.
Longpre Leon, (L & Bro) bds Barclay House.
Longpre Louis, (L & Bro), bds Barclay House.
Loomis Louis, sawyer. h 801 Fraser.
Loose William, (Parker & L). h 115 S Saginaw.
Lord George, druggist, 116 N Water, h 116 Centre.
Lotry John, sailor, h 314 N Jackson.
Love James, h 324 Fitzhugh.
Luddington Edwin W, sawyer, h 301 S Monroe.
Lutcke Henry, carp, h 220 S Jefferson.
LUXTON THOMAS, harness maker, 115 S Water, h 601 N Saginaw.

Lydan Daniel, lab, h 621 Howard
Lynch John, shoemaker, bds 213 S Water.
Lynch Timothy, lab, bds 310 N Van Buren.
Lyons James, lab, h 108 Eleventh.
Lyons Michael, lab, h 311 N Jackson.

M

Main Samuel, teamster, h 205 Sixth.
Maloy Michael, lab, h 101 Twenty-Second.
Mannausan R S, propr Milliken House, 311 S Water.
Manna William, clerk, bds 204 N Washington.
Mapes Samuel M, lab, bds 1009 S Water.
Marr Michael, lab, corner Woodside Avenue and Plank Road.
MARSTON & HATCH, (J M & H H H) lawyers, 201 N Water
MARSTON J M (M & Hatch) h 516 Tenth.
Maser L, (Oppenheim & M) res Detroit.
Masonic Hall, 212 N Water.
Masterson Thomas, lab, h 507 Eighth.
Mather M N, (Colburn & M) h 116 N Saginaw.
Mather Mrs M N, milliner, 116 N Saginaw, h same.
Maxwell A C, lawyer, 310 N Water, h 615 Fourth.
Maxon C A, dentist, 114 Center, h same.
McClellan Alexander, blacksmith, h 316 N Adams.
McCloud Norman, lab, h 321 S Adam.
McCormick Herbert, bds 1701 S Water.
McCormick James J, lumber manuf, h 1701 S Water.
McDermott Francis, tailor, bds 222 N Van Buren.
McDermott John, boots and shoes, 112 Third, h 916 Center.
McDonald Daniel, lab, h 403 Fraser.
McDonald John, lab, bds 125 S Water.
McDonald N, joiner, bds 204 N Washington.
McDonell A, (Grier & McD) h 123 S Adams.
McDonell N C, lab, bds 307 S Water.
McDougle Allen, millwright, h Fraser's Second Addition.
McDowell C, (McD & Park) h 124 S Washington.
McDowell Christopher, machinist, bds 633 S Water.
McDowell John, machinist, 702 S Water, h 633 S Water.
McDowell John Jr, machinist, h 623 S Washington.
McDowell Nelson, machinist, bds 623 S Washington.
McDOWELL & PARK, (C McD & E P) liquor dealers, Third st. near the bridge.
McEwen John, clerk, bds Wolverton House.
McEwen William, lumber manuf, h 702 Center.
McGardle John, carp, h 218 S Washington.
McGill James, carp, h 624 N Washington.

J. Z. NEWCOMB, Jobber and Retail Dealer in Dry Goods,

McGilvery John, livery stable, 414 N Saginaw, bds Wolverton House.
McGraw James, lab, bds 307 S Water.
McHale Michael, grocer, 737 S Water h same.
McHenry John lab, bds 125 N Water.
McIntosh James, lab, h 307 N Jackson.
KcKay A, saloon, bds Globe Hotel.
McKay Alexander, conductor S R R, h 612 Sixth.
McKay John, lumber inspector, bds 612 Sixth.
McKay, Mrs Delia, h 510 Fourth.
McKie George C, carp, h 912 Fifth.
McLeod A, harness maker, bds 801 Fourth.
McLeod Angus, lab, h 801 Fourth.
McMahon Martin, shoemaker, bds Barclay House.
McMann Martin, shoemaker, bds Barclay House.
McMath John, painter, h 514 S Saginaw.
McNamara John, lawyer, 310 N Water, bds 204 N Washington
McNeal Daniel, lab, h 617 S Adams.
Mead James, mason, h 619 S Adams.
Mead Leroy, bds 619 S Adams.
Meisell August, lab, h 601 S Jefferson.
Meisell Henry, clerk, h 603 S Jefferson.
Meisell William, lab, h 603 S Jefferson.
Meilminn August, fisherman, h 307 S Saginaw.
Meilminn G, fisherman, h 311 S Saginaw.
Meister B L, dry goods, 302 N Water, h 119 S Saginaw.
Methodist Episcopal Church, 208 N Washington.
Mercer & Dunbar,)W M & E L D) civil engineers and surveyors, 405 N Water.
Mercer William, (Hotchkiss & M) and (M & D) h 416 N Adams .
Merrill Norman, clerk, bds Monroe.
Merrett Edgar H, sawyer, 815 S Water.
Michillod Louis, tailor, h between Eleventh and Thirteenth.
Middaugh William W, (M & Whittemore), h 601 S Water.
Miller A, machinist, bds Saginaw.
Miller Angus, lumber manuf, h 316 S Washington.
Miller Frederick, tailor, h 413 Sixth.
Miller Gunder, (Simons & M) h 210 Center.
Miller Henry, lab, h 103 Bowery.
Miller James J, contractor, h 224 Broadway.
Miller Mrs Caroline, h 802 Twenty-Second.
Miller N, machinist, bds Saginaw.
Mills Warren, with Barse & Morris, bds Wolverton House.
Misner Herman, bds Jefferson.
Molat William, carp, bds 501 Fraser.
Monroe Albert C, millwright, bds 201 Center.
Monroe Byron, lab, h 622 N Jefferson.

Monroe Charles W, bds 301 Center.
Monroe J Hyde, clerk, bds 217 Third.
Monroe J L, (Hart & M) h 208 Fifth.
Monroe Mrs M, h 201 Center.
Monroe William R, lumber inspector, bds 201 Center.
Montreal House, R. Robdux, propr, 125 S Water.
Monture Mrs E, h 222 S Washington.
Moore Andrew, lab, h Fraser's Second Addition.
Moore Henry C, bds 310 N Washington.
Moore Henry sailor, h 523 S Adams,
Moore Walter, sailor h 911 Adams.
Morgan French (cold) barber, bds Third.
Morris Frank, lab, h 722 S Saginaw.
Morris H L, (Barse & M) h 808 Center.
Morris M, peddler, bds Milliken House.
Morrison James, bds 904 Seventh.
Morrison John, blacksmith, h 323 S Adams.
Morrison Thomas, lab, bds 904 Seventh.
Moulthrop Clark, commission merchant, h 302 N Saginaw.
Moulthrop G, lumber manuf, h 220 N Jefferson.
Mount, carriage maker, bds 204 N Washington.
Mudge Uriah, blacksmith, h 801 Third.
Muland Cornelius, lab, h 635 S Jefferson.
Muledy John, h, Fraser's Second Addition.
Munger A S, (Munger & Co) County Treasurer, h 310 N Madison.
Munger C, (Munger & Co) h 314 S Madison.
Munger & Co (C M & A S Munger) dry goods and groceries, 309 N Water.
Munn Thomas, millwright, h s side Center.
Munroe George H, sailmaker, 509 N Water, h same.
Murphy Lawrence J, tailor, bds Milliken House.
Murphy Thomas, mason, h 510 S Saginaw.
Myers F A, sailor, h 622 N Jefferson.
Myers John, lab, h 425 Fitzhugh.

N

Nabert Mrs Gustina, h 110 N Saginaw.
Nabert Otto C, tinner, bds 110 N Saginaw.
Nagle Francis, lumberman, h 309 S Madison.
Nash Rev H B, h 521 Fraser.
Nell Lawrence, teamster, h 402 N Van Buren.
NEWCOMB J Z, dry goods, 103 S Water, bds 202 N Madison.
Newman Samuel, furnishing goods and yankee notions, 315 N Water. bds Wolverton.
Nicholas George, boiler maker, h 613 S Monroe.

Nicholson Mrs Z, tailoress, h 208 Fourth.
Nickeal Adam, carp, h 211 S Saginaw.
Nickels Charles, carp, h 115 S Saginaw.
Nickel Henry, carp. h 115 S Saginaw.
Nickels Valentine, brewer, 521 S Water, h same.
Niles Samuel D, lumber inspector, h 515 Fourth.
Noble Joseph H, bookkeeper, h 105 Thirteenth.
Nolan Godfrey, carriage maker, h Fraser's Second Addition.
Noud James, liquor dealer, 424 N Water, h same.
Nusselt John, lab, h 312 N Jackson.
Nuth W H R, grocer, 211 S Water, h same.

O

O'Conner Edward, grocer, 410 N Water, h Washington.
O'Conner Wm, (Kilduff & O), 209 S Water, h same.
O'Brien John, h 323 S Washington.
O'Brien William, carp, bds 323 S Washington.
Ogeh Lenhardt, farmer, h east end of Nineteenth.
Omsteen William, carp & joiner, bds 117 N Jefferson.
Oppenhiem A, (O & Maser), h 801 Centre.
Oppenhien & Maser, (A O & L M), dry goods & clothing 210 N Water.
Orcutt Wesley, joiner, bds 108 S Monroe.
Orien Michael, carp, h 815 Fourth.
Orton Benjamin F, clerk, bds N Water.
Ouellete Peter, sawyer, h 301 Fraser.
Overhult B, engineer, h 1601 S Water.

P

Padget J C, photographer, 304 Center, h same.
Padley Richard, shingle manuf, h 412 N Adams.
Palmer John, lab, h 401 Howard.
Palmer P L, engineer, h 223 Howard.
Panny David, sawyer, h 101 Williams.
Park Edwin, liquor dealer, h 316 Fourth.
PARKER & LOOSE, (Wm P & Wm L), furniture, h 115 Center.
Parker William, (P & Loose), 115 S Saginaw.
Parshall John M, engineer, h 615 S Jefferson.
Parson Thomas, lab, h 219 Howard.
Partridge B F, civil engineer, h 908 Center.
Parrot Patrick, (sheriff), h 611 S Water.
Patterson John, machinist, h Washington.
Patterson John, sawyer, h 104 Fraser.
Payne C, lab, h S side Seventh, outer lots.
Pegley Rowley, (Cross & P), bds Wolverton House.
Peltee P N, sawyer, h 315 Eighteenth.

J. Z. NEWCOMB, Jobber and Retail Dealer in Dry Goods,

Penfield Warren, engineer, h 508 Fraser.
Perkins Benjamin, grocer, 1301 S Water, h 102 Broadway.
Perkins B F, (Lewis & P), 118 Center, h 205 N Washington.
Perry Hiram, lab, h 308 S Adams.
Peterkin John, saloon keeper, bds Wolverton House.
Peters Henry, carp, h 406 Center.
Petherick Wm W, painter, h 411 Eighth.
Phillips, Brooks & Stevens, (T C P, J B & R H S), groceries & provisions, 216 Center.
Phillips J P, lumberman, bds Wolverton House.
Phillips J W, bds 325 N Washington.
Phillips T C, (P, Brooks & Stevens), h 315 Ninth.
Phrp John, blacksmith, h 638 S Saginaw.
Pinco Hiram, sawyer, h 813 S Water.
Ploof Charles, lab, bds 612 N Adams.
Ploof Charles, sawyer, h 623 N Adams.
Ploof Philip, sawyer, h 612 N Adams.
Pluff Alexander, lab, h Fraser's Second Addition.
Pomeron F, capt tug U S, h 613 S Monroe.
Pomeroy Charles H, clerk, bds 212 N Washington.
Pontine Robert, ship carp, h 305 S Madison.
Porter Alexander, lab, h 406 N Van Buren.
Powell William E, miller, bds Fraser's Second Addition.
Powers G, h 316 N Washington.
Pratt Charles, sawyer, h 416 S Saginaw.
Prentiss Albert, supt L S S W, h 524 N Madison.
Presbyterian Church, 513 S Washington.
Prindwill Michael, tailor, bds 310 N Van Buren.
Prolx Nock, lab, bds 407 S Water.
Prosser T C, h 510 Sixth.
Purcon J, clothing, 204 N Water, h Saginaw.

R

Raap William, butcher, bds 604 Fraser.
Rahel John, lab, h 416 N Jefferson.
Randall Albert M, carp & joiner, bds 204 N Washington.
Randall C S, h 212 S Saginaw.
Randall S S, carp & joiner, bds 204 N Washington.
Rassingthwaighte Edward, millwright, h 306 N Madison.
Ray B F, machinist, h 206 S Madison.
Raymond Henry, h 310 N Washington.
Raymond Henry S, Post Master, 313 N Water, bds 310 N Washington.
Raymond Jacob, engineer, h 225 Howard.
Reaume Charles, blacksmith, 424 N Saginaw, h 606 N Jefferson.
Redmond John, boots & shoes, 213 S Water, h same.

Reed A J, stave dealer, bds Wolverton House.
Reice Daniel M, clerk, h Saginaw.
Reif George, lab, h 315 N Jackson.
Reilly Edgar, clerk, bds Saginaw.
Reilly John S, sawyer, h east end of Twenty-Second.
Remender Frederick, lab, h 1009 Third.
Renmann A, lab, h 407 Third.
Reuther William, pastor Lutheran Church, h 319 S Washington.
Rhoads Charles, watch maker, bds 204 N Washington.
Rice James, tailor, h 222 N Van Buren.
Rich Moses, lab, bds 624 N Washington.
Richardson Joshua J, (col'd), barber, 105 S Water, h Seventh.
Richardson Robert, carp, h 424 Fraser.
Ritche Mrs. Margaret, h 301 S Saginaw.
RIVETT & BRO, (C R & D A R) blacksmiths, 124 S Saginaw.
RIVETT CHARLES, (R & Bro), bds 216 S Jefferson.
RIVETT D A, (R & Bro), h 216 S Jefferson,
Rivet E, shoemaker, bds 216 S Jefferson.
Rivet John, blacksmith, bds 216 S Jefferson.
Rivis Peter, saloon, 307 S Water, h same.
Roach & Smith, (W J R & T S S) boots & shoes, 221 S Water.
Roach W J, (R & Smith) h 623 S Adams.
Robb Herman B, joiner, h 321 William.
Robinson Charles, fireman, h 319 William.
Robinson William, lumberman, h 108 S Monroe.
Rogers H B, shingle manuf, h 201 S Jefferson.
Rogers Wm R, lab, h 410 Fitzhugh.
Root Orville, machinist, h S Water.
Rosa John T, brewer, 729 S Water, h same.
Rose William, carp, bds 402 Tenth.
Ross A C, machinist, h Saginaw.
ROUECH A N, propr Globe Hotel, 202 N Water.
Rouech Charles, clerk Globe Hotel, 202 N Water.
Rouech Geo H, clerk Globe Hotel 202 N Water.
Rouech Christian J, clerk, bds Globe Hotel.
Rouse J M, h 1202 Center.
Royce Rev Fayette, rector Episcopal Church, bds 512 N Water.
Rumzy Charles, lab, bds 402 N Jefferson.
Rupley Jacob, cooper, h 702 Eleventh.
Russel Frances, mason, h 109 Fraser.
Russel Hiram, mason, bds 109 Fraser.
Rutan Peter, music teacher, 116 Center, bds Globe Hotel.
Ryan James, plasterer, h 310 N Van Buren.

S

Sarvann A, lab, bds 629 S Monroe.
Saunders Arthur, clerk, bds 512 N Water.

Saunders George, lab, bds 624 N Washington.
Saxlinger John L, butcher, h 603 Ninth.
Scheurman Charles, dry goods & groceries, h 601 Center.
Scheurman Richard, clerk, h 412 Fourth.
Scherer Joseph, saloon, 401 N Water, h same.
Schmidt George, lab, h 633 S Monroe.
Schmidtz Charles, moulder, bds S Water.
Schmidtz John, boiler maker, h 509 Ninth.
Schmidtz William, lab, h 403 N Jackson.
School House 510 S Saginaw.
School House 401 S Adams.
Schrader Julius, lab, h 622 S Jackson.
Schram Martin, brewer, 125Bowery, h same.
Scott Andrew, h 906 S Water.
Seely Mrs A S, h 506 N Saginaw.
Senecal A, painter, h N Jefferson.
Seviart Louis, lab, h 629 S Monroe.
Sexlinger Geo L. butcher, h 424 S Madison.
Shadick Conrad, carp & joiner, h 906 Sixth.
Shank Franklin, carp & joiner, h 609 S Washington.
Shank Henry, carp & joiner, bds 609 S Washington.
Shannon Isaac, carriage maker, h 618 S Adams.
Shannon Isaac A, carriage maker, 111 Sixth, h 618 S Adams.
Sharp John H, carp, h 211 N Van Buren.
Sharp Samuel C, clerk, bds Wolverton House.
Sharp William T, carp, h 211 N Van Buren.
Shaw A S, tinsmith bds Wolverton House.
Shaw Hugh, lab, bds 1009 S Water.
Shearer & Co, (James & George S) stave manuf, cor Water & First.
Shearer George H, (Jas S & Co), h 532 N Saginaw.
Shearer James & Co, (Jas S, Geo H S & G W Lloyd) lumber manuf, 602 N Water.
Shearer James, (Jas S & Co), h 222 N Water.
Sheppard Benjamin, clerk bds Washington.
Sheppard W H, tinsmith, h 425 Third.
Sherman Mrs T H, h 503 S Water.
Shindehette Henry, saloon, 116 Third, h same.
Simons I, salt boiler, h 405 Fifth.
Simons Jacob, lab h 116 S Madison.
Simons Philip, (S & Watson), h S end Madison.
Simons & Watson, (Philip S & James W), dry goods & groceries 112 Center.
Simons Frederick, (S & Miller), h 601 Sixth.
Simons & Miller (F S & G M), meat market, 210 Center.
Sirmyer John, clerk, h N Van Buren.
Skutches Henry, pastor Catholic Church, h 410 N Washington.

Slagg Henry, machinist, bds 633 S Water.
Slater Frances W, carp, h 517 Second.
Sloan Robert, lab, h 409 N Jefferson.
Smith, Baker, & Brown, (J S, C B & J O B), commission brokers, Park and McDowell's Dock, near bridge.
Smith David T, (col'd], h 705 S Washington.
Smith George (E, S & Hart], h 402 Second.
Smith Grove, sawyer, h 613 S Washington.
Smith & Hart, (Geo S & B B H), flour & feed, 107 Fourth.
Smith James, machinist, bds 633 S Water.
Smith John, boiler maker, h 312 S Adams.
Smith John, engineer, h 607 S engineer, h 315 N Van Buren.
Smith Moses, carp & joiner, bds 613 S Washington.
Smith S C, h 314 S Adams.
Smith Thomas, (Roach & Smith), h 514 S Saginaw.
Smith William, engineer, h 614 Fifth.
Smith William, farmer, h east end twenty-second.
Soamaran Andrew, carp, h 618 N Saginaw.
Spaulding J L, printer, h 202 Fourth.
Spear William, salt well borer, h 617 S Monroe.
Stodotleman Frank, engineer, h Ninth.
Stonton E, real estate dealer, h 511 S Water.
Stevens G D, clerk, bds 211 S Water.
Stevens J V, (Brook & S), 200 N Water.
Stevens R H, (Phillips, Brooks & S), 216 Center.
Stewart A L, bakery, 115 Fourth, h 115 N Jefferson.
Stillman Frank, lab, h 411 Ninth.
Stinbaurer, brewer, h 425 S Saginaw.
Stockle John, lab, h 604 Fraser.
Stony Clemence, carp, h 408 N Jefferson.
Street J F, clerk, h 615 S Saginaw.
Styninger John, tinsmith, h Saginaw.
Sullivan & Little, (O D S & J H L) groceries, 302 Center.
Sullivan Miss Helen, teacher, bds 601 S Madison.
Sullivan O D, (S & Little), h 601 S Madison.
Summerville Samuel, carp, h Fraser's Second Addition.
Sutherland S B, cooper, h 313 William.
Sweet J W, (Cusson & S) h 408 N Saginaw.
Syring Wliliam, lab, h 121 Bowery.

T

Tate Thomas, mason, bds 125 S Water.
Tatz George, lab, h 213 S Saginaw.
Taylor Thomas, carpenter and joiner, h 403 Fraser.
Tennant James W, carpenter and joiner, h 210 S Madison.
Tharrig Henry, lab, h 301 First.

J. Z NEWCOMB, Jobber and Retail Dealer in Dry Goods,

Thomas J R, physician, 308 Center, h same.
Thomas Mortimore, insurance agent, bds 122 N Washington.
Thompson Daniel F, bds 112 Eighth.
Thompson David H, carp, h 501 Howard.
Thompson Ralph, lab, bds 904 Seventh.
Thompson Richard, lab, bds 904 Seventh.
Thorn Benjamin F, clerk, h 212 N Saginaw.
Thornthwait Joseph, lab, h 110 Bowery.
Thorsby Charles lab, h 616 Twenty-Second.
Tilton William M, lab, h Fraser's Second Addition.
Timmis J, clerk, h 401 Third.
Tischner Felix, brewer, 209 S Saginaw, h same.
Titt Daniel, lab, h 619 N Adams.
Tripp A W, milkman, h 204 Eighth.
Trombley A, bds 602 Jefferson.
Trombley Alexander, carp, h 602 N Jefferson.
Trombley Benjamin S, clerk, bds Globe Hotel.
Trombley Daniel butcher, h 111 Bowery.
Trombley John, sawyer, bds 111 Bowery.
Trombley William, lab, bds 111 Bowery.
Trombley, Z, carp, h 524 N Jefferson.
Truedell Joseph, blacksmith, h 202 Seventeenth.
Tucker, S, salt manuf. h cor. Woodside Avenue and Plank Road.
Tuddington Benjamin F, engineer, h 410 S Washington.
Turner Edwin H, cabinet maker, bds 506 N Saginaw.
Tushner Daniel h 625 S Monroe.

U

Ueberroth Leonhard mason, h 712 Sixth.
Underwood William, carriage maker, bds 618 S Adams.
Underwood William, tailor, 207 Third, h same.
Union School House, 211 N Adams.

V

Van Arp Cornelius, clock maker, h 809 Third.
Van Etten George H, salt manuf, 310 N Water, bds N Water.
Van Haren Frederick, lab, h 409 N Van Buren.
Van Idestina Peter, ship carpenter, h 507 S Monroe.
Van Paris Louis. lab, h 624 N Van Buren.
Vanstienberg U, produce dealer, h 509 S Jackson.
Van Stratum Gottfried, clerk, h 401 Fourth.
Van Zeman Tyce, lab, h 416 Second.
Varner Robert, carp, h 301 Eighteenth.
Vassault Thomas, clerk, bds Wolverton House.
Valentine Albert, mason, bds 204 N Washington.
Valentine George W, mason, h 623 N Jefferson.

Valentine William B, mason, h 409 S Washington.
Valieres Stephen, lab, bds Milliken House.
Volk Francis, lab, h 310 Eighth.
Von Hemel F, farmer, h east end of Nineteenth.
Von Hemel Peter, farmer, east end of Nineteenth.
Vosburgh Charles, sailor, h 802 Sixth.
Vosburgh Frank, sailor, bds 802 Sixth.
Vosburgh Henry, sailor, bds 802 Sixth.
Vosburgh Loren, sailor, bds 802 Sixth.

W

Wagoner John, lab, h 401 Howard.
Wagoner, Joseph, carp, h 701 Fourth.
Wait David, carriage manuf, 107 N Adams, h Center.
Walch Thomas, lab, h 410 Woodside Avenue.
Walker James, salt manuf, h Fraser's Second Addition.
Walker Theodore, h 319 S Water.
Walthausen & Bro, (F V & W W) druggists, 117 N Water.
Walthausen, F V, (Walthausen & Bro) bds 401 Center.
Walthausen William, (Walthausen & Bro) h 401 Center.
Walther Alpheus, tinner, bds Center.
Walther Lawrence, cooper, h Woodside Avenue.
Walther Pius, shoemaker, bds Center.
Walton Andrew, lumber inspector, 116 N Water, h 110 S Adams.
Wanless George, engineer, h Fraser's Second Addition.
Wanless Henry, harness maker, bds Fraser's Second Addition.
Ward E C, machinist, h 626 S Adams.
Ward James, printer, bds 619 S Washington.
Ward Lawrence, lab, bds 125 S Water.
Ward William, saw maker, 302 S Water, h 619 S Washington.
Warden Peter, fireman, h 603 Howard.
Watkins George, builder, 408 Fifth, h 117 N Jefferson.
WATKINS T W, (W & Carney) h 102 N Washington.
WATKINS & CARNEY, (T W W & R J C) inspectors and shippers of lumber, 124 S Water.
Watson James, (Simons & W) h 101 Broadway.
Webber, ——bds 104 N Washington.
Webber John K, carpenter and joiner, h 617 Fraser.
Webster N H, dentist, 310 N Water, h 311 S Vanburen.
Webster Samuel, sawyer, h 313 N Jefferson.
Wehner H, harness maker, bds N Washington.
Weidemann J B, (Kaiser & Co) h Third.
Wells Oscar, lab, h 306 Third.
Wentz Henry, machinist, h 324 N Jackson.
Wentz Joseph H, engineer, h 324 N Jackson.
Wertheimer Morris, clothing, 113 S Water, bds Milliken House.

J. Z. NEWCOMB, Jobber and Retail Dealer in Dry Goods,

West David, millwright, h 612 N Saginaw.
Weston Robert, lab, h 622 S Adams.
Westover & Colver, (W W & D C) lumber dealers. 225 S Jefferson.
Westover J W, bds 125 N Washington.
Westover Luther, lumber dealer, h 125 N Washington.
Westover William, (W & Colver) h 225 S Jefferson.
Wetmore E A, teamster, h 801 Third.
Wheeler Charles C, carpenter and joiner, h 319 S Water.
Whille Shepard, carpenter and joiner, h 313 S Saginaw.
White Henry, boilermaker, h 609 S Monroe.
Whiting John, butcher, h 912 Fifth.
Whiting J W, carpenter and joiner. h 501 Monroe.
Whitman John, butcher, h 325 N Jackson.
Whittemore Charles E, tinner, bds 210 Fifth.
Whittemore J F, carp, bds 210 Fifth.
WHITTEMORE & MEDDAUGH, (W W & W W M) cabinet manufy 116 S Saginaw, sales room 202 Center.
Whittemore Nathaniel, County Clerk, h 210 Fifth.
Whittemore W C, accountant, h 111 N Jefferson.
Whittemore Walter, (W & Meddaugh) bds 210 Fifth.
Wider John, lab, h 632 S Jackson.
Wight J C, Pastor Presbyterian Church, h 602 S Washington.
Wight, boiler maker, bds 624 N Washington.
Wigle Eli, Pastor Methodist Episcopal Church, bds 212 N Washington.
Wiles Robert lab, h 202 Eighth.
Willet Joseph, lab, h Fraser's Second Addition.
Willey J F, livery stable, 322 N Saginaw bds Wolverton House.
Wilkin & Co (F G & S V Wilkin) clothing, 301 N Water.
Wilkin F G (Wilkin & Co) res East Saginaw.
Wilkin S V, (Wilkin & Co) bds Wolverton House.
WILLIAMS DAVID R, painter, 301 S Water, h 222 S Madison.
Williams Edward, lab, h Woodside Avenue.
Williams E Y, lumber inspector, 116 N Water, h 405 Third.
Williams Francis, lab, h 618 N Washington.
Williams James, lab, h 113 Fraser.
Williams James, sawyer, h 617 N Saginaw.
Willis Mrs L J, h 702 Twenty-Second.
Willson James, cabinet maker, h N Van Buren.
Wilson John S, h 1505 S Water.
Wilson J, painter, bds Globe Hotel.
Wilson Thomas, drayman, bds 624 N Washington.
Wilson William D, lab, h 224 S Vanburen.
Winkler Michael, sawyer, h 717 Fourth.
Wintermeyer Jacob, sawyer, h 205 Sixth.
Wipper Henry, carp. h 222 Howard.

Wipper John, lab, bds 222 Howard.
Wispinter John C, clerk, bds Seventh.
Witeman Albert, engineer, h 514 N Saginaw.
Witthauer Bernard, Register of Deeds, cor Center and Jefferson.
WOLVERTON HOUSE, A Dann, propr, 321 N Water.
Wood Edgar A, harness maker, bds 601 N Saginaw.
Wood Edwin, watchmaker, bds 204 N Washington.
Wood George, blacksmith, h near Water and Watson.
Wood John, clerk, bds Wolverton House.
Wood John, painter, h 215 S Madison.
Wood Joseph, clerk, bds Wolverton House.
Wood L. lab, h 401 Howard.
Wood P H, lab, h 321 N Adams.
Woolson J O, h 216 Fourteenth.
Wright David, boarding house, 1009 S Water.
Wyatt Will, clerk Wolverton House.

Y

Yales, Miss M L, 510 S Saginaw, bds Adams.
Yawkey E F, stoves and tin, 419 N Water, bds Madison.
Yawkey John H, lumber inspector, h 221 N Madison.
Yawkey William C, inspector and shipper of lumber, 405 N Water.
Young D, shoemaker, bds 221 S Saginaw.
Young H, (cold) barber, 123 S Water, h 725 S Jefferson.
Young John, lab, h 120 S Madison.
Young Peter, cooper, bds 424 N Madison.
Young Henry, lumber inspector, h 608 N Washington.
Yuirian Bertrand, lab, h 201 Sixth.

Z

Zauner & Helbig, (L G Z & O H) physicians, 303 S Water.
Zauner L G, (Z & Helbig) h 909 Twenty-Second.
Zehner T N, jewelry, 206 N Water, h 1003 Center.
Zerwis & Goebel (S Z & H G) proprs Forest City House, 202 S Washington.
Zerwis Simon, (Z & Goebel) h 202 S Washington.

[The following Notices were received to late for insertion in their proper place.—PUBS.]

C. R. HAWLEY & Co. commenced business here in December, 1865. They have a store 22x85, and two stories high, well filled with a complete assortment of goods in their line of trade, consisting of Dry Goods, Carpets, Boots and Shoes, Caps and Gents' Furnishing Goods. These gentleman having had a large experience in the mercantile business, know well the wants of their customers, and are amply prepared to furnish everything in their line of business as all must be convinced who visit their extensive establishment, at wonderfully low prices; their motto being "quick sales and small profits." The attention which these gentlemen give to their business is fast winning for them a place among the best business houses of the Valley.

The business of W. H. DOWNS, was established here in February, 1865. His store is 25x80, and well stocked with Boots and Shoes, and Gents' Furnishing Goods. The stock of Boots and Shoes is the largest and best assorted in the city, as all will be convinced who visit his store, and having had a large experience in the business, he is a good judge of the articles in which he deals, and none but the best goods are purchased by him.—He employs the best workmen in his custom department, and has the name of making the best of "fits." The repairing is neatly done, and attests the superior mechanical skill of his workmen. By his gentlemanly and fair dealing he has secured a large trade and a fair pecuniary reward. Success to him is a foregone conclusion, which is always the reward of upright dealing.

A. DANN, proprietor of the Wolverton House, is an old landlord, having had over twenty years experience. His table is always supplied with the best the market affords, and his customers are made to feel at home in his comfortable quarters. Charges moderate.

BARSE & MORRIS,

WHOLESALE AND RETAIL DEALERS IN

HARDWARE,

Cutlery, Stoves, Iron, Steel, Nails, Belting, Packing, Paints, Oils, Glass and Builders' Hardware.

Also, Manufacturers of Tin, Copper and Sheet Iron Ware.

310, North Water Street,

C. V. B. BARSE, Olean, N. Y.
H. S. MORRIS, Bay City, Mich.

BAY CITY, MICH.

McEWEN & FRASER,

MANUFACTURERS OF

Pine Lumber.

Mill, 308, North Water Street,
BAY CITY, MICH.

GEORGE CAMPBELL,

Architect and Builder.

All Jobs in the Building Line, promptly executed.

Office, 308, North Water Street.

BAY CITY.

BUSINESS DIRECTORY.

Agents—Insurance.

BUSH BENJAMIN F, 301 N Water.
DENISON C H. 309 N Water.
DRAKE JOHN, 116 N Water.
JUDSON, JOHNSON & CURREY, 116 N Water.

Artists, Ambrotype & Photograph.

Padget J C, 304 Centre.

Architects & Builders.

CAMPBELL GEORGE 308 N Water.
Cusson & Sweet, 215 N Washington.
Eicnemeiyer Edward, 309 Sixth.
Foster Milo, h 112 S Washington.
Holland & Gregson, 111 S Adams.
Tennant J W, 410 N Saginaw.
Watkins George, 408 Fifth.

Bakers & Confectioners.

Arnold Frederick, 114 Fifth.
Arnold Godfried, 215 S Water.
Steward A L, 115 Fourth.

Banks and Bankers.

FIRST NATIONAL BANK, 212 N Water.

Barbers.

Groeffort William, (col'd), 311 N Water.
Richardson Joshua J, (col'd), 105 S Water.
Young H, (col'd), 123 S Water.

Blacksmiths.

Davidson James, 739 S Water.
Eddy Samuel L, 120 S Water.
Fordon John A, 116 S Water.
Reaume Charles, 424 N Saginaw.
RIVETT & BRO, 124 S Saginaw.
Wait David, 115 Center.

Boiler Makers.

Davidson & White, S Water.
JOHNSON O, 202 Woodside avenue.

Booksellers & Stationers.

Doughty George, 301 N Water.

Boots & Shoes.

CATHCART & Co, 105 S Water.
DOWNS W H, 308 N Water.
Fountain Louis, 117 Fourth.
McDermodd John & Co, 112 Third.
Redmond John, 213 S Water.
Roach & Smith, 221 S Water.
Sullivan & Little, 302 Center.

Brewers.

Nickels Valentine, 321 S Water.
ROSA JOHN T, 729 S Water.
Schram Martin, 125 Bowery.
Tischner Felix, 209 S Saginaw.

Butchers.

Brooks & Stevens, 208 N Water.
Helbig G, 117 Fourth.
Kouser & Co, 401 N Water.
Simuns & Miller, 210 Center.

Carriage Manufacturers.

Fordon John A, 116 S Water.
Shannon Isaac A, 111 Sixth.
Longpre & Bro, 312 N Saginaw.
Wait David, 107 N Adams.

Civil Engineers & Surveyors.

BUSH B F, 301 N Water.
Hotchkiss & Mercer, 405 N Water.
HUGGINS ANDREW, 116 N Water.
Mercer & Dunbar, 405 N Water.

Cigars & Tobacco Manufacturers & Dealers

FRANK ERNST, 206 N Water.

Clothing—Manufacturers & Dealers.

LOEVENSTEIN, A, 120 N Water.
Purcon J, 204 N Water.
Wertheimer Morris, 113 S Water.
Wilkin & Co, 301 N Water.

Dentists.

Maxon C A, 114 Center.
Webster, N H, 310 N Water.

Drugs and Medicines—Dealers in.

CROSS & PEGLEY, 101 S Water, cor Center.
Lord George, 116 N Water.
Walthausen F V & Bro, 117 N Water.

Dry Goods—Dealers in.

Binder & Co, 211 N Water.
GRISWOLD H, 109 S Water, (will remove to 100 S Water first August.
HAWLEY C R & Co, 111 S Water.
Meister B L, 302 N Water.
Munger & Co, 309 N Water.
NEWCOMB J Z, 103 S Water.
Oppenhein & Mason, 210 N Water.
Simons & Watson, 112, Center.

Fancy Goods & Notions.

Crandell Frank, 107 S Water.
Newman Samuel, 315 N Water.

Flour and Feed.

Smith & Hart, 107 Fourth.

Foundries and Machine Shops.

McDOWELL JOHN, 702 S Water.

Furniture—Manufacturers & Dealers.

Bloedon Louis, 413 N Water.
PARKER & LOOSE, 116 Center.
Whittemore & Meddaugh 116 S Saginaw, salesroom 202 Center.

Groceries and Provisions—Dealers.

Aplin & Bro, 117 S Water.
BINDER & Co, 211 N Water.
DELZELL & DENISON 301 N Water.
Gustin H A, 317 N Water.
HART & MONROE, 405 N Water.
Heuman Leonard, 119 N Water.
Kilduff & O'Conner, 209 S Water.
Lewis & Perkins, 118 Center.
McHale Michael, 737 S Water.
Nuth W H R, 211 S Water.
O'Conner Edward, 410 N Water.
Perkins Benjamin L, 1301 S Water.
Phillips & Brooks, 216 Center.
Sullivan & Little, 302 Center.

Gunsmiths.

Ajgy John, 111 Fifth.

Hardware, Stoves and Tinware—Manuf's and Dealers.

Barse & Morris, 310 N Water.
Beach H G, 203 N Water.
Jennison C E, 201 N Water.
Yawkey E F, 419 N Water.

Harness, Saddles and Trunks.

Hemstreet H M, 214 Center.
LUXTON THOMAS, 115 S Water.

Hotels.

Barclay House, 202 Third.
Forest City House, 202 S Washington.
GLOBE HOTEL, 202 N Water.
Milliken House, 311 S Water.
Montreal House, 125 S Water.
Oswego House, 201 Second.
WOLVERTON HOUSE 323, N Water.

Justices of the Peace.

CORBIN CHARLES F, 310 N Water.
DENISON CHAS H, 309 N Water.
McNamara John, 310 N Water.
Kinderman C, 418 N Water.

Lawyers.

Beckwith & Cook, 301 N Water.
BIRNEY HON JAMES, 217 N Water.
DENISON CHARLES H, 309 N Water.
GRIER & MCDONELL, 301 N Water.
MARSTON & HATCH, 201 N Water.
MAXWELL A C, 310 N Water.
McNamara John, 310 N Water.

Liquor Dealers—Wholesale.

McDowell & Park, Third st, near bridge.
Noud James, 424 N Water.

Livery.

McGilvary John, 414 N Saginaw.
Willey J F, 322 N Saginaw.

Lumber—Inspectors, Manufacturers and Dealers.

BRADLEY H M, 522 S Water.
BRADLEY N B, 1001 S Water.
Gates & Fay, 202 S Water.
Hotchkiss & Mercer, 405 N Water.
Jackson G K, 202 S Water.
McCormick James J, 1701 S Water.
McEWEN & FRASER, 308 N Water.
Shearer James & Co, 602 N Water.
Walton Andrew, 116 N Water.
WATKINS & CARNEY 124 S Water,
Westover & Colver, 225 S Jefferson.
Williams E Y, 116 N Water.
YAWKEY WM H, 116 N Water.

Lime Burners.

Correon J, 1802 S Water.

Milliners and Dressmakers.

CORBIN MISS E R, 115 S Adams.
Freeman Mrs E O, 306 Third.
Hemma Miss Janette, 401 Center.
Mather Mrs M N, 116 N Saginaw.

Newspapers.

BAY CITY JOURNAL, (weekly), 202 Fourth.
BAY CITY SIGNAL, (weekly), 211 N Water.

Painters, Paper Hangers and Glaziers.

Brown & Barrett, 113 Fourth.
Colbern & Mather, 212 Center.
WILLIAMS DAVID K, 301 S Water.

Physicians.

CROSS THOMAS, 101 S Water, cor Center.
Griswold H S, 122 N Washington.
Gunn D B, Barclay House.
Johnson M, 302 N Jefferson.
Kindermann Constantine, 418 N Water.
Landon H, 300 N Water.
THOMAS J R, 308 Center.
Zauner & Helbig, 303 S Water.

Planing Mills and Sash and Door Manuf.

CARNEY T & Co, 723 S Water.

Sail Makers.

Munroe George H, 509 N Water.

Saw Manufacturers.

Ward William, 302 S Water.

Watchmakers and Jewelers.

Doughty George, 301 N Water.
Zehner T N, 206 N Water.

M. E. CHURCH BAY CITY.

The first Minister that was stationed as Pastor at what was then called Lower Saginaw, was Rev. G. Bradley ; it was in the year 1851-2. At this time the Church was built. In the years 1853 and 1854, Rev. J. Cogshall was appointed Pastor, and he reporced a membership of ten in number. And in the same year a Sabbath school was organized.

In the years 1855 and 1856 Rev. T. J. Joslin was appointed Pastor, and succeeded in building a Parsonage.

In the years 1857 and 1858, Rev. Wm. Benson was appointed Pastor.

In the year 1859 the Rev. E. Klumpp, was appointed Pastor; and then Rev. J. C. Wathey was appointed two years. In the year 1863, Rev. E. Castor was appointed Pastor. In the year 1864 Rev. H. O. Parker was Pastor, and in the years 1865 and 1866, Rev. Wm. Fox, was appointed Pastor.

We have now a membership of over 100, and the Sabbath school numbers about 100.

BAY CITY FIRE DEPARTMENT.

1861.

Chief Engineer—H. M. Bradley.

Ass't Engineer—Charles Merrill.

1864.

Chief Engineer—Andrew C. Maxwell.

1st Ass't Engineer —J. H. Little.

2d " " Bernard Witthauer.

Red Rover Fire Company,—*Foreman*—J. N. Sweet—*1st Ass't Foreman*—Chris. Heinzman; *2d Ass't*—Edward O'Connor.

On the 14th of April Mr. Little resigned and John Harding was appointed to fill vacancy.

1865.

Chief Engineer—Charles H. Denison.

1st Ass't " Thomas Howes.

2d " " A. N. Rouech.

RED ROVER FIRE CO.—*Foreman*—William T. Kennedy; *1st Ass't Foreman*—Charles Rivett; *2d do*—Jacob Knoblaugh.

PROTECTION FIRE CO.—*Foreman*—W. B. Valentine; *1st Ass't*—B. Boutell; *2d do.*—E. F. Yawkey.

On the 9th of May the following officers were confirmed by the Council.

Chief Engineer—Charles H. Denison.

1st Ass't " William Fox.

2d " " Benjamin Boutell.

In October the Fire Department disbanded and William T Kennedy was appointed Chief Engineer with instructions to re-organize.

Chief Engineer—William T. Kennedy.

1st Ass't " Edward T. Williams.

2d " " William Fox.

3d " " William B. Valentine.

Steam fire Engine Company, 60 members.—*Foreman*, Henry Hutchinson; *1st Ass't* H. S Raymond; *2d do*, James W. Watson; *3d do*, Thomas Pitts; *President*, Henry Hutchinson; *Secretary*, R. J. Carney; *Treas.*, Harvey J. Clark.

Hook & Ladder Company, forty members—*Foreman*, Conrad Fieger; *1st Ass't*, Conrad Hage; *2d do*, Henry Lutzke.

Sack & Bucket Protective Association, thirty members. This Company is not yet fully organized.

HISTORY OF PORTSMOUTH.

The history of Portsmouth being so closely interwoven with that of Bay City repetitions must necessarily occur, but we will endeavor to avoid them as much as possible.

The village of Portsmouth is beautifully located on the east bank of the Saginaw river adjoining Bay City on the south; being about six miles south of Saginaw Bay, and being so closely connected with Bay City the dividing line between the two places is not discernable to the stranger.

It is a thriving place and contains about two thousand inhabitants. Its principal business is the manufacture of Salt and Lumber. There are in operation at the present time six Salt Blocks, four saw mills and one planing mill and flouring mill, connected together. Merchandizing is carried on to a considerable extent; there being eight stores containing a variety of stock, such as is usually kept in country villages. There are three blacksmith shops; three wagon maker shops and two shoemaker shops. There are two Churches, one a Methodist and the other a Baptist. Education is not neglected here, there being one school containing two hundred and eighty pupils under the superintendance of one Principal, who has two asistants.

The village was first laid out and named by Albert Miller, Esq., in 1836. In Feb., 1837, it was replotted and enlarged by the "Portsmouth Company." In 1856, Wm. Daglish was employed to re-survey the place and make a new map. The former Plot being found incorrect. The first settlers of Portsmouth were

Joseph and Meador Tromble, who located here in 1834 and built a log house near where the "Center House" now stands for the purpose of trading with the Indians. They afterwards *entered* a tract of land on the present site of the village. In 1843 Meador Tromble sold his interest to James McCormick and removed one mile up the river on what is known as Tromble's Addition of Portsmouth. The next settler who became identified with the place was Albert Miller who came from Saginaw in company with B. K. Hall and others for the purpose of erecting a lumber mill. The mill was erected, and put in operation in 1837, being the second mill on the river. Thomas Rogers came the same year, and was the first blacksmith. His wife was the first physician in what is now called Bay County, and her memory will long be endeared and cherished by those who were the recipients of her many acts of humanity and kindness.—She is now a resident of Bay City, highly respected and beloved for her many virtues. In 1841 James McCormick came here from Saginaw, and in company with his son, James J. McCormick, purchased the interest of B. K. Hall in the lumber mill before mentioned, which business he continued until his decease, occurring in 1846, Jesse M. Miller came here in 1850 and is now a resident. Capt. Joseph F. Marsac came here from Detroit in 1838, and Capt. John S. Wilson came here in 1841.—The first school taught was in a small house on the corner of Fremont avenue and Water street and for many years afterwards the residence of Judge Miller. David Smith, now of Tuscola County, was the first teacher, who commenced his school in the year 1843, with six scholars, named respectively, Peter and Hial Rogers, Andrew J. Crutchfield, William Tufts, Elizabeth and Wm. R. McCormick. The first store was opened in 1850 by C. L. Russell on Water street, in connection with his lumbering business. This store has since been enlarged and is now carried on by M. & H. Bunnell.

The first hotel was the "River House," and Daniel Chappel was its landlord, which duties he dispensed with "ability" and to the satisfaction of the public. This house was afterwards named the Center House and is now known by that name.

The first vessels built here were the "Essex" and the "Bay City." The former was built in 1857 and the latter in 1858.

Having thus given a hastily written sketch of the village and its early settlement, we will conclude by remarking, that few places possess more natural advantages than Portsmouth; its location; its almost unexhaustible supply of salt and lumber; together with the enterprise of its citizens, must in a few years cause it to join hands with Bay City and together, extend their borders to Saginaw Bay and rank among the large and important cities of the west.

PORTSMOUTH DIRECTORY.

Abbreviations.—For ab., read *above*; bds,, *boards*; bet., *between*; carp., *carpenter;* cor., *corner;* col'd *colored;* E., *East* h., *house;* lab., *laborer;* manuf., *manufacturer;* manufy., *manufactory;* N. *north*; propr., *proprietor;* res., *residence;* S., *south.*

The word *Street* is implied.

A

Adams James, lab, bds 301 First.
Adams James, lab, bds 104 Kossuth.
Allen E, lumber dealer, bds 225 Water.
Alyea Warren, teamster, h 316 Tuscola.
Avery James H, millwright, h 1904 Water.
Avery Morrison A, millwright, h 1906 Water.
Baker Alexander, lab, h 609 Second.
Baker Mrs M, seamstress, h 311 Lafayette.
Baldwin Henry; lumberman, h 321 Water.
Baptist Church, 214 Fremont.
Beckwith B F, salt manuf, h 625 First.
Bedell B C, grocer, bds 111 Second.
Bedell J G, grocer, 102 First, bds 111 Second.
Bedell Mrs C, h 111 Second.
Bedell M N, grocer, bds 111 Second.
Beebe S C, joiner, h 215 Tromble.
Beebe William, joiner, h 523 First.
Bennett Mrs Mary, h 501 Fremont.
Bialey J M, tailor, 109 First, h 210 Second.
Bird A, bds 310 Second.
Bird Mrs Margaret, h 824 Seventh.
Bird Mrs P, h 310 Second.
Black John, lab, h 310 Second.
Boiteu George, (Chapman & B) h 219 Fifth.
Boyse Jacob, lab, h 611 Water.
Braddock A C, salt manuf. h 503 First.

Braddock Charles, shingle manuf, h 518 First.
Braddock & Co, salt manufy, s end of Water.
Braddock Edward, butcher, h 110 Burnett.
Braddock H A & Co, lumber manufy, 1518 Water.
Braddock H A, lumber manuf, h 701 First.
Brannan Daniel, lab, h 108 Salt.
Brazzelton L N, (cold) barber, 306 First, bds 301 First.
Briggs David, lab, h 707 Water.
Britton Theodore, soap manuf, h 1824 Water.
Brooks Andrew, lime burner, h 124 Water.
Brown John E, lab, h 616 Lafayette.
Brown Mrs U A, h 602 Sixth.
Brown William, lab, h 401 Tuscola.
Bunnell & Co, (M & H B) grocers, 920 Water.
Bunnell H, (B & Co) bds 219 First
Bunnell, M, (B & Co) h 219 First.
Burnett Hamilton, carpenter and joiner, 111 Burnett, h 524 First.
Burtch Jonathan, ferryman, h 201 Fifth.
Burtch Miss,, teacher, bds 201 Fifth.
Campbell Lawrence. lab, h 201 Lafayette.
Campbell Moses, h 101 First.
Center House, Albert Coggshall, propr, 325 Water.
Chapman & Boiteu, (W A C & G B) boots and shoes, 120 First.
Chapman William A, (C & Boiteu) h 524 First.
Clark Russel, machinist, h 423 Sixth.
Clay Michael, lab, h 607 Water.
Coggshall Albert, propr Center House, 225 Water.
Comstock John S, sawyer, h 303 Fifth.
Cooper Milton, blacksmith, h 108 Kossuth.
Crampton George, boarding house, 216 South.
Crampton John, boarding house, 104 Kossuth.
Cummings, A L, teacher, h 1703 Water.
Cunningham Patrick, lab, bds 301 First.
Daglish William, lawyer, 911 Water, bds 202 Fremont.
Davison Michael, sawyer, bds 215 Tuscola.
DeForest Stephen, millwright, h 306 Sixth.
Demon George, lab, bds 1625 Water.
Dobson Robert W, lab, h 707 Water.
Dodge Samuel, shoemaker, h 315 Webster.
Dunham & Johnson, (N D & A Johnson), dry goods & groceries 109 First.
Dunham N, (D & Johnson), h 301 Tromble.
Durfee Harvey W, sawyer, h 825 Seventh.
Easton P, spile driver, h 2001, Water.
Edmonds Joseph, mason, h 601 Jefferson.
Edwards G, lab, bds 401 Tuscola.

Ellis G H, carp & joiner, h 1822 Water.
Ellis Wm H, lab, bds 1822 Water.
Ellison Henry, sawyer, h 812 Broadway.
Fagirat John, cooper, h 411 Polk.
Fleck J J, lab, bds 707 Water.
Flynn John, lab, h 813 Seventh.
Forcill Joseph, lab, bds 2001 Water.
Fowler Andrew, lab, bds 108 Salt.
Frost George, farmer, h 401 Jefferson.
Gale A W, lab, h 313 First.
Garrison Garrett, engineer, h 210 Trombly.
Gillott J B. (G & Till), 201 Water.
Gillott & Till, (J B G & A Till), grocers, 201 Water.
Gladwin & Bro, (H L & C A G), groceries & provisions, 602 First.
Gladwin H L, (G & Bro), 602 First.
Gladwin C A, (G & Bro), bds Trombly.
Green Robert, lab, bds 707 Water.
Grisdale James, sawyer, h 116 Tuscola.
Handy Mrs R A, h 215 Burnett.
Hansel John, gardner, h 702 Jefferson.
Hayden & Co, salt manufy, 1917 Water.
Hayden Henry, Supervisor, bds 301 First.
Hawkins John W, farmer, h 625 Second.
Heath Martin, lab, h 609 Second.
Hennesey Patrick, school teacher, h 316 Tuscola,
Henry Samuel, engineer, h 1607, Water.
Hewitt Calvin A, mason, h 1724 Water.
Hopkins Daniel, sawyer, h 810 Broadway.
Hotchkiss William, shingle sawyer, h 713 Broadway.
Hutchinson Mrs A, h 618 Washington.
Ingle George, mill wright, h 1119 Water.
Ingle John, millwright, h 1125 Water.
Jenkins Mrs B, milliner, 109 Tuscola, h same.
Johnson Alonzo, (Dunham & J), bds 425 First.
Keeppe D, lab, bds S end of First.
Keith Daniel, lab, h 201 Lafayette.
Kelly Thomas, farmer, h 125 Third.
Kent William, h 315 Jefferson,
Kerwin James, lab, bds S end First.
Kinney Byron, cooper, bds S end First.
Knight Caspar, wagon maker, h 901 Tuscola.
Langdon E G, lumber dealer, h 301 Water.
Lennard Charles, lab, bds 502 Harrison.
Lennard John C, sawyer, h 502 Harrison.
Lewis George, L & Peters), bds 225 Water.
Lewis & Peters, lumber manuf, 510 Water.

Lyon Mrs Elizabeth, h 522 Sixth.
McCormick William K, lumber insp, 115 McCormick, h same.
McDade W H, blacksmith, 401 First, h 105 First.
McGee Louis, sawyer, h 1601 Water.
McLane Andrew, sup't Portsmouth salt works, h S end of First.
Maitland John, lab. bds 201 Lafayette.
Mallet Abraham, lab. bds 601 Tuscola.
Mallet Paul, lab, h 601 Tuscola.
Manley Samuel, lab, h 116 Lafayette.
Marble Hiram, joiner, h 702 Fremont.
Marks E B, sawyer, h 819 Sixth.
Marsac Charles, bds 1909 Water.
Marsac Frank, bds 1909 Water.
Marsac Joseph, h 1909 Water.
Mason James C, groceries & provisions, 202 Water, h Washington.
Meloy Alexander, cooper, h 1123 Water.
Merrill Charles A, millwright, h 202 Jefferson.
Methodist Church, 510 Fremont.
Miller Abram, bds 309 Sixth.
Miller A J, engineer, h 325 Third.
Miller Albert, lumber manuf, 1012 Water, h 309 Sixth.
MILLER Hon ALBERT, h 202 Fremont.
Miller J M, farmer, h 125 First.
Moore J S, shingle sawyer, h 511 First.
Munday Joseph, lab, h 313 Lafayette.
Munyan A L, (M & Bro), bds 608 First.
Munyan & Bro, (A L & H F M), groceries & provisions 225 First.
Munyan H F, (Munyan & Bro), h 608 First.
Murphy Mathew, lab, bds 607 Water.
Murphy Patrick, lab. bds 607 Water.
Newcombe Abram D, lab, h 819 Seventh.
O'Conner Dennis, saloon, 216 Water, h same.
Oatman Frances, (O & Son), bds 415 Polk.
Oatman Myron, (O & Son), h 415 Polk.
Oatman Nelson, (O & Son), bds 415 Polk.
Oatman & Son, (M & T O), builders, 110 & 112 Washington.
Parmley James, millwright, h 701 Water.
Parmley Miss L A, school teacher, bds Water.
Parmley M, millwright, bds 425 First.
Peters William, (P & Lewis,) 510 Water.
Pine Ambrose, lab, bds 216 Burnett.
Pine Benjamin, lumber dealer, h 216 Burnett.
Pine Samuel, teamster, bds 216 Burnett.
Portsmouth Ferry, Jonathan Burtch propr, 202 Water.
Portsmouth House, Mrs H Raby propr, 302 First.

Post Office, 109 First.
Pringle Sanford, propr, Union House, 101 First.
Quigley John, engineer, bds S end First.
Quinn John, lab, h 611 Water.
Raby Mrs Hannah, propr, Porstmouh House, 302 First.
Raby William, bds 302 First.
Randall Peter J, h 406 Harrison.
Rutherford Chas, carp, bds 401 Tuscola.
Sanford J S, h 305 Sixth.
School House 725 Water.
Schrader William, lab, h 615 Tuscola.
Shawl G P, farmer, h 904 Broadway,
Shilling George, clerk, bds 219 First.
Shilling John, carpenter, h 901 Tuscola.
Smith Charles W, fisherman, h 211 Water.
Smith D D, teamster, h 814 Broadway.
Smith George W, saw filer, h 424 Third.
Smith James, sawyer, h 1121 Water.
Smith John C, sawyer, h 801 Sixth.
Smith Mary A, h 325 Water.
Smith Sylvester S, sawyer, h 416 Tuscola.
Southworth Charles G, lumber manuf, h 1924 Water.
Southworth W H, lumber dealer, h 1005 First.
Stevens A & Co, lumber & salt manuf, 1624 Water.
Stevens A, (S & Co), h 1625 Water.
Stevens John F, blacksmith, h 710 Tuscola.
Stevenson Thomas, farmer, h 115 Water.
Sutton Jacob, foreman, salt block, h 601 Second.
Swaley Frederick, lab, h 201 Lafayette.
Swain James, brewer, 212 Water, h same.
Taylor Frances, boarding house, S end of First.
Thomas George W, lab, h 2012 Water,
Thompson Henry, machinist, h 315 Second.
Thorp George, carriage maker, 401 First, bds 405 First.
Till A W, (Gillett & T), 201 Water, h same.
Timm John, lab, bds 825 Sixth.
Trombly Meddaugh, h 1421 Water.
Trombly Peter, fisherman, h 1421 Water.
Vosburgh Henry, saloon, 116 Tuscola, bds same.
Watkins Stephen, carp & joiner, h 1803 Water.
Watkins Thomas G, carp, bds 1803 Water.
Wathworth L, carp, h 1005 First.
Watrous A W, cabinet maker, h 910 First.
Watrous & Brother, (Jas & O A W), proprs shingle manufy 1924 Water.
Watrous James, (W & Bro), h 2009 Water.
Watrous O A, (W & Bro),) h 2005 Water.

Webb C W, blacksmith, 110 Third, h 625 Broadway.
Webb Thomas C, teamster, h 810 Seventh.
Westbinder, h 401 Washington.
Westcott Harvey, lab, h 412 Second.
Whipple William, lumber dealer, h 425 First.
Whiting Albert, lab, bds 2001 Water.
Williams S, shingle sawyer, bds 511 First.
Winterhalter George, engineer, h 1201 Water.
Winterhalter Michael, land agt, 304 First, h 825 Sixth.
Withey Lafayette, h 501 Polk.
Withey Russell, lab, h 501 Polk,
Wright Frank, lab, bds 301 First.
Wright Luther, mason, h 323 Second.

WENONA DIRECTORY.

ABBREVIATIONS.—For ab., read *above*; bds., *boards*; bet., *between*; carp., *carpenter;* cor., *corner;* col'd *colored;* E., *East* h., *house;* lab., *laborer;* manuf., *manufacturer;* manufy., *manufactory;* N. *north*; propr., *proprietor;* res., *residence;* S., *south.*

The word *Street* is implied.

Allord Hiram C, mason, h Lynn.
Arnold & Co, planing mill, river.
Arnold David G, planing mill, river.
Arthur Robert, lab.
Ashley Frederick, carp.
Aubry O, blacksmith.
Babcock Dennis, carp, h Lynn.
Bates George, lumber insp, bds River.
Benedict Wm H, lab.
Bentley John O, sawyer, bds River.
Boyd W C, lumber insp, bds River.
Boynton E. H. painter, h Lynn.
Brock Martin W, carp & joiner, h Lynn.
Brown N, grocer, h John.
Buchanan Stephen A, carp & joiner bds River.
Burt J H, cabinet maker, h Lynn.
Campfield John, machinist.
Campbell Rev D B, pastor Presbyterian Church, h River.
Carson George, lab, bds River.
Chambers Miss Helen, school teacher.
Chambers Mrs H.
Chambers William, carp.
Chandler Mrs Sarah.
Chase John A, physician, h Lynn.
Clark N, grocer.
Coffin Henry, carp.
Cook Mrs. Mary.
Cooper John, lab.

Corbitt James, sawyer, h River.
Courtier Charles, lab, bds Lynn.
Craft W O, carp.
Cullan Cormick, bds Lynn.
Daily Andrew, carp, bds Lynn.
Davis James, lumber insp.
Davis Thomas, lab, h Lynn.
DEAN WARREN H, (Sage, McGraw & Co), res Toledo.
Davenport James T, sawyer.
Eli Charles, lab.
Emery John G, millwright, h River.
Emery N, millwright,
Emery Temple, millwright, bds River.
Ewen William, carp & joiner, bds Lynn.
Fairfield Isaac, butcher, h River.
Ferguson W G, carp & joiner, h Lynn.
Gardiner E U, fisherman, h Lynn.
Gilbert Joseph, carp.
Golden John, shoemaker, h Lynn.
Grant A, lab, bds River.
Gregory William, clerk, bds River.
Griest J D, painter, bds Lynn.
Grover John, carp.
Harrington Alfred, sawyer, h River.
Harrison Francis, carp.
Harrison George, carp.
Hollenbeck J, Fireman, bds Lynn.
Hurlacer John, cooper.
Johnson R, teamster, bds Lynn.
Johnson William, lab.
Jones Nathan, carp.
Lankey F, blacksmith.
Larkins James, blacksmith, bds Lynn.
Lyon Frederick, telegraph operator, bds River.
Mahar William, mason, bds River.
Man John, lab.
Markham Henry, lab, h Lynn.
Matevi Joseph, lab, h Lynn.
McGraw John, (Sage, McGraw & Co), res Ithica, N Y.
McGraw Thomas, (Sage, McGraw & Co), res N Y City.
McLane William, lab.
Moose Louis, lab.
Morlatt Paul, lumberman.
Morrison John, carp,
Nash Samuel, sailor bds Lynn,
OSTRANDER H A, lumberman, bds River.
OSTRANDER JOHN B, lumberman, h River.

Orolowbright O, engineer, bds Lynn.
Pangburn Myron, engineer, h River.
Phillips Thomas, teamster, h River.
Plum J H, clerk, h River.
Post Office, cor River and Midland road.
Robinson C, teamster, h River.
Root C, (Sweet & R), h River.
Rounsvell L, engineer, h Lynn
Russell A T, carp.
Russell D B, carp, h Lynn.
SAGE H S, (S, McGraw & Co), res Brooklyn, N Y.
SAGE, McGRAW & Co, (H S S, John McG, Thomas McG & W H Dean), proprs lumber manufy, near bridge, & store corner River st.
Shear John W, millwright, bds River.
Simons Joseph.
Simpson Daniel, millwright.
Simpson James, lab.
Smith George.
Smith William, carp.
Stark F, farmer, h Lynn.
Strong Patrick, lab, bds Lynn.
Swart William, drugs & boots & shoes. Lynn, h same.
Sweet Benjamin, (S & Root), h River.
Sweet O, lab, bds River.
Sweet & Root, boarding house, River.
Telegraph office, cor River & Midland road.
Thomas Gilbert, lab, bds River.
Thomas William, lab, bds River.
Tromble A D, sawyer.
Vanboorhees William, sawyer.
Webster Miss Helen, milliner.
Wheeler H H, grocer.
Williams J H, book keeper, bds River.
Winter George, sawyer.
Yokley William, carp.

EVERETT HOUSE

Opened, 1864--Enlarged, 1865.

No. 219, Genesee, Corner of Franklin Street,

EAST SAGINAW, MICH.

SMITH & CROUSE, - - PROPRIETORS.

Choice Location--Ample Accommodation for Guests.

CPSIA information can be obtained
at www.ICGtesting.com
Printed in the USA
LVHW111704260322
714493LV00002B/261

9 783752 579055